SWEETBITTER

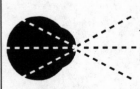

This Large Print Book carries the
Seal of Approval of N.A.V.H.

SWEETBITTER

STEPHANIE DANLER

THORNDIKE PRESS
A part of Gale, Cengage Learning

GALE
CENGAGE Learning·

Farmington Hills, Mich • San Francisco • New York • Waterville, Maine
Meriden, Conn • Mason, Ohio • Chicago

GALE
CENGAGE Learning·

Thorndike Press, a part of Gale, Cengage Learning.

LIBRARY OF CONGRESS CATALOGING-IN-PUBLICATION DATA

Names: Danler, Stephanie, author.
Title: Sweetbitter / by Stephanie Danler.
Description: Large print edition. | Waterville, Maine : Thorndike Press, 2016. | Series: Thorndike Press large print core
Identifiers: LCCN 2016022070| ISBN 9781410493439 (hardcover) | ISBN 1410493431 (hardcover)
Subjects: LCSH: Young women—Fiction. | Self-realization in women—Fiction. | New York (N.Y.)—Fiction. | Large type books.
Classification: LCC PS3604.A5376 S94 2016b | DDC 813/.6—dc23
LC record available at https://lccn.loc.gov/2016022070

Published in 2016 by arrangement with Alfred A. Knopf, a division of Penguin Random House LLC

Printed in Mexico
1 2 3 4 5 6 7 20 19 18 17 16

For my grandparents
Margaret Barton Ferrero and
James Vercelli Ferrero

Eros once again limb-loosener
whirls me
Sweetbitter, impossible to fight off,
creature stealing up.
— Sappho, translated by Anne Carson,
Eros the Bittersweet

"Let us now cast a philosophical glance at
the pleasure or pain of which taste may
be the occasion."

— Brillat-Savarin,
translated by Anne Drayton,
The Physiology of Taste

CONTENTS

■ ■ ■ ■

SUMMER

■ ■ ■ ■

I

You will develop a palate.

A palate is a spot on your tongue where you remember. Where you assign words to the textures of taste. Eating becomes a discipline, language-obsessed. You will never simply eat food again.

I don't know what it *is* exactly, being a server. It's a job, certainly, but not exclusively. There's a transparency to it, an occupation stripped of the usual ambitions. One doesn't move up or down. One waits. You are a waiter.

It *is* fast money — loose, slippery bills that inflate and disappear over the course of an evening. It can be a means, to those with concrete ends and unwavering vision. I grasped most of that easily enough when I was hired at the restaurant at twenty-two.

Some of it was a draw: the money, the sense of safety that came from having a place to wait. What I didn't see was that the time had severe brackets around it. Within those brackets nothing else existed. Outside of them, all you could remember was the blur of a momentary madness. Ninety percent of us wouldn't even put it on a résumé. We might mention it as a tossed-off reference to our moral rigor, a badge of a certain kind of misery, like enduring earthquakes, or spending time in the army. It was so finite.

I came here in a car like everybody else. In a car filled with shit I thought meant something and shortly thereafter tossed on the street: DVDs, soon to be irrelevant, a box of digital and film cameras for a still-latent photography talent, a copy of *On the Road* that I couldn't finish, and a Swedish-modern lamp from Walmart. It was a long, dark drive from a place so small you couldn't find it on a generous map.

Does anyone come to New York clean? I'm afraid not. But crossing the Hudson I thought of crossing Lethe, milky river of forgetting. I forgot that I had a mother who drove away before I could open my eyes, and a father who moved invisibly through the rooms of our house. I forgot the parade of people in my life as thin as mesh screens, who couldn't catch whatever it was I wanted to say to them, and I forgot how I drove down dirt roads between desiccated fields, under an oppressive guard of stars, and felt nothing.

Yes, I'd come to escape, but from what? The twin pillars of football and church? The low, faded homes on childless cul-de-sacs? Mornings of the *Gazette* and boxed doughnuts? The sedated, sentimental middle of it? It didn't matter. I would never know exactly, for my life, like most, moved only imperceptibly and definitively forward.

Let's say I was born in late June of 2006 when I came over the George Washington Bridge at seven a.m. with the sun circulating and dawning, the sky full of sharp corners of light, before the exhaust rose, before the heat gridlocked in, windows unrolled, radio turned up to some impossibly hopeful pop song, open, open, open.

Sour: all the puckering citrus juices, the thin-skinned Meyer lemons, knobbed Kaffirs. Astringent yogurts and vinegars. Lemons resting in pint containers at all the cooks' sides. Chef yelled, This needs acid!, and they eviscerated lemons, leaving the caressing sting of food that's alive.

■ ■ ■ ■

I didn't know about the tollbooths.

"I didn't know," I said to the tollbooth lady. "Can't I squeeze through this one time?"

The woman in the booth was as unmoved as an obelisk. The driver in the car behind me started honking, and then the driver behind him, until I wanted to duck under the steering wheel. She directed me to the side where I reversed, turned, and found myself facing the direction from which I had just come.

I pulled off into a maze of industrial streets, each one more misleading than the next. It was irrational but I was terrified of not being able to find an ATM and having to go all the way back. I pulled into a Dunkin' Donuts. I took out twenty dollars and looked at my remaining balance: $146.00. I used the restroom and rinsed off my face. *Almost,* I said to my strained face in the mirror.

"Can I get a large iced hazelnut coffee?" I asked. The man wheezing behind the counter masticated me with his eyes.

"You're back?" He handed me the change.

"Excuse me?"

16

"You were in here yesterday. You got that same coffee."

"No. I. Did. Not." I shook my head for emphasis. I imagined myself getting out of the car yesterday, tomorrow, and every day of my new life, pulling into the Dunkin' Donuts in motherfucking New Jersey, and ordering that coffee. I felt sick. "I didn't," I said again, still shaking my head.

"I'm back, it's me," I said to the tollbooth woman, rolling the window down triumphantly. She raised one eyebrow and hooked her thumb into her belt loop. I handed her money like it was nothing. "Can I get in now?"

Salt: your mouth waters itself. Flakes from Brittany, liquescent on contact. Blocks of pink salt from the Himalayas, matte gray clumps from Japan. An endless stream of kosher salt, falling from Chef's hand. Salting the most nuanced of enterprises, the food always requesting more, but the tipping point fatal.

A friend of a friend of a friend, his name was Jesse. A spare bedroom for $700 a month. A neighborhood called Williamsburg. The city was in the grips of a tyrannical heat wave, the daily papers headlined with news of people dying in Queens and the outer boroughs where there were blackouts. The cops were passing out bags of ice, an evaporating consolation.

The streets were wide and vacant and I parked my car on Roebling. It was mid-afternoon, there wasn't enough shade, and every business seemed closed. I walked over to Bedford Avenue to look for signs of life. I saw a coffee shop and thought about asking if they needed a barista. When I looked through the window the kids on laptops were thin lipped, pierced, gaunt, so much older than me. I had promised myself to find work swiftly and unthinkingly — as a waitress, a barista, a whatever-the-fuck-job so I could feel planted. But when I told myself to open the door my hand objected.

The waterfront skyline was plastered with skeletons of high-rises, escalating out of the low buildings. They looked like mistakes that had been rubbed out with an eraser. Creaking above an overgrown, abandoned lot was a rusted-out Mobil gas sign — all around me ambivalent evidence of extinction.

This new roommate had left the keys at a bar near the apartment. He worked in an office in Midtown during the day and couldn't meet me.

Clem's was a dark spot on a bright corner, the air conditioner rumbling like a diesel motor. It anointed me with a drip when I walked in, and I stood blinking in the airstream while my eyes adjusted.

There was a bartender leaning heavily against the back counter with his boots up on the bar in front of him. He wore a patched and studded denim vest with no shirt underneath. Two women sat in front of him in yellow print dresses, twirling straws in big drinks. No one said anything to me.

"Keys, keys, keys," he said when I asked. In addition to his body odor, which hit me in the face on my approach, this man was covered in terrifying — demonic — tattoos. The skin of his ribs seemed glued on. A mustache as defined as pigtails. He pulled out the register, threw it on the bar, and rummaged through the drawer underneath. Stacks of credit cards, foreign change, envelopes, receipts. The bills fluttered against the clamps.

"You Jesse's girl?"

"Ha," one of the women said from down the bar. She pressed her drink onto her forehead and rolled it back and forth. "That was funny."

"It's South Second and Roebling," I said.

19

"Am I a fucking real estate agent?" He threw a handful of keys with plastic colored tags at me.

"Aw, don't scare her," the second woman said. They didn't look like sisters exactly, but they were both fleshy, rising out of their halter necklines like figureheads on the prow of a ship. One was blond, the other brunette — and now that I was looking, their dresses were definitely identical. They murmured inside jokes to each other.

How am I going to live here? I wondered. Someone is going to have to change, them or me. I found the keys marked 220 Roebling. The bartender ducked down.

"Thank you very much, sir," I said to the air.

"Oh, no problem, madame," he said, popping up and batting his eyes at me. He opened a can of beer, pushed his mustache up, and ran his tongue around it while looking at me.

"Okay," I said, backing away. "Well, maybe I'll come in again. For like . . . a drink."

"I'll be here with bells on," he said, turning his back on me. His stench lingered.

Just before I stepped out into the heat I heard one of the women say, "Oh god," and then from that bartender: "There goes the fucking neighborhood."

20

■ ■ ■ ■

Sweet: granular, powdered, brown, slow like honey or molasses. The mouth-coating sugars in milk. Once, when we were wild, sugar intoxicated us, the first narcotic we craved and languished in. We've tamed, refined it, but the juice from a peach still runs like a flash flood.

I don't remember why I went to that restaurant first.

I do remember — in perfect detail — that stretch of Sixteenth Street that gave away so little: the impersonal, midcentury teal of Coffee Shop, the battalion of dumpsters between us and Blue Water Grill, the bodega with two small card tables where they let you drink beer. Always uniformed servers buying Altoids and energy drinks.

The alley where the cooks lined up to smoke cigarettes between services, the recesses of the alley where they smoked pot and kicked at the rats tearing through the trash. And just beyond our line of vision we could sense the outlines of the scrawny park.

What did the Owner gaze at when he built it? The future.

When I got there they told me a lot of

21

stories. Nobody went to Union Square in the eighties, they said. Only a few of the publishing houses had moved down there. That city has been replaced by another city. The Whole Foods, the Barnes & Noble, the Best Buy — they got stacked right on top of it. In Rome, they dig for a subway and find whole civilizations. With all the artists, the politicians, the tailors, the hairdressers, the bartenders. If you dug right here on Sixteenth Street you'd find us, younger, and all the stale haunts, and all the old bums in the park younger too.

What did those original servers see when they went to the first interviews in 1985? A tavern, a grill, a bistro? A mess of Italy, France, and some burgeoning American cuisine that nobody really believed in yet? A hodgepodge that shouldn't have worked? When I asked them what they saw, they said he'd built a kind of restaurant that hadn't been there before. They all said that when they walked in, it felt like coming home.

Bitter: always a bit unanticipated. Coffee, chocolate, rosemary, citrus rinds, wine. Once, when we were wild, it told us about poison. The mouth still hesitates at each new encounter. We urge it forward, say, Adapt. Now, enjoy it.

■ ■ ■ ■

I smiled too much. At the end of the interview the corners of my mouth ached like
stakes in a tent. I wore a black sundress and
a pilled cardigan, which was the most
conservative and professional thing I owned.
I had a handful of résumés folded up in my
purse, and my loose plan — if that's even
the right word for the hesitant brand of
instinct I forced myself to follow with a
sense of doom — was to walk into restaurants until I got hired. When I asked my
roommate where I should look for a job, he
said the best restaurant in New York City
was in Union Square. Within a minute of
getting off the train I developed giant wet
half-moons of sweat in the cardigan, but the
top of my dress was too revealing to remove
it.

"Why did you choose New York?" asked
Howard, the general manager.

"I thought you were going to ask me why
I chose this restaurant," I said.

"Let's start with New York."

I knew from books, movies, and *Sex and
the City* how I was supposed to answer. I've
always dreamed of living here, they say.
They stress the word *dreamed,* lengthen it,

23

to make it sound true.

I knew so many said: I came here to be a singer/dancer/actress/ photographer/painter. In finance/fashion/publishing. I came here to be powerful/beautiful/wealthy. This always seemed to mean: I'm stopping here to become someone else.

I said, "It really didn't feel like a choice. Where else is there to go?"

"Ah," he said. "It's a bit of a calling, isn't it?"

That's all. *Ah.* And I felt like he understood that I didn't have endless options, that there was only one place large enough to hold so much unbridled, unfocused desire. *Ah.* Maybe he knew how I fantasized about living a twenty-four-hour life. Maybe he knew how bored I had been up until now.

Howard was in his late forties with a cultivated, square face. His hair receded finely, emphasizing bulging eyes that told me he didn't need much sleep. He stood squarely on athletic legs, balancing a prominent belly. Judicious eyes, I thought, as he tapped his fingers on the white tablecloth and assessed me.

"You have nice nails," I said, looking at his hands.

"It's part of the job," he said, unswayed. "Tell me what you know about wine."

24

"Oh, the basics. I'm competent in the basics." As in I knew the difference between white and red wine and it couldn't get more basic than that.

"For example," he said, looking around the room as if plucking a question from the air, "what are the five noble grapes of Bordeaux?"

I pictured cartoon grapes wearing crowns on their heads, welcoming me to their châteaux — Hello, we are the noble grapes of Bordeaux, they said. I debated lying. It was impossible to know how much honesty about my ignorance would be valued.

"Mer . . . lot?"

"Yes," he said. "That's one."

"Cabernet? I'm sorry, I don't really drink Bordeaux."

He seemed sympathetic. "Of course, it's a bit above the average price point."

"Yep." I nodded. "That's totally it."

"What do you drink?"

My first instinct was to list the different beverages I drank on a daily basis. The noble grapes were back in my head, dancing, telling him all about my Dunkin' Donuts iced coffee.

"What do I drink when?"

"When you purchase a bottle of wine, what do you tend toward?"

25

I imagined myself purchasing a bottle of wine, not based on price or proximity to the checkout line, not based on what animal was on the label, but by an internal matrix of my own taste. That image was as laughable as my noble grapes, even if I was wearing a cardigan.

"Beaujolais? Is that a wine?"

"It is. Beaujolais, c'est un vin fainéant et radin."

"Yes. That."

"Which cru do you prefer?"

"I'm not sure," I said, batting my eyelashes forcibly, falsely.

"Do you have any experience as a server?"

"Yes. I've been working at that coffee shop for years. It's on my résumé."

"I mean in a restaurant. Do you know what it means to be a server?"

"Yes. When the plates are ready I bring them out and *serve* them to customers."

"You mean guests."

"Guests?"

"Your guests."

"Yes, that's what I meant." He scribbled on the top of my résumé. Server? Guests? What was the difference between a guest and a customer?

"It says here you were an English major."

"Yes. I know. It's generic."

26

"What are you reading?"

"Reading?"

"What are you reading right now?"

"Is that a job question?"

"Perhaps." He smiled. His eyes made an unabashed, slow circle around my face.

"Um. Nothing. For the first time in my life, I'm reading nothing." I paused and looked out the window. I don't think anyone, even my professors, had once asked me what I was reading. He was digging, and though I had no idea what he was looking for, I decided it was better to play. "You know, Howard, if I can call you that, when I was leaving for here I packed a few boxes of books. But then I really started looking at them. These books were . . . I don't know . . . totems of who I was. . . . I . . ."

My words had a point, I had just felt the point coming, I was trying to tell him the truth. "I left them behind. That's what I mean."

He rested his cheek on an aristocratic hand. He listened. No, he perceived. I felt perceived. "Yes. It's startling to look back on the passionate epiphanies of our youth. But a good sign perhaps. That our minds have changed, that we've evolved."

"Or maybe it means we've forgotten ourselves. And we keep forgetting ourselves.

And that's the big grown-up secret to survival."

I stared out the window. The city passed on, obliviously. If this went badly I would forget it too.

"Are you a writer?"

"No," I said. The table came back into focus. He was looking at me. "I like books. And everything else."

"You like everything else?"

"You know what I mean, I like it all. I like being moved."

He made another note on my résumé.

"What do you dislike?"

"What?" I thought I'd misheard him.

"If you like being moved, what do you dislike?"

"Are these normal questions?"

"This isn't a normal restaurant." He smiled and crossed his hands.

"Okay." I looked back out the window. Enough. "I don't like that question."

"Why?"

My palms were damp. That was the moment I realized I wanted the job. That job, at that restaurant specifically. I looked at my hands and said, "It feels a little personal."

"All right." He didn't skip a beat, a quick glance at my résumé and he was on track.

"Can you tell me about a problem at one of your last jobs? At that coffee shop, I suppose. Tell me about a problem there and how you solved it."

As if I had dreamed it, the interior of the coffee shop dissolved when I tried to recall it directly. And when I tried to remember punching in there, tried to remember the sink, the register, the coffee grinds, the objects faded. And then her fat, gloating, vindictive face appeared.

"There was this awful woman, Mrs. Pound. I mean it, she was insufferable. We called her The Hammer. From the second she walked in everything was wrong, the coffee scalded her or it tasted like dirt, the music was too loud, or her blueberry muffin had poisoned her the night before. She was always threatening to shut us down, telling us to get our lawyer ready each time she bumped into a table. She wanted scrambled eggs for her dog. Never tipped us a cent. She was dreaded. But then, this was a little over a year ago, she had her foot amputated. She was diabetic. None of us ever knew, I mean, why would we know? And she would wheel by in her wheelchair and everyone was like, Finally, The Hammer is done."

"Finally, what?" Howard asked.

"Oh, I forgot that part. We didn't have a

ramp. And there were stairs. So she was finished, more or less."

"More or less," he said.

"But, the real part of the story. One day she was wheeling by, and she was glaring, I mean, hateful. And I don't know why, but I missed her. I missed her face. So I made her coffee and I ran after her. I wheeled her across the street to the park and she complained about everything from the weather to indigestion. From then on it was our thing. Every day. I even brought the scrambled eggs in a to-go container for her dog. My coworkers made so much fun of me."

The Hammer's swollen, varicosed legs. Flashing her stump at me from under her housedress. Her purple fingers.

"Does that answer your question? The problem was not having a ramp, I guess. The solution was to bring out the coffee. I'm sorry, I didn't explain it very well."

"I think you explained it perfectly. That was a kind thing to do."

I shrugged. "I really liked her actually."

The Hammer was the only impolite person I knew. She put me in that restaurant. I felt it then but didn't understand it. It was her niece's daughter who was a friend of a friend of my new roommate in Williamsburg. Our goodbye had been tearful — on my end, not hers. I promised to write her letters, but the weeks were eclipsing our small relationship. And as I looked at Howard and the perfectly set table and the tasteful hydrangea arrangement between us, I understood what he meant by *guest,* and I also knew that I would never see her again.

"Did you move here with anyone? Girl-friends? A boyfriend?"

"No."

"That's very brave."

"Is it? It's been two days and I feel pretty foolish."

"It's brave if you make it, foolish if you fail."

I wanted to ask him how I would be able to tell the difference and when.

"If you're hired here, what do you want the next year to bring you?"

I forgot that I was being interviewed. I forgot about my negative bank account, my pit stains, and the noble grapes. I said something about wanting to learn. About my work ethic.

I was never good at the future. I grew up with girls whose chief occupation was the future — designing it, instigating it. They could talk about it with so much confidence that it sounded like the past. During those talks, I had contributed nothing.

I had visions, too abstract and flat for me to hang on to. For years I saw a generic city lit up at night. I would use those remote, artificial lights to soothe myself to sleep. One day I was quitting my job with no sense of exhilaration, one day I was leaving a note for my father, pulling out of his driveway, slightly bewildered, and two days later I was sitting in front of Howard. That was the way the future came to me.

The vision that accompanied me on my drive was a girl, a lady actually. We had the same hair but she didn't look like me. She was in a camel coat and ankle boots. A dress under the coat was belted high on her waist. She carried various shopping bags from specialty stores and as she was walking, pausing at certain windows, her coat would fly back in the wind. Her boot heels tapped on the cobblestones. She had lovers and breakups, an analyst, a library, acquaintances she ran into on the street whose names she couldn't call to mind. She belonged to herself only. She had edges, boundaries, tastes, definition down to her eyelashes. And when she walked it was clear she knew where she was going.

As I thanked him and we reviewed my contact information, I didn't know what had transpired, whether it was good or bad. It took me a moment to even remember the name of the restaurant. He held my hand too long and as I stood, his eyes traveled down my body, not like an employer's, but like a man's.

"I dislike mopping. And lying," I said. I don't know why. "Those are the two that come to mind."

He nodded and smiled — what I wanted to call a private smile. The backs of my legs were damp with sweat and as I walked away I felt his eyes unabashedly on my ass. At the door, I rolled my cardigan off my shoulders, and arched as if stretching. No one knows how I got the job, but it's better to be honest about these things.

Taste, Chef said, is all about balance. The sour, the salty, the sweet, the bitter. Now your tongue is coded. A certain connoisseurship of taste, a mark of how you deal with the world, is the ability to relish the bitter, to crave it even, the way you do the sweet.

II

The space was aesthetically unremarkable, even ugly in places. Not ragged by any means — the paint fresh, the dust banished — but defiantly past its peak. The art was dated, gaudy, some of it honestly preposterous, purchased in the eighties or whenever. The dining room had three levels, as if it had been built during different periods and linked together as an afterthought. Tables cluttered on one side of the room, sparse on the other. The cumulative effect was like someone hadn't quite made up his mind, but insisted on having you over anyway.

The owner told me at orientation, "There are many endeavors to bring pleasure to people. Every artist assumes that challenge. But what we do here is the most intimate. We are making something you take inside you. Not the food, the experience."

Two areas of the restaurant were flawless: first, three café-style tables in the front framed by a large window at the entrance. The tables were set in the day's changing light. Some people — I mean *guests* — hated to be next to the entrance, to be sectioned off from the main dining rooms. But some of them wouldn't sit anywhere else. These tables were often held for the most poised guests — rarely a sloucher or anyone in denim.

The Owner said, "Running a restaurant means setting a stage. The believability hinges on the details. We control how they experience the world: sight, sound, taste, smell, touch. That starts at the door, with the host and the flowers."

And then, the bar. Timeless: long, dark mahogany, with stools high enough to make you feel like you were afloat. The bar had soft music, dim lighting, tinkling layers of noise, the bumps of a neighbor's knee, the reach of someone's arm by your face to take a glittering martini, the tap of a hostess as she escorted guests behind your back, the blur of plates being passed, the rattle of drinks, the virtuoso performance of bartenders slapping bottles into the back bar while also delivering bread, while also taking an order with the requisite substitutions and complications. All the best regulars came in and greeted the hostess saying, Any space at the bar tonight?

"Our goal," he said, "is to make the guests feel that we are on their side. Any business transaction — actually any life transaction — is negotiated by how you are making the other person *feel.*"

The Owner looked and spoke like a deity. Sometimes the *New York Post* referred to him as the mayor. Tall, tan, handsome with perfect white teeth, effortless articulation, and gorgeous gesticulation. I listened to him accordingly, with my hands in my lap.

Yet there was a tension I couldn't quite put my finger on. Something false about making guests "feel" that we were on their side. I looked around the room and suddenly everything looked like currency to me: the silver, the wooden beams, the regal floral arrangement crowning the bar. Jesus, I thought, you can get rich by making people *feel* good about spending their money. We weren't on their side; we were on the Owner's side. All the emphasis on details, all the jargon — it was still just a business, right?

When orientation was over, I wanted to catch his eye and let him know that I got it. I wanted to ask someone how much of that money I would be taking home. Then I approached him at the exit and he looked me in the eyes. I stopped. He said my name though I hadn't told him. He shook my hand and nodded like he had already forgiven me for all my shortcomings and would remember my face forever.

He said, "We are creating the world as it should be. We don't have to pay any attention to how it is."

When I got the job I didn't actually get the job. I got to train for the job. And the position was "backwaiter," which wasn't the same as being a server. Howard led me up a narrow spiral staircase in the back of the kitchen and deposited me in the locker room. He said, "You're the new girl now. You have a certain responsibility."

He left without clarifying what that responsibility was. In the corner of the windowless room sat two older Latino men and a woman. They had been speaking in Spanish but were now staring at me. A small electric fan shuddered behind them. I tried a smile.

"Is there somewhere I can change?"

"Right here mami," the woman said. She had unruly black hair, held back by a bandana. Rivulets of sweat made track marks down her face. She pursed her lips. The men with their outsized, destroyed faces.

"Okay," I said. I opened my locker and stuck my face into it, blocking them from my sight. Howard had told me to buy a white button-down shirt, and I put it on over my tank top to avoid undressing. The shirt was as breathable as cardboard. Sweat ran down my back and into my underwear.

They began talking again, fanning themselves, walking to a small sink and splashing water on their faces. The room was stacked with chairs in the back, and along the walls were pairs of Crocs and clogs covered in white splotches, with heels worn down to nothing. There was no air, my chest contracted.

The door burst open and a man said, "Are you not hungry? Are you coming?"

I looked at the three in the corner to make sure he was talking to me. He had an adolescent, tame face, but was irritated, his brows narrowed together.

"No, I'm hungry," I said. I wasn't, I just wanted something to do.

"Well family is almost over. How much more primping do you have left?"

I shut my locker door and put my hair back in a ponytail.

"I'm done. Are you in charge of me?"

"Yes, I'm in charge of you. I'm your trailer. First lesson, if you miss family, you don't eat."

"Well it's nice to meet you. I'm —"

"I know who you are." He slammed the door behind us. "You're the new girl. Don't forget to clock in."

There were tables in the back dining room set with stainless steel sheet trays and bowls so big I could bathe in them. Macaroni and cheese, fried chicken, potato salad, biscuits, an oily green salad with shredded carrots. Pitchers of iced tea. It looked like food for a large catered event, but my trailer handed me a white plate and started helping himself to family meal. He went and sat at a table in the corner without inviting me to follow. The staff had taken over the back dining room. They came from every department: the servers in aprons, people in white coats, women removing headsets, men in suits, tugging at ties. I sat near the servers, in the very last chair — it was the best seat if I needed to run.

Preshift turned out to be a turbulent affair. A frazzled, skittish manager named Zoe was looking at me like it was my fault. She kept calling out numbers or names — things like "Section 6" and "Mr. Blah-blah at eight p.m." but the servers talked right through her. I nodded deafly. I couldn't touch my food.

The servers looked like actors — each perfectly idiosyncratic, but rehearsed. It all felt staged for my benefit. They wore striped shirts of every color. They were performing, snapping, clapping, kissing, cutting each other off, layers of noise colluding while I sank into my seat.

Howard walked up with wineglasses hanging like spokes from his hand. A young man in a suit trailed behind him with a bottle of wine wrapped in brown paper. The servers passed around the glasses with tastes of wine, but one never made it to me.

When Howard clapped his hands everyone went silent.

"Who would like to begin?"

Someone called out, "Pinot, obviously."

"New World or Old?" Howard asked, scanning the room. His eyes fell on me for a second and I dropped my face to my plate. I remembered every time a teacher had called on me and I didn't know the answer. I remembered wetting my pants in the fourth grade and thought that if he called on me I would again now.

"Old World," a voice called out.

"Obviously," someone else said.

"It's old. I mean, it's got age — look, it's beginning to pale."

"So we're talking Burgundy."

"It's just a matter of deduction now, HR." This man lifted his glass and pointed it to Howard. "I'm onto you."

Howard waited.

"A little austere to be Côte de Beaune."

"Is it off?"

"I was thinking it might be off!"

"No, it's perfect."

They stopped talking. I leaned forward to see who had said that. She was in the same row as me, behind too many people. I saw the bowl of her glass as she pulled it away from her nose and then brought it back. Her voice, low, ponderous, continued:

"Côte de Nuits . . . hmm, Howard, this is a treat. Gevrey-Chambertin, of course. The Harmand-Geoffroy." She put the glass down in front of her. From what I saw, she hadn't taken a sip. The wine caught the light rebelliously. "The 2000. It's actually showing really well."

"I agree, Simone. Thank you." Howard clapped his hands together. "Friends, this wine is a steal, and don't let the difficult 2000 vintage put you off. Côte de Nuits was able to pull off some stunning wines

41

and they are drinking well, today, right now, this minute. As far as this gift goes, pass it on to your guests tonight."

Everyone stood up together. The people around me stacked their plates on top of my full one and left. I held them to my chest and pushed through the swinging doors in the kitchen. Two servers walked by on my right and I heard one of them say in a false singsong, "Oh, the Harmand-Geoffroy, of course," and the other girl rolled her eyes. Someone walked by on my left and said to me, "Seriously? You don't know what a dishwasher looks like?"

I moved toward a trough laden with dirty dishes that ran the length of the room. I set my stack down apologetically. A tiny, gray-haired man on the other side of the trough huffed and took my stack, scraping the food off of each one and into a trash can.

"Pinche idiota," he said, and spat into the trough in front of him.

"Thank you," I said. Maybe I had never actually made a mistake before in my life and this is what it felt like. Like your hands were slipping off of every facet, like you didn't have the words or directions and even gravity wasn't reliable. I felt my trailer behind me and spun around to grab him.

"Where do I —" I reached out for an arm

42

and noticed too late that it wasn't striped. It was bare. There was a static shock when I touched it.

"Oh. You're not my person." I looked up. Black jeans and a white T-shirt with a backpack on one shoulder. Eyes so pale, a weatherworn, spectral blue. He was covered in sweat and slightly out of breath. I inhaled sharply. "My trailer person I mean. You're not him."

His eyes were a vise. "Are you sure?"

I nodded. He looked me up and down, indiscreetly.

"What are you?"

"I'm new."

"Jake." We both turned. The woman who knew the wine stood in the doorway. She didn't see me. Her gaze distilled the kitchen light to its purest element.

"Good morning. What time does your shift start again?"

"Oh fuck off Simone."

She smiled, pleased.

"I have your plate," she said, and turned into the dining room. The doors swung back violently. And then all I could see was his feet pounding the last few stairs.

They showed me how to fold. Stacks of plastic-wrapped, blindingly white linens.

Crease, turn, crease, fold, fan. Wrap with napkin bands, stack. The servers used that time to catch up, engaging in full conversations. Crease, turn, crease, fold, fan. I was lulled into a trance by the motions, by the lint gathering in my apron. No one addressed me. At least I can fold napkins, I said to myself, over and over.

I watched Jake and Simone. He stood at the end of the bar hunched over his plate with his back to me, and she talked without looking at him. She tapped the screen at the computer terminal. I could tell they were attached far underneath the surface of the restaurant. Maybe because they weren't laughing, or bantering — there was no performance. They were just talking. A girl with a button nose and a debutante's smile said, "Hey," and stuck her chewing gum into the napkin on my lap, and the trance was over.

I didn't look up for weeks. I asked to work as many days as possible, but there was an alarming delay in money while the new paycheck cycle started. And when it came it was training pay. Nothing. With my first paycheck I bought a used mattress for $250 from a couple moving out a few apartments down.

"Don't worry," they said, "no bugs. It's full of love."

I took it, but that to me was more disturbing.

On the other end of the linen spectrum came the bar mops. Every new trailer opened the session with, "Did someone explain bar mops?" And when I said yes they said, "Who? So-and-so always fucks it up. I have a secret stash." I learned four different and elaborate systems for managing what were essentially rags they kept under lock and key.

There were never enough. We could never attain healthy bar mop equilibrium. The kitchen always needed more, or the guy in the back never got set up before service, or the bartenders went on a cleaning spree. Invariably you forgot to save some for yourself. The victim of this bar mop negligence got to yell at you. When you asked a manager for more, they got to yell at you too, for burning through bar mops before service even started. If you begged — and everyone begged — the manager would unlock the cupboard and count out ten more. You told no one about the ten extra bar mops. You hid them, and then doled them out heroically during emergencies.

■ ■ ■ ■

"The kitchen is a church," Chef screamed at me when I asked my trailer a question. "No fucking talking."

Silence was observed in the kitchen. People entered on tiptoe. The only person allowed to directly address Chef during service was Howard — sometimes the other managers tried to do it and got their heads bitten off. The silence probably helped the cooks, but it made learning anything difficult to impossible.

In between shifts I went to the Starbucks that smelled like a toilet and drank one cup of coffee. On my evening off, I bought individual Coronas from the bodega and drank them on my mattress. I was so tired I couldn't finish them. Half-empty bottles of warm beer lined my windowsills, looking like urine and filtering sunlight. I put slices of bread from the restaurant into my purse and made myself toast in the mornings. If I had a double I took naps in the park between the shifts. I slept hard, dreaming that I was sinking into the ground, and I felt safe. When I woke I slapped myself to get the grass marks off my cheeks.

■ ■ ■ ■

No names. I didn't know people. I grabbed whatever characteristics I could: crooked or fluorescent teeth, tattoos, accents, lipsticks, I even recognized some people by their gait. It's not that my trailers were withholding information. I was just so stupid that I couldn't learn table numbers and names at the same time.

They explained to me that this restaurant was different — real paychecks first of all, and health benefits, sick days. Some non-salaried servers even got hourly raises. People owned homes, had children, took vacations.

Everyone had been there years. There were senior servers who would never leave. Debutante-Smile, Guy-with-Clark-Kent-Glasses, Guy-with-Long-Hair-and-Bun, Overweight-Gray-Hair-Guy. Even the back-waiters had been there at least three years. There was Mean-Girl, and Russian-Pouty-Lips, and my first trailer, whom I called Sergeant because of the way he ordered me around.

Simone was Wine-Woman, and a senior server. She and Clark-Kent-Glasses had been there the longest. One of my trailers

47

called her the tree of knowledge. Every pre-shift the maître d' rearranged the seating chart because regulars demanded to sit in her section. The servers would line up to ask her questions, or they sent her to their VIP tables with a wine list. She never looked at me.

And Sweaty-Boy, Jake? In those weeks of training I didn't see him again. I thought maybe he didn't work there, had just been filling in that day. But then I came in to pick up my first check on a Friday night and he was there. I put my head down when I saw him. He was a bartender.

"So I heard you're a barista," drawled Guy-with-Long-Hair-and-Bun. "That makes my training day real easy."

It was like arriving to a coffee station on another planet. Everything silver, futuristic, elegant. More intelligent than me.

"Ever worked on a Marzocco before?"

"I'm sorry?"

"The machine, the Marzocco. It's the Cadillac of espresso machines."

All right, all right, I thought. I know how to make fucking coffee. Even a Cadillac was still a car. I picked out the portafilters, saw the grinder, the tamper.

"You know the four Ms? What kind of

espresso were you guys using?"

"The kind that got dropped off in big bags," I said. "It wasn't exactly a gourmet place."

"Oh shit, okay, I heard you were a barista. No big deal, I'll train you and we'll check in with Howard after —"

"No. No." I twisted the portafilter out and discharged the spent espresso into the trash can. "Where are your bar mops?" He handed me one and I wiped the basket. "You guys use timers or what?"

"We use our eyes."

I exhaled. "Okay." I turned on the grinder, wiped the steamer wand, flushed out the group head. Twenty-five seconds was a perfect shot of espresso. I would count it myself. "One cappuccino, coming right up."

I studied the menu, I studied the manual. At the end of every service a manager asked me questions. I found that even if I didn't know what on earth a Lobster Shepherd's Pie was, even if I couldn't imagine it, if I knew it was the Monday night special I was going to pass my trails. Even if I didn't know what the fuck our tenets meant, I repeated back to Zoe perfectly, "The first tenet is to take care of each other."

"And do you know what makes a fifty-one

percenter?"

Zoe was eating the hanger steak at her desk in the office. She swirled a piece of it through mashed potatoes and frizzled leeks. I was so hungry I could have slapped her.

"Um."

I forgot that the Owner had said to me: "You were hired because you are a fifty-one percenter. That's not something we can train for — you have to be born with it."

I had no idea what that meant. I looked at the choking sign on the wall. The man asphyxiating in the sign looked calm and I envied him.

Forty-nine percent of the job was the mechanics. Anyone can do this job — that's what I was always told about waitressing. I'm sorry, *serving.*

You know, just memorize the table numbers and positions, stack plates up along your arm, know all the menu items and their ingredients, never let the water levels drop, never spill a drop of wine, bus the tables cleanly, mise-en-place, fire orders, know the basic characteristics of the basic grape varieties and basic regions of the entire wine world, know the origins of the tuna, pair a wine with the foie gras, know the type of animal the cheeses come from, know what is pasteurized, what contains gluten, what contains nuts, where the extra straws are, how to count. Know how to show up on time.

"And what's the rest of it?" I asked my trailer, out of breath, dabbing paper towels into my armpits.

"Oh, the fifty-one percent. That's the tricky stuff."

I flung off my sweated-through work jeans, twisted the top off a Pacifico because they were out of Corona, and sat on my mattress with the manual. I am a fifty-one percenter, I said to myself. This is Me:

- *Unfailingly optimistic:* doesn't let the world get him or her down.
- *Insatiably curious:* and humble enough to ask questions.
- *Precise:* there are no shortcuts.
- *Compassionate:* has a core of emotional intelligence.
- *Honest:* not just with others, but most essentially with oneself.

I lay back on the bed and laughed. Rarely, but sometimes, I thought about my old coworkers back in nowhere — where our training consisted of learning how to switch on the coffeepot — watching me sweat and run and parrot back this manual, unable to see five feet in front of me. They watched me spend every clocked-in moment blind and terrified, and then we laughed about it.

The corner of South Second and Roebling was crowded with Puerto Rican families in their lawn chairs with adjacent coolers. They played dominoes. Kids screamed through the stream from a detonated hydrant. I watched them and thought back to that coffee shop on Bedford from the first day. I could probably walk in there now. I would say, Yeah I've worked on a Marzocco — oh, you don't know it?

But it wouldn't be enough. Whatever it was, just being a back-waiter, a server, a barista — at this restaurant I wasn't *just* anything. And I wouldn't call it being a fifty-one percenter because that sounded like a robot. But I felt marked. I felt noticed, not just by my coworkers who scorned me, but by the city. And every time a complaint, a moan, or an eye roll rose to the surface, I smiled instead.

III

And one day I ran up the stairs into the locker room and a woman from the office followed me. She carried three hangers hung with stiff, striped Brooks Brothers button-downs. They were the androgynous kind of shirt that straddles the line between the boardroom and a circus.

"Congratulations," she said in monotone, like her clothes. "These are your stripes."

I put them in my locker and stared at them. I wasn't training anymore. I had a job. At the most popular restaurant in New York City. I fingered the shirts and it happened: The escape was complete. I put on navy stripes. I thought I felt a breeze. It was as if I were coming out of anesthesia. I saw, I recognized, a person.

She stopped me on my first steps into the dining room, holding a glass of wine in her hand. I had the fleeting impression that she had been waiting for me a long time.

"Open your mouth," Simone said, her head raised, imperious. Both of us looked at each other. She painted her lips before each service with an unyielding shade of red. She had dark-blond hair, untamable, frizzy, wisped out from her face like a seventies rock goddess. But her face was strict, classical. She held the glass of wine out to me and waited.

I threw it back like a tequila shot, an accident, a habit.

"Open your mouth now," she commanded me. "The air has to interact with the wine. They flower together."

I opened my mouth but I had already swallowed.

"Tasting is a farce," she said with her eyes closed, nose deep in the bowl of the glass. "The only way to get to know a wine is to take a few hours with it. Let it change and then let it change you. That's the only way to learn anything — you have to live with it."

I had the next day off and wanted to celebrate. I took myself to the Met. The servers were always talking about the shows they saw — music, film, theater, art. I didn't know a single thing they mentioned though

I had taken an Intro to Art History course in college. I went because I needed something to contribute during napkin time.

I don't know how long I had been in the city, but when I got off the train at Eighty-Sixth Street I realized how narrowly I had been living. My days were contained to five square blocks in Union Square, the L train, and five square blocks in Williamsburg. When I saw the trees in Central Park I laughed out loud.

The lobby of the Met — that holy labyrinth — appropriately took my breath away. I imagined being interviewed ten years from now. Not like with Howard where I was tested, but interviewed with admiration. My amicable interviewer would ask me about my origins. I would tell him that for so long I thought I would be nothing; that my loneliness had been so total that I was unable to project into the future. And that this changed when I got to the city and my present expanded, and my future skipped out in front of me.

I stuck to the Impressionist galleries. They were paintings I had seen a hundred times reproduced in books. They were the rooms that people dozed in. Your body could go into a kind of coma from the dreamscapes, but if the mind was alert, the paintings galvanized. They were almost confrontational.

"And that confirmed what I had always suspected," I told my interviewer. "That my life before the city had only been a reproduction."

After I ran out of rooms I started again. Cézanne, Monet, Manet, Pissarro, Degas, Van Gogh. "This is what I want," I said, showing my interviewer the painting of Van Gogh's cypresses. "Do you see how, up close, it's blurry and passionate? And from a distance, whole?"

"And what about love?" my interviewer asked me, unprompted, as I stared at Cézanne's apples. For a second I saw Simone's red lips asking the question.

"Love?" I looked around the gallery for the answer. I had wandered out of Impressionism, into early Symbolism. Where a moment earlier I could have sworn the room was crowded, it was now nearly empty except for an elderly man who stood with a cane and a younger woman holding his arm in support. When I was driving to the city I had said to myself, I'm not one of those girls who moves to New York to fall in love. Now, in front of a jury of Symbolists, Simone, and the old man, my denial felt thin.

"I don't know anything about it yet," I

said. I moved next to the man and his friend. His huge ears looked like they were carved of wax, and I was sure he was deaf. He was too at peace. We looked at Klimt's woman in white, *Portrait of Serena Lederer,* the title said. She certainly wasn't one of his most daring, and stood in contrast to his later gold-leafed, erotic works. But though she looked like a virginal column, she had in her face a restrained joy. I remembered something about an affair between the artist and the model, rumors that her daughter was actually Klimt's. She stood above the three of us, unconcerned with being stared at. The old man smiled at me before he walked off.

"Show me," I said to the woman in white. We regarded each other and waited.

I got off the train and the streets were glowing. I went to the wine stall in the mini-mall on North Fifth and Bedford. The man behind the counter had long hair and tired, hanging eyes. He turned down the Biggie he'd been blasting when I came in.

I looked at every single bottle, but I didn't recognize anything. Finally, after ten minutes, I asked, "Do you have an affordable Chardonnay?"

He had paint all over him and a cigarette

behind his ear. "What kind of Chardonnay do you like?"

"Um," I swallowed. "France?"

He nodded. "Yeah, that's the only kind, right? None of that Cali shit. How's this? I have one cold."

I paid him and held the bag to my chest. I ran home, crossing to the opposite side of Grand Street so I wouldn't be contaminated by the demons lounging outside of Clem's. I ran up my four flights of stairs too, ran into the apartment, stole Jesse's wine key and a mug, and ran up the last flight, pushing out onto the roof.

The sky was like the paintings. No, the paintings were trying to represent this sunset. The sky was aflame and throwing sparks, the orange clouds rimmed with purple like ash. The windows in each high-rise in Manhattan were lit up like the buildings were burning down. I was out of breath, overtired from the museum. My heart drummed. A voice said, You have to live with it. Another voice said, You made it, you made it, and at the same time, in a blistering chorus I said, *Made it where? Live with what?*

I walked in on them in the locker room. Simone had been speaking loudly, sitting in

58

a spare chair in her stripes with her legs crossed. He was standing in front of his locker, buttoning his shirt. They both looked at me, startled.

"Sorry. Do you want me to come back?"

"Of course not," she said. But neither of them said anything else. The silence was accusatory. He dropped his pants, stepped out of them, and turned back to Simone.

"Ignore him," she said. It sounded like an order, so I obeyed. I looked away.

"Pick up" was the call.

"Picking up" was the echo.

"Six and six, table 45, share," Chef said. His eyes didn't leave the board of tickets in front of him. "Pick up."

I put my hands in front of me and grabbed. Another sweltering day. Air conditioners all around the city were giving up. As I pushed into the tepid dining room I noticed the ice was melting in the oyster tray in my hands. Pale blue bodies amid sloshing ice chips. It looked disgusting. And six and six meant nothing to me. I had forgotten to check the day's oysters. I forgot the table I was going to. Simone flooded by me and I reached for her.

"Excuse me, Simone, sorry, but which are which oyster? Do you know?"

"Do you remember when you tasted them?" She didn't look at the plate.

I hadn't tasted them when they had been passed around at family meal. I hadn't looked at the menu notes.

"Do you remember tasting them?" she asked again, slowly, like I was dumb. "East Coast oysters are brinier, more mineral. West Coasts are plumper, creamier, sweeter. They're even physically different. One has a flat cup, the other tends to be deeper."

"Okay, so which are which on this plate?" I held the plate closer to her face but she wouldn't look.

"Those are covered in water. Take them back to Chef."

I shook my head. Absolutely not.

"You're not going to serve those. Take them back to Chef."

I shook my head again but sucked in my lips. I saw it all unfolding ahead of me. His anger at me, his yelling about the waste, my embarrassment. But I could look at the menu notes while I waited for the new ones. I could hear the table number again. I could figure it out.

"Okay."

"Next time look at them but use your tongue."

■ ■ ■ ■

The managers maintained power by shifting things. They came into a server's station and moved their dupe pad, moved their checks, rearranged the tickets on the bar. They pulled white wines out of the ice bucket, wiped them down, and reinserted them in a new pattern. They would pause you when you were running, obviously in a hurry, and ask you how you thought you were settling in.

Simone maintained power by centrifugal force. When she moved, the restaurant was pulled as if by a tailwind. She led the servers by her ability to shift their focus — her own focus was a spotlight. Service unfolded in her parentheses.

"What's that bartender's name again? The one who only talks to Simone?" I asked Sasha. I was casual about it.

Sasha was a backwaiter. He was otherworldly beautiful: broad alien cheekbones, blue eyes, bee-stung, haughty lips. He could have been a model, except he was barely five foot four. His gaze was so cold, you knew he had been everyone: a rich man, a poor man, in love, abandoned, a murderer, and close to death. None of these states impressed him much.

"That bartender? Jake."

He was Russian, and though he was clearly fluent in English, he didn't bother to adhere to its rules. His accent was both elegant and comical. He rolled his eyes at me while he cut bread.

"Okay, Pollyanna, let me tell you few truths. You're too new."

"What does that mean?"

"What you think it means? Jakey will eat you for dinner and spit you out. You even know what I'm speaking of? You're not bouncing around after that."

I shrugged like I didn't care and filled the bread baskets.

"Besides. He's mine. I'll cut your fucking throat if you touch him and I'm not a joker."

"Silence in the kitchen! Pick up."

"Picking up!"

The kitchen was a riot of misshapen, ugly tomatoes. They smelled like the green insides of plants, like sap, like dirt.

There were tomatoes of every color: yellow, green, orange, red-purple, mottled, striped, dotted. They were bursting. "Seaming" is what Chef called it, when the curves and indentations pulled apart from each other, but not completely, like parted lips.

"Heirloom season," Ariel sang out. She was also a backwaiter. She always had pounds of eyeliner on, even if it was the morning. She had bangs and dark-brown hair that she twisted up onto her head and held with chopsticks. She was still named Mean-Girl in my head because she wouldn't speak to me during training, only pointed and gave exasperated sighs. But today she was passing out dripping bar mops to the line cooks from a bucket of ice water. They wrapped them around their heads like bandanas or slung them over the backs of their necks. That didn't seem like something a Mean-Girl would do. In fact, I hadn't seen anyone do something that compassionate with their bar mop stash. I heard from my own head, Our first tenet is to take care of each other.

She handed me a bar mop. I put it on the back of my neck and it felt like rising out of a soggy cloud into clean air.

"Pick up."

"Picking up," I said. I looked expectantly to the window but there were no plates lined up. Instead Scott, the young, tattooed sous chef, passed me a sliver of tomato. The insides were tie-dyed pink and red.

"A Marvel-Striped from Blooming Hill

Farm," he said, as if I had asked him a question.

I cupped it while it dripped. He pinched up flakes of sea salt from a plastic tub and flicked it on the slice.

"When they're like this don't fuck with them. Just a little salt."

"Wow," I said. And I meant it. I had never thought of a tomato as a fruit — the ones I had known were mostly white in the center and rock hard. But this was so luscious, so tart I thought it victorious. So — some tomatoes tasted like water, and some tasted like summer lightning.

"What are heirlooms?" I asked Simone as I ran to get behind her in line for family meal. She had two white plates in her hand and I felt a shiver of expectation looking at that second plate. I noted how she made her own — a generous tongful of green salad and a cup of the vichyssoise.

"Exciting, isn't it? The season? They're rare or unique breeds of plants and animals. Once all our tomatoes were like that. Before preservatives and supermarkets and this commercial food production hell we're living in. Breeds evolved in places based on one evolutionary principle: they tasted better. The point is not longevity or flawless-

64

ness. All of our vegetables were biologically diverse, pungent with the nuances of their breed. They reflected their specific time and space — their terroir."

On the second plate she took the biggest pork chop on the bone, a scoop of the rice salad, and a wedge of gratin potatoes. She said, "Now everything tastes like nothing."

They conjoined in my mind. It wasn't that they were always together. Theirs was an oblique connection, not always direct. If I saw one, my eyes started to move, looking for the other. Simone was easy to find, ubiquitous, directing everyone — she seemed to have some sort of system where she divided her attention between the servers equally. But I had a harder time tracking him, his alliances, his rhythms.

If they were in the restaurant together they had one eye on each other and I had one eye on them, trying to understand what I was seeing. It wasn't like they were the only fascinating people at the restaurant. But they were an island if the rest of us were the continent — distant, inaccessible, picking up stray light.

"Pick up."

My eyes snapped open but I was the

barista today, the kitchen was far away. Howard looked at me from the Micros terminal. He was waiting for me to make him a macchiato but I was overthinking it. I threw the first two shots away.

"I'm hearing Chef scream, 'Pick up' in my sleep," I said, swirling the warm milk. It was as glossy as new paint. "Punishing myself I guess."

"Thanatos — the death drive," Howard said. He laid a napkin over his arm and inspected a bottle of wine on the service bar. "We fantasize about traumatizing events to maintain our equilibrium. Lovely." He took the macchiato and smelled it before taking a sip. He regarded me. The other managers wore suits but somehow everyone in the restaurant always knew that Howard was the man in charge — as if his suits were cut from a finer fabric.

"It's compulsive but we actually find the painful repetition pleasurable." He took another sip.

"It doesn't sound pleasurable."

"It's how we self-soothe. How we maintain the illusion that we are in control of our lives. For example, you repeat 'Pick up' in hopes that the outcome each time will be different. And you are repeatedly embarrassed, are you not?" He waited for me to

66

respond but I wouldn't meet his eyes. "You are hoping to master the experience. The pain is what we know. It's our barometer of reality. We never trust pleasure."

Every time Howard looked at me I felt bare. A coffee ticket printed up and I used it as an excuse to turn around.

"Are you dreaming about work often?" he asked. It felt like he spoke it into my neck.

"No." I slammed a portafilter to empty it and I could feel him walk away.

But I was. The dreams were tidal, consumptive, chaotic. Service played over in my head, but no one had faces. And I heard voices, layered on top of one another, a cacophony. Phrases would rise then evanesce: Behind You, Pick Up, To Your Right, To Your Left, Picking Up, Candles, Can You, Now, Toothpicks, Pick Up, Bar Mops, Now, Excuse Me, Picking Up.

In my dreams these words were a code. I was blind and the directives were all I had to pick my way through the blackness. The syllables quaked and separated. I woke up talking: I couldn't remember what I had been saying, only that I was driven to keep saying it.

Terroir. I looked it up in *The World Atlas of Wine* in the manager's office. The definition was people talking around it without identifying it. It seemed a bit farfetched. That food had character, composed of the soil, the climate, the time of year. That you could taste that character. But still. An idea mystical enough to be highly seductive.

Ignore him. That's what I did. When Jake came into family meal late and took his seat next to Simone, when he pulled up on his bike outside the front window, when he called harshly out for bar mops, I looked away.

But I started to hear things, all of it unverifiable and improbable. Jake was a musician, a poet, a carpenter. He had lived in Berlin, he had lived in Silver Lake, he had lived in Chinatown. He was halfway through a PhD on Kierkegaard. They called his apartment "the opium den." He was bisexual, he slept with everyone, he slept with no one. He was an ex–heroin addict, he was sober, he was always a little drunk.

He and Simone were not a couple though their magnetic, unconscious way of tracking each other seemed to indicate otherwise. I knew they were very old friends, and that she had gotten him the job. Some nights a cherubic strawberry blonde that Sasha called Nessa-Baby came and sat in front of

Jake at the bar as service was winding down.

He knew part of his job was to be looked at. He was a quiet bartender. There was a submissiveness to his beauty that was nearly feminine, a stillness that made one want to paint him. When he worked the bar he submitted. Women and men of all ages left business cards and phone numbers with their tips. Guests gave him gifts for no reason — that kind of beauty.

If he rolled up his shirtsleeves, you could see the edges of tattoos that spoke to another private body he kept. It was the sight of his arm resting on the beer tap that changed me. The beer was acting up. The kegs were probably too new, not cold enough. Just foam, no beer. Jake let the foam pour while he talked to a guest. The drain was full of foam, it ran over to his feet, a spreading white pool. His sleeve was rolled up, the tendons of his forearm tensed from shaking cocktails. I remembered that static shock when I touched him. I felt the shock in my mouth. His inappropriate forearm and the foam cascading, his manner too casual, too condescending.

"That's a lot of beer to waste," I said. My voice surprised me, ringing out over my vow of silence.

He looked at me. Perhaps it was raining

69

that night, a stifling tropical storm. Perhaps someone struck a match and held it to my cheek. Perhaps someone cleaved my life into before and after. He looked at me. And then he laughed. From that moment on he became unbearable to me.

You will encounter a fifth taste.

Umami: uni, or sea urchin, anchovies, Parmesan, dry-aged beef with a casing of mold. It's glutamate. Nothing is a mystery anymore. They make MSG to mimic it. It's the taste of ripeness that's about to ferment. Initially, it serves as a warning. But after a familiarity develops, after you learn its name, that precipice of rot becomes the only flavor worth pursuing, the only line worth testing.

IV

The sardines are insane tonight.
It's true, Chef called him a faggot.
HR is freaking out.
Have you been to Ssäm bar yet?
No, the best Chinese is in Flushing.
I'm playing a show Wednesday.
Scott is on fire.
I was obsessed with Chekhov.
I'm obsessed with Campari right now.
I need to get my cameras out again.
I'm fairly well known in the experimental
    dance world.
Table 43 is industry — Per Se?
If one more bitch cuts me off to ask for
    Chardonnay —
If one more person asks for steak sauce —
What the fuck?
Carson is in again — without the wife.
That's twice this week.
Sometimes I think, Fuck the pooled house.

71

I'm not jealous.
Technically I texted first. But he responded.
You don't get it.
I'm on day three — I feel great, high all the
    time.
Will you water 24?
Will you drop bread on 49?
Move.
Fuck off.
Fuck you.
It's like the rude Olympics in here today.
They're just French.
And after I took the LSAT, I was like wait, I
    don't want to be a lawyer.
I still paint sometimes.
I just need space. And time. And money.
It's so hard in New York.
Allergy on 61.
It's not really romantic.
I'd fuck the mom.
Does she come in drunk?
It's just lemon, maple syrup, and cayenne.
It's just Nicky's martinis, never drink more
    than one.
I just need representation.
It's like banging against a brick wall.
I need soupspoons on 27.
Chef wants to see you — now.
I'm dropping soup now.

What did I do?

Fuck — the midcourse.

"Pick up."

The tickets came from a printer on Chef's right. They flew into the air like an exclamation and fluttered down in a wave. He yelled: "Fire Gruyère. Fire tartare. Hold calamari. Hold two smokers."

From that code the cooks on the line went into action. Chef lined up the tickets, bouncing from foot to foot like a child who had to go to the bathroom. He was a small man from New Jersey but classically trained in France. He screamed anecdotes at the cooks, recalling "real" kitchens where chefs would slam you in the head with a copper pan if you couldn't chop the parsley fine enough. Chef's voice was too loud and he couldn't really control it. The servers and managers were always complaining that you could hear him from the dining room. Everyone, even Scott, his number two, kept their eyes averted if he was on a tirade. The man paced the kitchen red-faced, primed for explosion.

The line cooks were a blur of movement while essentially staying in one place. Everything was within arm's reach in their stations. Sweat funneled off their eyelashes.

There were open flames or salamanders at their backs and heat lamps in the pass at their front. They wiped the rim of each plate before passing it to Chef, who inspected it mercilessly, eager to find smudges of stray sauce or olive oil.

"Pick up!"

"Picking up."

I was the food runner, I was next. I covered my hands with bar mops. The plates heated up like irons, I expected them to glow.

"I heard you don't know the oysters yet," said Will, startling me. Will was Sergeant, the guy who'd been in charge of me on my first day. Even though I had my stripes now, he still seemed to think I was his project.

"Jesus," I said. "Everything is a lesson around here. It's just dinner."

"You don't get to say that yet."

"Pick! Up!"

"Picking up," I responded.

"Pick up!"

"Louder," said Will, nudging me forward.

"Picking up," I said, harder, hands out-stretched, ready.

It was all one motion. The roasted half duck had been in the window for going on five minutes while it waited for the risotto, the plate baking. At first, as with all burns, I felt nothing. I reacted in anticipation. When the plate shattered and the duck thudded clumsily onto the mats, I cried out, pulling my hand to my chest, caving.

Chef looked at me. He had never really seen me before.

"Are you kidding me?" he asked. Quiet. All the line cooks, butchers, prep guys, pastry girls watched me.

"I burned myself." I held out my palm, already streaked with red, as proof.

"Are you *fucking* kidding me?" Louder. A rumbling, then quiet. Even the tickets stopped printing. "Where do you come from? What kind of bullshit TGI Fridays waitresses are they bringing in now? You think that's a *burn*? Do you want me to call your mommy?"

"The plates are too hot," I said. And then I couldn't take it back.

I stared at his feet, at the mess on the floor. I bent over to pick up the beautifully burnished duck. I thought he might hit me. I flinched, but held it out to him by its leg.

"Are you retarded? Get out of my kitchen. Don't even think about setting foot in here again. This is a church." He slammed his hands on the stainless steel in front of him. "A fucking church!"

His eyes went back to the board and he

said, quiet again, "Refire, duck, refire risotto, on the fly, what the fuck are you looking at Travis, keep your eyes on your steak before you turn it to cardboard."

I set the duck on the counter next to the bread. The grating noise of tickets printing, of plates being thrown around, of pans hitting burners, it all throbbed with my hand. In the locker room I went to the sink and ran lukewarm water on it. The mark was already starting to disappear. I cried and continued crying while I changed out of my uniform. I sat on a chair and tried to calm down before I went back downstairs. Will opened the door.

"I know," I yelled. "I fucked up. I know."

"Let me see your hand."

He crouched next to me. I opened my palm and he put a bar mop filled with ice cubes into it. I started crying again.

"You're okay, doll." He patted my shoulder. "Put your stripes on. You can work the dining room."

I nodded. I put on fresh mascara and went downstairs.

The mezz was seven two-tops on a balcony over the back dining room. The stairs were narrow, steep, treacherous. "A lawsuit waiting to happen," they told me. I took them one at a time, up and down, and still soups spilled onto rims, sauces slid.

Heather was Debutante-Smile, and she got in trouble weekly for chewing gum on the floor. She was from Georgia, with a delicate southern accent. They told me she had the highest tip average, and everyone blamed the accent. I thought it might be the gum.

"Sweetness" — she snapped her gum at me — "start the stairs with your left foot when you go down. Lean back."

I nodded.

"I heard about Chef. It happens."

I nodded again.

"You know, nobody is from here. We were all new. And like I always say, it's just dinner."

From a section of the handbook I neglected to read: Workers were to receive one complimentary shift drink after they clocked out. Workers were also to receive one complimentary shift coffee per eight-hour shift.

When this translated off the page, quantities increased, entitlement ran rampant. But I didn't know that yet. They wound us up, they wound us down.

"Take a seat, new girl."

Nicky was definitely talking to me. I had just clocked out and changed. I was cracking my wrists and heading toward the exit.

It was still a touch early. Cooks were plastic-wrapping the kitchen, servers swiping the final credit cards and waiting in the hutches. The dishwashers piled trash bags at the exit of the kitchen. I saw them peeking out, trembling like sprinters, waiting for the signal that they could take the bags to the curb and go home.

"Where?"

"At the bar." He wiped down a spot.

Nicky was Clark-Kent-Glasses. He was the first bartender they hired, and they said he'd be there until they shuttered the place. His glasses were often crooked, and at odds with the crookedness of his bow tie. He met his wife at the bar ten years earlier and she still came in and sat in the very same seat on Fridays. I heard he had three kids, but I couldn't really comprehend it, he seemed half child himself. He had an unpretentiousness and a Long Island accent that had been drawing people to the bar for decades.

"You want me to sit like a regular person?"

"Like a regular old person. What do you want to drink?"

"Um." I wanted to ask how much a beer cost, I had no idea.

"It's your shift drink. A little thank-you from the Owner at the end of the night."

He shook the amber, watery remains from a cocktail shaker into his glass. "Or a big thank-you. What do you like?"

"White wine sounds all right." I climbed onto a stool. Earlier in the night, midrush, Nicky had asked me if I had any common sense. I thought about it all night. I had no idea what to say to him, especially now that I was stripeless, except, Yes. I think I do have common sense.

"Yeah? Nothing particular?"

"I'm easy."

"That's what I like to hear from my back-waiters."

I blushed.

"Boxler?" he asked, and poured me a taste. I lifted it to my nose and nodded. I was too nervous to actually smell it. He poured me a glass, and I watched as he left his hand there, the wine surging past the pour line we used for guests. The glass now seemed a goblet.

"You did better tonight," said a voice behind me. Will jumped up onto the bar stool next to me.

"Thank you." I sipped my wine before I could undo the compliment. The Albert Boxler Riesling, not from Germany, but from Alsace, one of the high-end pours at twenty-six dollars a glass. And I was drinking it. Nicky had served it to me. To thank me. I rolled it through my mouth the way Simone had taught me, pursing my lips and cupping my tongue and almost making an inward whistle. I thought it would be sweet. I thought I tasted honey, or something like peaches. But then it was so dry it felt like someone had pierced me. My mouth watered and I sipped again.

"It's not sweet," I said out loud to Nicky and Will. They laughed.

"This is nice," I said. An hour ago these were incredibly privileged seats, occupied by the kind of people who spent thirty dollars on an ounce of Calvados.

Will had changed his tone with me since my burn. He was careful, or perhaps protective. I thought maybe he wanted to be my friend. He wouldn't make a terrible first friend. He wore a khaki shirt, reminiscent of safaris. He had a long arrowhead nose and bovine brown eyes. He spoke rapidly, nearly slurring. Those first trails I thought it was because he was in a hurry. Now I saw that he didn't want to show his teeth. They were square and yellowed, and the front left one was cracked.

He pulled out a cigarette. "Are we all clear?"

"Yes, sir." Nicky slid him a bread-and-butter plate. I panicked when Will lit up — I barely had memories of a time when you could smoke inside restaurants. He asked if I wanted one. I shook my head. I glued my eyes to the back bar, pretending to be absorbed in the memorization of the Cognac bottles. The two of them traded incomprehensible insults about two baseball teams from the same place.

"You say hi to Jonny tonight?" Nicky polished glasses from a never-ending pile on the bar. They were stationed like soldiers that progressed to the front only to be replaced by more in the back.

"He was here? I missed him."

"He was next to Sid and Lisa."

"Christ, those two. I stayed as far away as possible. Remember that Venice-is-an-island argument?"

"I thought he was going to hit her that night."

"If I was married to that, I'd do worse than hit her."

I kept an impassive face. They must be talking about their friends.

"What are you drinking, Billy Bob?"

"Can I get a hit of Fernet while I think

81

about it?"

"This. Is. It," said Ariel, slamming the glass racks down on the corner of the bar. The glasses jangled like bells and her hair flew up.

"You've got your hair down already?" Nicky asked. His voice was harsh but his eyes playful.

"Come on, Nick, please, I'm done, you know I'm done. Don't I look done?" She ran her fingers through her long hair, scratching at the scalp like she was trying to undo a wig. She flipped her hair to one side and leaned over the bar, feet coming off the ground.

"Come on Nick, snip, snip." She made a scissors motion with her fingers.

Ariel looked like trouble with her hair down. She had gone from quirky to something from the underworld, her hair well past her breasts, kinky from being knotted up all night. Her bangs were flat on her forehead and slashes of liquid eyeliner that once had swung rebelliously away from her lids were now smudged and battered.

During services Ariel worked with the energy of a bird, through a series of chirps, clicking noises, phrases half sung. She became frantic easily and recovered just as easily, whistling.

"Okay, you're cut, Ari. But I do need two bottles of Rittenhouse and one bottle of Fernet."

" 'Kay, I'll bring the rye but homeboy here can get his own Fernet." She eyed Will's glass, which had a black liquor in it, reeking of oversteeped tea and bubble gum. "You drink it, you stock it."

"Fuck off, Ari." Will exhaled smoke toward her.

"Fuck you, darling." She flounced away. Will shot back his drink.

"What's that?" I asked.

"Medicine." He burped. "It's for the end of a meal. Incredible . . . curative properties for the digestive tract."

He reached over the bar and started to fill a water glass with beer. Nicky stopped working and watched.

"I just fucking cleaned that, Will, if you spill one fucking drop . . ."

The beer shook in Will's hand, and the head rose an inch out of the glass. A hush. It kept rising but didn't spill.

"I'm a pro," Will said.

"Misery," said Ariel. She put two bottles of rye on the bar and pulled out the stool on the other side of Will. She was in a black slip, or maybe she thought it was a dress. Her bra was neon yellow like a traffic sign saying Proceed with Caution.

"Hm . . . what is open?" She tucked her legs under her and reached into the speed rack behind the bar.

"Can you animals get off my bar? I'm trying to clean."

"Is that Gigondas still good? When did we open it?"

"Two nights."

"Pushing it."

"Worth considering."

Nicky put up a glass and a black bottle with an insignia at the top and went back to his cleaning.

"Self-service tonight? You poured for the new girl."

"Ariel, I'm not fucking around, you barely stocked. She doesn't even know her head from her asshole yet and I think she could have done a better job. You've put me back twenty minutes."

"It looks like you picked the wrong night to be bartender, old man." Ariel emptied the wine into her glass, smelled it, and flipped open her cell phone.

If Nicky had spoken to me like that I would be flattened. But nothing happened. There wasn't even residual tension. Nicky yelled, All clear, into the kitchen and the porters sprang from behind the doors. They ran bags down the line behind the bar, an endless caravan of black bags to the curb. They propped the door open and the hot, dark air rushed in, as sticky as fingers running over my face. Misery. I drank my Riesling. Medicine.

"It's been really hot," I said. Nobody responded.

"Summer," I said.

Droning came in from the streets, then a rustling. For a second I thought it was the claustrophobic noise of the cicadas from my childhood. Or the wind bending branches. Or the moans of cows in fields. But it was cars. I wasn't used to it yet — the elimination of nature, the brimming whine of overheating machinery.

I shifted a little toward Will, wanting to seem open in case anyone talked to me. Will and Ariel were on their phones and Nicky was cursing to himself behind the bar. I thought about taking my phone out. It was new. I had left my old one on my dresser back home. I wondered what my father had done with it, with the boxes of books. Though I was also fairly certain he hadn't opened the door to my room. When I got my new phone, the area code felt like a badge: 917. I dutifully copied everyone's contact information into it. But I didn't have missed calls or messages. No one even asked me to cover shifts yet.

"I don't have an air conditioner," I said.

"Really?" Will shut his phone and turned to me. "Seriously?"

"They're expensive."

"Misery," Ariel interjected. She leaned around Will and looked at me inquisitively. "What do you do?"

"Oh, I have big windows and a fan. When it's really bad, like that stretch last week, I take cold showers to get the sweat —"

"No," she said. Her eyes said, You fucking idiot. "What do you *do*? In the city. Are you trying to be something?"

"Yes," I said. "I'm *trying* to be a back-waiter."

She laughed. I made Ariel laugh.

"Yeah, after that the sky's the limit."

"What do you do?"

"I do everything. I sing. I write music. I have a band. Willy here is trying to make a film. A claymation version of *À Bout de Souffle.*"

"Okay, that was one idea, it's not the worst idea."

"No, it's very admirable, a week of sculpting clay to get the right look of boredom —"

"Ariel, I can't be offended that you don't

86

understand anything about art. I blame first, your gender, second, the system —"

"Honestly though, Will, tell us the truth. You're just masturbating, right? In that little dark room with your clay Jean Seberg?"

Will sighed. "I will admit, it's hard not to." He turned to me. "I actually am working on something else. I'm writing a feature —"

"The comic-book one? The hero's journey? The exploration and reaffirmation of the patriarchal narrative?"

"Ariel, do you ever shut the fuck up?"

She smiled and rested a hand on his shoulder. She picked up her glass of wine and was about to sip when she said, "Oops," and turned to us.

"Cheers," she said gravely.

"Cheers."

"No, in the eyes, new girl."

"Look her in the eyes," Will said, "or she'll put a hex on your family."

I looked in her blackened eyes and said cheers like it was an incantation. Our three glasses touched and I pulled a mouthful of wine. The joints in my spine softened, like butter going to room temperature.

Then three things happened, seemingly at once.

First, the music changed. Lou Reed came over the speakers like a mumbling, beloved poet-uncle.

"You know I saw him once at the Gramercy Park Hotel — have you seen what they fucking did over there? That, my friends, is a rotten omen if ever there was one. So anyway, I'm sitting there and it's like, Lou-fucking-Reed, and I'm thinking, Thank you for teaching me how to be human, you know?"

I tried to keep listening. I nodded when Ariel looked at me. But the song was as intimate as a faucet dripping in the night.

Next, the bar stools filled. The cooks, the closing servers, the dishwashers, all out of their uniforms now, commandeered them. Everyone looked sloppy and criminal without their stripes. To see the scarred hands of the cooks against rumpled polos or old heavy-metal T-shirts, you wondered what it would be like to see one of them on a subway, without knowing they had a secret authoritative life in whites.

Simone walked down the line, her hair untied. I tried to catch her eye but she went to the far end of the bar with Heather, and who I now understood to be Heather's boyfriend, Parker, the man who'd initiated me on the coffee machine. Simone didn't look like a statue of herself anymore. She wore plain leather sandals and she swung one off her foot once she crossed her legs.

And finally, Chef banged out of the kitchen with a baseball cap and a backpack on. All his rage had melted away, leaving a man who looked like a dad on his way to a minivan. Everyone said, Good night, Chef, in a forceful singsong. He waved without looking. He barreled through and exited the building.

A curtain came down as Nicky reappeared behind the bar in a white undershirt and turned the lights up. The restaurant where I worked turned into a social club after hours. The bartenders weren't performing bartender anymore. They were mixing drinks with playful proportions. The cooks weren't looking over their shoulders for Chef, or walking numbly into hot pan handles. They were rolling joints, giggling, punching each other. The servers were stretching their arms and shoulders, comparing knots in their necks, stirring drinks with a finger, while complaining in one long, loving torrent about Howard, Zoe, dissecting the guests with a tone of passive contempt. I started to be able to tell when they were talking about regulars, because they would all want to outdo each other, demonstrating that they were the favorite.

Too dazzled to contribute, I watched them. It was the duality of everyone that floored me. Simone with her simple softness, her tired eyes. Will and Ariel snipping at each other. The talking got louder as the drinks receded. I kept looking at the open door, thinking a stranger would walk in and want a drink, or that the Owner would decide to pass down Sixteenth Street on his way home from an event and catch us and call the police. I'm new, I'm blameless, I would say with hands up. No one else seemed concerned. It made me wonder who really owned the restaurant.

"Black Bear?" Scott yelled down the bar to Ariel.

"No, Park Bar. Sasha just texted, he has a corner."

"No más Park Bar," he said. Jared and Jeff, two of his line cooks, started laughing.

"No you did not fuck the new one — Vivian?"

"Vivian!" they shouted. They raised their glasses.

"Full of shit," Ariel yelled. She turned to me and said, "Fuck. I thought she was gay."

"Too slow, Ari," said Will.

"Oh we'll see about that." She put her

hand on top of mine and said into my eyes, "They always start off straight. That's part of the fun."

I laughed. Petrified.

"What time is it?" I asked. A wall of exhaustion hit me with the drinks. It seemed to be a good moment to excuse myself. I didn't know who was going to clean this all up so the restaurant would be blank and sterile for the morning. When I looked down the line I saw Simone. She was texting and I thought, It's too late for her to be texting. That was when I first realized she was older. An image of him hit me in the back of my throat, just from habit. Who did Jake turn into when they turned the lights up? The shift drink — the first liminal space between work and my apartment, a space that I could project onto for hours, a space of inevitability where I would catch up with him eventually.

"It isn't two yet," Ariel said. As if something switched at two.

"Do you do this every night?"

"Do what?"

I nodded toward my glass of Boxler that refilled itself every time my eyes were averted. To the half-empty wine bottles that lined the bar for consumption. To Nicky eating cocktail olives while he and Scott told each other to fuck their mothers. To Lou's gravelly serenade coasting down on us through a film of smoke. To the row of us, unkempt, glassy and damp, sweating drinks in our hands.

"This?" Ariel waved away the smoke in front of my face, waved it away like it was nothing. "We're just having our shift drink."

V

When I started they told me, You have no experience. New York experience is all that counts.

Well, I had a little now. A structure presented itself to me, like the grid of the city. There was the GM, there were managers. There were senior servers, servers, backwaiters. The backwaiters originally functioned as a holding pen where aspiring servers awaited transcendence, but there was so little internal movement, most of them seemed contented where they were. I had Heather to thank for my position — she had talked a reluctant Parker into serving after six years of backwaiting. That's the only reason I existed.

The backwaiter had three kinds of shifts: food running (the carrying of plates), dining room backwaiter (the busing and resetting of tables), and beverage running (assisting with the drinks), which included a fair amount of barista work. I noticed that even though we rotated the shifts, people showed an affinity for one area and developed a schedule around it.

Will was an excellent food runner, with his Yes-Chef-No-Chef military mentality, his eyes-to-ground focus. So while he was a backwaiter, he also had some loyalties in the kitchen, which he exhibited in several annoying ways, such as partaking in kitchen beer, and complaining about "FOH" as if he weren't one of the front of house.

Ariel loved the freedom of being dining room backwaiter. She waltzed around, picking up a few plates, topping off a few waters, polishing a few knives and nudging them into place on the newly set table with first a look of pinched frustration, and then placidity when it came together. And while this wasn't true of all backwaiters, Ariel was generally trusted to talk to the guests. If the rest of us so much as said "Hello" to a table, a scolding was sure to follow.

Sasha was too good at his job to stay still. He got bored easily. If you put him in the kitchen, he could run your plates, drop off ice at the bar, and bus two tables on his way back in — all in the same amount of time it took me to find position 3 at table 31. It worked against him — I saw Ariel,

Will, even the servers slack when they were on with him.

Which left me. For several reasons I gravitated toward the bar. First, because I noticed that there was a spot open to be *the* beverage runner. Second, because I had an aptitude for beverage running, cultivated over many years making hearts in mediocre lattes. The third reason was that it was a chance to get away from Chef in the kitchen. The fourth, or first, or only reason was that Jake was a bartender.

I assisted the servers in delivering their drinks to tables. I assisted the bartenders in keeping their bar stocked. I brought up crates of wine and beer, buckets of ice, ran the glass racks, the bar bus tubs, polished the glasses. If you were slow, the drinks were slow, and if the drinks were slow, the turn times lagged and we made less money. And then, about an hour and a half into each turn, the first espresso ticket would print. And then I was under it for the next thirty minutes.

At the end of the night the bartender made a stocking list and I put the whole thing back together again. Some people dreaded beverage running because it was a pure shit show for most of the night — you got hit with the drinks on the initial rush and the coffee on the tail end. Yes, my neck, my hands, my legs hurt. I loved it.

There was only one problem with my new position. The manual labor, the coffee — fine, that was the forty-nine percent of it. The fifty-one percent of beverage running was wine knowledge.

"Appetite is not a symptom," Simone said when I complained of being hungry. "It cannot be cured. It's a state of being, and like most, has its attendant moral consequences."

The first oyster was a cold lozenge to push past, to push down, to take behind the taste buds in the back hollow of the throat. Nobody had to tell me this — I was the oyster virgin, my fear told me what to do when the small wet stone came into my mouth.

"Wellfleet," someone said.

"No, too small."

"PEI."

"Yeah, some cream."

"But so briny."

Briny. PEI. A code. I took a second oyster in my hand, inspected it. The shell was sharp, sculptural, a container naturally molded to its contents, like skin. The oyster flinched.

I suspended it on my tongue this time. Briny means salty. It means made by the ocean, it means breathing seawater. Metallic, musky, kelp. My mouth like a fishing wharf. Jake was on his third, flipping the shells over onto the ice. Swallow, now.

"I'm going West Coast, it's too creamy," someone said.

"But clean."

"Kumamotos. Washington, right?" he said.

"He's right," said Zoe, smiling like a fool for him.

I wrote it down. I heard him say, "Do you like them?"

I was sure he was talking to me but I pretended to be confused. Me? Do I like them? I had no idea. I took gulps of water. The taste stayed. In the locker room I brushed my teeth twice, stuck my tongue out to the mirror, wondering when the residue would go away.

That Sunday afternoon I was positive Mrs. Neely was dead, that she had died at table 13. I stayed away but kept her in my vision until another server went and revived her. She asked for more sherry for her soup. A shot glass for her soup, a glassful for herself.

She was nearing ninety, born and still living in Harlem. She took the bus down to Union Square every Sunday in stockings, high heels, and a hat. She had a burgundy pillbox with silk flowers, and a cornflower-blue fascinator edged in lace. She had been a Rockette at Radio City Music Hall.

"That's why I still have these legs," she said, pulling her skirt up to her thighs.

"I dined at Le Pavillon. Henri Soulé, that bastard, he ran the door like a dictator. But I went, everyone went. Even the Kennedys went. Child, you don't remember. But I remember. They really cooked your food back then. Where's the cream, I say. The butter, the green beans, honey, you didn't even need to chew."

"I wish I could have been there," I said.

"The haute cuisine, it's done, it's dead. Al dente. That's what they do now." She paused and looked around the table. "Did my soup come?"

"Um. Yes." I had cleared it myself ten minutes ago.

"Now, I haven't had my soup yet. I need my soup."

"Mrs. Neely," I whispered stupidly, "you already had the soup."

Suddenly Simone was beside me, sweeping away my inefficiencies, making me irrelevant. I drew back as Mrs. Neely narrowed in on Simone.

"Tell the chef I'd like my soup now."

"Absolutely, Mrs. Neely. May I bring you anything else?"

"Oh you look tired. I think you would do to drink a little old wine. Some good old wine, like some sherry."

Simone laughed, her cheeks colored. "I think that's exactly what I need."

Partly in the handbook, but mostly just understood: You could sleep with anyone, except those above you. You couldn't sleep with anyone on salary. Anyone that could hire or fire you. You could sleep with anyone on your level. All the hourlies.

Anything slightly more romantic than sex had to be disclosed to Howard, but the sex passed freely below the surface.

I asked Heather about her and Parker. She wore a small vintage engagement ring — his grandmother's — but they hadn't set a date yet.

"Parker? Oh, I remember my first trail, seeing him from down the bar, and I said, Oh lord, look at Trouble. We were both betrothed to other people. He was engaged to — I'm not kidding — a Debbie Sugarbaker from Jackson, Mississippi, a lawyer-something, plain as white bread. Don't you ever tell him I told you. Once we started talking, I thought, Here we go. My real life is coming for me, gunning at me like a train."

"Wow," I said. My life, my train.

"This place is a love shack, darlin'. Try to keep your panties on."

The interior of Park Bar was dark and the decorations minimal. But watching over us, high up near the ceiling, was a huge reproduction of a painting that felt familiar. I told them I'd seen it before but that might have been a lie. Two boxers in a ring, mid-conflict, midinjury. Action everywhere, blows landing, receding. Except the faces. The two boxers' faces were blurred together, one solid mass.

Will had finally asked me to join them for a post-shift-drink drink, or Shift Drink Part Two. I hung close to him while Nicky locked up the restaurant. People said their good-byes, discussed which trains were running, flagged down cabs. I remembered Ariel's voice daring me — "It isn't two yet" — and I checked my phone: 2:15 a.m. They headed into the parking garage across the street from us. Oh do you have a car? I asked. Will said, No, we're going to Park Bar. Ariel hummed into the echo. We walked

100

farther underground. Rubber soles on cement, oil stains, gasoline fumes. The guard waved to Will. We ascended and we were on Fifteenth Street under a huge lit-up sign that said PARK. And there was, indeed, a bar.

No one asked me if I did coke. Ariel asked me if I wanted a treat and I said sure. *I had done it* seemed to be the same as *I do it.* I caught the subtext that everyone did a little bit of coke and nobody had a problem. If I had any inclination to think about it the noise in Park Bar ran right over it. It was crowded and Will and Ariel knew everyone.

Scott and the cooks held up a table in the corner. I recognized some of the prep guys. We moved toward the table and I set my purse by them just like Ariel. I saw people that had been cut earlier, people who worked the a.m. Ariel pointed to different tables and said, "Blue Water, Gotham, Gramercy, some retards from Babbo, and so on." I nodded.

Will held on to my elbow as we made our way to the bar, where Sasha sat next to a Dominican man with huge diamond stud earrings.

"Oh look who finally graced us from her present!" Sasha said, and shocked me by kissing me on both cheeks. The other man introduced himself as "Carlos-at-your-service." He was a busboy at Blue Water Grill and he sold drugs to every server within a ten-block radius.

The line for the bathroom ran in humid pairs, some ear-piercingly loud, some whispering as they waited. It wound around the room. After two sips of my beer, Ariel took my hand and we joined the line. When our turn came, we shut a flimsy door, hooked it, and locked the handle. She dipped a key into a small plastic bag and handed it to me. Someone banged on the door.

"Wait your fucking turn motherfucker!" she screamed. She dug the key around and took a bump herself.

"What do you think of Vivian?"

"The one Scott was talking about?"

"Don't listen to him. He's lying, they're all fucking homophobes."

"She's pretty," I said. "She has great tits? I don't know. I don't feel anything. Can I have some more?" Ariel handed me the bag and I pyramided up the powder. "Are you *gay* gay or just half gay?"

"Jesus, you're something. Where do you come from? Okay, stick this in your mouth."

She stuck the key in my mouth like a pacifier. It tasted like battery acid and salt.

"You good babe? How do I look? Torrid?

Like a natural disaster?" She ruffled her hair up like she'd been in an electrical storm. I nodded. She kissed me on the forehead, and where she kissed tightened, first in my skin, then in my skull, then in my brain. A saccharine, sentimental drip ran down my throat, and I was blinded by how stupid I had been not to see that everything was absolutely, one hundred percent going to be okay.

The boxers panted furiously above my head, I could hear them: *let me go, let me go.* They put on *Abbey Road* and I wanted to tell everyone at the bar about how for my sixth birthday I knew I wouldn't have a party because my father didn't believe in birthdays but I stole two pastel Hallmark invitations from the grocery store by slipping them into the back of my jeans and I used all my colored pencils to decorate them and addressed one to John Lennon and one to my mother, asking them to please come to my house for tea on my birthday, and the night before my birthday I put them in the empty planter next to the front door and I went inside and I prayed on my knees next to my bed and I begged God to come and deliver the invitations to John Lennon and my mother, I promised him I would never cry again, I would always finish my dinner, and I wouldn't even ask for another birthday for the rest of my life, and I went to bed holding an unendurable, trembling joy in my arms, thanking God for his hard work tracking the two of them down, thanking him for knowing how badly I needed them, and when I woke in the morning and the cards were in the planter, wet and mushy, I threw them away and I didn't cry in front of my father, but later in school I started crying at my desk and couldn't stop and they sent me to the nurse and I told her I knew that God didn't exist and they called my father to come pick me up, and I heard the nurse arguing with him and then she said to him, exasperated, "Do you know that today is her birthday?"

Instead I said, my voice coming out of me with brusque clarity: "On certain days, I forget why I came here." They nodded empathetically. "Do I need to *justify* myself all the time? Justify myself for being alive and wanting more?"

They introduced me to Terry, who bartered free drinks for free bumps. He was pushing forty, his hair balding from the top down so it was still long on the bottom, and he tucked it obsessively behind his ears. He raged like a bull in a pen back there, flirting, singing, snapping at the bar back. When

I was introduced he pointed to his cheek so I kissed him and he gave me a beer.

He said, "On this day in 1864, General Grant surveyed General Lee's army and knew he was sending his men to their deaths. He told his soldiers, There will be no surrender, gentlemen. And we think we have it rough."

I thought, Is that even true? But instead I said, "At least they had something to fight for."

He shrugged. "I may have made some bad life choices. Who can tell?"

A dagger of morning prowled outside the open windows. The air revived itself, my bones braced like something new was coming. We reentered the line for the bathroom, passing the bag between our back pockets, our hands lingering longer, a feeling of clouds, ominous, pads of melancholy on our fingertips, impending headaches. . . . Mundane, yes, but thrilling to me, all of it.

"All right. What is Sancerre?" Simone's brown eyes, serpentine.

"Sauvignon Blanc," I answered, my hands crossed in front of me on the table.

"What is *Sancerre*?"

"Sancerre . . ." I shut my eyes.

"Look at France," she whispered. "Wine

105

starts with the map."

"It's an appellation in the Loire Valley. They are famous for Sauvignon Blanc."

"More. Put the pieces together. What is it?"

"It's misunderstood."

"Why?"

"Because people think Sauvignon Blanc is fruity."

"It is not fruity?"

"No, it is. It's fruity, right? But it's also not? And people think you can grow it anywhere, but you can't. Popularity is a mixed blessing?"

"Continue."

"The Loire is at the top. It's colder." She nodded and I continued. "And Sauvignon Blanc likes that it's cold."

"Colder climates mean a longer growing season. When the grape takes a longer time to ripen."

"It is more delicate. And has more minerality. It's like Sancerre is the grape's true home?"

I waited for affirmation or correction. I did not know half of what I'd said. I think she pitied me, but I received a grim smile and, finally, a half glass of Sancerre.

After service the dishwashers rolled up the

sticky bar mats and the smell of rot rose from the blackened grout in the tiles. The kitchen was a hollow amphitheater of stainless steel, still, but holding the aftereffects of the fires and banging and shouting.

The kitchen boys were scrubbing every surface, rubbing out the night. Two servers sat on the lowboy, eating pickled red onions from a metal tin. Leftover ice cream sat on the bread station, turning to soup.

"Hey, new girl, I'm in here."

Me? Jake was in the doorway of a walk-in. He had a cup full of lemon wedges in his hand. His apron was streaked with wine, his shirtsleeves were rolled high and I could see his veins.

"Are you allowed to be in there?" What I meant is, Do you ever think about me the way I think about you?

"Did you like them? The oysters?"

When he said the word *oysters,* their flavor flamed on my tongue, as if it had been lying dormant.

"Yes. I think I do."

"Come in here." His tattoos showed themselves as he pressed the door open wider. I passed under his arm, looking back to make sure Simone wasn't watching. I had never been in any space alone with him.

"Are we going to get locked in?" What I

meant is, I'm scared.

Inside there were two open beers, the Schneider Weisse Aventinus, a bottle I'd pulled for the bar but never tasted. The beers were propped against a cardboard box labeled Greens but filled with littleneck clams. We were in the seafood closet. Crimson tuna fillets, marbled salmon sides, snowy cod. The air nipped at my skin, smelling like the barest trace of the sea.

"What's that tattoo?" I asked, pointing to his biceps. He pulled his sleeve down.

Jake dug through a wooden crate labeled with masking tape, Kumamotos. He pulled out two tiny rocks, discarded the debris that clung to the outside. A strand of seaweed stuck to his pants.

"They look so filthy," I whispered.

"They're a secret. Quite a leap of faith." His voice was quiet with the motor of the fridge, and I involuntarily shivered and moved toward him. He pulled a blunt knife out of his pocket and wedged the tip into an invisible crack. Two switches of his wrist and it was open.

"Where did you learn to do that?"

He pinched a lemon over it and said, "Take it quickly."

I flipped the shell back. I was prepared for the brininess. For the softness of it. For the rigidity and strangeness of the ritual. Adren-alized, fiercely private. I panted slightly and opened my eyes. Jake was looking at me and said, "They're perfect."

He handed me the beer. It was nearly black, persuasive as chocolate, weighty. The finish was cream, it matched the oyster's creaminess. The sensory conspiracy made the blood rush to my head, made my skin break out in goose bumps. Ignore him. Look away. I looked at him.

"Can I have another?"

In bed I could feel the pain in my back dif-fusing into the mattress. I touched my neck, my shoulder, my biceps. I could feel where my body had changed. I clicked on my cell phone: 4:47 a.m. The black air wouldn't move, it wouldn't shift in or out the window. The heat was an adhesive — even the fan couldn't disrupt it.

I went to the bathroom and saw my shirt-less roommate passed out on the couch. His chest was slick with sweat and he was snor-ing. He had an air conditioner blasting away in his room. Some people were morons.

The bathroom was a narrow room of tiny brown tiles, brown grout and brown, moldy ceiling corners. I turned the shower on to cold and stepped in and out of it, gasping and sighing, until my skin was stiff. I put my towel on top of my sheets and lay down sopping wet. The heat landed again like tiny gnats on my skin.

I touched my abdomen, my thighs. I was getting stronger. I touched myself and I felt like stone. I saw Jake in the locker room dropping his pants, his tattered boxers, his pale legs. I thought about the sweat on his arms, of how violently he shook the cocktail shaker, of the sweat adhering his white T-shirt to him the day I first saw him. And when I tried to picture his face it was blank. It had no features except eyes. It didn't matter. I came abruptly and gratefully.

My body shone in the distressed streetlight. I was used to being alone. But I'd never been aware of so many other people, also alone. I knew that all over the south side of Williamsburg people were staring at their ceilings, praying for a breeze to come and cure them, and like that I lost myself. I evaporated.

VI

You burned yourself. You burned yourself by participating.

On the wineglasses that came out in gushes of steam, on the espresso machine's milk-scum-covered steamer wand, on the leaky hot-water faucet of the bar sink, on the china plates searing themselves in the heat lamps at the pass.

On the webbings of hands, on your fingertips, on your wrists, your inner elbows, strangely right above your outer elbow. You were restocking printer tape and had to move behind Chef, but caught your skin on the handle of a copper saucepan. You yelled, it spun and fell to the floor. Chef sent you out of the kitchen and you reset tables for the rest of lunch.

The burns healed and your skin was boiled.

Knicks in your knuckles from tearing the foil unprofessionally from wine bottles.

Scott said, "The skin gets so tough, even a knife won't scratch it." He grabbed a plate out of the salamander with his hands to really illustrate the point.

By the time we waddled up to the bar it was well past midnight and we were as tattered as the dining room floor. It had been a hard one. The dishwasher broke in the middle of service and two of us were pulled to hand wash the glasses in scalding water. Then the air conditioners, usually mediocre at best, bottomed out. The technicians arrived as we sat down for our shift drinks. They propped open the door and we all looked wistfully at the street. No change in temperature arrived.

Nicky let the backwaiters have gin and tonics as rewards. My fingers were thoroughly poached, the muscle between my thumb and index finger throbbing from polishing. I didn't even have the energy to contemplate sitting next to Jake and Simone. I took my stool next to Will wearily. An empty bottle of Hendrick's stood on the bar like a mascot.

Walter sat on the other side of me. We had never overlapped. He was a large, elegant man in his fifties with a chic gap between his front teeth. He looked as tired as I felt, the lines around his eyes amplifying with each exhale. He asked how I was settling in and we made small talk. But when I told him I lived in Williamsburg, he grunted.

"I lived there," he said.

"You? With all the dead-eyed slouchers?"

"In the late eighties — were you born then? Six years. God it was appalling. And look at it now. The trains used to stop running. Some nights we walked the tracks."

"Ha!" Nicky slapped the bar. "I forgot about that."

"It was a straight shot, the quickest way." Walter finished his drink and pushed it toward Nicky. "Can I get a scooch for this story?"

"We had the whole building," Walter said as Nicky emptied out a bottle of Montepulciano into his glass. "Three floors. My share was $550, which was not a little bit of money. I was with Walden . . . Walden and Walter of Williamsburg. We thought that was cute. Walden needed space for his paintings, they — well." He looked at me. "Even you have probably seen them. The canvas itself took up a wall. He built them indoors and we broke them down to get them back out. And then his collage phase began in earnest. One of the floors we kept as a junk shop. Car fenders, defunct lamps, chicken coop wiring, boxes of photographs." Walter chuckled softly into his wine. "This was so long ago, before his, what do they call it?"

Everyone at the bar was listening with their heads down, except Simone, who watched him patiently.

"His materialist phase," she said.

"Ah, Simone remembers! If you ever forget something about your story, Simone will remember." They looked at each other, not unkindly. "They called it his coup d'état. The beginning of his love affair with Larry Gagosian. Me-te-or-ic. And all the Williamsburg stuff, now I suppose it's technically his juvenilia, worth millions. He dicked around with garbage and I sang opera in the bathtub."

"I miss your singing," Simone said.

"The third-floor skylight was missing. When it rained it was like the Pantheon, a column of water and light in the middle of the room. The floor rotted in this glorious black circle. It grew moss in the spring. They tried to sell it to us for $30,000. I am not kidding. We thought, Jesus, who would buy a place on Grand Street and Wythe? I assumed the river would swallow it up."

He stopped. I took a tiny sip of my gin and tonic, which was too strong for me though I would never admit it.

"There are condos there now," I said. I didn't know what else to say. My head was getting difficult to prop up. "All these half-finished, empty buildings. They'll never fill them. There are no people."

"You are condos, new girl," Sasha said.

Walter stared into the bottom of his glass. "Fucking holes in the ceiling. Frozen pipes all winter, showering at the Y. We tossed crackheads out of the entryway weekly — *weekly*. One of them tried to stab Walden with a steak knife — *our* steak knife. And sometimes I wish we would have stayed."

I rode the L train, back and forth. Back and forth. In the beginning, I made eye contact with everyone. I applied mascara, I counted my cash tips on my lap, I wrote myself notes, ate bagels, redistributed the cream cheese with my fingers, moved my shoulders to music, stretched out on the seats, smiled at flashes of my reflection in the train windows.

"Your self-awareness is lacking," Simone said to me one day as I was leaving. "Without an ability to see yourself, you can't protect yourself. Do you understand? It's crucial to your survival that you pause the imaginary sound track in your head. Don't isolate your senses — you're interacting with an environment."

I learned how to sit still and look at nothing and no one. When someone next to me on the train started talking to themselves, I was embarrassed for them.

I was working the dining room the first day Mrs. Neely didn't have her wallet. I was replenishing the silver and I heard her exclaim. She threw her purse up on the table with her needle-thin arms and her knife fell to the floor. It sounded like an alarm. The surrounding tables turned. She pulled out slips of paper, crumpled Kleenex, several tubes of lipstick, her MetroCard.

Simone picked up the knife and put her hand on her shoulder. Mrs. Neely sat back down but her hands continued to flap in front of her face. "Well I . . . well I . . . Well."

"You know, I believe we found it," Simone said, catching one of Mrs. Neely's erratic hands. "You are all set. I noticed you didn't finish your lamb today, was it all right?"

"Oh it was underdone. I don't know what you pay that chef for if he's not able to cook a lamb. I attended a dinner with Julia Child once, and we had lamb. James Beard, he could cook a lamb, my dear."

"Thank you for telling me. I will pass it along." Simone picked up the check. I hadn't seen Zoe come up next to me. Simone approached us.

"There's no wallet," she said and sighed. "I'll go ahead and comp it."

"I should check with Howard first," Zoe said carefully.

"Excuse me?" Simone turned to her. I backed up.

"The situation is entirely out of control. It deserves a conversation. Chef is completely fed up — double orders of soup, lamb sent back three times? It's getting worse."

Simone stiffened, I felt it from a few feet away. Zoe kept her hands clasped behind her back, enforcing composure. A silence bubbled between them and I knew Zoe would break it first.

"You can't just comp entire meals every week, Simone. That's not your call. And it's gone beyond the restaurant's responsibility. Do you remember when she fell? That's on us. Where is the line? Where is her family?"

She engrossed me. She flickered.

"Every week, Zoe. For twenty *fucking* years. You're looking at her family. I'm taking care of the meal."

There was now a small orbit of us around the hutch and when Simone turned we scattered. I ran into the kitchen and Ariel had wide eyes.

"Shit," she said. "Queen Bee is getting written up for that. Picking up!"

When I would finally get to taste the wine at the end of our lessons, I would say idiotic things like, Oh I get it now. Simone would shake her head.

"You're only beginning to learn what you don't know. First you must relearn your senses. Your senses are never inaccurate — it's your ideas that can be false."

I didn't know what a date was and I wasn't an anomaly. Most of the girls I knew didn't get asked out on dates. People got together through alcohol and a process of elimination. If they had anything in common beyond that they would go out and have a conversation. When Will asked me to get a drink in the late afternoon on my day off, I thought that placed us firmly in the friend arena, like getting coffee.

We met at a tiny space called Big Bar, four booths and a few stools doused in red light. When he opened the door for me and he put his hand on the small of my back I thought, Oh fucking fuck shit fuck, is this what a date is?

"Kansas," he said. I smiled. It wasn't awful, being somewhere besides the restaurant

118

and my room. To be talking to another human without doing fifteen other things at once. Not awful at all.

"It all makes sense."

"Does it? You were getting the Midwest vibe?"

"I wasn't actually. My radar is all off — everyone seems like they were born and raised in the restaurant. But now it makes sense."

"Because of my charm?"

"No, because of your manners."

"Charming manners?"

"Utterly," I said and drank my beer. It is a strange pressure to be across from a man who wants something that you don't want to give. It's like standing in a forceful current, which at first you think is not too strong, but the longer you stand, the more tired you become, the harder it is to stay upright.

"How long have you been here?"

"I came for film school like, god, five years ago? That's depressing. I promised my mom I would move back as soon as school was over, and I feel like I'm running against the clock. She's livid."

"Is she? It's so impressive that you got out, that you're doing what you want."

"She thinks family is impressive."

I swallowed. "Maybe she's right."

"Your parents know you're here?"

"What does that mean?"

"I don't know. You give off this runaway vibe, like you're all huddled up inside yourself."

"I'm flattered. I'm pretty sure my dad knows."

"Pretty sure? What about your mom? Her little baby girl in the big city?"

"My mom doesn't exist."

"Doesn't exist? What does that mean?"

"That means I don't want to talk about it."

Will's eyes became concerned and I thought, Don't do that. That's not why I told you. It's not something to fix.

"What happened to film school?" I asked.

"You come here for one thing, you end up absorbed by another. I have all these ideas, it's just . . . Well. It's hard to retain the original vision, which is usually the most pure, you know?"

"Yeah." I didn't.

"You really came here for nothing?"

"I wouldn't say for nothing."

"What did you do in school?"

"I read."

"Any particular subjects? Are you always this difficult?"

I sighed. It wasn't as intense as Howard's interview. "I majored in Lit. And I came here to start my life."

"How's it going? Your life?"

I paused. He seemed like he really wanted to know. I thought about it. "It's kind of fucking amazing."

He laughed. "You remind me of the girls back home."

"Oh yeah? I'm vaguely insulted."

"Don't be. You're not jaded."

I thought, You don't know me, but I smiled politely. "I'll catch up soon. Just let Chef scream at me a few more times and I will go completely numb."

"He's got a hard job."

"Really? The only thing I see him do is yell. I've never even seen him cook!"

"It's different at that level. He's not a line cook anymore, he's running the whole fucking business. I know he misses cooking every single day."

"The other day he told me to stab my fucking tickets or he'd stab me. I mean, how is that allowed?"

"He didn't say that to you."

"He did! I cried by the ice machines."

"You're a little sensitive."

"He's a monster."

Will put his hands up, surrendering, smiling. I liked him. The truth was that he reminded me of people back home too — nice, open-book people. Thinking of Chef reminded me of the restaurant and that I could talk freely because I wasn't in it.

"You know, Simone is kind of helping me with wine."

"Ugh." He scrunched up his face. "I would be careful with Simone's help."

"Why? She's so smart. She's so fucking good at her job. You ask her questions all the time."

"Yeah, when I'm desperate. Owing Simone a favor is like being owned by the mafia. Her help is a double-edged sword."

"Are you being serious right now?"

"I would just be careful what you tell her. She and Howard have this weird thing where she reports on all the servers. Everyone thinks they're fucking. Once Ariel told Simone something about Sasha and then Sasha got written up. And she has these creepy relationships with Howard's girls, and then they disappear in the middle of the night. I don't know, she's fine, but she's been there too long, she gets bored, makes trouble."

"I don't believe that. I get the feeling that she's genuinely interested in helping me." It's not that I expected Will to get her. She

122

probably barely tolerated him. But the rest of it disoriented me. "What are Howard's girls? What do you mean they disappear?"

"Never mind, doll," he said. He finished his beer, and I knew I had to decide if we were staying for another round. It felt like a mistake to get drunk before four p.m., but it would be worth it if I could get him to keep talking.

"Maybe you softened her up," he said and his eyes went past me. "Speak of the devil. I forgot this was her neighborhood."

I turned and there she was, in a black shift dress, looking so petite I would have looked right past her. I flipped back into the booth, chafing. This wasn't Park Bar; this was my day off. I wanted Simone to think I was nude modeling for painters or drinking absinthe with musicians, or at the Guggenheim, where she'd told me to go, or even that I was alone at a bar with a book being sophisticated. How could I have been stupid enough to be drinking with Will?

"Do you think she heard us?" I whispered. "We should go."

"What? You were just saying —"

"I'm sick," I said. "I mean, I don't feel well. This beer isn't sitting well. I have to go home."

"Are you okay?"

"Will, I'm sorry, we can do this again, but I —" I could feel her eyes on us, there was no way to miss us in the four hundred square feet. I took a breath and felt a hand on my shoulder.

"Aren't you two a lovely pair." She held a paperback book with a French title in her hand and smelled like gardenias. I wished Will would die.

"We're not. We were just talking about work stuff," I said. "Sorry, hi Simone. I like that dress. Lovely to see you too."

"So you're off today, huh?" Will said, a little coolly, I thought.

"Yes, I'm just meeting a friend. And I think Jake will be by later."

I finished my beer. "I —"

"I finally got her outside of work," Will said, showing me off.

"Oh, is she so elusive?" Simone said with a derisive smile.

"I'm not." I stood up. "I'm just, upset, I have an upset stomach, I mean." I pulled up my purse and put five dollars on the table. "Will, I'm sorry, next time."

I did not look back. Once I hit Second Avenue, I threw my arm up. I understood why taxis were so essential to life in the city, even with those of us who couldn't afford them. Desperation.

■ ■ ■ ■

As I started up the stairs to find more straws, Jake was coming down. He brushed the back of his hand against my hand. I stared at it, but my hand looked the same. There had been an explosion, but no collapse. I spent the next five hours sleepwalking, wondering whether he had touched me with intention.

Everything was over my head. The senior servers, the bartenders especially, had doctorates in talking shit to guests. They could skim any topic. You couldn't stump them. The briefness of these interactions meant their casual expertise was never exposed as groundless.

As I overheard it, to be good at this job you needed to know the city, but also how to leave the city. Which was hard for me to imagine, since I found the idea of traveling to the Upper West Side daunting. Everyone had a cursory knowledge of the East Coast weekend retreats: not just upstate and Connecticut, but unlisted antiques stores in the Hudson Valley, small towns in the Berkshires, lakes in the Northeast Kingdom. Beaches were their own category, divided mainly between the Hamptons and the Cape, and again, the specific towns were identity badges.

You knew which shows were at which galleries, and it was a given that you attended the museums regularly. When asked whether you had seen Manet's execution paintings (and you were going to be asked by someone taking a late lunch after visiting MoMA), you were either on your way or had already seen them in Paris. You had opinions about opera. If you didn't, you politely implied it was too bourgeois. You knew what was playing at Film Forum, and you corrected anyone who lumped Godard and Truffaut together.

You knew trivia from the guests' lives: where couples got married, where men traveled for business, what kinds of projects they were working on and the deadlines. You knew where they'd gone for undergrad and what they'd dreamed of doing while they were there. You knew names of the towns where they kept their mothers in Florida. You asked about the absent colleague/husband/wife.

You knew the players on the Yankees and Mets, you knew the weather, more about predicting the weather than any meteorologist. You were a compendium of disposable information that people burned up while they drank and escaped their lives.

And the most peculiar part was how none of it mattered to them. One push through the kitchen doors and they were back to food, sex, drinking, drugs, what bar had opened, what band was playing where, and who had been drunkest the night before. Once I saw someone throw a rag in Scott's face over a spaghetti carbonara dispute, but I don't know if anyone held a political belief.

They were so well versed in that upper-middle-class culture — no, in the *tastes* of upper-middle-class culture — they could all pass. Even most of the cooks had gotten an Ivy League education at Cornell before they spent a second fortune at CIA. They were fluent in rich people. *That* was the fifty-one percent of it.

Scott and his cooks sat on a lowboy post-shift, drinking beer. Scott was bitching about Chef: how threatened Chef was by his food, how out of touch Chef was with what was happening in Spain, how Chef had dried up a decade ago. Chef called Scott's food "subversive" and it was clear that Scott wanted us to see that as a compliment. Jeff and Jared nodded, worshipping. As I eavesdropped I felt an unexpected swing of loyalty toward Chef, toward his food and the restaurant he'd built, even if it was "hopelessly out of date."

The back of house had separate kitchen beer, which sat all night in an iced-down bus tub. One of the interns drained and refilled the ice during service — that task was actually in his job description, I asked him. The beer was genius. The boys could be cut, burned, or crying, but within their line of vision was a bucket of beer that was just theirs.

"New girl, come here, Santos likes you." They had the newest prep guy that I hadn't met yet. His skin was stretched and skinny, like a child in a growth spurt's. He didn't look much past fifteen.

"Be nice, guys," I said. I jumped up on the lowboy.

Jared put his arm around Santos and said, "I love Santos. He's our new friend. Show the new girl that dance we taught you. The dance like a pollo."

Santos smiled but looked at the floor and didn't move.

"Ah he's being shy now. Want a beer?"

Santos took one and they gave one to me as well. I swung my heels against the door. I saw Santos slipping under a fence at the border. Making himself as thin as a coin and rolling through a crack in the wall. They had told me it was so expensive they could only pick one to go. And that once that one landed, it was too dangerous to ever go back.

"Cuántos años tiene?" I asked.

"Dieciocho," he said defensively.

"No es verdad? Eres un niño. De dónde eres?"

"Mexico," said Scott. He finished his beer in three gulps and opened another. "You know I'm not hiring any more filthy Dominicans. Right, Papi?"

Papi was the troll-like man who had spit at me the first day. He nodded with hooded eyes and a vacant smile.

Santos said timidly, "Hablas español?"

"Sólo un poco. Puedo entender mejor que hablar. Hablas inglés?"

He looked at the kitchen boys to see their reaction.

"Not impressive," said Scott. "Everyone speaks Spanish here. Bueno, yes?"

They opened new beers and Jared said, "Papi, do the pollo dance."

Papi knocked out his elbows and flapped them like a chicken and yodeled. He spun in a circle and the boys clapped.

"One more time, Papi, show Santos how the pros do it."

Scott saw that I wasn't laughing and seemed embarrassed. His eyes said, These are the rules here. "He's wasted. They steal bottles of whiskey and hide them in the dry goods."

"Oh," I said. We drank our beers. Until that moment I'd been the girl they tricked into dancing like a pollo. Santos looked at me with grasping, runny eyes, the kind of eyes that take in everything and have no defenses. I knew how badly he needed a friend. I shook my head and asked for another beer. I looked at Santos appraisingly and said to the boys, "He's brand-new, isn't he?"

■ ■ ■ ■

AUTUMN

■ ■ ■ ■

I

You will stumble on secrets. Hidden all over the restaurant: Mexican oregano, looking cauterized, as heady as pot. Large tins of Chef's private anchovies from Catalonia hidden behind the bulk olive oil. Quarts of grassy sencha and tiny bullets of stone-ground matcha. Ziplock bags of masa. In certain lockers, bottles of sriracha. Bottles of well whiskey in the dry goods. Bars of chocolate slipped between books in the manager's office.

And people too, with their secret crafts, their secret fluency in other languages. The sharing of secrets is a ceremony, marking kinship. You have no secrets yet, so you don't know what you don't know. But you can intuit it while holding yourself on the skin of the water, treading above deep pockets, faint voices underneath you.

They folded napkins and I refilled pepper

mills on table 46. They talked as they did every day. I listened in my trance as I did every day. Up front, at the café tables, Howard and a young woman sat in interview fashion. I kept thinking about my cardigan, and how they must have all been there that day but I'd seen no one. I couldn't remember the interior of the restaurant besides the hydrangeas and Howard's hands that sat on the table. This one was not wearing a cardigan.

"They can't be serious, interviewing her."

"Maybe she got lost on her way to Coffee Shop."

"Or that place in Times Square where they wear bikinis."

"Hawaiian Tropic, don't hate."

A few peppercorns slipped through my fingers when I tried to funnel them. They bounced on the floor, popping when the servers walked over them. Fine, spicy gravel around my feet.

"They make crazy money there."

"You wear a bikini. It's one step away from a strip club."

"But an important step."

"Listen, I will personally volunteer to train her."

"I bet you will."

"When she looked in the mirror was she

like, This is an interview outfit?"

"Does she think her tits look real?"

"Jealous?"

"I bet Jake fucks her first."

I dropped more peppercorns, they scattered. I took a new handful and they stuck to me.

"No, she's kitchen material."

"Not Asian enough."

"Why don't they put a sign up that says you must be *this* much Asian to enter?"

"She's straight off the boat."

"But what boat?"

"Ask Sasha if she's Russian."

"There's no way Zoe will let Howard hire her."

"Please, Zoe's interview outfit wasn't much better."

"I bet this girl has a lot of experience."

"Yeah, at what would be my question."

"Enough," I said. I stood up and wiped my palms off on my apron. They all turned to me, surprised I was there. "Don't be mean. We can just be honest. I'm sure she's a very nice girl, but she's too pretty to work here. She'll never make it."

Jake behind me. I felt him like a few degrees of temperature change, a prickling. He said into my shoulder:

"That's what we said about you."

■ ■ ■ ■

"This is the glory month, hmm?" Simone said, transfixed over a crate of chanterelles. They were sheathed in dirt, her fingers streaked with it.

Yes, those were luminous September days. The afternoon light pearling, the mood alert, turned-on, compassionate. Out in the Greenmarket people circled patiently, holding cartons of prune plums, ears of the last silken corn, thin-skinned lavender eggplants. The air vibrated like the plucked string of a violin.

"I knew from those rains last week, I just knew it. Look at these." She passed one to me and I inhaled. She wiped the tip of my nose and I drew closer to her. Simone unheated, unrigid, as if we had no work to do. The crease of concentration between her brows ironed out. Her attention felt like a warmer current of water.

"I've put together a stack of books for you, including that wine atlas you're always peeking at in the office. You can have an old copy of mine, you should have one at home. I've been meaning to bring them but perhaps you can come by my apartment, since it seems you're in the East Village on your days off."

I cringed again at being caught with Will on the outside. "I'm happy to come. Whenever."

"And it's time for you to open a bottle of wine."

"Not for a table!" I saw myself being pushed overboard, Simone with a knife at my back, the sea black, turbulent, bottomless.

"God no. Not for a table. We can practice tonight after close."

There was a low white fridge that they called the cheese larder. Next to it sat the day's cheeses. Orange spotted rinds, ashy cones, teal-veined cheeses all breathing under a mesh dome. She took a wood-handled spade and dug into them. I looked around to see if we would be caught, but the kitchen was miraculously empty. She went around a corner and came back with a cluster of grapes. Their musk was a solo performance — all the other scents dimmed.

"Spit the seeds." She spit two black seeds into her hand. I had already bitten them, bitter and tannic.

"Mine didn't have any."

"One of the three fruits native to North America, that distinctive Concord musk. The great irony of our country is that we produce the greatest table grapes in the world and yet can't seem to figure out how to make wine. Arturo?"

A dishwasher was going by, carrying a bus tub of muddlers, cocktail shakers, strainers.

"Arturo, do you mind asking Jake to make an Assam? He knows how I like it. Thank you."

Arturo smiled and winked at her. This was the same man that growled at me when I asked him where to put the recycling. I hadn't seen Jake come in — did he just appear when Simone needed her tea made? His effect must have shown on my face.

"Did you want one?"

I shook my head though I very much wanted Jake to make me tea the way I liked it.

"Ah. Well. Do you know what abundance is?"

I shook my head again and plucked another grape.

"You have been taught to live like a prisoner. Don't take, don't touch, don't trust. You were taught that the things of the world are flawed reflections, that they don't demand the same attention as the world of the spirit. It's shocking, isn't it? And yet, the world is abundant — if you invest in it, it will give back to you tenfold."

"Invest what?"

She spread some cheese on a cracker and nodded while she chewed.

"Your attention, of course."

"Okay." I looked closely at the cheese, the grapes. The grapes had a veil of dust on them, the cheese a veil of mold, reminders of the elements that shaped them. The kitchen doors swung open. Jake had not only made it, he'd brought it himself.

"One Assam," he said. He had brewed it in a tall water glass and lightened it with milk.

"Thank you, darling."

He surveyed the food Simone had laid out and smirked. He took a grape.

"Is school in session?" he asked, looking between us.

"We're just having a chat," she said smoothly.

"A chat over Camembert." He spit the seeds onto the floor next to my feet. "I wouldn't trust it, new girl."

"My love, aren't you needed?"

"I think I ought to stay put to protect this one. She's already got quite an appetite for oysters. Ten more minutes with you and she'll be reciting Proust and demanding caviar for family meal."

My heart stopped. I thought those oysters

were ours. But Simone betrayed nothing. She wore the same satisfied face she had when she accepted compliments from guests at the end of the meal. He was fearless with her. I couldn't imagine anyone else in the restaurant teasing her to her face.

"I don't need protection," I said suddenly. Stupidly. They turned on me, and I shrank.

The same thin-lipped, austere smiles. But through Simone's eyes, as she appraised him as having the potential to be related to her, I saw a streak of adoration pass and land on him — it was so unmistakable it was almost hued.

"Sometimes I feel like you guys are related or something."

"Once upon a time," he said.

"Our families were close," she explained.

"She was the girl next door —"

"Oh Jesus, Jake —"

"Now she's my warden —"

"I'm quite benevolent —"

"And omniscient, omnipotent —"

"Yes, it's quite a burden —"

"And now I've got a classic case of Stockholm syndrome."

Their laughter was closed, held back from me, laughter that ran along a private line. He left abruptly and Simone looked at me.

"Where were we?"

"You're the girl next door?"

Any lingering lightheartedness faded. That was reserved for him.

"We're from the Cape. We grew up together in a way."

"Okay," I said. "Do you like his girlfriend?"

"Jake's girlfriend." She smiled.

"Yeah, that Vanessa or something."

"I do not know a Vanessa or something. Jake's a private man. Perhaps you should ask him."

I reddened and put my hands in my apron, mortified. "I just thought it must matter. If you thought she was cool or whatever. 'Cause you guys are close."

"Have you thought about what you want from your life?"

"Um. I don't know. I mean, honestly . . ."

"Do you hear yourself?"

"What?"

" 'Cool or whatever,' 'Um, I don't know,' 'I mean, honestly.' Is that any way to speak?"

God, I was melting. "I know. It's a problem when I'm nervous."

"It's an epidemic with women your age. A gross disparity between the way that they speak and the quality of thoughts that they're having about the world. They are taught to express themselves in slang, in clichés, sarcasm — all of which is *weak* language. The superficiality of the language colors the experiences, rendering them disposable instead of assimilated. And then to top it all, you call yourselves 'girls.' "

"Um . . . I don't know what to say now."

"I'm not attacking you, just calling your attention to it. Isn't that what we are discussing? Paying attention?"

"Yes."

"Did I scare you?"

"Yes."

She laughed and ate a grape.

"You," she said. She grabbed my wrist and pressed two fingers onto me as if taking my pulse and I stopped breathing. "I know you. I remember you from my youth. You contain multitudes. There is a crush of experience coursing by you. And you want to take every experience on the pulse."

I didn't say anything. That was in fact a very eloquent expression of what I wanted.

"I'm giving you permission to take yourself seriously. To take the *stuff* of this world seriously. And to start *having*. That's abundance."

I waited for her to go on. Nobody had ever spoken to me like that in my life. She cut me a piece of the cheese and handed it to me — "The Dorset," she said — and it tasted like butter but dirtier, and maybe like the chanterelles she kept touching. She handed me a grape and when I bit it I found the seeds with my tongue and moved them to the side, spit them into my hand. I saw purple vines fattening in the sun.

"It's like the seasons, but in my mouth," I said. She humored me. She cracked whole walnuts with a pair of silver nutcrackers. The skins on the nuts felt like gossamer wrappings. She brushed the scattered shells onto the floor, with the grape seeds, the pink cheese rinds.

Let's be generous and say that I understood about seventy percent of what Simone said to me. What I didn't misunderstand was the attention that she gave me. Or that by being close to her, I was always in proximity to him. There was an aura that came from being under her wing, with its exclusive wine tastings and cheese courses — the aura of promised meaning.

When she touched my pulse I felt so vulnerable, like she could stop it if she wanted to. I had an awareness that I would die. I hid from that thought, as I had trained myself to do, but it came back to me when I was walking home from the train late that night. The silent purples of the warehouses and oily black of the river seemed to be watching me. The streets seemed to be breathing, then they seemed to be disappearing. I could see them being erased. I had that feeling of never having existed at all, which I could only call my sense of mortality. It inflamed me. More. That was the result: *more* got into my bloodstream and ran rampant.

"Hey, Fluffer, come get the list," Nicky said. Some nights that man came in here to play, his hair newly shorn, his ears sticking out, looking like an eight-year-old wanting to be chased. And some nights he clocked in looking so tired he was gray. "Never have kids" was all he said to me when I asked if he was feeling okay. But tonight he had run around with an impish smirk on his face as if he'd just gotten laid.

"What did you call me?"

"Fluffer. That's your name. You look like a Fluffer."

"My name is Fluffer." I stated it, confused.

"It fits."

I took the list from him. "Like a fluffer in a porno? The girl that sucks dick in between takes to keep the guys hard?"

"There she is!" He clapped his hands. "See, you're not so new after all. So let's go, Fluff, I don't wanna be stuck here all night."

I put my head down. I was about to walk away, but I had a sensation I hadn't felt in weeks. I started laughing. Really laughing. It came up from my feet.

"You're saying I make you hard, Nick?"

He pulled his glasses down his nose and regarded me.

"Nah, you're not my type. But you kept me going all night, that's for sure." He winked at me. "You did all right tonight."

I ducked into the cellar with the milk crate. The sign above the door said Beware of Sediment and I started laughing again. It took me a long time to restock. I was still terribly inefficient. But I brought up bottles he hadn't put on my list, things I'd seen him sell and knew he needed. I swept the room too, still grinning.

A lot of what I couldn't place about Simone was explained to me with the sentence, "She lived in Europe."

I don't know how a phrase so vague explained why Simone could drink without getting drunk. Why she had such an affected way of speaking, like a retired professor at her country estate, even in the midst of thirteen emergencies. Why she could wander

into and out of conversations like a character in a Chekhov play who has been listening but hasn't actually *heard* a thing. Why
she was at once disheveled and precise. Her
lips blinkering red lights.

She started at the restaurant when she was
twenty-two. She had left before, more than
once. I heard rumors: She had been engaged
to the heir of a champagne dynasty . . . they
moved to France . . . She left him and
wandered the uncharted bulk-wine back-
woods of the Languedoc and Roussillon,
the lavender-soaked filthy roads to Marseille, a slow boat to Corsica . . . back to
the city, back to the restaurant . . . refer-
ences to hard-baked afternoons in lemon
groves in Spain, to time in Morocco . . .
How she was engaged a second time to a
regular at the restaurant, a publishing scion,
but again she had ended up staying and
he'd never returned . . .

Hints of this from her, but mostly I heard
it from others. The wreckage of powerful
men added to her presence. I only knew that
she was not of my world. She had barely a
trace of the city, of the struggle, on her. Just
the dust, which she shook off with a
thoughtless dignity.

The sky was so blue.

It's only been five years.

My skyline was never marked with an absence.

Remember that wine school? Windows on the World?

I had been underneath them, on the F train coming from Brooklyn, just one hour before.

I was late for high school but glued to the TV.

I had taught a class there — on Rioja — on the night of September tenth.

Chef made soup.

So I heard something and looked out my window — you know I'm on the East Side.

It was too low. But it was steady and went by almost in slow motion.

The Owner set up a soup kitchen on the sidewalk.

No, I haven't been down there.

The smoke.

The dust.

But the sky was so blue.

My buddy was the somm at the restaurant — we came up at Tavern on the Green together.

You guys never talk about it.

I was going into a class called, I'm not
    joking, Meanings of Death.
I always wondered: If I had been here,
    would I have stayed?
And I thought, New York is so far away.
My cousin was a firefighter, second-wave
    responder.
Nothing on television is real.
But am I safe?
Because what else is there to do but make
    soup?
But I really can't imagine it.
I was pouring milk into my cereal, I looked
    down for one second . . .
I was asleep, I didn't even feel the impact.
A tide of people moving up the avenues on
    foot.
Blackness.
Sometimes it still feels too soon.
It's our shared map of the city.
Then the sirens, for days.
We never forget, really.
A map we make by the absences.
No one left the city. If you were here, you
    were temporarily cured of fear.

It was well past two a.m., it was Park Bar,
and I needed to stop drinking. The tables
were dizzy, I said to them, It's too early,

spinning tables, calm down! Will took my elbow and then we were in the bathroom. He sat on the toilet and pulled me onto his lap.

I took two bumps using my wine key. I took them off the knife that cut the foil so cleanly for Simone. I had been practicing in the mirror. The bottle can't move, it can't wobble as you cut, tear, insert, twist, push, spin, twist, pull. Don't hide the label. Cultivate stillness. Gentility when you remove the cork. Give the wine some grace, some space to breathe, Simone said.

"She can swirl wine in her glass. Without moving her hands," I said.

"What?"

"Nothing."

My eyelids dropped, blackness. I felt him rubbing small circles on my back.

"You're making me sleepy," I said.

"That's good," he said, and I thought I felt his head touch my shoulder, thought I felt him twisting me toward him.

The drip flooded down my throat, dirt, Splenda, sulfur, my eyes ventilated. I sat up and unlocked the door. The tables had resolved themselves. Park Bar had large windows, and on evenings when the temperature of the air complemented the temperature of your skin, they opened them and let the street mingle.

Jake was outside smoking. He was presumably meeting Vanessa, who usually sat at a table with other servers from Gramercy. His T-shirt had once been white and was now nicotined, eroding, neckline torn. He only ever wore the same black jeans that gaped at the knees, the bottoms cuffed high over rough leather boots. The streetlight hit his collarbone. He turned and sat in one of the windows, Vanessa standing above him, her arms crossed, her face turned toward the park. His spine in his shirt, like some ancient draped artifact.

I shook Will off me. He went out to smoke with Jake. I sat next to Ariel and Sasha. We only sat at the bar now that something was clearly going on between Ariel and Vivian. It was just Terry tonight though, unfurling postrush.

"How are you holding up, babe?" Ariel asked.

"Better. I'm probably just tired." I pretended to stretch my neck and looked at Jake.

"Don't do it," Ariel said. I turned back to her, fixed my hair.

"I'm not doing anything."

"You're looking for trouble."

"Look." I lowered my voice so Sasha

150

wouldn't hear me. "He's very attractive. But whatever, right? Why is everyone so afraid of him?"

"Because he's textbook, that's why."

"Baby Monster," Sasha said, hitting me hard on the shoulder. "You been for reals hungry? I tell you what the fucking problem in America — when I first got here I ate M&M's for three days, that's all, I think I'm dying in some fucking hellhole in Queens and rats eat my face. Now I'm a fucking millionaire, but you don't forget hungry like that."

I twisted a napkin and sealed my eyes to the black lacquer of the bar. I felt it — Jake's absence. I stretched my neck again and looked out the windows. Just the wind dusting up the bare street.

"I'd like to read it," I said to Ariel. She heard me. "The textbook, I mean."

Will came up, ordered drinks, and looked at me. "You want one more, right?"

II

"Fuck brunch."

Scott was bloated, red-eyed, but standing. The rest of his crew were walking bent in half.

"It's not technically brunch," I said. Chef always said brunch wasn't a meal, and I loved passing that on to the servers from Coffee Shop and Blue Water who had to stand outside on their patios serving eggs Benedict.

"Fuck lunch."

"I knew you were in trouble, Scott. I told you it was time to go home. You wanted to stay."

I had left Park Bar at three thirty a.m. right when the cooks were getting another round of Jägermeister shots. I had taken one and thought I might throw up on the floor. Instead I threw myself into a cab and threw up in my own toilet like an adult. I was proud of myself.

I'd volunteered to cut the butter. The hot knife slipped into the chilled sticks effortlessly. The pats clung to the wax paper. It had the same orderly rhythm of folding napkins, repetition and satisfying progression. My fingers were shiny.

"Fuck brunch forever." Scott moaned. "Where's Ariel?"

"She's dining room today. Sorry you're stuck with me."

"Get Ariel, I need her treats."

"Treats?"

"It's an emergency," he yelled.

"Okay, okay, I'll find her."

She was standing at the service bar having an espresso and talking to Jake.

"Hey Ariel," I said, turning to the side so he wouldn't think I was trying to look at him. "Scott needs you. In the kitchen."

"We're in a war," she said. She was beaten up around the eyes, but fairly fresh for someone who'd only slept a few hours.

"Whatever," I said. I wished my hair was down so my neck and cheek weren't so vulnerable. Jake in the mornings, before service, precaffeine rush, bags under his eyes. Not interested, I told him with the angle of my head. "He just said it was an emergency."

She went into the kitchen like she was

ready for a showdown but Scott was abject. He leaned over his station with his head in his hands.

"What's up Baby Chef?" Usually they would start fighting, he especially hated that name, but he moaned instead.

"I need help."

"Apologize for hitting on her."

"Ariel, I wasn't. I swear. That girl loves cock, I can't help it."

"Bye-bye," she said and stuck up her middle finger, the nail painted black.

She turned to leave and he yelled, "I'm sorry, I'm sorry, I will never look at her again, I have a small dick, I'm insecure, I'm untalented, I'm stupid, I will cook you whatever you want for breakfast."

She stopped.

"Steak salad. And dessert. And whatever new girl wants."

"Fine. Hand them over."

"You're disgusting. But you're not untalented. I want to be fair about this." She clapped her hands. "Okay, beverages first."

Sundays had a candid feeling. There were no laws, no stakes. Howard and Chef were both off, as was most of the senior staff. Scott ran the kitchen and Jake was the most senior on the floor. It was his only day shift, and it was clear he was in a fog for the entire service. It was also Simone's day off. The people who remained on this pared-down crew were usually mildly hungover at best, actively ill at worst.

Ariel pulled down a stack of clean quart containers and headed into the wine cellar. Those quarts, which once housed minced garlic, shallot vinaigrette, aioli, tuna salad, shredded Gruyère, they came back as "beverages."

"It's just Sancerre on ice, splash of soda and lemon. Stick a straw in it and it looks like seltzer."

"I need the treats, Ari, I could've had Skipper make beverages."

"Skipper?" she asked me.

"Barbie's little sister." I shook my head. "I've given up. Each one is better than the last."

She had a handful of blue pills.

"Two for you because you're huge, and we will split one because we are tiny." She broke a pill in half and handed it to me.

"I haven't eaten," I said. "Also, what is it?"

"Adderall. Fixes everything. Obviously."

Obviously. I took my half and sucked on my straw. I felt dizzy as soon as I swallowed. It wasn't noon yet.

"Delicious."

Scott gulped his down in two sucks and handed the quart back to her. He was sweating, breathing hard, and I had a vision of him collapsing during service, a bear keeling over.

"Refill, refill."

"You're going to have to teach Skip how to do this stuff — I have work to do," Ariel said, but took the quarts and headed back into the wine cellar.

"What do you want?" Scott looked at me sideways.

"What?"

"What. Do. You. Want. To eat."

"Um." At my hesitation he moved on to other tasks and I saw the precious opportunity slipping away. "What's in the omelet?"

"I have zero fucking idea, what do you want in the omelet?"

"Chanterelles," I said.

Scott made a disapproving grunt but didn't deny me. He reached into the lowboy and started cracking mottled brown eggs into a clear bowl. He turned up the heat under a small black skillet. The yolks were a vivid, livid orange.

"They're nuclear," I said, leaning in to watch. Last night's booze radiated off him. But Scott's tattooed hands took flight from muscle memory: he frothed the eggs with a fork in two swipes, touched his finger to the pan to feel the heat. He turned the flame down and slid the eggs in, he dipped his hand into the salt and flung it, he tipped the pan to all the points on a compass, letting the wet egg slide under the set edges.

The chanterelles had been prepped earlier, they were waiting, wet and caramelized. He spooned them into the middle. He rolled the eggs, using only the tine of a fork and the movement of the pan. It was all one motion. The skin of the omelet was flawless.

Ariel came up with new beverages for us. Her eyes flashed when she saw my omelet and we dug into it from opposite ends. I sipped my wine through a straw. I saw whole peaceful countries built on perfect omelets and white wine spritzers. Nations at war drinking before noon and then napping.

"Is that Scott's chaser?" I pointed to a fourth quart container.

"No, it's Jake's. Will you drop it off?"

I shook my head.

"Come on, babe, por favor, I'm super behind."

"It's on your way," I whispered.

"Take him the drink and stop being a cunt," she whispered back.

"Ugh," I said. "Too early for the c-word."

I wiped my mouth with a bar mop and ran my tongue around my teeth for stray bits of parsley. As I picked up the drink, the first ticket came through, as grating as a lawn mower starting.

Ariel said: "It's never too early for the c-word."

Scott said: "Fuck brunch."

I said: "Cheers."

My last sip of wine was still humming in my throat as I approached him. He was leaning against the back bar with his arms crossed, face toward the window. There was no one to serve yet. I put the drink down. I tapped my fingers on the bar and decided to leave it at that, but then said, "Jake."

He turned gradually, surprised. He didn't move.

"This is for you. From Ariel," I turned to leave.

"Hey, I need bar mops." He took a sip. The key to dealing with Jake was that I told myself it was all in my head. He rarely engaged with me. The problem with that method of disavowal was the oysters. I thought maybe something had shifted, but I didn't trust it. But when he asked me for more bar mops it was obvious. He was flirting.

"I already gave you the par for the bar," I

said carefully.

"I need more."

"There aren't any more."

"So we're going into a busy Sunday lunch service with no bar mops on the bar? What is Howard going to say about that?"

"He's going to ask why you wasted all your bar mops."

Jake leaned forward on the service bar, close to me. He smelled sour and fragile, and said, "Get me fucking bar mops."

I rolled my eyes and walked away. But my stomach flipped, it kept flipping. How many times had Nicky said that to me and I just nodded.

My secret stash was in my locker — as far as I knew I was the only one to have thought of this. Since the management kept them locked up, I figured I should as well. I finished my beverage before I dropped them off. He was annoyed by the six new guests in front of him, and I said to myself, Leave the bar mops, walk away. Instead I said, "Jake" — the charge I got from demanding his attention, from making him look at me — "can you make me an Assam?"

I don't think I said it well before. His teeth were slightly crooked and when we did last call he would unbutton the top of his shirt, his throat pulsing like something that had been caged. His hair was irreverent after eight hours of bartending. He drank like he was the only person who understood beer. When he looked at you, he was the only person who understood you, sipped you, and swallowed. Someone told me his eyes were blue, someone else that they were green, but they were gold in the center, which is entirely different. When he laughed it was rare and explosive. If a song came on that affected him, let's say Miles Davis's "Blue in Green," he would shut his eyes. His eyelids would flutter like he was dreaming. He was making the bar and guests disappear. He would disappear too. He could turn himself off like a switch and I stood in the dark, waiting.

It was in the autumn that what they called "our people" returned. In thirty years, Nicky had never forgotten a regular's drink. If they caught his eye when they walked in, the drink would be ready before they had pocketed the coat check ticket.

Simone had never forgotten an anniversary or a birthday. She would be silent throughout the meal, only to appear at the end with complimentary desserts, Happy Anniversary to Peter and Catherine, or whatever, written in chocolate ganache. But she had a million tricks the other servers emulated. When a guest particularly enjoyed a bottle of wine she made a pressing of the wine label, scraping it onto a clear sticker and putting it into an envelope. Sometimes she and Chef signed it. I couldn't figure out the exact cause-and-effect relationship but her wine sales were leaps ahead of everyone else's.

We had support. At every preshift the hostess reminded us of who was coming, their table preference, their likes, dislikes, allergies, sometimes gave a summary of their last meal, especially if it had been questionable. But whatever computerized tracking system they used — and I'm sure it was top of the line — it couldn't stand up to the senior servers and their memories. Their innate hospitality. Their anticipation of others' needs. That was when service went from an illusion to a true expression of compassion. People came back to the restaurant just to have that feeling of being taken care of.

They had to be kept at a distance, that was key to the relationship. The intimacy was confusing because the line was so firmly drawn, no matter how many times the regulars wanted to believe that they were family. From Walter: "Regulars are not friends. They are guests. Bob Keating? A racist, and a bigot. I've waited on him for a decade and he has no idea that he's being served by an old queen. Never show yourself."

From Ariel: "Never go out with regulars. Sometimes they ask about my shows and it's so awkward. These people don't even like music. Or, oh god, once this woman wanted to get a nightcap and Sasha recommended Park Bar as a joke, and she was actually there. Just not right."

From Will: "The biggest mistake I made in my first year was to accept opera tickets from Emma Francon. I thought, This is awesome, I put on my suit. I know she looks good for her age, but there is a twenty-year gap there, I thought it was totally innocent. *La Traviata,* a hand job in the taxi, followed by two nights where she totally embarrassed herself at the bar. We never saw her again. Howard was not happy."

From Jake: "They're all better looking with a bar between you and them."

"I forget your hand doesn't naturally go that way," said Will, catching me. He crossed his arms and watched.

I was in the server hutch by the handicapped bathroom, out of view, practicing my three-plate-carry. Some of the backwaiters could do four-plate-carries, three plates solidly fanned up one arm and one in the other. The plates were organized, so they could flick down the first plate to position one and use the now-free arm to arrange the other plates from open-armed swoops on the left side of each guest. The plates were always placed according to the way Chef designed the dish, like a painting hung properly on a wall.

I put the second plate on my wrist and it dipped.

"There are three prongs," Will said. "Your pointer and middle together, the soft part right here," and he touched the bottom of my palm where it went to my thumb, "and this — your steering wheel." He pulled my pinkie up vertically.

It felt wrong. My pinkie deflated.

"Maybe my hands aren't big enough."

"It's not optional. Chef is going to keep thrashing you until you can do it. It's like you're half a food runner right now. If the kitchen boys can do it, you can do it. It's not a Mexican secret."

"She's shrinking again," said Nicky. Will nodded gravely and we all stared at her.

Even I noticed that Rebecca was acting strange. She was a hostess and we had barely any overlap, but she was polite, deferential once she saw that I was aligned with Simone.

Overnight she developed the whiff of an unstable woman, something like plumeria body lotion from the drugstore. She scooped together compositions at family meal, then talked instead of ate. She hovered, hawkish, as we finished our food.

Simone said, "There's a moment in every female's career when her wit blackens." I saw it with Rebecca. Instead of laughing she began to say, "Ha," as if writing a message over a great distance.

I woke up past noon to two emails from her. They were addressed to everyone, the entire staff, the Owner, everyone at the corporate office. The first gave her notice. She had worked, gotten home, and written to tell us that it would be her last shift. No going-away party necessary. Thanks.

The second email went like this: "Hi guys! First of all, I can't tell you how lucky I feel to have worked with you all. I'm going home to California for a while, but I'm going to miss everyone so much! But second of all, Howard and I have been sleeping together for four months. He is the reason I quit.

164

Thanks for understanding and thanks for the memories! XO, Becky."

My shock was total — I looked around my room for someone to reflect it back to me, but I was alone. I texted Will immediately: Howard's girls? What the fuck happened?!

A text back from Will: I know! What a crazy bitch!

A text back from Ariel: Textbook insane anorexic, I hear she's checking into a hospital in CA.

And that was the consensus. I felt that some gross, unignorable injustice had occurred. But I said her name to Simone and she began talking about Pinot Noir. There was a lot of: Can you fucking believe that? And then head shaking. I kept an eye on Howard all night. He worked the floor in a pink tie, weaving around like cursive.

"How's it going?" I asked him while I made him his macchiato. "Weird night?"

"Did you know that the word *weird* pertains to fate? It's Old English, and relates to having the ability to bend or turn fate? But the first popularized usage was Shakespeare —"

"Macbeth," I said. "I remember now. The Witches. Right?"

"Very quick." He smiled, threw back his

espresso, and passed me the empty cup. "I wasn't wrong about you."

Sasha was a tough nut to crack. He loved watermelon-flavored Smirnoff, Jake, cocaine, and pop music. Those subjects provided just enough overlap between us for me to occasionally warrant his attention. He finally asked me to do a line with him one night at Park Bar and I was thrilled to cement the friendship. I'd heard that his father had died back in Moscow a few weeks before and that he couldn't go back because he didn't have a green card yet. He was married to a beautiful Asian girl with blue hair named Ginger, but he didn't know where she was living and the paperwork had stalled. When we got into the bathroom I offered my condolences. He narrowed his eyes like a threatened animal. We snorted coke and I told him I wanted to visit Moscow and he said, "Oh you just a real idiot. That's all."

After that he started offering me his cheek to be kissed when he arrived at the restaurant. His favorite thing to say to me was, "What you think?" and then state something I had believed as if it were utter madness.

He caught me by the ice machine rubbing the bags under my eyes with ice cubes.

"You crying? Oh my god, angel-face, what you think, you're supposed to be happy? Why you think that?"

"I'm not crying. I'm just tired."

"Yeah, no shit, that's life," he said, exasperated. He started scooping ice. He hurt my feelings all the time but was open about my stupidity, so I loved him.

"But I'm tired *all* the time."

"You want a disco-nap, pumpkin?"

I shook my head. He shrugged.

"Don't worry, Baby Monster. You still innocent."

"What does that mean?"

"I don't know, what you think it means? When the trial comes, you will be not guilty."

"That's what you think innocent means?"

"It's not purity, sweetheart, if that's what you thinking." He blinked twice like he knew everything about me.

"I don't know that I'm innocent exactly, but . . ."

"But what? You wanna be the victim too? When you grow up you gonna own all that mess. That's being an adult, pumpkin-face. You got the booze, the sex, the drugs. You got your under-eye concealer. Maybe you're tired 'cause you lying to yourself all day. Or you just fucking Jake all night like a little slut?"

He looked at me and waited, smiling. As if he expected me to answer. I started giggling. He slid toward me, conspiratorial.

"Oh yeah, like you such a good girl."

My eyes full of kinetic energy, my skin sensitized to anticipating motion. Specks of dust taking off from bottles, shadows darting onto the floor, glasses listing over the edges of counters and caught just in time. I knew exactly when someone was going to appear from a blind corner. The Owner called it the Excellence Reflex. The reflex was to see beyond my line of vision, to see around and behind myself. The breath between consciousness and action collapsed. No hesitations, no projections, no order. I became a verb.

III

"What time is it?"

I leaned toward the touch-screen terminal where Simone was breaking down an order. Her hand shot out and covered my eyes.

"Never look! Once you look it stops moving altogether. It's best to be surprised when it comes."

"It's only seven twenty!"

"You're a silly, rebellious thing, aren't you? Is it so difficult to accept the present tense?"

"Seven twenty. I'm not going to make it."

"We will turn at eight and be so busy you'll forget who you are. One of the many joys of this profession."

"No, Simone, really. I've already had three coffees and I'm sleeping behind my eyes. I can't do it."

"Do you think you're here as a favor to us?" She reviewed her order and tapped her fingers. She sent it through and I heard the

169

phantom sounds of a ticket being printed. Mechanically I started toward it and she shook my shoulder.

"You are paid to be here. It's your job. Look alive."

I pushed through the kitchen doors, my arms leaden.

"Pick up," said Scott. He squinted at the tickets. The funny thing about Scott expediting was that he couldn't see that well, had probably needed glasses for years.

"Picking up." When I approached I said in a quieter voice, "Oh man, I'm not going to make it."

"You don't have a choice. Table 49: calamari 1, Gruyère SOS 2, and I need a follow."

"I'll come back for it, 49 is quick."

"We're cutting into a new wheel of Parmesan later. If that makes you feel better."

"Oh goody, I have something to live for."

"Okay bitch, I just uninvited you."

"I'm sorry. I'm so tired."

"Sounds like a personal problem," he said as I took the plates away.

I approached table 49. They were the hungry sort of guests who had spotted me from across the room and were beckoning me with their anxiety. I tried to smile Calm down, I have your fucking food, you're not going to fucking starve to death, it is a restaurant for fuck's sake. When we laid plates down we were to say the full names of the dishes. I usually sang them to myself all the way to the table. As I swung in to the left, open-armed, I said, "Seat 1 calamari, seat 2 Gruyère SOS, and a follow. Table 49. Enjoy."

I looked at them expectantly. I waited for the gratifying looks the guests gave when they knew they could eat. It's their version of applause. But the two guests looked at their plates confused, like I had spoken another language, which I realized with a bolt of shame up my middle that I had.

"Oh my god! I'm sorry!" I laughed and their faces eased up. "That's not what I meant to say."

The woman seated closest to me at position 1 nodded and patted me on the wrist.

"I'm new," I said.

The man at position 4 looked at me and said, "What about the food for seats 3 and 4?"

"Yes sir, absolutely, it should be coming right now."

I ran up to Ariel at the barista station.

"Jesus, Ariel, help me god, I need a treat and a coffee."

"I'm five deep, it's the end of the first

turn." She moved erratically between tickets and cups, trying to line her drinks up, but then turning back to the tickets. I had tried to show her my way of organizing coffees for a rush, but nobody listened to me.

"Please. I'm sorry. Whenever you can."

"Fluff, I need two Huet on the fly."

"Okay, sure, yes, right now."

I kept my eyes down as I ran through the kitchen and down the stairs to the cellar. Scott called out to my back, "Follow? I need a fucking follow."

"I can't, ask Sasha!" I yelled back. But I was already in the cellar, insulated, dim, mold stitched into the corners. Quiet. I leaned against a wall. I felt tears and said, Don't stop moving. The Huet was one of the "no markings" boxes that were impossible to find. I thought it was probably at the bottom of a stack of five and I accepted it. I grabbed my wine key and used the knife to tear into boxes, shoving them to the ground when they weren't the right bottle.

Dust flew.

"I'm just tired," I said to the room. I pulled two Huet and made a mental note to come back and clean up the brutal unpacking job. As I ducked out Will walked past with a bucket of ice.

"You scared me," he said, slowing down.

"You need help with those?"

"No, Will, it's just two bottles."

"Jesus, sorry I asked."

"No, I'm sorry. I'm really off tonight."

"You're off every night," he said and hiked the bucket to his shoulder. "That's your thing."

"That hurts my fucking feelings," I said but he didn't turn.

"Am I running the food tonight?" Scott yelled as I came up. "Did we not schedule a backwaiter?"

"I'm sorry," I said, holding up the bottles in front of my face as a defense.

"I did it!" I presented the bottles to Nicky.

"You want a medal? I need clears on bar 4 and 5. I can't get down there and I'm getting nothing from Sasha tonight. Have you seen him? Bar 4."

"Okay, yes. Um. But Nick? I'm not great at clearing. I can't three-plate yet. I can try. I mean, I can do it."

"Yeah, no shit, Fluff, I'm not asking."

"Your espresso, Skip," Ariel said. "It has the sprinkles in it." She handed me a water glass as well so I could pour a splash in — it was a trick I learned from her, it cooled down the shot so you could take it quicker. I gagged. The grains of Adderall stuck to my tongue.

"Delicious. Adore you. Angel."

"Can you get me the glass rack? I'm almost out of flutes, these fucking idiots —"

"Ariel, no I'm super weeded, I have to bus —"

"You're fucking drinking espresso, I'm fucking weeded."

"Okay, okay." I held my hands up. A man in a navy suit holding a glass of Champagne knocked into me.

"I'm sorry," I said with my meekest smile.

"Hey," he said, "I know you!"

He didn't, but I nodded and tried to move past him.

"Isabel! You were at Miss Porter's with my Julia. Julia Adler, do you remember her? You're all grown up! I haven't seen you since you were a child."

"Um, I'm sorry, that's not me."

"No, it's you, of course it's you. Your parents were in Greenwich."

I shook my head. "I don't know what Miss Porter's is, I don't know a Julia, my name is not Isabel, my parents aren't in Greenwich."

"Are you sure?" He narrowed his eyes and pointed the flute at me. I didn't know how to defend myself, since I didn't know Isabel. Or exactly what I was being accused of. In my bones I thought, The customer is always right.

"But that's funny, isn't it?" I said, trying to appease him. "We all look like other people, you know?"

I smiled, big, with all my non-Isabel teeth, and pushed past him.

It was crowded. The bar didn't have orchestrated turns the way the tables did. Stools were vacated and refilled immediately by people on their second drink, ready to order ten minutes ago. There was no grace period. Already the next round of guests was pressing into the backs of the current diners, hovering when desserts were dropped, stalking people that had asked for the check. And this was the weekend — these weren't our poised regulars. Loud, anxious, steaming. I pushed myself into a group, a man and two women, all of them reeking of cigars. He said, "She's getting in tomorrow. So I'm on my best behavior tonight. The boss is back." The women smirked and leaned their glasses in closer.

Music ran too loudly through the speakers. I looked at Nick, who was looking at Ariel, mouthing for her to turn it down. The music amplified the guests, they screamed above it, gesticulated harder, everyone suddenly grotesque.

"Are you all done?" I asked the couple at bar 4. I winced. The Owner made it very clear that "Are you all done?" was awful verbiage.

"I'm sorry," I said. "I meant, may I?" I offered my palms to them. They were young — late twenties — but fully polished, aspiring to appear older. She had a sharp, severe bob, a pink silk dress, scornful eyebrows. He was square-jawed but conventional, and reminded me of rugby. They must have been fighting, because she looked at me like I was intruding, and he looked relieved. I stuck one arm between them, trying to gain access.

"I'm sorry," I said again, groping for the first plate. "I'm just going to . . . if you don't mind . . ." I pushed my shoulder between them and the girl twisted in her seat, sighing. PR? I thought. Assistant to an assistant? Gallery front-desk girl? What the fuck do you do for a living? I pulled the largest plate first. I grabbed the silverware off the others and stacked them next to the lamb chop bones and gratin grease. Someone bumped into my back and I clenched my teeth. But nothing budged.

I leaned into the boy as I reached. I gave him a helpless look and he stacked two far plates on top of his plate and moved them toward me.

"Careful," the girl said, "or you'll end up

working here."

It's never too early for the c-word, I thought. The boy put his hands in his lap.

We weren't allowed to half clear, everything had to go at once. I took his stack, but they were uneven, since like me, he didn't understand how to clear. I knew it was too many plates — not for Will or Sasha, but too many for me. My arm started burning. I made a lunge for her bread-and-butter plate. The knife, still buttered, slid onto her lap and she screamed.

"Oh god, I'm so sorry. It's just butter. I mean, I'm sorry." She looked at me, mouth open, horrified, as if I had assaulted her.

"It's silk!" she wailed.

I nodded but thought, Who wears silk while they eat? She threw the knife back up on the bar, and I saw the grease sinking into the fabric. I couldn't grab it, my hands were fully loaded. The song ended. I swiveled to look for help.

Two plates slid off my stack and hit the floor. The precise, unmitigated snap of breaking. The room halted, no noise, no motion.

Sasha was next to me, smiling like he had found me at a crowded party.

"Pop-tart made a mess," he said under his breath. "Who taught you how to clear?"

"No one," I said, and shoved my plates at him. "Where were you?"

He went past me toward the couple, offering her club soda, napkins, a business card, and promising to take care of the dry cleaning. I picked up the pieces of the broken plates. The man in the navy suit who had called me Isabel caught my eye, and I moved my shoulder up in front of my face.

"Butterfingers, huh?" said Scott when I went to the broken-glass bin. "Pick up."

"I'm sorry. I'm not good at clearing. I told him."

"Pick up!"

Ariel flew into the kitchen and yelled at the dishwasher, "Papi, vasos, vasos, come on."

Will came up the stairs from the cellar with flattened boxes, a broom, and a full dustpan.

"Don't worry about the wine room," he said to me. He pushed the broom into my hands. "The maid will get it."

"I was coming back for it," I said. "I'm sorry."

My breath jumped hurdles. Each one shook me. My eyeballs vibrated and I couldn't hold on to an emotion: rage, shame, exhaustion, dehydration, hunger — a cradle of twitching wires in my chest. I

178

kept blinking, not knowing if my eyes had dried out or if they were about to run over. There was a hand on my back and I had a vision. I was going to throw this person up against the pastry cart with superhuman strength. I would hold a knife at their throat and scream, Don't fucking touch me. It would roar out of me. And everyone would have to listen, and nobody would ever touch me again.

"Breathe," she whispered. "Your shoulders."

Simone's hand smoothed the line from my neck to my shoulders, like she was smoothing out a tablecloth. She squeezed and it shot pain into my elbows.

"Pick up!"

"Will you inhale? And now out."

When I exhaled I thought I might black out.

She said into my ear, "You need to stop apologizing. Do not say you're sorry again. Practice. Do you understand?"

"Pick up, are you fucking deaf?"

I ran a bar mop over my face and nodded for Simone. She squeezed again and gently moved me forward. I covered my hands with the bar mop.

"Picking up."

■ ■ ■ ■

The day I could three-plate-carry came and went. It wasn't some sort of victory. No one congratulated me. We started from zero at the beginning of each service, and wiped the board clean at the end. But movements became sleeker, elongated. I became aware of being onstage. I gave a trail of my fingers as I set down each plate, as if performing magic.

I became aware of the ballet of it. The choreography never rehearsed, always learned midperformance. The reason you felt like everyone was staring at you when you were new is because they were. You were out of sync.

The way Jake used his foot to catch the sliding glass door of the white-wine fridge, or how Nicky tapped the pint glasses apart when they stuck together from the heat of the dishwasher and flipped them in his hand before he started a drink, the way Simone poured from two different bottles of wine into two different glasses and knew when each glass was full, how Heather flew through the Micros screens like she had written the program, the way Chef absent-mindedly slapped the silent printer and it burped up a ticket, the way Howard could direct us with his eyes from the top of the stairs, how everyone ducked under the low pipe going into the basement.

"You'll know you have the job when it becomes automatic," Nicky said to me early on.

We said, "Behind you," and the person nodded. They already knew. The "behind you" was more for the guest, a formality. We tracked each other's movements with touch, all of us all over each other. If I fell out from under the spell, I went with one of Sasha's tenets that I overheard him declaim to a sixty-year-old woman at table 52.

"I'm sorry about the mess," she'd said, sweeping bits of food off the table.

Sasha shone down on her. "You and me, darling? We the beautiful people. We don't never apologize."

IV

Figs in my locker. Four of them, in a small brown basket. They were gilded like an offering. A slap from another sun-soaked world. I pushed them to the back and laid an old *New Yorker* over them. I knew that no one was supposed to see them.

When my shift was over I put them gently in my purse. I felt like I had stolen something. I paused at the service bar and looked at him. He was talking to Flower-Girl at the entrance, where she was replacing branches that weren't going to last the weekend. Normally she bothered me — she was girlish, her bicycle had a basket, she always wore dresses and a beribboned headband. I had no doubt she had been in a sorority. But I had figs and an entire evening. No, I had a secret.

"You. Want a drink?" he asked, tucking a bar mop into his belt loop. I searched his face for anything — amusement, annoyance, affinity.

"What goes well with . . . ?" I almost said it. What goes well with figs? I suddenly understood how saying something out loud could murder it. That the privacy was what made it voluptuous. That the silence was a test.

"The sunshine," I said. "I want to take it to go."

He nodded with barely raised eyebrows and reached for a bottle of sparkling and I knew the figs were from him.

"In my personal opinion, the wine should never get in the way." He poured the Crémant Rosé into a to-go coffee cup. "Of the sunshine."

"I think Simone would say that a wine that isn't in the way isn't really a wine."

"Who cares what Simone would say?"

"Um . . ." I searched his face. "Me?"

"What would you say?"

"I don't know." I sipped the wine through the plastic lid. It tasted like sparkling Capri Sun. "This is delicious. It will be perfect with the sun. Thank you."

Look at me, I thought. Parker came up and started asking him about beers and he was gone. But we had a secret. As I walked out, Flower-Girl was gazing up at her arrangement.

"I'm glad you fixed that," I said to her. I put my sunglasses on. "They looked terrible."

I ended up walking home. That to-go cup. The ambrosial twilight tumbled off the cliff-sides of buildings, pooling on sidewalks. Every face I met, hypnotized, facing west. When I got to the park I found a bench and held my figs. Each one with a firm density that reminded me of flesh, of my own breasts. There was a teardrop at one end and I put it on my tongue. I felt undressed.

I tore them apart. They were soft, the pink interior lazily revealing itself. I ate them too quickly, rapaciously. I got up, tossed the empty cup and basket in the trash can. At that moment a chubby little girl and her mother came up the subway steps into Union Square. The girl put her hand to her mouth.

"Oh mama, oh mama!" she yelled and pointed to the sky.

"What do you see?"

"I see a city!"

I decided to walk.

Dreadlocked men playing chess and nod-ding to themselves, dogs slumped against dead-eyed kids with tears tattooed on their faces, the bursts of commuters up from the subways, dilating into the streets, the garbage cans overflowing with plastic water bottles and trashed New York dailies, a woman screaming into a cell phone while adjusting her bra, three blond men on a corner holding a map between them, speaking German, the sidewalk quaking as the N, Q, R trains ran in and out of the station underneath, a smoky, acrid cloud next to a gyro cart, tables laid with paperbacks, cheap leather, bulk T-shirts, the leftovers of lives, and then dehydrated carnations, left in the middle of the sidewalk, fossilized in plastic, irradiated with light. Everyone stepped around them, tenderly. I moved out of their way as well.

As I walked, I repeated the street names like they had the permanence of numerals: Bond, Bleecker, Houston, Prince, Spring. Lust rubied my blood, gave me the gait of an uncaught criminal, and I felt like I could walk forever.

"Maybe I'll stay here," Jake said. I heard him from around the corner of the hutch and his tone was barbed so I stopped.

"Well of course you're not staying," Simone said.

"You don't listen to me —"

"That's because Thanksgiving is not optional."

I thought about circling back, but they were silent and I had the impression that they were mouthing words to each other, or they had stopped talking because they knew I was there.

I entered and put my water pitcher down. I looked between them. Heather came in right behind me and went to the silver.

"Everything okay in here?"

"I'm good," I said cheerfully, keeping my back to Jake. "Simone, I have a question. Will you show me who eats here?"

"Ooooh, she's hunting," said Heather. She handed me her lip gloss and I put it on, confused.

"She's not hunting." Simone stared at me.

"Hunting for what?"

"You're too young for that," said Jake.

"Youth is a prereq for wife-number-two, Jakey. She's going to peak real soon," Heather said, rubbing her lips. "You wouldn't be the first to marry up."

"You're just trying to get fucked by an old guy?" Jake asked.

"You guys are terrible," I said, getting hot and wondering what I had walked into. "Never fucking mind."

"No," Simone said. She walked away from

Jake and I thought I saw a trace of annoyance on him. I assumed that expression was for me. "I have a moment if you're ready."

I nodded.

"But no talking. And grab an extra napkin."

"For what?"

"The Eriksons just sat on 36. You'll see. Let's start a sweep."

We stood at the top of the stairs, surveying the expertly coiffed heads of the guests spread below us.

"In the early years the restaurant was surrounded by publishing houses and literary agencies that had moved down here for the cheaper rents. The Owner befriended them and we became the de facto headquarters for their lunch meetings. Many have moved elsewhere, chased out of here by inflated rents. But they have remained loyal, and we treat them accordingly."

She made tiny motions with her chin and eyebrows and directed my gaze toward different tables in the room. "Editors are soigné, midlevel employees you want to take note of. They generally ask for the same table as their bosses but we're not always able to accommodate.

"37, Richard LeBlanc, he's an original

investor, with his own venture capital firm. He's more important because he and the Owner were roommates in college. 38, the architect Byron Porterfield with Paul Jackson, architecture critic for *The New Yorker.* 39, a sort of general Condé Nast table, today those gentlemen work at *GQ.* The man in sunglasses at 31 is the photographer Roland Chaplet, and the man whose eyes keep rolling back into his head is his gallerist Wally Frank. 33, Robert and Michael, you will notice a Vieux Télégraphe on the table, it's Michael's, never pour for Robert, he doesn't drink. They just adopted a little girl from India, they bring her on Sundays, she's an angel. 34, Patrick Behr, former editor at *Saveur,* incredible food writer, hmm, I hope Parker told Chef, they are drinking the . . ." She paused, having met Patrick's eyes, and left me. My head spun.

"Now the napkin," she said when she returned. She led me toward table 36. "Good afternoon, Deborah, Clayton. What a pleasure. I'm glad we didn't lose you to California."

"Always nicer leaving LA than arriving," said Clayton, a fat man with an orange tan. His wife was long necked, razor thin, and wore big sunglasses.

"Simone, tell me, is it possible to get the

188

burger without the bun? Or have you come up with a gluten-free alternative?"

"Deborah, let me see what I can do. Last time you had it wrapped in lettuce."

"In LA they call that 'protein-style,' " she said.

"Before you make any decisions, may I tell you about the specials?"

While Simone pointed out the specials, Deborah took her napkin and put it on her lap. Simone handed her another one without pausing her recitation.

"I don't get it," I said when we got back to the hutch.

"She doesn't eat. When service is over both napkins will be in the bathroom trash can, full of food."

"No way." I looked back at the woman. "But . . . I mean . . . why come here? Why spend the money?"

"Are you not listening to me?" Simone asked while entering orders into the computer. "Everyone is here because everyone else is here. It's the cost of doing business."

Simone's tour further enforced that I was on a pedestal at the center of the universe, and perhaps Deborah Erikson's extra napkin was the first stranger's secret that I learned how to carry. The life of this woman

was so insidiously but totally disturbed —
and she was buffered from it by a staff of
people, of which I was now one. After
service I went to the tiny front bathroom
and dug through the trash. French fries,
four gnocchi, wilted lettuce, and an entire
rare burger, the napkin stained with blood.

I started writing letters to no one. I thought
I was writing toward the center, a place that
did nothing but receive. After I wrote them
in my head I floated them toward the bridge
and left them there for the wind to carry
the rest of the way. They weren't interesting
enough to write down. It was just the feeling of conversation I was after.

I cursed Nicky under my breath while I
unloaded the boxes of glass-bottled water
that we got from Italy. The bottles were
shapely, green, exotic, weighed a ton. The
offices were quiet and the door to Chef's
office was ajar.

He was sleeping with his jaw cracked
wide, head hanging off the back of his chair.
A glass of brown liquor was in his lap,
nestled against his stomach. It jiggled with
each breath. He was red-faced and perspir-
ing even in repose. His desk covered with
yellow and blue invoices. A half-empty

bottle of George T. Stagg bourbon was perched on his desk, still with the bow on it.

Next to him was a stack of the night's expired menus. He changed the specials every day. The mornings were filled with printing, with changes, edits. Behind him was a paper shredder, the bin half removed and overflowing. A four-foot-high trash can touching the desk was full of paper. And here he was at midnight shredding what he had spent all day creating. I was touched by his sleep. The scope of his job expanded, it filled up the room. I leaned in farther and saw more, clusters of shredded dinner menus all over the floor, tumbleweeds, as tangled as hair.

"I think it's really good," I said, and I closed the door.

When I fell down the stairs I didn't see it coming. There are falls that address you directly: You, young lady, are about to eat shit. The warning provides some opportunity for correction. This fall gave no such dispensation. It was predetermined and fact.

I fell down the fucking stairs. As I stepped, my foot went through the stair as if it were air. There I was, full of momentum, carrying stacked plates in both hands, and hugging a mess of linens in my armpit. I stepped like I owned the stairs, until they disappeared. My clogs flew up and out. The load I was carrying meant I didn't brace or catch myself.

I came down hard and bounced to the last step. A full flight. I saw darkness. Gasps erupted all over the restaurant, chairs scraping the floor. When I opened my eyes the couple on table 40 looked at me with pity, but also an unmistakable resentment. I was an interruption.

"Oh fuck," I said. "Those fucking stairs."

Later I was told I screamed it.

I tried to stand but my left side was completely numb. My breathing gave way to crying. I burrowed into it, like a child, self-pity and anger merging.

Surrounded: Heather, Parker, Zoe, Simone. Even Jake's absence wasn't a consolation. Hands on my back. Santos with the broom and dustpan. Questions flying at me, someone telling me to quiet down. When Simone pulled strands of linguine out of my hair, I got up and limped to the guest bathroom. I slammed the door and lay on the floor and I said while crying, Enough.

"Terroir?" Simone repeated. She lifted her eyes sleepily from her glass to the wine bottles that lined the back bar. "Earth. Literally, it translates into *land.*"

"But it's something else, whenever I look it up it's always like this magical designation."

"There's no word for it in English. Like tristesse, flâneur, or la douleur exquise, words full of gray. The French do ambiguity so much better than Americans. Our language relies on fixedness because that's what the market demands. A commodity must always be identifiable."

"We *sell* wine, Simone," Nicky said. He seemed to think it his role to take her down a peg every now and then. "It qualifies."

"Wine is an art, Nick. I know big words scare you, but that one only has three letters," Simone replied. Of course, whenever he came at her, she swatted him away.

"Here we go," he said. He burned the ice with boiling water and made a show of not listening.

"Okay, so what is it?"

"Nick, where is the Billecart? Let's revisit it." She inspected champagne flutes. She held them to the lamp and tossed them aside. By the fourth one she was satisfied. "Will, those need to be repolished."

I looked at him sitting next to me. He didn't move. I got up and grabbed fresh cheesecloth and started polishing.

"Champagne is the fulcrum of the terroir debate. It expresses two disparate positions. The first is that this is proof of terroir's existence: the chalk content in the soil, the cold northern climate, the slow second fermentation. These wines can only come from one place in the world. You taste it" — she sipped — "and you know it's Champagne."

I stopped polishing and sipped the glass she poured for me. The wine surged like an electrical current. My lips like I kissed sparks. Jake came out of the kitchen in his street clothes and sat in my former seat next to Will, clapping him on the back. The wine, barbed, invigorating.

"And yet," she continued, "what is it an expression of? It's a multibillion-dollar corporation, you're tasting a brand. There are no plots, no vintages. What is this wine doing to express the irregularities of the place, its complications, the difference in the topsoil between Reims and Aube? What are these wines doing to express the differences in the way the individual growers take care of their grapes?"

"Why don't the growers make their own wine?"

"Exactly!" She looked proud of me. "There is a small movement, a contingency of farmers and growers that are making estate-bottled Champagne. It's a very small production and they don't have the funding to compete with Moët and Veuve. They are still hard to find here, but" — she poured us more — "it's only a matter of time before the quality speaks for itself. Before the terroir speaks for itself."

Jake, Will, Sasha, and Nick were looking at us. Simone smiled at Jake and said, "Champagne is a trick. You think you are tasting the essence of a place, but you're being sold an exquisite lie."

"What are you two talking? Whatsoever nobody gives a fuck," said Sasha, blowing perfect Os of smoke. He said in a falsetto, "Hello, look at me, I'm the Queenie and the little Princess and we whisper terror in the corner."

"You think people have terroir?" I asked. I was thinking of her and Jake and their Cape Cod and the oysters I had tasted. I heard a hiccup and turned.

"Oh dear," she said.

"Stop," Jake said and held his hand up. Had Jake hiccupped? Not possible, I thought. It was too human, too accidental. He stared at his beer in front of him, meanly, and the room turned sour. We all waited to see if he would do it again.

"Hey, I've got this method," Will said, putting a hand on his shoulder. Jake shook it off immediately and kept looking at his beer.

"In Russia, there is only way —"

"No," he said. I looked at Simone to see if it was a joke. It was the fucking hiccups. She was watching him. He hiccupped again and shut his eyes.

"No listen, dude, it's easy. First you hold your breath."

"I can handle this," Jake said seriously.

"Is this a joke?" I asked.

"It's just hiccups, Jake, my kid gets them all the time," said Nick.

"I don't like them."

I turned to Simone and whispered, "He doesn't like them?" and she shook her head and whispered back, "It's from when he was a child. It's about not being able to catch his breath."

He was obviously having trouble holding his breath and we waited. Sasha reached behind the bar and said, "Hey, old man, get me the juices from the little pickles. My grandma taught me."

"Just swallow three times."

"No," said Nick, pouring sugar onto a teaspoon. "Take this."

"You drink a cup of water upside down," I said inaudibly.

"Jake," Simone said and he held his hand up to her again. He hiccupped and his whole chest shook. She bit her lip.

"Stop being a pussy," Will said.

Jake hit his hand on the bar and we froze. Then he gripped the bar with both hands and shut his eyes, taking long breaths. Nicky walked away. He hiccupped again.

I took my flute and walked off like I was going to the kitchen. But I turned once I was past him. My reason fled, my sense of propriety. As I started creeping back I saw Simone shake her head at me. And I thought, Perhaps your way is not the best way. Maybe the two of you have grown too serious if he can't handle the hiccups.

I moved with purpose, with stealth. I crouched down to a squat and inched behind his stool. Once I was close enough to see the hairs on his arms, I sprang.

"BOO!" I said, and slammed my hands onto his shoulders. I laughed. I stopped when he turned his face slightly. He was not laughing. He looked murderous.

"Sorry," I said. I went back to the kitchen, busing my flute, growing more ashamed with each step. The only comfort I had as I changed my clothes was that someday I would be far, far away from the restaurant and I wouldn't remember how I had acted like a child. He should be embarrassed, I said. The fucking hiccups, what a narcissistic little boy. *He* should be the one running away. But no, it was me, hiding in the locker room until I was calm.

When I came back down he and Simone were gone. Relief.

"Such a moody little bitch, right?" Sasha said, shaking his head.

"You want one more?" asked Will, turning the stool next to him.

"That was stupid," I said.

"Let's shut it down," said Sasha, picking up the plates holding everyone's ashes.

"Park Bar?"

I hesitated.

"Come on, Fluff, you won this round." Nicky shut off the lights and said, "He didn't have another one after that. You cured him."

The ramifications of my fall down the stairs appeared on my left hip, my lower back, my cheek from where the entrée plate hit me. The bruises bubbled to the surface of my skin before they colored. My skin like that of a nearly liquefied nectarine, the pulp rolling around under the thin surface. If you bit it, the whole thing would burst.

V

Then one day I learned that there was an invisible ravine running up the city, as deep as the Grand Canyon, narrower at the top. You could walk in tandem with a stranger on the sidewalk and not realize that he or she was not on the same cliff-side as you.

On one side, there were the people who lived there, and on the other side, terminally distanced, were the people who had made homes there.

The first time I saw a home was on an Indian summer day when I took up Simone's offer to let me borrow her *World Atlas of Wine* and a few other books she thought might be helpful in my ongoing quest to speak of New World versus Old World; to identify when Brettanomyces is to be encouraged or when it is to be abhorred. She lived in the East Village, on Ninth between First and A.

I had been in New York long enough to

know that servers, even the senior ones, didn't make enough to live alone in the East Village. Simone had been in the same apartment for over twelve years. I didn't understand exactly how rent control worked, but I gathered that if you stayed in the ghetto long enough, eventually you would be living for free, or something like that.

An old, ornately fire-escaped and charred building. Four flights of stairs. I clocked details like I was assessing it to move in, imagining taking the garbage out, or my laundry. I thought that Simone and I might be making the essential transition — daytime, both of our days off — and I imagined the invitations she would bestow on me: Let's go to the Russian baths together and gossip. Or we can get a pedicure and read trashy magazines. Or, best of all, she would ask if I had eaten — I hadn't on purpose — and she would say, Let's grab lunch, and take me to a hole in the wall in Alphabet City where they spoke French and she would order couscous and we would drink cheap white wine, and she would explain the difference between the crus in Beaujolais again but when she did she would be telling me about her life, thinly veiled, and I would respond, constructing stories of my own terroir for her, all my experiences clicking into order around her words.

"Oh hello you," she said softly. She seemed surprised to see me, as if I were unexpected. She wore a short, patterned robe over men's briefs and a wifebeater. Simone's legs. Simone's loose, low breasts. It always surprised me how small she was when she wasn't at work. Simone's smells: coffee, powdery night-blooming flowers, unwashed hair, and the barest trace of cigarettes. I moved minutely past the doorway, afraid to breathe.

I could take it all in from the threshold. It was a tiny studio with a wall of windows onto Ninth Street, which light had already passed over by midday. In front of the windows was her living space, although study would be a more appropriate term. There was no couch, no television, no coffee table. There were bookshelves halfway up the walls and then books horizontally stacked on top. Dominating the center of that area, framed between the windows, was a massive round wood table. More books stacked on that table, empty wineglasses, vases of flowers in various states of bloom and decay. A mortar and pestle amid white pillar candles. A motley mix of chairs surrounded it and in the corner a cracked leather club chair that had two blankets, one in a Native American pattern, one the loose cotton weave found in Amish shops. There were collections of papers in portfolios next to the chair, metal filing tins filled with papers torn out from magazines and newspapers. The walls were painted a light gray and covered in framed prints, the most notable a nude woman reclining. I moved instinctively toward the woman, wondering if it was her, though I knew at the same time Simone wasn't the kind to put herself on the wall. She dropped a record-player needle into place, and jazz startled the room into the present tense.

"Did you run here?" she asked, gesturing toward my blouse. My shirt was soaked through.

"Kind of. I walked."

"That's lovely." I wanted her to recognize that I had walked over the bridge, that I lived just across the river from her. I wanted her to ask me about my house, which now had to exist in relation to her house. "Water? Coffee?"

"Both please. No couch?"

"Couches make people lazy. I'm sure if I had one I would never get anything accomplished."

Just what is it that people got accomplished on their days off? She seemed like a writer — her apartment had the worn aura of a writer's apartment or a painter's if I could find some canvases, but she never spoke of specific projects. And she never spoke of writing, of sitting down with pen to paper. While she was at work that was where she existed completely, never half in her head. She spoke often of art, she spoke often of food, she spoke often of books.

"Are you a writer?"

"Hmm. A writer. I try to engage in the task of setting something true on paper. But if you take art too seriously you wind up killing yourself. Do you know what I mean?"

I love you I wanted to say. I grunted. She padded into the kitchen, which was miniature. The ceiling was lower because of a lofted, hidden bed, and everything seemed shrunken to accommodate it. The refrigerator was diminutive as well. Next to it, a row of hanging tarnished copper pans.

"Wow. You really have it," I said. I walked past her to a large cast-iron tub that sat on the far side of the kitchen, against a window into the air shaft. The air turned humid although Simone didn't seem damp at all. There was a clothesline of lingerie drying, and bottles of detergent mixed with her shampoo and Dr. Bronner's soap. The tub had two curtains that were pulled back and a handheld showerhead that had been mounted to the wall. I remembered him. I looked at the clever but amateurish way the shower had been constructed and I knew he had been there. I wished his handprints would show themselves, develop all over the apartment.

"Ah. I must admit I still love it. When I saw the place the landlord was telling me he could enclose it all, make it into a proper bathroom, tear out the tub. And I insisted on keeping it. I was very romantic back then. I thought I would drink wine in the tub, drink coffee in the tub, hold court in the tub. I knew I had to have the place. It's the only one left in the building that's still like this. The landlord apologizes every time he sees me." She laughed and handed me a glass of water. "It's maybe a little sad that it still gives me so much pleasure?"

"You really drink wine in the bath?"

"I've had many wild nights in that tub. Wild nights, wild nights, my luxury."

"Isn't that dangerous? What if you passed out?"

"I don't think I drink as much as you, my love."

"Ha ha," I said and I felt an echo of our work selves, our banter. I knew she was magic. I had known from the first time she spoke to me. I was right, her lips were still quite red though she was unmade.

"You look so excited, little one — do you want to get in it?"

I'm not sure what she meant but I jumped in the empty tub under a garland of lace underwear. I lay back and surveyed the scene. Simone was filling the kettle, absorbed in whatever coffee ritual she had.

"This place is amazing. You can't ever leave," I said. It felt like nothing in the apartment had ever been transient — it had all been born here. The gray walls were a curtain, and the city felt remote, like a city in Europe, not the one where I did trivial, daily battle. My mind stilled. All at once I was exhausted, every switch in me went to Off. My eyelids flickered, then dropped.

I opened them after what I assumed was a few seconds but a pot of coffee sat on the counter in a Chemex and I could hear her talking softly on the phone, sitting on her windowsill. I sat up, my head pounding, and felt like I might pass out. She got off the phone. I saw a mug had been poured for me. Next to it sat a small pitcher of milk and a bowl of brown sugar with a spoon. The mug was garish turquoise and said Miami.

"I'm sorry. That was weird."

"Not at all. It's a nice tub. Aren't you glad I kept it?"

She started moving through her books with her eyes and hands, as if she were tracing a pattern in the air. She was in jeans now, but still in the wifebeater, and she had her glasses on. The coffee was hot and the light had shifted. I had no idea how long I'd been out but the light told me I had overstayed. The spell of softness had broken. She pulled books from the shelves and stacked them on the table.

"Miami?" I said, hopeful, holding the mug out.

"How much can you carry?"

"I'll take the L back, so whatever you want." I was dazed. "It's only one stop."

"Hmm . . ."

"Do you want to go to lunch?" I asked too loudly. "I mean, do you want to go to lunch with me? I mean, take you out to lunch. For the books. For having me over."

"That sounds lovely, but I'm afraid I have plans today. Another time."

I wanted to cry. "Well, I'm going to have lunch. Is there a good place for me? By myself. To have lunch."

"Um . . ." She seemed distracted. Lunch, Simone! I wanted to scream. Food! Take me seriously. "There's Life Café on the park. You might like that. You can sit outside. It's nice out — is it nice out? God, it's getting late."

She nodded at the stack, six books, two larger than any textbook I had in college. She went to the kitchen and got plastic grocery bags. She tapped her lips, scanning the room, concentrating.

"And here." She skipped to a shelf and pulled a slim volume.

"Emily Dickinson?"

"It's time to revisit the patron saint of wild nights."

"Emily Dickinson?"

"Just enjoy it. And really look at those maps of France. Nothing will teach you about the wine but the land. Keep an eye out for stories — wine is history, so look for the threads."

"Okay." I couldn't move. Her energy was pushing me toward the door but I didn't want to go. I looked around the room, grasping.

"Well, thank you for the coffee. What kind of coffee is that?"

"It's excellent, right?" She opened the door and stood to the side. I stepped into the hallway.

"Can I come back?"

"Of course, of course," she said but it was too enthusiastic. "Soon. And for a proper meal." When she said *Soon* it sounded like *Never.*

"See you tomorrow."

She was already shutting the door. I made it to the bottom flight of stairs before I started crying.

Sometimes my sadness felt so deep it must have been inherited. It had a refrain, and though I evened out my breathing by the time I got to First Avenue, the refrain wouldn't leave me. It was guttural and illogical and I repeated it endlessly like a chant: Please don't leave me, please don't leave me, please don't leave me. All the way home, against the bored, anorexic kids on Bedford Avenue, against the lurid tinkling of bodega music, and the dull thunder of the J train on the bridge. I heard myself say it out loud when I got into my bedroom. I kicked the mattress that lay on the floor. That's when I realized how far away I was. I saw the ravine. I had traveled a great distance, just one stop away. Please don't leave me. I guess it made sense — I had never felt more alone.

On Monday morning Flower-Girl came armed with cinnamon sticks, bay leaves, and waxed apples. The cooks came out of the kitchen on fake errands so they could look at her. Her voice was like a Disney princess's when she said hello to me. Birds twittering. But the arrangements turned out understated and, it pained me to say, beautiful.

I walked the Greenmarket stalls during my break. The leaves were riotous but I couldn't focus on them. I only saw apples. Stacked, primed for tumbling. Empires, Braeburns, Pink Ladies, Macouns. Women in tights, men in scarves. Vats of cider, steaming. I bought an apple and ate it.

Did I understand the fragrance and heft? The too-sweetness of the pulpy flesh? Had I ever felt the fatality of autumn like my bones did now, while I watched the pensive currents of foot traffic? A muted hopelessness pressed on me. I lay under it. At that point I couldn't remember the orchards, the blossoms, the life of the apple outside of the city. I only knew that it was a humble fruit, made for unremarkable moments. It's just food, I thought as I finished it, core and all. And yet it carries us into winter. It holds us steady.

Jake checked the lights twice, swaying as he came up. He threw on his leather jacket, it thudded onto his shoulders. One lapel had a massive pin, a gold anchor. Then everyone in unison put on leather jackets. I imagined them calling each other, saying, Today's leather jacket day. Where did they get them?

"Are you going for one?" someone asked him.

"One sounds all right," he said.

We went outside. The air tasted of steel knives and filtered water. An actual chill like a warning.

The bar was four deep. The crowd was different — loud, blandly preppy and undergraduate. We walked into a dank cloud of perspiration. I split off from Will and Ariel and made my way to the back corner. Limbs in my face, my hands wedging into the crowd. Someone grabbed my fingers. I yanked my arm back and when I threw my purse on the floor I turned and yelled, "I can't breathe."

I forgot how tall he was. When I turned Jake was up against me like it was the subway during rush hour, my nose lined up with his clavicle. The leather blotted out my vision. Someone pushed him from behind and my nose touched his chest. Bergamot, tobacco. I looked up at him. Shit.

"Hey," I said.

"Hi there," he said.

I sucked in my lips. He didn't move to go anywhere. Not to the bar, to the bathroom, not even to remove his coat.

"Excuse me," someone screeched and pushed him again. He braced his arms above my head. His sweat, his smell.

"Don't say I never did anything for you," said Ariel, shoving through and handing me a beer.

"Thank you," I said. I put it to my forehead. "I don't think I can be in here tonight."

"Suit yourself, Skip. Tell me before you leave." She looked back and forth between us. "So I know you're safe or whatever. Vivian's dying up there."

I gulped the beer. Wait out the silence, that was my plan. He would say something.

"We can split this," I said. He took the bottle, tilted it, I watched his Adam's apple, and he handed it back to me. His eyes were asking me a question. I nodded.

"You never talk to me," I said.

"I don't?"

"No. You don't seem to like me."

"I don't?"

His eyes colorless, cloudy, collected. His teeth wine stained. He leaned in. "You're very affected by things. A gust of wind throws you. You take everything seriously."

His breath like malt and violets, gripping.

"I do," I said.

"I like that."

"But you don't seem to take anything seriously."

He scanned the room and his eyes came back to me every few seconds when someone bumped into us.

"Sometimes," I said, "I feel like we're talking. But we're not talking."

He reached out and grabbed a piece of my hair. He twirled it around his finger. I was not breathing.

"How's that bruise?"

"It's fine," I said. I turned my cheek away even though it had nearly faded. He dropped my hair. "I'm going to sue. Those stairs are idiotic."

He nodded, patient. Wolfish cheekbones, angular, ascetic face. Rings on long fingers, a rose, a half skull, a gold Mason seal.

"Is that Yorick?" I asked, pointing to his skull ring.

"That's a problem," he said. He took the beer from me. "I don't flirt with girls who read."

He smiled, knowing he had me. Something expert and sadistic in him, wrapping and unwrapping me. I looked away, I looked back. I started to say something, stopped. I moved toward the bathroom but didn't move. He passed the beer back to me and I took a gulp.

"You're confused," he said. "I can see it all over your face."

What to say? Duh? "I'm just trying to do a good job."

"In life?"

"Yes, in life."

He took the beer back and finished it in a long pull, looking me up and down. Was it my ripped jeans and gray T-shirt? My Converse? Where was everyone else?

"I want . . . I mean, I want more than to do a good job. I want to take each experience on the pulse."

"Ha!" He slammed the wall above me. "She's quoting Keats to you? You're too malleable to be around her."

"I'm not a child," I said, but felt cheated.

"You're not a child," he repeated. "Do you know the difference between wanting experiences and having them?"

"You don't know me," I said. But I wanted him to. I tried to drink the beer but there was nothing there. My hairline prickled in sweat. I pulled my scarf off, choking myself for a second. With the air on my neck I felt careless. I pushed my chin up, dropped my head back, and blinked at him.

"Your eyes. It's unmistakable," he said. He thumbed my cheekbone. "Veiled melancholy has her sovereign shrine."

His hand moved up my cheek, flushing me, into my hair, where he tugged, his fingers dry, nonchalant. His other hand pressed into the bruise on my thigh, as if he could intuit the blood below the skin.

When he kissed me I said, Oh my god into his mouth but that, like everything else, was swallowed up.

At that moment there was no Jake, no restaurant, no city. Just my desires running flagrantly, power-drunk, through the streets. Merciless, all of them. Was I a monster or was this what it felt like to be a person? He didn't just use those absurd, softly sketched lips, but his teeth, his tongue, his jaw, his hands pressing me down, eventually grabbing my wrists, compressing me. I fought back. I grunted. I hissed.

I don't think it was pretty kissing. When it was over I felt like I had been beaten. Dazed, angry, still itching. He went into the humid crowd to get a beer and didn't come back. I stood there staring at the boxers in the painting for I don't know how long, until Scott asked if I was hungry and I said, "Starving."

■ ■ ■ ■

We streamed through the door of the Sichuan place in lower Midtown. I looked for a
clock on the wall and luckily couldn't find
one. Nothing to bear down on the plastic
tablecloths, nothing to remind me that this
night would end.

The restaurant was fairly full, a mixed
crowd for so late in the night, some of them
looking respectable, some of them looking
like us, used up and nervy. None of the diners met each other's eyes, following a law of
anonymity built into brightly lit, late-night
places.

Yes, we were starving. Scott waved the
menus away and we got the waiter's attention — he proceeded to order an obscene
amount of food off the "real menu," which
wasn't printed.

Two-dollar beers that tasted like barely
fermented, yeasty water. We salivated. There
was no coursing — in ten minutes plates
started pounding the spinning tray at the
center of the table and we fought among
ourselves. Conch in a hallucinatory Sichuan
oil, a nest of cold sesame noodles, a wild,
red stew that Scott called ma po tofu, cold
tripe ("Just eat it," Scott said, and I did),

crackling duck, dry-sautéed green beans, skinny molten eggplants, cucumbers in scallion oil . . .

We sweat, we breathed harder, our eyes ran. More napkins. The sauces ran. More rice. I touched my lips, numb and electrified. My stomach bloated out, a hard alien ball. I thought about throwing up so that I could eat another round.

"What would your last meal be?" I asked suddenly. That was a night when I thought it would be all right if my life ended.

"A really long omakase. Like at least thirty-four courses. I want Yesuda to cook them himself. He puts the soy sauce on with a paintbrush."

"Salmon pastrami from Russ and Daughters. A ton of bagels. Like three bagels."

"In-N-Out double double."

"I'm thinking about a Barolo, something really ripe and dirty, like from the eighties."

"ShackBurger and a milk shake."

"My mom's was veal scallopini and a Diet Coke."

"Nonna's Bolognese — it takes eight hours. She makes the pappardelle by hand."

"A roast chicken — I would eat the entire thing by hand. And I guess a DRC. When else would I taste that kind of Burgundy?"

"Blinis, caviar, and crème fraîche. Done

and done. Some impossible Champagne, Krug, or a culty one like the Selosse, drunk out of the bottle."

"Toast," I said, when my turn came. I tried to think of something more glamorous, but toast was the truth. I expected to be mocked. My suburban-ness, my stupidity, my blankness.

"What on top?"

"Um. Peanut butter. The raw kind you get from the health-food stores. I salt it myself."

My clumsiness. My dullness. Instead they all nodded. They treated my toast reverentially. Which was exactly how I thought of it when I made it in the morning. I ate it standing up in the narrow kitchen, which had one pan, paper plates, and a toaster. A small window at the end where I could scan the buildings and watch pigeons on telephone wires. Sometimes I had two pieces. Sometimes I ate it naked, leaning up against the window.

"I'm going to throw up."

We all agreed.

"Nightcap?"

We all agreed.

The bill was nothing and the table was destroyed. We left a pile of cash on the spinning tray and rolled ourselves into the ample night.

VI

Jake acted like nothing had happened, so I acted like nothing had happened harder. One evening we were alone in the glass-and-cardboard labyrinth of the wine cellar. I could hear him moving behind a stack of boxes higher than my head. I heard an unconcerned grunt. His knife tore into the tape. Scrape of cardboard on cement. Taps of glass on glass.

How easy it would be to say, Hi. To say, Hi, do you remember me? To say, Can you help me find the Bricco Manzoni? To say, Oh geez, this place is a mess. To say, Kiss me again like that, right now.

Footsteps above us loosening dust from the ceiling. I stopped doing everything and listened to him. He left carrying six bottles of wine in his hands, ducking at the low door. Beware of Sediment, I would have said, if he had looked at me.

I woke in the mornings inwardly hysterical at the possibility of seeing him. I took great pleasure in subduing it. I practiced composure. He was teaching me a previously unknown patience. It was about him, but it was also not him. I longed for satiation but was terrified of it. I wanted to live in this queasy moment of fantasy for as long as possible. My body was agitated and possessed, but I found the Bricco, I broke down the case. I held it in my body — the precarious balance between the quotidian and Technicolor madness.

"Amateur night," Ariel yelled. Park Bar was filled with lumpy women strapped into flammable dresses, grown men in faded face paint. A pair of vampire fangs in an empty glass with lime rinds. A gold-chained, clown-shoed pimp sat in a corner, around him all the usual tarnished whores. Will, our own Peter Parker, had morphed into Spider-Man. He asked me to cover his Halloween shift, saying that it was his favorite holiday, and I thought he was being sarcastic. Not only had I not participated in Halloween as a child, I found adults who clung to it especially odd. But he owned a full costume and had been drinking with his friends Batman, Robin, and Wolverine since the early afternoon. He crouched on a bar stool and shot webbing at me, ignorant of how the red fabric clung to his beer belly.

Vivian was indecent. I had spent many nights appraising her with Ariel, who was critical by default, but also smitten. Sometimes I forgot Vivian was like me — a person, perhaps soulful, ambitious, or something. Tonight she was "tit soup" — that's what she called it. She overflowed everywhere, the waistband of her fishnets cutting into her hips above little black shorts.

"What are you, sweet pea?" she asked over the bar.

"I'm inoffensive," I yelled back. She didn't hear me but pretended like she did and said, "Cool."

"This is kinda sad, no?" But Ariel wasn't paying attention to me either. She threw a cocktail cherry at Vivian, who was midconversation with a knight and princess. She caught it and popped it in her mouth and winked at Ariel.

"Cunt!" Ariel yelled and laughed.

Vivian laid out tequila shots and a bowl of candy corn on the bar. As soon as I took my shot my stomach gurgled. It had been hours since I had eaten. I was doomed.

"Total amateur night," I said, chewing a slimy handful of candy corn. "Is someone getting a bag or what?"

"I think Spidey has plenty."

Will was talking to Scott and the kitchen guys in the corner, wringing his hands. We all had our tics when we were high: Will wrung his hands, Ariel blinked rapidly, and I said, "No, wait," over and over again. They mimicked me all the time. "No, wait, guys," and I always sounded like the slow child when they did it.

"Nice costume," said Scott. "Are you a teenage boy?"

"In your dreams, Scott." I tapped Will on the shoulder. "Willy babe, do you have treats for me?"

"Trick or treat!" he yelled and slid his arm over my shoulder. He followed me, babbling, into the bathroom line.

"What are you saying?" I flipped on the lights and locked the door. It smelled like shit. "God, someone destroyed this place."

Will was sweating, his face greenish against his red suit. His eyes chased light around the bathroom. He looked frightening.

"Sit down, babe," I said, putting him on the toilet.

"You never watched that movie."

"I'm getting to it." I held my hand out and he started wringing his hands.

"You're too busy now."

"I'm not, Will, I'm getting to it. Are you going to share or what?"

"I'm a sharer," he said. "I have five brothers and sisters." He reached into his sock and his head fell into the sink.

"Ouch." I grabbed his forehead and straightened him up. "I know. You have five brothers and sisters and you are right in the middle. You hold it all together." I kissed him on the forehead and took the bag.

"Most men lead lives of quiet desperation."

I looked at the bag — it was nearly empty. "Okay, okay, Thoreau. You're out."

"You should watch that movie."

"Did you do this all yourself?"

"Nah, I'm a generous guy."

"That's true, darling. No one would argue with that. I'm going to finish this." I took out my compact — there was just enough for a serious line. I looked at myself in the mirror as I came up. The truth was that sometimes I felt nothing. I did the coke and told myself that I was high but I was just numb. That's why I looked in the mirror. When I was really flying I couldn't stop searching for my eyes in any reflection. I thought I was beautiful, I thought my eyes had secrets. That night I looked plain. I picked my eyelashes in the mirror and I saw Will staring at me, his eyes bulging out.

"Are you okay? Do you need air?"

"I'm in love with you." The words smashed together when he said it, but it was one of those unmistakable phrases. It was built that way so you could never take it back.

"Excuse me?"

"I'm in love —"

"God, no, never mind, don't say it again." He put his hand over his mouth and fell backward, hitting the toilet handle. It flushed profoundly.

"Don't be stupid, Will." My voice sounded angry. I looked in the mirror and my eyes were vibrating. "You're a fucking nightmare talking like that."

"I'm sorry," he said. His head wilted on his neck.

"Don't be sorry," I said. Of course tomorrow I would pretend like nothing had happened. Jake had taught me about that. I would be kind. But as I hit him on the back, I realized I was actually angry. "Don't be sorry, just don't be stupid, okay?"

I guided him out and dropped him on a bench near the door. He sat calmly, swiveling his head around as if he had just woken up. I sat on a bar stool next to Ariel and concentrated on my fingernails kneading into the wood on the bar.

"Did you ever read Djuna, I forget," she said, totally coherent, chewing on a cherry stem.

"Yes."

"I gave *Nightwood* to Vivi. I'm trying to get her to read more."

"That's good." There was a tequila shot in front of me and I took it. "That should fuck her up for a minute."

Ariel smiled. "You finished the bag, huh?"

A stethoscope on the bar. A cape hanging on a stool. Costumes wearing away then finally discarded as we approached another harsh morning. I listened to everyone, peeling back the black paint from the bar in strips. I could do it, if I wanted to. That's what I was thinking. I could talk about Billy Wilder and Djuna Barnes and the new bone-marrow dish at the gastropub in the West Village and whether you knew so-and-so from that university, oh it's just a little school called fucking Harvard, and isn't it sad how the city is changing, every day for the worse, and of course radicalism is the only vehicle for change, and oh yes, revolution is intrinsically violent, but what is violence anyway, it all boils down to pheromones, we are just chemical mixtures, but when you meet that person you just *know,* you know?

"Fake," I yelled. No one looked at me. Maybe I hadn't said it out loud. "We're all just waiting around to become real people — well guess what Vivian — we're not. Remember the phonies?" She nodded, her face like a sequin. "You don't remember. You need to read more.

"Fuck you," I said to a man I didn't recognize. "You want to repeat the names of things? You want to make out?"

That person disappeared.

"I serve people!" I yelled out above the music.

"Sasha, you think my life is easy 'cause I'm pretty? It's not. I get a fucking door opened for me now and then. Being pretty . . . well . . ."

"I wanna fuckin' record this shit right now."

"It sucks."

"Baby Monster, how 'bout you shut your face 'fore I break your face."

"I hate you," I said to Will, but he was asleep on coats.

Maybe it was that he'd said it in the bathroom. Was that me now? The Park Bar bathroom with its one dreary bulb and scratched-out mirror, scummy faucet, and

STD-infected walls? A bathroom where I ran the water and threw up on countless occasions? Love?

But it was Jake, really. Will and Jake were friends, or friendly, as much as Jake could be friends with anyone. They drank together, acted like old comrades, had their safe subjects to chat about (rare Dylan recordings and Vietnam War trivia). But Will gossiped like a teenager. Everyone at the restaurant did. It was entirely possible — likely even — that Jake and Will had discussed this "love," a word now irreparably tied to the Park Bar bathroom. Perhaps Jake had told Will to express his feelings. Perhaps Jake had told him I wasn't worth it. What Jake certainly hadn't said was, Stop, I like her.

"Ari," I yelled. She turned away from her conversation. I shot back more tequila and reached behind the bar for the bottle. I heard glass shattering as I pulled it up. "Look, skulls." I pointed to the bottle. "It's spooky. Get it? Death."

Ariel pinched me hard on the underarm but didn't yell at me. "What's wrong with you?"

"Can we share a cab home? I'm about to be really drunk."

I shut my eyes and she patted my head.

"Sure, Skip. Whatever you want."

I picked my head up and looked toward the door. Just leave, I thought. It was bitterly cold that night and the wind knocked on the sealed windows. Instead of my reflection there was a spiteful, sparkling face floating in the dark window, looking at me with a tightened jaw, judging.

The park became threadbare as the vendors thinned out at the Greenmarket. The farmers made bets on the first frost. The windows in my room were always shut, old T-shirts stuffed into the cracks. I tapped at a decrepit, cold radiator, watched it like an oracle. But what really signaled the change in the seasons was that the bugs moved inside. The fruit flies first. They hovered around the lids of the liquors at the bar, around the sink drains. Fruit flies dispersing when you picked up a damp rag. A spray of black specks on the cream-colored walls. Zoe addressed it at preshift and assigned everyone extra side work.

"Fruit flies are an emergency," she said and struck her fist forward for emphasis.

That was what had me with yellow gloves on up to my elbows, holding a roll of paper towels and a nameless spray bottle of blue. I shuffled toward Nicky and the bar sink.

"You look great, Fluff, now down on your hands and knees."

"I don't understand," I said, but what I meant was, Why me?

"You're a woman, I thought cleaning was intuitive."

He poured the watery remains of a cocktail into a glass and handed it to me.

"Liquid courage."

"What's under there?" I took the drink down.

"You think I know? The last time I cleaned under that sink was in the late eighties."

I sighed and knelt. As I descended the air changed. Dank, uncirculated, a whiff of citrus.

I peeked in under the sink. It was dark.

"I can't see anything."

Nicky handed me a flashlight. A drain is made of two drains, Zoe told me. The first was in the sink, and the second was in the floor. There was a gap between them. That air gap was called a stopgap I found out later. It prevented water, sewage, anything from the pipes from backing up directly into the sink.

I pointed the light and saw pens, wine corks, foil, scraps of paper, forks, coins. I swung the light, looking for the floor drain. When I found it I gasped and clicked the light off.

Nicky was leaning on the bar, looking at me.

"What'd you find?"

"Nick, this is bad."

His "behind you"s became demonic. The best-case scenario was that it was the start of his shift, late afternoon, and he was still groggy, grumpy, avoiding eye contact. I could pretend to ignore him. It was worse if he was caffeinated. If he had been sipping on the Crémant, if his appetite had awoken.

"Behind you," Jake said. I froze at the back bar, where I was dusting the aperitif bottles. Feather duster on Suze. Eyes on Lillet. Tributaries of dust sparkling beneath the hanging lamps.

First his shoulder, then the indolent expanse of his chest. His thumb grazed my elbow. I held my breath until the whole thing was over.

"Behind you," he said. I froze at the pass, where I had been stacking clean quart containers. It was a narrow passage. The butane flames clicked in front of me. Behind, the staccato hits of knives on plastic cutting boards. My arm was raised and I collected it to my side and waited.

He placed his hand on my lower hip, or

my upper thigh, or along the bottom seam of my underwear. He pushed me, moved me, and caught my hip with his other hand. Anyone else would have allowed me to move. Anyone else would have waited. He scraped roughly by.

"Excuse me," he said. I did not have the weapons to fight back.

"Don't strangle the bottle, my love," Simone said. She sat at an empty table in the mezz, her hair unfastened, the remains of a Burgundy in a glass in front of her, a gift from one of her tables. I had helped her finish her side work and now I opened wine while she watched. I relaxed my grip.

"You're twisting the label away, keep it toward me."

"I'm not turning it."

"In Sicily you're cursing a person when you hold the wine with the label turned away from them. Stop staring at it, look at me."

"It's not that turned. It's better than before."

"I don't care about better than before, I care about correct."

I grabbed a new bottle. I took the knife of my wine key and ran it around the lip.

"I can't wait until everything is a screw top."

"Bite your tongue. You're twisting it again."

"How do I get the knife all the way around without twisting it?"

She took the bottle from me and demonstrated, swiping the knife clockwise, then flipping her wrist open, the knife going from inside to out, and finishing the cut. The foil top popped off. She grabbed another bottle of the Bourgueil Cabernet Franc. We had a bottle of each of the house wines so I could really practice.

"Why do you know so much?"

"I've been doing this a long time."

"No, everyone here has been doing this a long time. You know what I mean."

"I find it impossible to do anything without investing in it. Even server work."

"This job was supposed to be easy."

"All jobs are easy for people averse to using their brains. I'm in a slight but stately minority who believes that dining is an art, just like life."

I had made the cut. The foil cap came off in one perfect piece. I looked at her expectantly.

"Again" was all she said.

"But it's not just that this job is hard.

Most mornings I wake up thinking, I need an adult."

"That's you. You're the adult."

"No, you're my adult," I said and she smiled. "I don't know. I haven't done laundry since I moved here. I'm not lying."

"That can happen in the beginning. Drop it off, pick it up."

"I used to work out. Run at least."

"That happens too. Join a gym."

"I never go to the bank, I lose all my cash tips."

"That's just Park Bar, little one. Balance," she said, gesturing toward the bottle I held almost horizontally. I leveled it, "floated it," as she said, in midair.

"You could talk to Howard."

"Excuse me?"

"You can schedule a one-on-one with Howard. All the managers have mandatory meetings but Howard opens it up to the servers as well. You can review your progress, or just vent about work. Ask him life questions."

"Um . . ." I looked at her, trying to see what she meant. I felt like I was standing at the edge of something, or maybe back against something, and I remembered what Will had said about Simone and Howard. I thought of that anorexic hostess, Rebecca. I couldn't even remember her face, all I recalled was her name on the schedule. "That's a little weird, right? Besides, that's why I have you."

"I'm serious. He could advise you in ways I can't."

"Why can't it be you?" I put the bottle down. "I don't want to talk to him."

"I see how hard it is for you to open up to people, but Howard is someone that could help you."

"Help me what? Get all my friends in trouble? Have a nervous breakdown and move back home? Get transferred to another restaurant?"

Howard wasn't so terrible. But his indifference with Rebecca, the way he erased her, upset me. And it felt like Simone was sending me away.

"Oh," she said. She cooled considerably. "I wouldn't go in for gossip. He has mentored a lot of girls like you."

"Girls like me?" I looked at my hand, where a cut on my index finger had reopened.

"Young women, I'm sorry. Young women like you who have moved to the city and . . ." She waved her hand in the air.

"And what?" It came out loudly. Will looked up from the dining room below and

233

I waved. *And what?*

"Listen, I will set it up for you, you can talk to him while I'm gone."

"I don't want to, Simone," I said. My tone changed and I saw it affect her. I was telling her I wouldn't. She touched her hair.

"Of course," she said. "Well, you will need to continue working on your form for wine service. May I at least ask that you practice that?"

"You're going somewhere?" Had she said that? They let Simone leave the restaurant?

"Yes, it's that time."

"What time?"

"Little one, it's nearly Thanksgiving. Jake and I are going home."

Jake and I, Jake and I, Jake and I disappear.

"Jake kissed me," I heard myself say, like a stranger was telling on me. I had been so restrained. Of course, I wanted to tell her immediately. I wanted to see if she already knew. But it was like the figs, the oysters. More than anything I wanted to accumulate moments between *us* — just Jake and me.

"Yes, he did." She regarded me with a passive reception to my words. I couldn't find any causes for the cloud of tension that had grown during the lesson, but there it was, coloring the room.

"I don't know," I said. Shut the fuck up, I told myself. "I don't know what it means."

Simone sighed. She was silent a long time looking at me. "What do you think it means?"

I shrugged. Anything I thought of to say out loud would be juvenile when it landed in front of her.

"A woman needs to be in her right mind to be kissed. I tell him that all the time. Otherwise all hell breaks loose."

People hear what they want to hear. I heard, I tell him that all the time. All the time, all the time, Jake and I. My finger was bleeding and I put it in my mouth.

"Have a great trip, then," I said. I gripped the rails and started down the stairs.

"Enjoy the holiday," she replied when I was halfway down.

Let me try to say it again: sometimes when he spoke to you he mumbled. You had to lean in to hear what he was saying. He repeated himself often. We were drinking the last quarters of open bottles of Cabernet Franc, and Jake poured them over ice cubes and it tasted like thyme and cranberries, and I said, When do you head home for Thanksgiving? And he said, Soon. I leaned in and said, When? He turned, lined me up in his sights, and said, Soon. I said, nearly falling off my stool, When? We should hang out before you go, and his arctic eyes said to me, Babe, I've already gone.

I was polishing knives at the front hutch when I heard my name. It sliced me, my name that I hadn't heard in months. Suddenly I saw the version of myself who had never come to the city, never fallen down the stairs, or said anything stupid. She was safe and as good as dead.

It was a kid I had gone to college with. I couldn't remember his name. He was in a suit. They always wore a suit when they came in with their parents. Or at least a sports jacket and tie. My instinct was to run into the kitchen and pretend I hadn't heard. But I thought Simone might be watching. I smiled warmly.

"You work here?" he asked, incredulous.

"Yes. Yes, I do." I tried to see my new self. All I could see was the red and white stripes of my shirt. Why did I wear the red one, which always reminded me of Waldo and clowns? I split and watched us from the top of the stairs, I split and watched us from the ceiling, I split and watched us from halfway across the country.

"That's so funny!" he said.

236

"Yeah, it's hilarious."

"Do you live here?"

"Not in the restaurant."

"Ha, yeah. That's so cool you moved here. You live in the city?"

"In Williamsburg. It's a neighborhood. In Brooklyn."

"Oh, I've heard of it. It's like the hip spot, right?"

Not the part I live in, I thought. But I knew what I was supposed to say. "Yes. Lots of . . ." — the words wouldn't come together — "artists, very . . . up and coming."

"What else are you doing?"

Inevitable. Why hadn't I practiced this situation? Was it possible that I had ferociously recited menu ingredients to myself on the subway, but had never come up with a tagline about my life? Had I completely erased the world outside these walls?

What else am I doing? I am learning about food and wine and how to taste terroir and how to pay attention.

"I'm doing this," I said. I paused. His expectation hung on me. "And I'm working on some projects."

"What kind of projects?"

Jesus, his curiosity was baffling. Other industry people knew when to let it go, they understood the subtext.

"Mixed-media stuff. You know, all the different mediums. Um. Fragments. The human condition. The failure of language. Love. I'm at the gathering stage right now."

"Fascinating," he said, smothering me with his earnestness. "This must be the perfect place to gather material."

I wanted to say, My life is full. I chose this life because it's a constant assault of color and taste and light and it's raw and ugly and fast and it's mine. And you'll never understand. Until you live it, you don't know.

Instead I nodded and said, "Yeah, it's perfect."

"Yeah . . . that's great." When he said *great* it sounded like *sad.* I steeled myself. The only way out of this was hospitality.

"Are you dining with us?"

"Yeah, I'm in the back with my dad and uncle. I was just looking for the bathroom. We're in from Philly for the afternoon. This place is his favorite. It's really famous, you know that?"

I smiled. "Well I'll come say hello. And I will let Chef know you're here. Please, let me show you the restrooms."

I walked him over and he seemed to understand that it was time for me to return to my glamorous life as an artist who was

238

accidentally polishing knives in a stripy pirate's blouse.

He started to leave but turned back and said, "Hey, do you think you could be our waitress? That would be so fun!"

So fun! If only I knew how to tell him I wasn't even a fucking waitress.

I never would have recognized him. I didn't belong to his world anymore. We called them the Nine-to-Fivers. They lived in accordance with nature, waking and sleeping with the cycle of the sun. Mealtimes, business hours, the world conformed to their schedule. The best markets, the A-list concerts, the street fairs, the banner festivities were on Saturdays and Sundays. They sold out movies, art openings, ceramics classes. They watched television shows in real time. They had evenings to waste. They watched the Super Bowl, they watched the Oscars, they made reservations for dinner because they ate dinner at the normal time. They brunched, ruthlessly, and read the Sunday *Times* on Sundays. They moved in crowds that reinforced their citizenship: crowded museums, crowded subways, crowded bars, the city teeming with extras for the movie they starred in.

They were dining, shopping, consuming,

unwinding, expanding while we were working, diminishing, being absorbed into their
scenery. That is why we — the Industry
People — got so greedy when the Nine-to-
Fivers went to bed.

"Yeah, you in the marge now," said Sasha.
He had watched the whole interaction with
unconcealed delight. "What, you think you
like your friends? You never be like them
again, honey pie. Look at you — you think
you dip your toe in the pool? No bitch, you
in the pool. You drowning in the pool."

"I'm in the marge."

"Yeah, like you in the marge with the fat-
ties and the fags and the freaks and that
guy that sleeps on the bench."

"You mean I'm in the margins of society?"

"Yeah, what you think I fucking mean?
Well, whatsoever, you an old hag now, just
like me."

I saw him that night at Park Bar. When I
looked at the schedule I saw that they were
both off for the next two weeks. Flower-Girl
was there in a turtleneck dress and tights
and riding boots, looking fresh from some
polo match, but otherwise it was just us.
Everyone else was filmed in oil and dust. I
ignored him bowed against the wall talking

to Will. I went to join Ariel and Vivian at the bar and as soon as I sat I felt it: he was gone. Every beautiful animal knows when it's being hunted.

I sat down next to Terry — it wasn't busy enough for two bartenders. Ariel and Vivian were bickering so I turned to him. He was drunk. He leaned into me, winking, his voice as fuzzy as his stretched-out cotton sweater.

"Hey, new girl. You know the straw that broke the camel's back? Is that the same thing as the last straw?"

He touched his fingers to mine. I don't know if he meant to. I put my hands in my lap. My beer was flat but I knew I would drink all of it.

"Absolutely. It's absolutely the same straw."

He nodded, impressed that I knew.

Not being able to swipe into the subway when people are backing up behind you. Waiting for him at the bar. Leaving your purse open on a stool with a mess of bills visible. Mispronouncing the names while presenting French wines. Your clogs slipping on the waxed floors. The way your arms shoot out and you tense your face when you almost fall. Taking your job seriously. Watching the sex scene from *Dirty Dancing* on repeat and eating a box of gingersnaps for dinner on your day off. Forgetting your stripes, your work pants, your socks. Mentally mapping the bar for corners where you might catch him alone. Getting drunker faster than everyone else. Not knowing what foie gras is. Not knowing what you think about abortion. Not knowing what a feminist is. Not knowing who the mayor is. Throwing up between your feet on the subway stairs. On a Tuesday. Going back for thirds at family meal. Excruciating diarrhea in the employee bathroom. Hurting yourself when you hit your head on the low pipe. Refusing to leave the bar though it's over, completely over. Bleeding in every form. Beer stains on your shirt, grease stains on your jeans, stains in every form. Saying you know where something is when you have absolutely no idea where it is.

At some point I leveled out. Everything stopped being embarrassing.

■ ■ ■ ■

WINTER

■ ■ ■ ■

I

You will kiss the wrong boy. It was an easy prophecy. They were all the wrong boy. The night before Thanksgiving was a drinking holiday you didn't know about until you moved to the city. The streets in the Village were clogged with people, server people, the shops closed, orange- and yellow-papered windows darkened. No one had anywhere to go. A celebration ensued, mildly destructive, mildly bored — it was a night of driftings and nowheres.

You threw up and kept drinking, pulled the trigger and doused the trigger. Throwing up was effortless, like nothing, kissing like nothing. Your head full, then emptied, ready to be kissed.

You were on Will's lap, staring at his buttery lashes. You knew you shouldn't be but his arms enclosed you while he told you

245

about the latest movie script he had written. He modeled the superhero after you. You: in red patent-leather boots. You: able to jump buildings and shoot lightning out of your eyes. Sunrise came like an undisclosed verdict. The wind was salient, persistent, and you shivered. You were blown out on cocaine, sitting on a rooftop and he tasted like a malt shop. Every time you pulled away, his eyes were welling like puddles in his face. You opened a beer warmer than the air, spilled your beer on your shirt. The sky rushing up now, anxious, and you knew you were doing something wrong. You kissed him harder and the sky abated. When you had sex you were totally dry and it felt like scratching. For one second, every face you'd ever seen, you forgot.

Pigeons flew in diminishing waves between the low buildings. The sun rose. It said, Now that you've done this, you can never have that. Now that I'm like this, I can never go back.

The first time I came into work really hungover — *ill* hungover — my shoes were gone. It had a muddled logic that I accepted. When I woke with my head rattling I knew that every step of my day would be harder than normal. It was the day after Thanksgiving. I was the three p.m. back-waiter, but the trains were running irregularly, and while I had heard one sighing into the station as I ran down the stairs, my card was out of money. Which is to say, I was late.

I had seen the sun come up. Two mornings in a row actually, I had watched in real time as the night weakened and the authoritative blue of morning, flat as a sheet, hung itself in the east. There are many romantic reasons to watch the sunrise. Once it started, it was hard to leave. I wanted to own it. I wanted it to be a confirmation that I was alive. Most of the time, however, it felt condemning.

The door to the locker room opened but I didn't look up. I was on my hands and knees looking for my clogs. Server clogs were indestructible with a utilitarian ugliness. They were built for labor, for standing on tile for fourteen hours. They were not cheap.

"You're late," he said. I turned to Will and he looked as sick as I felt or maybe it was the bleak light in the locker room.

"Will, I can't talk, I can't find my shoes."

"I can't, I can't, I can't."

"Please."

"When in your life did you get so good at

disappearing?"

"Will. The sun was up. I had been saying I needed to leave for hours."

"You said you were going to the bathroom."

"I meant the bathroom in my apartment."

"You seemed like you were having a nice time."

"Please, let's not talk about this."

"I was having a nice time."

"Yes."

"It's funny because you laugh like a little girl one second —"

"Will, stop."

"Is your phone broken?"

I started opening every unlocked locker.

"I texted you yesterday. We had a big dinner. With turkey and all the stuff."

"I was busy."

I had spent Thanksgiving Day napping, masturbating, ignoring phone calls from distant relatives who probably didn't even know I had moved, and watching all three *Godfathers.* I had pad Thai for dinner. As a gesture of holiday goodwill they turned on the heat in my building. Every ten minutes the radiator sounded off like a firecracker and within an hour I had to open all the windows. My roommate had invited me to his mom's house in Armonk. It was a pitiful moment, in that he pitied me enough to invite me, and I pitied him for having familial obligations. I probably would have been a nice buffer and we could have had a real conversation for the first time. But the parade of it, the shallow, ancient family dramas, the hours of being polite. I waved him off happily.

Scott texted me that the cooks were going out in Williamsburg. It was already ten p.m. but he promised to pay for a car home if I came. So I brushed my hair. They were raging when I got there, drinking whiskey hard, like taking bullets to the throat. I couldn't keep up, I kept up. Scott ladled me into a car at seven a.m.

"My shoes are gone," I said, incredulous.

"Maybe we can grab a beer tonight. Take it easy."

"I'm not drinking again. Ever."

"You just need hair of the dog. Ask Jake to slip you something. Or wait, he's gone."

"Lovely," I said under my breath.

Will squatted next to me as I looked in the dark space under the lockers. I wanted to hit him. You did this to yourself, I said, my eyelids twitching.

"But you *did* have a nice time the other night."

I didn't answer. Was I going to get written

249

up for being late? I had worn my Converse to work, there was no way I could wear them on the floor. Ariel and Heather were both on the schedule later, so I couldn't steal their shoes, and Simone's were too big for me.

"I wore them literally two days ago," I said. "I wore them, I put them in the corner, under the coats."

"But that's not where they go, doll, they go in your locker."

"But they make everything in my locker dirty." My teeth hurt. Something in my back felt broken. "I *usually* put them by the coats."

"You went out with the cooks last night?"

"How do you know that?"

"Scott told me you were wasted. He said you fell down in the middle of a crosswalk."

"He was wasted," I said. I didn't know if that had happened. It might have happened. When Will said his name, I faintly remembered making out with Scott, and felt injured.

"You're cute when you're hungover."

I took a deep breath.

"Will. I am very sorry. For any misinformation. I mean, misleading. I mean I'm sorry if you have ideas. It's been a very . . . tipsy week."

"What does that mean?"

"It means I don't quite feel I'm in control of my life. I've been hitting it a little hard, you know?"

"Okay," he said. He thought about it. "You can lean on me."

"No, that's not what I'm saying. I'm sorry if I did anything."

"Sorry you did what? Which part?" Will thought we were flirting. I didn't know when exactly my guard had lowered with him, it had been high since his confession in the Park Bar bathroom, but it had been whittled away by time, cocaine, and beer. And work had been lusterless since they left.

"I don't even know, Will. I don't remember a thing."

"Ah," he said. He stood up. "Chef threw them out."

"What?"

"Yesterday. Every year whatever is left out over the holiday gets thrown out. There's a note on the bulletin board. Check the trash cans in the alley. Maybe the garbage hasn't been picked up yet."

I stared at him as he left. "Sorry," he said, "you should have told the maid."

And there they were. Three bags into my search, with curdled milk and clotted food and disintegrating paper towels.

■ ■ ■ ■

The floor drain under the sink was the fountainhead. Decomposing fruit, crusts of bread, wine dregs, and general backwash congealed to an opaque gray slime. It seemed ridiculous that we didn't know about it sooner, as water barely passed through it. This slime, this primordial sludge, was the home base for all sorts of insects that weren't allowed in the restaurant. Namely the fruit flies.

They weren't so menacing in and of themselves. But they had a disturbing blind tenacity when they landed. They moved away in thick clusters when you swatted them and then settled again in the exact same spot. I had nightmares about them landing in my hair, covering my face.

I told Zoe the first time. She nodded and nothing happened. Then it was my turn again for the drain side work and I marched up to the office where she was picking at a filet mignon of tuna.

"Zoe, I can't clean that drain."

"What drain?" she asked.

"The drain. The one I told you about, the disgusting one where the fruit flies live."

"You never told me that."

"Yes I did, it was like weeks ago."

"No one said anything to me." She stood up, annoyed, and straightened her blazer. "We can't solve problems if we don't work together. I need you to perform your side work, and inform management if you're not able to."

Never once had I thought of her as a real authority figure. She was Howard and Simone's puppet, the poor desk slave who made sure the drop was correct and had to arrange the server schedule every week. Which meant everyone hated her.

"I'm very sorry, but I did inform management. You can't pay me enough to touch that." I laid the yellow gloves down. "You should see for yourself."

Maybe it was because Simone was gone, or maybe I was worn a little thin. I thought for a second she would write me up. But she shrugged her shoulders and shook them, like she was warming her body up. She picked up the yellow gloves.

"The bar sink?"

When we got downstairs Nicky was rinsing down and wiping out the speed rack, one of the last steps of closing. He saw Zoe's gloves and said, "I wouldn't disturb them. Can this wait five minutes?"

"No, I've been informed of a serious situation."

"Yeah, like a month ago, Zoe —"

"Enough." She put a hand up. She went behind the bar and grabbed a flashlight and a fork. I don't know what the fork was for — protection? She sank down and two seconds later, she screamed, covering her face. They soared up in a cloud and I sprinted back into the kitchen.

Some nights if Terry was feeling particularly loose, he let Ariel put on her music while we cut lines on the bar and helped him put up the stools.

"Did I tell you the one about polar bears?" he asked. I finished my line and passed him my cut-up pen.

"Yes, the canned peas."

"Shit, you need to get a new bar."

"You need to get new jokes, old man."

He passed it to Sasha. Ariel stood looking out the windows, her body tense. Vivian was supposed to meet us two hours ago. I wiped my nose. Every muscle in my body clenched then released and my legs gave out. I sank, and then sat on the floor.

"Whoa," I said. "It's strong."

"Who gonna take care of Baby Monster tonight? Not me, I have a date in twenty minutes."

"You have a date at four a.m.?" Terry asked.

"I say to him four fifteen," Sasha said, checking the clock. "You think too early-ish?"

"Terry, can we get one more?" Ariel asked. Her eyeliner made black notches in her face.

"Ari, come on, I'm all cleaned up."

"I'll make it, I'll clean it, come on, Skip here is tripping her face off, we all need to wind down."

Terry looked toward the street and he and Ariel exchanged a loaded glance.

"I'm not tripping my face off. I'm cool," I said from the floor. My palms were sweating and it was delicious, running them on the cold, gritty tile.

"Negronis!" Ariel demanded, pushing behind the bar.

"Wait, you guys, wait, show me!" I bolted up. I pulled down a stool, and it felt so light.

"The lesson is thirds," she said as she poured Campari into a jigger. She locked her eyes on me and said in a low voice, "And of course, it is a lesson of life as well."

They started laughing.

"Stop guys, don't make fun of her. Thirds is an important lesson! Like a cappuccino," I said. "I mean, ideally, the perfect cappuccino, it's one-third espresso, one-third milk, one-third foam, but I mean, ideally, you want the foam and the milk to be perfectly integrated, um, aerated actually —"

"There she is," said Will. He pulled down a stool and sat next to me and I hugged him, generously, an overflow of the love I had burrowed within me and needed the drugs to interpret.

"Now she got diarrhea in her mouth," Sasha said.

"No, wait, guys, it's a lesson —"

"The lesson of thirds," said Terry. "I ever tell you guys about the two German girls I took home? It wasn't as fun as you would think. Even before the gonorrhea."

"One time I took too much Special K and ended up with two fat, ugly motherfuckers, not a good time," Sasha said and pointed at me. "Don't touch that shit."

"Threes, threes, the three amigos," I said. "No, sorry, the five amigos."

"Jesus, Skip, will you shut up and make a pretty little line." Ariel scrolled through her iPod. "Then we're done."

"Are you high?" I asked Ariel. I turned to Will and Sasha. "Wait, are you high? Is anyone high?" I made the line the way she taught me, about the length of a cigarette, evenly distributed with sharp, tapered ends.

"I'm *high.*"

Ariel passed me a Negroni and it tasted like cough syrup. "Medicine. Hey guys, I think I hate my job." They laughed. "No I'm serious, isn't it kinda depressing and dirty in there lately?"

"What you think, everyone look, Alice just wake up and oh fuck, no wonderland."

"Maybe you should hit the pause button every now and then," Will said, and I turned away from him.

"I'm putting on your favorite song, Skip."

Ariel was aggressive about music. She had made me a few CD mixes, the depths of my ignorance presented in sixteen tracks. It never ended well. For her, the enjoyment of music was contingent on its obscurity. Once people knew about it, she discarded it, moved on. And yet she was always trying to educate me. Every time I told her I liked a song she had shown me, she put on a disappointed smirk and said, "You *would.*" Which I thought had been the point.

"You don't know my favorite song," I said. When I caught her eyes they were like rain-washed windows I couldn't see inside. Worry fluttered through me and I took another drink.

"No LCD," Terry said, hitting his hand on the bar for emphasis.

"I will shoot myself, Ari," said Will.

"Fuck you, fuck your mothers, if you talk shit on James Murphy I will fucking kill you."

The song came on. "Heartbeats." I clapped my hands.

"Oh, I *do* like this song!"

"Why you squeal like a piggy?"

"Sasha, come on, it's *my* song." I moved my shoulders and shut my eyes, dizzy, white cloudbursts inside my lids. I pulled Sasha off the stool. I swung my hair in front of my face like Ariel taught me, my body dilated under the water of the synthetic bass. It was an apathy dance. I heard Ariel singing, and when Will took my hand and spun me, I smiled, lip-synching.

To call for hands of above, to lean on . . . wouldn't be good enough for me, oh.

All the movement stopped and I looked toward the door. Vivian stood, wobbling, cautious. I waved and looked at Ariel, who had a glass in her hand. It went flying by my face and into the wall next to Vivian.

The sound came seconds later. I had already watched it explode and shower the floor, no snapping, nothing clean, full disintegration. During the delay in sound I covered my eyes.

"Where the fuck have you been?"

"You're out, Ari," Terry yelled. "God fucking damn it."

Vivian looked bored. Ariel grabbed a handful of straws and threw them before Will grabbed her by the shoulders.

"I'm sorry, I'm sorry," I heard someone call out above the music. The song ended and I realized it was me. Vivian walked to the bar, not looking at Ariel, and sighed as she brought up the hand broom.

"Sorry, Terry," she said.

"Oh, she's sorry, *Terry*?" Ariel wrestled as Will held her arms down.

"Let's go, string bean, party's over." Sasha grabbed her purse and Will picked her up and went to the door. Sasha waved to someone out the window. "Oh and look, Victor-baby is here."

"I know you," Ariel yelled at Vivian, her voice shot and guttural, "I know everything about you."

Nearly five a.m. in the park. A frigid night that should have been blown over by sleep. Empty bottles rattled in the gutters, darkness lay thick as wax in the trees. We couldn't get Ariel to do anything but pace and rage and smoke. Sasha and Victor took off immediately. I thought, What's stopping me from leaving? Why can't I grab a taxi too? Do all the single people have to wait it out together?

Vivian was a sex addict — undiagnosed, but Ariel was familiar with the signs. Vivian was illiterate. She was tits and ass, barely queer. Ariel was embarrassed to be seen with her. Vivian had used her. For what was unclear.

"Take the down pill, babe," I said. I smoked with her for solidarity, but I was sick, sweaty, shivering, coming down hard.

"She's right, Ari, where's the Xanax?"

Ariel took two pills without stopping her tirade. She lit another cigarette before the first was finished. And just when I thought I was going to freeze to death on a bench in Union Square, her drugs kicked in.

She stumbled. Will grabbed her and her head dropped down to her chest.

"She took too much," he said. Ariel slapped him and started laughing.

"Like *too much* too much? Like we're going to the hospital?"

"No, just difficult-to-handle too much."

He put her down on the bench and we sat on either side of her. Her eyes were closed, her head cocked to the side. I put her hood on her and Will and I looked at each other. I remembered how delicately he'd touched my face when we kissed and felt repulsed and then sad.

"Thank you for being nice to me," I said.

He lit a cigarette and looked across the park, not taking the bait.

"Does this happen?" I asked.

"It has happened. It doesn't happen all the time. She has all these meds. It gets complicated."

"I see that. You think Vivian is cheating?"

"No," he said loudly into Ariel's ear. But then he met my eyes and shrugged.

"Sucks."

We looked at her, looked at each other, then out at the park. I lifted my feet when I heard the rats. Neither of us wanted to deal with it. But I owed Will for getting me home safely more than once. We all owed Will, really. He never stopped watching over us.

"I'll take her. My place is closer to her place, she can walk in the morning."

"Aren't you like fifth-floor walk-up?"

"She's going to have to walk." I tapped her and she didn't move. "You're going to walk, Ari."

Wind came through the park and I could hear the trees bending, creaking.

"I haven't heard that in so long," I said, hushed, looking up. "They are speaking like real trees."

Ariel walked but her eyes were closed. I

261

guided her by our hooked arms. A cab materialized going south on Union Square West, a beacon of hope. The driver saw us and rolled down his window.

"No puke," he said. He had a drooping, ashen face, as if he'd been sleeping. I tried to open the doors but they were locked.

"Come on, she's fine."

He looked her up and down and Ariel said, "Fuck you."

"See, she's fine!" I said. "Please, I have cash, extra tip, por favor."

Ariel took up the far two seats. As soon as we settled in her head was on my shoulder. I held her hand and kissed it. The lit store windows turned SoHo into a lunar landscape, nothing human for miles. I watched each block present itself to me, and I thought, Who lives here?

When we turned onto Delancey, Ariel's head fell onto my breast. When I picked her head up, she kissed me. She was so soft. Kissing her felt like trying to stand on a mossy stone in a river, our lips ran over each other with no traction. Her hair drifted up as if we were underwater. After a minute I became aware of it, and I started trying to kiss her back, performing, asking myself if I liked it. But for the first few seconds all I knew was her mouth.

262

I couldn't lose myself in it again. I let it go over the bridge. There was no groping, just the fine edges of teeth and a feathery tongue, so yielding. I tilted my face down and told the driver to take the first exit. His eyes were locked on us in the rearview mirror.

"You have beautiful lips," I said, pulling a few strands of her hair from my mouth. She didn't open her eyes.

"Yes, yours are a shame too."

The driver took the turn too fast and her head smashed into the window on the other side. She moaned the rest of the way. I was patient with her on the stairs. I couldn't make her brush her teeth. She was asleep before I finished brushing mine, taking up the entire bed, her black hair splayed like spider legs on my pillow. *Who lives here?*

II

I heard the rain while I slept, heard the cars moving, like scissors shearing paper. It was my day off. I woke up out of breath, inflamed from the radiator. Someone was playing Édith Piaf out their window. It washed through the rain, the claustrophobic sky, and shot in my open window. It hit me in the chest right where old Édith intended it to land. I couldn't imagine another life.

They were both on today, their first shift back. He would be in at three p.m., although I imagined him coming in closer to three thirty. I couldn't find a rational reason to show up at work, but I felt calm for the first time in weeks, the wasted nights of their absence firmly behind me.

I masturbated, thinking of him on top of me, suffocating me, and every time I got close to coming he grabbed my face and said, Pay attention. Then my own body felt like a bag filled with sand and I fell back asleep.

When I finally got out of bed most of the shops were closing. The pavement was slick as I ran down Bedford and into the vintage shop. I bought the first one I tried on — the girl sized me up perfectly. It was mint condition, a black leather motorcycle jacket. When I saw myself in it, I thought, I want to be friends with her. I zipped it to my throat when a wind from the river shook rain from the branches. As I walked — I swear it — strangers looked at me differently.

Who knew winter meant vegetables? Chef. No asparagus shipped in from Peru, no avocados from Mexico, no eggplants from Asia. What I assumed would be a season of root vegetables and onions was actually the season of chicories. Chef had his sources, which he guarded. Scott walked through the restaurant in the morning with unmarked brown paper bags, sometimes crates.

He told me that the chicories would really brighten when the first freezes came. It sweetened their natural bitterness. I could barely keep track of them. The curly tangle of frisée didn't seem the same species as the heliotrope balls of radicchio, or the whitened lobes of endive. Their familial trait was a bite — I thought of them as lettuces that bit back. Scott agreed. He said we should be hard on them. Eggs, anchovies, cream, a streak of citrus.

"Don't trust the French with your vegetables," Scott said. "The Italians know how to let something breathe." I helped him wash frisée, my hands stiff and frozen. The salad spinner was an appliance nearly my size, and Scott let me sit on top of it while it ricocheted around. I was nearly positive we had made out, but he seemed uninterested in reliving it. My pride was stunned, but I was relieved to have a friendship with a man. I knew he was dating a bartender in Williamsburg, had just broken something off with a hostess, and had his eye on the new Asian pastry girl.

"What's this one?"

"The best one." He peeled off battered dark-green outer leaves and gave me a leaf from the inside. I used it as a scoop for the tapenade.

"Escarole," he said.

"And those outside leaves."

"Soup. Just wait."

Her distracted, concerned expression inspecting the server kit behind the bar. Those red lips. She seemed surprised to see

266

me when I ran out to family meal. I hugged her.

I wanted to say, I missed you. Instead I said, "Hi."

"Hello, little one." Reserved, but a satisfaction somewhere. I felt it. She missed me too. "Did you hold down the fort while I was gone?"

"Oh, Simone, it was awful, there are fruit flies and Zoe didn't listen to me and everyone got so drunk."

"Brown food, winter food, peasant food," she said, eyeing the soup. She only took one bowl — I knew he wasn't coming. I was watching her like she knew more than the schedule. "A soup made with the bitter scraps and bits, where the sum is always greater than the parts."

"Yes, whatever you say," I said. White beans, escarole, chicken stock skimmed until it was velvet, studded with sausage. I went back for seconds, then thirds.

I became terrified of drains. I skipped my eyes over them in the dishwashing station, I wouldn't look down in my own bathroom, I didn't even want to see the pipes. I thought I would see a break in them, an air gap, where everything from the underworld would crawl up into the open air, where they could teem, thrive.

It wasn't easy to catch Ariel outside of work. She seemed to have an expansive network within the city that went beyond the restaurant, probably because she was an NYU kid who'd never left. I often asked her about college in the city — when I tried to imagine it, I thought, But wait, where do you move when school is over?

When she said I could maybe, one day, come with her to a show, I didn't get my hopes up. When she said, Do you want to come to a show this Thursday? I corralled my excitement.

But I found myself in a closed-up office building on the West Side below Fourteenth Street and from the bleak gray exterior I was ready to be underwhelmed. Ariel and I doused in green and red light, making our way into a basement, where the drums tapped like a switch, echoes and duplicates colliding with the walls. A ragged-looking middle-aged guy with gray hair paced the stage. He took lines of coke off a record that a little pixie held in the air like a serving platter. Whenever I heard electronic music I thought of a man locked up in a room with computers, never of musicians — but I was watching it, with instruments, with a band that traded chemistry between themselves and the crowd. They released a song like a tidal wave.

New York in the seventies it was not. No disco decadence, drag queens, nudity, or androgyny. But even with this basement's lack of glamour, I was aware of being truly relevant — within my time and of my time. Plain-faced kids with outsized glasses, girls in gritty fur vests and boots, deep, unmovable veins of apathy and inattention that made them care more about the next ten minutes than the next ten years. They — I guess it was "we" now — wanted dance music with a knife's edge, ironic lyrics that crossed accidentally into sincere, like they crossed into the sincere, accidentally but every so often. Everyone was stripped down in the awkward peridot light, unselfconscious as they pogo-ed around.

Ariel wore a tiny crop top under her sweater, highlighting her pale ribs. It read Disco for Assholes, and I wondered if I could wear something like that. She was confetti, all over the room. People kept coming up to her, kissing her and screaming. A waifish, anemic blond girl kissed her on the lips and Ariel bit her and hissed. She smiled at me and I yelled, "That's not how you kissed me."

" 'Cause you're a baby, baby!" She spun. "Amazing?"

"Amazing!" I yelled back. Self-deprecating, sentimental, sarcastic music and I felt like I was breaking out of a corset. I was going to dance all night.

The crowd diffused my sixth sense for Jake. He was there, next to me, he was the person Ariel jumped on, the person holding her hair off her neck while they spoke. This intimacy was surprising, but not as surprising as just him. Jake in the real world. He was supposed to be tethered to the restaurant where I imagined him when I wasn't at work. Ariel cupped her hands over her mouth and tunneled words into his ear. Jake had his eyes on me and he nodded. I stopped dancing. She took his hand and pulled him away, but not before he gave me a tiny, condescending wave with his fingers. He was back.

And I knew he wouldn't leave, not like the other nights at the restaurant or Park Bar when I turned my back and he was vacuumed out by the night. No.

Unplanned, unmediated, this was a regular Thursday night, with no shift at the restaurant behind or ahead of me, and Jake and I were at the same place. A cool place, where cool people went — the pressure was lifting, I started dancing again — and I screamed for the band because I knew this song, it was *my* song, and I felt the source of the city's adrenalized, fatal energy. It was me.

"You're really sweating," he said when I came up to the bar. "You're kind of a crazy dancer."

"I am," I said, flatly. I meant to say coquettishly, *I am?*

"You're into them?" he asked. He gestured toward the band. I nodded and shrugged, a subtle look that meant either (a) they're so overrated or (b) they are like God. The look depended a lot on what Jake thought.

"What are you doing here?" He gave me back that same amorphous shrug and nod. As if to say, I go places. I wanted to ask, What places?

"Did you work today?" Banal. I couldn't think of anything else to say. A song started and I turned toward the stage.

"Let's go."

"What?"

"Let's *go*. Come on, if you keep dancing you're going to hurt someone. Or yourself."

"Let's go?" I held my hand to my ear. All I heard was that he had been watching me dance.

"Ari's good, she met up with her people."

"Her people?" I yelled.

He shook his head at me like I was a fucking idiot, which I was, a deaf bobble-head trying to hear him, trying to see the tattoo on his collarbone. He had his glasses pushed up on top of his head, his hair suspended, a scientist pulled out of the laboratory. He grabbed me by the back of the neck and moved me toward the exit.

It was pattering rain outside, translucent, needle rain, pricking my cheeks, collecting like quartz on my wrists where the light hit them, our two exhalations coming in cold clouds.

"Do you have an umbrella?"

"I don't believe in them," he said. He walked over to his bike, chained against a tree. There was a plastic bag over the seat.

"But you believe in protecting your bike seat?"

Almost had him. Almost had a laugh.

"I didn't know it was a choice to believe in umbrellas."

"All beliefs are a choice," he said. He rolled his bike and I walked next to it.

"That's really deep, Jake." I loaded it up with sarcasm, but what I thought was, You're romantic.

Raindrops perched on his eyebrows, on the lenses of his glasses, on his ears. I was suddenly very sober and scared.

"Are we going to Park Bar?"

"Is that the only bar you've been to?"

"Um, no." Yes, more or less.

"I'm taking you to dinner."

He's taking me to dinner. I watched my feet until my laughter made it impossible, and I covered my mouth.

"I am," he said, "why are you laughing?"

"You're taking me to dinner?"

"Are you a fucking parrot? Stop repeating everything I say." But he couldn't finish it. He laughed.

"Jake, I would looooove to go to dinner with you." Heads down, frizzy rain, rocking with laughter. It wasn't funny but it took some time to stop appearing that way. When it ended we looked away from each other and I stared into ground-floor apartments. I bumped into the bike.

I wondered if we were going to the restaurant. All the servers got vouchers, monthly allowances that you could spend or accrue. I would get one too after I'd been there six months. It was such an incongruity to see your coworkers sit at the bar. They treated themselves like royalty with their fake money, ordering everything on the menu, rubbing elbows with the regulars, sharing their bottles of Burgundy. It scared me to think about — watching from the other side. Watching the bar tickets drag, knowing that Chef was screaming at someone about my entrée, watching Howard, or god forbid Simone, going over my order with the server, while I was drinking or talking with my mouth full.

But what if Jake opened the door for me? What if the hostess's eyes flashed when she saw him, and then settled on me? Her disappointment would be so satisfying. I would let Jake order. I watched the oyster plate drop down in front of us, Nicky bringing out two Negronis. Then that anchovy-and-escarole salad everyone talked about, Chef would probably send out the foie gras torchon with candied kumquats, Simone would want us to drink Sauternes with that, she always dropped off half glasses to her soigné tables. Every time I rose from my seat a backwaiter would come and refold and fan my napkin, and Jake would look marvelously unkempt without his stripes, like a wealthy degenerate and I would be —

"I have a thing about shitty diners," he said. He stopped in front of the plate-glass windows and gaudy lights of a diner somewhere on Sixth Avenue. He pulled open a door and said, "I love them."

A half-moon, radiating yellow, revolved

above us, but the sign had so much sparkling plumage I couldn't read the name of the place. There were a few others inside, a nondescript trench coat at the bar, an older couple in a booth. Jake took me to the counter, to the corner, and jumped on the stool while I tried to flatten my hair. He pulled off his soaked green army jacket and his shirtsleeves were short enough that I could see tattoos. There was the key on the inside of his biceps, which I saw now was heavily scarred, the bottom of a buffalo that I assumed covered his shoulder. The tail fins of what I assumed was a mermaid descending down the back of his right biceps.

"That one doesn't look like the others," I said, pointing to the key.

"Yeah, it fell out partially." He pulled down his shirtsleeve.

"The key to your heart?" I asked playfully, stupidly.

"Sure, princess," he said. He scanned the menu and I shut up.

To our right sat a couple not much older than me. She had long, ironed platinum hair, with sooty roots. She wore a fake flower crown. The guy was so hairy I couldn't make out his face. Bearded, long hair sticking out from under a woolen cap, wearing red-and-black flannel. They looked familiar to me, probably from my neighborhood.

"I think they were at the show," I said.

Jake looked visibly pained. "They are everywhere."

"Says the guy with American Spirit cigarettes and the bike."

A terse smile. "Did someone learn what a hipster is? Very good, new girl."

What I knew was that they lived in Williamsburg and the label was pejorative. And I knew that I would never be one. Even in my leather jacket, I couldn't blend in. I cared too much about the wrong things. The waitress behind the counter threw two giant menus at us and walked away.

"No specials?"

Jake studied the menu. When she came back he ordered us both black coffees and Coors Lights.

"Steak and eggs," he said. He waited for me. I hadn't even looked.

"What's good?" I asked her.

"Nothing," she said and smiled. She was firmly into her fifties, pillowy, and had drawn Egyptian cat eyes with black eyeliner through her wrinkles.

"A turkey club, I guess," I said. "Is that a good choice?"

She took our menus. Jake didn't look at

me, like he thought he'd made a mistake. I told myself to just be normal, casual, two friends at a diner, totally cool.

"She was enthusiastic. How was home?" I asked, not meeting his eyes.

"Home?"

"For Thanksgiving?"

"Fucking brutal per usual. There's a reason there's so many suicides out there during the winter."

"But you got to see your family?"

"I don't have any family. I go to Simone's."

I had a dozen questions to ask: What does that mean? What happened to your family? What is Simone's family? Why didn't you stay here? I finally said, "I don't have any family either."

"Should I believe that? A little Jane Eyre alone in the world?"

"I thought you didn't flirt with girls who read."

He coughed and said, "I'm not."

A month ago I had seen Jake eat a steak topped with foie gras. The cooks made fun of him behind his back because he was thin, and made him disgustingly decadent food as a dare. He ate nonstop while he worked, but I held a certain regard for his palate because of Simone. Then I watched him

277

wolf down a cindery steak and eggs at midnight and I realized he was a brute who was always hungry. He was the master of indifference and she was the master of attention.

"So," I said, grinding the cardboard sandwich down into the plate. "When did you move here?"

"Seven, eight years ago? I don't know, I can't remember."

"And you've been at the restaurant the whole time?"

"About five years too long."

"You don't like it."

"These places have a shelf life."

"But no one leaves."

He shook his head rather sadly. "No one leaves."

He pushed my coffee toward me and I sipped — weak, watery.

"Cinnamon — am I right, Nancy?" he said to the waitress. She ignored him. "They put cinnamon in the blend."

"I don't think her name is Nancy." I pushed the coffee away.

"A snob already? That was quick."

"No."

I picked the white bread out of the sandwich, dipped it in the mayonnaise, and crumbled up bacon with my fingers. Inedible, but I probably couldn't have touched it anyway. So many times I imagined this, and now that I was living it, I couldn't fit myself into the scene. I glanced at Flower-Crown and Lumberjack as they got ready to leave. I tried to see us through her eyes. I tried to see us as a couple that always ate at these stools, us inside an Edward Hopper painting.

"So," I said. His eyes were on his rapidly disappearing food. "What neighborhood do you live in? Do you like it?"

"Are you interviewing me?"

"Um, I wasn't trying —"

"No, it's fine, I get it. Just let me put on my suit if you want to play." He tucked his hair behind his ears and cleared his throat. "The time in my life that best exemplifies my totalitarian — I mean, *hospitalitarian* — attitude was when I carried drunk old Neely —"

"Okay, I get it. You don't want to tell me where you live." He went back to his food. "You carried Mrs. Neely?"

"Many a time, many a time. She's as light as a feather." He cleaned his plate completely, pushed it away. He burped and turned to me. Finally. "Chinatown."

"That's cool. I hear it's really cool down there."

"Cool?"

"I don't know. Is that not the right word? Is that like, what a hipster would say?"

"No, cool is fine," he said. "Yes, it's a cool place. It was much *cooler* seven years ago, and it was actually cool ten years ago, before I even got to the city. You see, what those kids over there" — he pointed at the empty booth — "don't realize is that cool is always past tense. The people who lived it, who set the standards they emulate, there was no cool for them. There was just the present tense: there were bills, friendships, messy fucking, fucking boredom, a million trite decisions on how to pass the time. Self-awareness destroys it. You call something *cool* and you brand it. Then — poof — it's gone. It's just nostalgia."

"I see," I said, though I don't know that I did.

"Those two — to go back to our apt illustrations — they want to play dropouts, want to live 'La Vie Bohème.' They want to eat at blue-collar diners, ride their bikes like fucking apes, tear their clothes, discourse on anarchy. And they want to shop at J.Crew. They want dinner parties with organic artisanal chickens and they want their fucking Southeast Asia sojourns, and their jobs at American Express. They come here, but they can't finish their plates."

I took another leaden bite. "You can't have all those things?"

"Sweetheart, you can't make a set of aesthetic decisions without making an ethical one. That's what makes them fake people."

I forced my sandwich down.

"Don't worry. You're not like them."

"I know." It sounded defensive.

"None of us are. Even if you grew up in a country club — which I can tell you did — you're in the struggle now. That's authentic. And whatever your story is, I don't see mommy-and-daddy all over you."

"You think I grew up in a country club?"

"I know you did."

He drained me. "You don't know me."

"Maybe I don't. And you don't know me. And none of us know anything about each other."

"Well, I don't think that's useful. Sometimes people . . . I don't know . . . go out to dinner or get coffee or whatever the fuck . . . and get to know each other."

"And then what happens? They live happily ever after?"

"I don't know, Jake. I'm trying to find out." My head hurt, I propped it on my arm and took a big drink of flat beer.

"Don't get drunk."

"Excuse me?"

"You're sloppy when you drink."

Enough. I opened my throat and chugged my awful beer all the way down. It leaked out of the corners of my mouth and ran down my neck. When I finished I said, "Fuck you and good night."

"Hey, firecracker, give me a second."

A normal man, in this rough pantomime of a date, would put his hand on my hand and apologize. He would reveal just enough vulnerability to convince me to stay and keep digging. Jake of Chinatown, Jake of greasy diners, Jake of exuberant hair in an umbrella-less city — he put his hand under my shirt, right on my ribs, and pushed me onto the stool. He took his hand off me, his fingers had been freezing but I felt branded.

"You're incandescent when you drink. That too."

I exhaled. "A consolation."

"It's the truth. You can take it."

"It's something."

I had my purse in my lap but when the waitress came back I ordered another beer. My ribs, my life, my train.

"You read too much Henry Miller," I said to him. "That's why you think you can treat girls like this."

"You're a decade off, but yeah, I used to read too much Henry Miller."

"Who do you read too much of now?"

"I don't read anymore."

"Seriously?"

"You could call it a crisis of faith. I haven't read a book or even a newspaper in two years."

"Is that why you quit your doctorate?"

"Who told you that?"

"I don't know. Simone?"

"Simone did not tell you that."

"Yeah, she did." She hadn't. But I could tell by his sudden attention that it was true.

"But then you're the Anaïs Nin type, right?"

"Not really." I was, or had been, or always would be.

"We're both a couple of imperfect types." He smiled, and it was soft.

"You missed me," I said, not quite believing it as I said it, but knowing it.

"You want me to tell you that I missed you?"

"No, I want you to be nice to me, actually."

"I'm mean because you're young and need discipline."

"I'm sick of that," I said. "Young, young, young, that's what I get, all day every day.

But I know your secret." I lowered my voice and pushed myself toward him. "You're all terrified of young people. We remind you of what it was like to have ideals, faith, freedom. We remind you of the losses you've taken as you've grown cynical, numb, disenchanted, compromising the life you imagined. *I* don't have to compromise yet. I don't have to do a single thing I don't want to do. That's why you hate me."

He looked at me and I knew he was thinking about disciplining me.

"Do people tend to underestimate you?"

"I have no idea. I'm too busy trying not to fuck up."

He was still looking at me, my shoulders, my breasts, into my lap. To be turned over by his eyes was like being paralyzed.

"You know," he said, and leaned forward. Our knees touched. I could see his pores, the tiny blackheads around his nose and I remembered his up-close face. "I get this sense that you are extremely . . . powerful. I felt it when we kissed, I felt it when you were speaking just then. Like I had tapped into an electrical current. But then I watch you and you spend most of your sober hours holding it back. Maybe you don't have to compromise yet, but you're going to have to choose between your mind and your looks.

284

If you don't, the choices will become narrower and narrower, until they are hardly even choices and you'll have to take what you can get. At some point you decided it was safer to be pretty. You sit on men's laps and listen to their idiotic jokes and giggle. You let them give you back rubs, let them buy your drugs and your drinks, let them make you special meals in the kitchen. Don't you see when you do that, all the while you're . . ." He reached out and wrapped his hand around my throat. I stopped breathing. ". . . choking."

I held my head as still as a vase, something breakable that had a crack, and the crack was spreading. I said, "I felt it too. When we . . ."

His phone rang. It was the most intrusive sound I could imagine. Even Jake looked annoyed, but he looked at the number and jumped off his stool and walked to the bathroom and I continued to hold perfectly still.

The waitress came to clear the plates. She stacked them in the most disordered, haphazard stack I'd ever seen. Even I could do better. She threw them roughly in the bus tub. The plates landed with a crack and the silverware slipped with a slight splash into the juices that lived in the bottom of bus tubs. I had pitied her when we came in, but now I realized that we had the same job.

"Debbie," he called out to the waitress. "Nancy? Sandra?" He didn't sit back down on the stool, he was leaning against the counter now, and I knew our night was over. "I have to go," he said, "I was supposed to meet someone twenty minutes ago."

I nodded, perfunctorily. But I heard this: It wasn't some undeclared rule that kept him from taking me home all those nights I was practically begging for it. He was interested. It was that I wasn't living up to my potential.

"This is my treat. A belated holiday dinner. I heard you had a wild Thanksgiving. I'm sorry I missed it."

He pulled cash out of his wallet. He sent off a text while he drank his beer. I spun around on my stool, watched people duck into doorways out of the fluorescent rain.

"I'm different," I said, not caring about how simpleminded I sounded. I knew how he saw me — grasping, lost. I didn't know yet in which ways he was right or wrong.

But what he didn't know was that I had escaped. That I had gotten myself here. I helped myself to his beer. "I don't have to choose between my looks or whatever. I'm going to have everything. Didn't you say

286

that the aesthetic and the ethical must co-exist?"

I hit him with my knees. "Now. Where the fuck am I and how do I get home?"

III

"Did you know fish have a four-second memory?" Terry asked me. I was pretending to read an old *New Yorker* in the candlelight, my eyes scanning the same lines of a poem over and over again — *what will unleash itself in you when your storm comes* — but really thinking about the coke in my purse, how there was a nice weight to it there, with an entire evening ahead. I thought briefly about leaving before everyone got there, but the night was muddy and I couldn't see past it or through it or even to the next five minutes. The bar was empty so it meant that Terry was talking to me.

"Huh?"

"I always think of that when you guys come in here after your shift. Get it?"

"Yeah, Terry, I get it. We are the fish. And this is the fucking water."

This one had been Mrs. Neely's mother's:

288

it was a wine-purple velvet cloche, with gold embroidery that was nearly worn away. It hugged her tiny skull and lifted slightly so she could bat her eyes at me. Her mother, she told us, had been a legendary beauty. She attended all the art salons, held her own in conversation with W.E.B. DuBois and Langston Hughes. Quite progressive. She didn't have time to make art, supporting her children as a seamstress after her husband died, but she had an artistic flair for living.

"I don't understand it now," she said, taking both my hands in hers emphatically. "You didn't leave the house without a hat. We were not fancy people, my mother made dresses out of curtains, but I would have been indecent without my hats. My mama would have slapped a girl like you silly, the way you dress."

"I know," I said. I encouraged her to admonish me, and she loved to dole it out. "Girls now, they wear leggings. As pants. It's embarrassing."

"Just parading their coochies around town."

"Jesus! But yes. They actually do that."

"Where are the standards? How is a man going to know what to do with you?" She slapped the back of my hand. "You dressing like a boy, hiding your figure. You still hitting them on the playground so they'll look at you."

I nodded, totally unmasked.

"You know, style isn't frivolous. In my day it was a sign of your integrity, a sign that you knew who you were." I nodded, but she was looking beyond me. "Oh, there's my prince."

Sasha sauntered toward us like he was on a runway. Mrs. Neely applauded, her eyes watering.

"Neely darling, you are a vision, now why you talking to this trash?"

"Give me a kiss for goodness' sake." She offered up her cheek shyly and he kissed her on both sides.

"That's how they used to do it in Paris," she said.

"How's the lamb, my love?"

"Terrible, it was absolutely terrible." She looked troubled and gestured for us to come closer. "I swear, every time, worse and worse."

"Marvelous," said Sasha, shining his teeth on her.

"Sasha, will you take this beautiful young lady out on a date? She needs a real gentleman in her life."

"Yes, Sasha." I turned to him. A few weeks

ago he'd dropped his pizza on the ground and offered me fifty dollars to eat it. I did, and he paid me. Like a gentleman. "When are you going to take me out?"

We were both shaking with restrained laughter. Mrs. Neely laughed too, settled into her chair, regal.

I knew he was down there. He had just told Nicky he was going down to find a bottle of scotch, even though I had told him, for over a week, that we were out. I'd even asked Howard about it, and he'd told me it was back-ordered at the distributor. And yet Jake refused to believe it. I wondered if he was looking because he didn't trust my information or because he wanted to draw out this small duel between us.

So when Simone asked if someone could pull the Opus 2002 from the cellar for her, she had just been double sat, I said absolutely, tightened my ponytail, and ran. He didn't turn when I came in.

"It's not here," I said, walking purposefully to the California reds section.

"Those who would believe the words of women would be fools."

"Charming." I scanned the wall, but I already knew where the Opus was. I wished that I knew nothing, that I was wrong about the scotch, that we were out of Opus and we had to spend the rest of service in the cellar looking for bottles that didn't exist.

He grunted. I pulled the wine and went to peer over his shoulder at the mess of stray bottles I had already been through a thousand times.

"Hey," I said. "You're bleeding."

He had a cut on his forearm. He looked down, confused, and I reached out, instinctively, and brought his forearm to my mouth and licked the cut. My tongue metallic, salty, a spark. When I realized what I had done I pushed his arm back to him. I exhaled and he inhaled, his nostrils flared. My eyes said, I dare you. I felt tears, I felt bottomless, I felt liquid.

"Excuse me," she said. Simone stood in the doorway. I blinked at her, wondering what I was seeing. "The Opus?"

I looked at my hand and walked the bottle over to her. I waited for some sarcastic comment. "Well I would have just done it myself," is what Heather would say. Ariel would say, "What the fuck Skip, you fucking cunt." Either of those would have been acceptable. Simone said nothing but looked at us. She was silent and I knew I'd fucked up.

"You wanna peach treat?"

I looked at Heather dumbly. I had properly fucked up, so when the rest of the night took a turn toward chaos, I knew it was my fault. Tables ran over their turn times, they sat sipping water contentedly while the waiting parties tapped their feet and impatience, anxiety, frustration gathered in a prickly cloud. The most desired tables were refused. They were too close to the hutch, too close to the bathroom, too small, too isolated, too noisy. Servers were mishearing orders. They stood nervously outside the kitchen, avoiding telling Chef for as long as possible, making up circuitous stories of how it wasn't their fault. Chef slammed food into the trash dramatically until Howard stopped him and started gifting the mistakes around the room.

That Opus? I wanted to blame him but couldn't. *Somehow* I pulled the 1995, not the 2002. *Somehow* Simone presented it, opened it, and tasted them on it. *Somehow* Howard spotted it while making the rounds in the dining room. He said, "Ah, the '95, what an incredible bottle. How is it drinking this evening?"

The robust man at the table laughed darkly. "Better than the 2002 I ordered. Thanks for that."

"Did you hear?" Ariel asked, swinging past

me with plates. She came back a moment later with empty hands and said, "Simone fucked up for real."

I saw Howard and her in the hutch. His voice calm with none of his usual inquisitiveness, just sharp. "Highly allocated . . . massive loss . . . not like you."

No, I wanted to say, it wasn't like her, it was like me. But I watched Simone nodding, her lipstick worn through in the center of her lips where she was biting them. I felt sick. Heather came to pick up coffee and I confessed.

"Happens," she said, waving me off.

"But Simone —"

"It's her fault. She presented it, she said the vintage out loud, she pointed to it. She should have noticed. That's why she's a server and you're a backwaiter."

I was unconvinced.

"You wanna peach treat?"

"What's that?"

"Just a Xanax." She pulled out a peach-colored pill.

"You think I can do my job on that?"

"Pumpkin, a monkey could do your job on Xanax. And probably not fuck up as much. It's not a real drug."

Or a real job, I thought as I took it. Simone came up to the service bar.

"My cappuccinos on 43?"

"Already went," I said eagerly. I delivered them myself less than five minutes after she put the order in, putting it ahead of the five other tickets.

She turned to Heather. "Do you have another?"

She popped the pill in her mouth and swallowed without water.

"Simone," I said, "I'm sorry."

"Don't," she said cordially. "Heather, eighty-six the '95 Opus. That was the last bottle."

The pill was lodged in my throat. I kept swallowing, but it dissolved there, and it tasted like Jake's sour blood. He didn't speak to me for the rest of the night.

The espresso machine had always been a hot zone for us. The beverage runners were to clean it extra diligently. And I assumed the other backwaiters did. But after a cockroach crawled out of a portafilter I had just picked up, after I threw the whole thing at the wall, spraying coffee grinds everywhere, leaving a dent, after the bug walked away unharmed — well, I stopped taking my cleaning of the espresso machine so seriously.

Zoe was supposed to be our general in

this war, which meant she kept ordering different cleaning supplies, and kept yelling at different exterminators on the phone. Each new arrival promised eradication in hours, each orange jug with its skull and crossbones promised death. Zoe labeled spray bottles with masking tape specifying where they were to be used: Espresso. Bar Sink 1. Bar Sink 2. Zoe modified side work checklists, ordered special rags to clean out the ice machine, special blue strips of paper that we had to wear gloves to handle and hang in the fruit-fly area.

What Zoe didn't do was get rid of the bugs. I learned that every single restaurant in New York City had bugs, from uptown to downtown. I still would have eaten off the ground in the kitchen — the place was spotless. Part of our job was to protect the ignorance of the guests, who couldn't handle the hard truths of the city. We said: "It's just winter." "It's just the park." "It's just construction down the block." "It's the neighbors." All of that was true.

And yet, when Will found a prehistoric-looking cockroach popsicle, even I gagged. It was exquisitely frozen inside an ice cube. He had scooped it from the ice bin. We passed it around until it started to melt, our mouths open in wonder.

To that we said, "Fuck-*Ing*. Dis-Gust-*Ing*."

I did my part. I initialed Zoe's checklists that hung on clipboards above the stations. But one day I went to hang my apron on a hook and it dropped into a crack behind the freezer. When I looked down for it, the wall was covered. *Covered*. Families, generations of roaches breeding, feeding, dying, in the temperate exhaust from the freezer. I stopped fighting so hard. We were outnumbered.

"Oursins!" Simone exclaimed as she came into the kitchen. I kept doing my job, eyes down, scraping spent candles out of the votives. Somebody hadn't put enough water in them, they stuck to the sides even as I hacked away at them. I couldn't remember — it might have been me.

"What?" I asked, just in case she was talking to me. Our chats had tapered off lately.

"Chef, ils sont magnifiques," she murmured. The two of them leaned over a crate, rapt at whatever golden object was in there. It grated on me when she slipped into French with Chef or Howard or Jake. She would drop her voice so I heard only the curl of a romance language and knew I was being left out. I had apologized to her about the Opus again. I confessed to Howard a day later, and he had already forgotten about it. I had no choice but to wait her out until she directed her attention back at me, when she looked at me like I was as exciting as whatever was in the crate.

At preshift Chef said, "Tonight we have Plat de Fruits de Mer. Very traditional. Oysters, mussels, cherrystone clams, prawns — head on — and the small snails. But what takes it over the top is some spanking-fresh uni, in the shell."

Someone whistled, a few groans of desire.

"Seventeen orders. This is a hand sell, people; we're not printing it. $175 per tower."

"Per tower?" I yelled out. Everyone looked at me.

Howard continued. " 'Tis the season, my friends. People are celebrating. They have been waiting to dine with us. You are here because you're perceptive, so read your tables. See if this is what will make them rave about our restaurant. And do what you will, of course, but I highly recommend some Champagne, or perhaps a Chablis as an alternative . . ."

I followed her upstairs to the locker room, where she was digging through clean aprons with an obsessive tenacity to find the shorter ones she preferred. I was forcing a thaw, I knew it, but I was tired of waiting.

"Okay, so tell me."

"Tell you what?"

"The uni . . ."

"Excuse me?"

"I mean, *please* tell me about the uni."

"Uni is sea urchin roe, crowning the tower this evening."

"But why is it special?" I motioned with my hands for her to get on with it.

"You're getting a bit spoiled aren't you?"

"No!" I stood up straighter. "I don't like having to beg for information. Are you upset with me or something?"

"Don't be dramatic. Shouldn't you be focusing on your work?"

"I'm trying to."

She hitched a new apron high onto her waist, making her look momentarily maternal, pastoral. She re-marked her lips with her lipstick. I saw sprays of silver in her coarse hair. I saw inscriptions of her years around her mouth, a solid crease between her brows from a lifetime of cynicism. The posture of a woman who had stood in a casual spotlight in every room she'd ever been in, not for gloss or perfection, for self-possession. Everything she touched she added an apostrophe to.

"It's quite eerie," she said, inspecting her face, pulling up her cheeks. "When you begin to see your mother in the mirror."

"I won't know," I said.

"No, you won't. You will always look like a stranger to yourself."

She never dealt in pity. I didn't know what to say.

"Your mother must be pretty," I said eventually. "You're pretty."

"You think so?" She looked at me from the mirror, unimpressed.

"Why don't you want a boyfriend?" I had made two assumptions before I knew what was happening, first, that she didn't have a boyfriend, second, that it was because she didn't want one.

"A boyfriend? That's a sweet word. I'm afraid I am in retirement from love, little one."

She barely but definitely softened.

"In Marseille you could walk down to the docks in the mornings. They had urchins, still alive. An offhand exchange, a few francs for this delicacy. The rocks are littered with debris: empty shells opened with a knife, rinsed by salt water, and sucked dry on the spot. Men taking lunch with bottles of their hard house wine, watching the boats move in and out. It's the ovaries — the coral ovaries. They are supposed to transfer a great power when you consume them. Absolutely voluptuous, the texture, absolutely permanent, the taste. It stays with you for the rest of your life."

She went toward the door, pulling her hair back. She looked at me thoughtfully. "There are so many things to be blasé about: your youth, your health, your employment. But real food — gifts from the ocean, no less — is not one of them. It's one of the only things that can immerse you safely in pleasure in this degraded, miserable place."

"It's exhausting," Howard said as he put on a slate-wool overcoat, a fedora, and leather gloves. He looked like he'd walked in from the 1940s. He gazed toward the exit and smiled at me. "You really have to love it."

"Yes," I said. I swirled the milk and splashed it on the espresso. I knew exactly how to make his macchiatos. "It's like, physically tiring. But there is something else that really flattens me every night. I can't put my finger on it."

"Entropy," he said. Like I was the sixth person to ask him. He raised his eyebrows at me to see if I knew what it meant, and I raised my eyebrows back to say I was skeptical of his usage.

"Rather it's a case of mismatched desires. The restaurant, an entity separate from us, but composed of us, has a set of desires, which we call service. What is service?"

"It's exhausting?"

"It's order. Service is a structure that controls chaos. But the guests, the servers, have desires as well. Unfortunately we want to disrupt that order. We produce chaos, through our randomness, through our unpredictability. Now" — he sipped and I nodded that I was still with him — "we are humans, aren't we? You are, I am. But we are also the restaurant. So we are in constant correction. We are always straining to retain control."

"But can you control entropy?"

"No."

"No?"

"We just try. And yes, it is tiring."

I saw the restaurant as a ruin. I imagined the Owner closing the place, locking the door many decades from now and the dust and the fruit flies and the grease accumulating, no one working around the clock to clean the dishes and linens, the restaurant returning to its primitive, nonfunctional elements.

"Thank you," he said and put the cup down.

"You're a free man now?"

"That I am. I have some manly Christmas decorating to do."

I nodded. It had surprised me, the holiday erupting in the park, in Flower-Girl's ridiculous bar arrangement. It was hung with actual cookies from the pastry department. Even Clem's had strung up lights. I remembered how warm New York had looked in Christmas movies, how benevolent and rich the shop windows were, how everyone's humanity broke through just in time for redemption, just in time for faith. It didn't feel like that when I walked to work. It felt cold and forced.

"I guess I should go see that tree or something."

"Will you be around for the holidays?" he asked.

I thought, Um, you scheduled me the day before and the day after, where the fuck do you think I'm going to go, but I said, "Yeah. I'm here. Just relaxing. I hear it's very quiet."

"Well, if you find yourself restless, I host an orphans' Christmas every year. Don't worry, Simone does most of the cooking, I wouldn't subject anyone to mine. But it's a tradition. You are heartily invited. And it's not as boring as I've made it sound."

"Are you an orphan?"

"Ah." He smiled at me. "We are all orphans eventually. That's if we're lucky." He waved to someone at the bar who had spotted him and winked at me before releasing himself from our grip and into the free fall of the evening.

"Wait until the truffles hit the dining room — absolute sex," said Scott.

When the truffles arrived the paintings leaned off the walls toward them. They were the grand trumpets of winter, heralding excess against the poverty of the landscape. The black ones came first and the cooks packed them up in plastic quart containers with Arborio rice to keep them dry. They promised to make us risotto with the infused rice once the truffles were gone.

The white ones came later, looking like galactic fungus. They immediately went into the safe in Chef's office.

"In a safe? Really?"

"The trouble we take is in direct proportion to the trouble they take. They are impossible," Simone said under her breath while Chef went over the specials.

"They can't be that impossible if they are on restaurant menus all over town." I caught her eye. "I'm kidding."

"You can't cultivate them. The farmers used to take female pigs out into the countryside, lead them to the oaks, and pray. They don't use pigs anymore, they use well-behaved dogs. But they still walk and hope."

"What happened to the female pigs?"

Simone smiled. "The scent smells like testosterone to them. It drives them wild. They destroyed the land and the truffles because they would get so frenzied."

I waited at the service bar for drinks and Sasha came up beside me with a small wooden box. He opened it and there sat the blanched, malignant-looking tuber and a small razor designed specifically for it. The scent infiltrated every corner of the room, heady as opium smoke, drowsing us. Nicky picked up the truffle in his bare hand and delivered it to bar 11. He shaved it from high above the guest's plate.

Freshly tilled earth, fields of manure, the forest floor after a rain. I smelled berries, upheaval, mold, sheets sweated through a thousand times. Absolute sex.

That was why it took me some time to see the snow falling in the window at the end of the bar. Whispers rose among the guests, they pointed to the street. Their heads turned in a reverent row. Thin shards of truffle drifted down and disappeared into the tagliatelle.

"Finally," said Nicky, and replaced the truffle. He leaned back on the bar, wearing a handsome, self-satisfied smile. "You never forget your first snow in New York."

The first flakes lingered in the window, framed. For a second, I believed they would fly back up to the streetlights.

I came to love the Williamsburg Bridge, once I learned how to walk it. I was mostly alone, a few all-weather bikers, a few heavily bundled Hasidic women. I walked either in some dusky circumference of gray light or some blotchy, cottoned afternoon. It never failed to move me. I paused in the middle of the filthy river. I stared at the trash eddying in currents and clinging to docks like wine dregs cling to a glass. Simone had mentioned the orphans' dinner at Howard's to me. I thought of them all up there at Howard's on the Upper West Side. I thought of Jake in a Christmas sweater. I told them I was busy. Remember this, I told myself. Remember how quiet today is. I had the newspaper, which I would keep for years, and I was on my way to lunch in Chinatown by myself. As I contemplated the skyline this double feeling came to me as one thought, pressing in from either side

306

of the bridge, impossible for me to reconcile: *It is ludicrous for anyone to live here* and *I can never leave.*

IV

Sometimes I saw all of service condensed, as if I had only worked one night that stretched out over the months.

I kicked the kitchen doors open with the toe of my clog, I came up the stairs and Jake and I met eyes. I looped the dining room in sweeping, elongated arcs, both my biceps and wrists tense. I saw myself without a time lapse, the images still and laid on top of each other. All the plates of filet mignon of tuna streamlined into its essential form: *the* filet mignon of tuna, lapidary. All the napkins I ever folded in a totemic monument. And running through these still lifes, an unmistakable straight line, was the gaze with which I watched them, a gaze in which sometimes Jake or Simone would join me. That's all I remembered — these few images and watching them all from afar, a huge stillness, a giant pause. When I felt like this it was the easiest and most beautiful job in the world. But I knew it was never still, that it was always flawed and straying from the ideal. To romanticize it was to lie.

I heard it turn midnight from the wine room. A beckoning din came through the ceiling. Thumping on the floorboards, whistling. I ran up the stairs and there was a crowd at the service bar, where flutes were lined up. The regulars had left their stools to cheer with us. Simone brought me a glass of the Cuvée Elisabeth Salmon Rosé Champagne. I shut my eyes: peaches, almonds, marzipan, rose petals, a whiff of gunpowder and I had started a new year in New York City.

"You. In a dress."

That's what I wanted him to say. He didn't end up saying it, but I said it to myself many times as I greeted my reflection in the buildings going up Broadway. My high heels rocked me like roller skates, my hair that I had spent time blow-drying was whipped up, I was suddenly vulnerable to the weather, to uneven sidewalks. I nodded to the iron wedge of the Flatiron like a prestigious acquaintance. The dress was half a paycheck. A short, black silk tunic. I was still confused about the power of clothes — nobody had taught me how to dress myself.

When I tried it on and looked in the mirror, I was meeting myself decades from now, when I had grown unconquerable. All in a dress. I nearly returned it twice. I saw myself in the dark-green glass of a closed bank. I turned to my reflection: You. In a dress.

The owner closed the restaurant on New Year's Day. He rented out a bar and we all got to drink there with one giant, miraculous, unending tab. From the stories everyone had been rehashing, bad behavior abounded. Someone was going to get too drunk, and though Will and Ariel were both betting on me, I was determined to stay on the soberer side of wasted and had brought my own bag of coke to ensure it.

I had forgotten that there would be adults there. The Owner and his wife stood at the entrance, beaming down authority and warmth. Even they must have been hungover, but they were flawless. A small line had formed to greet them, and as he shook each person's hand his eyes didn't scan the room. His wife looked charitable and flashed a smile that drew you out of the ground.

I tiptoed around the line. I couldn't say hello. What if he didn't remember me? What if I started crying? I remembered orientation and I still couldn't believe that they had chosen me.

It went more or less according to plan. Baby blinis with caviar, foie gras crostini, broiled mussels in the shell, crab dip, oyster shooters — decadent and finger-sized from the Owner's new catering company. We greeted each other tentatively, checking each other out, marveling at the transformations of dress-up. Ariel in a miniskirt and a sweater she had cut into a crop. Will in a lavender button-down. Sasha in all black and sunglasses. We clung to the bar nervously, trying to get a little tipsy, suddenly scared to talk to these strangers. An hour into it, the entire room relaxed and laughter rang out coarsely from all over the room and the DJ turned up the music. Then the Superlatives started.

Of course I had voted. Zoe made sure we all voted when she passed out the ballots at preshift. There were some usual suspects: Prettiest Eyes, Cutest Couple. And there were the industry-specific prizes, Most Likely to Start a Restaurant. I figured it was another code I had to break — every category had a natural winner. Starting a restaurant — it had to be Nicky, he talked about ditching us and opening up his own bar all the time. Person You Want to Wait on Your

Mom was Heather because she looked and talked like a doll. As they announced the prizes I was the shallow spectator I had been in the beginning. Biggest Prankster was Parker — I had put Nicky for that one as well because I wasn't sure Parker even knew how to speak. Apparently he had been pranking the people he liked for years. I had yet to fall into that category. Most Likely to Make It to Broadway was Ariel. She stuck her finger in her throat and retched. Will went and got the award for her. Then Howard, in a top hat no less, said, "And the Person You'd Most Like to Be Stuck in an Elevator With . . . is . . . Tess!"

A polite smattering of applause and a wolf whistle. I clapped too. Everyone stared at me. It dripped into my head, from some neglected faucet, thickly, painfully, that I was Tess.

I had chosen Simone, after a thorough consideration. This is your elevator person, I told myself. It's not the person you made plans with, it's not where you thought you'd end up, but bam — the elevator sticks. Your life, a luscious pause, dictated by chance. All the tasks of the day are tossed away. You can't know when you'll make it out, but unlike the desert-island scenario, with the elevator you can be assured of an eventual exit.

Of course, I'd thought about Jake. There he was, all to myself. I thought of him pinning the four corners of me to the wall with his body. But the flaming center of my fantasy wasn't the sex. No, what I wanted to get to was after. We would still be trapped in the elevator. He would look at me. There would be no bar tickets, no crowds, no phone calls, no stripes. He would be forced to recognize me. I knew that if I could get him to *see* me, then both of us would stop being lonely.

But then I reconsidered. Chances are Jake would be in a mood. I had a sense of how he would react to feeling trapped. What if he fell silent? What if he was mean? Or worse, what if I bored him? The nakedness of the scenario scared me. So he was off my list.

With Simone, the mood in the elevator went from erotic to cerebral and I was relieved. Simone would recite Wordsworth, William Blake, or if I was feeling modern, Wallace Stevens, Frank O'Hara. Simone would explain how wines were made in the Jura in the 1800s and how it related to the cheeses. She would remember details of paintings she saw in Florence a decade ago, and the name of the trattoria where she took lunch afterward. She might even tell me a story about *their* salt-strewn, dune-grass-covered childhood.

I would make fun of myself and make her laugh. I would tell her stories of demented middle America, and how after I first read *The Catcher in the Rye* when I was ten years old I packed a backpack and ran away from home but returned after neighbors found me sleeping in their toolshed. Simone would unravel the universe and tell me why it was so hard to find meaning in our technological age, why cities rise and fall, why we are doomed only to repeat ourselves. And after all this prolonged contact, I would come away changed, with more of her on me, the lessons would be permanent.

"Tess?" Howard waved a generic certificate that one of the hostesses had decorated with gold stars. I stood up uneasily in my heels. I turned to look for someone, turned to look for someone, turned to look for someone.

I said thank you and took my seat again. But not before I gave my coworkers a real once-over. I tried to meet as many eyes as possible and ask them, Me?

"So did you vote for me or what?" I slid

myself down the bar to him, simmering, lacy, high. In my shoes I was closer to his eye line. Jake in a muted, worn-out flannel and wool slacks, his hair flat and greasy. Uncomfortable, hunched.

"I hate these things. Every year I say, never again."

"What's to hate? Free appetizers." I looked around the room at the strange group of people who had been chosen by the restaurant. The cliques came magnetically back together after the initial shocks of being out of context. The porters and dishwashers were wearing sports coats and they sat with their heavily made-up, animated wives. The cooks had taken over a corner of the bar, where they sipped on añejo tequila and paused for shots of mezcal. The floor around them was wet from spillage. The hostesses and pastry girls hovered around them like a protective layer of atmosphere.

The real grown-ups were at a table together — Howard had brought an age-appropriate date who did everything at half speed. She chewed each bite to completion before setting her fork down, reaching into her lap, and pressing her napkin to her lips lightly, not enough to disrupt her lipstick. Definitely not a restaurant person. There was Chef and his rather beautiful wife, there was Nicky and Denise, who had her cell phone out on the table — it flashed with updates from the babysitter. Simone had joined the table to talk to Denise, their knees turned toward each other. I thought about them in their twenties, Denise with no kids, just dating a bartender, Simone lighter, more prone to laughter. Parker and Sasha played quarters at our table, Ariel and Will were probably in the bathroom, and Heather was trying to get Santos to dance.

It was so predictable and lovely, my heart struggled to hold it.

"As if I don't see enough of these people," he said darkly. "And to be here on my day off. Giant waste of time."

"Why did you come?"

"It's not worth the black mark for non-participation. Besides" — he shot back his whiskey and nodded to the bartender for another — "free drinks."

Misha, the hostess we all still made fun of for her inflated breasts, walked by and stuck her arm out to me.

"Tess, congrats! The big win!" She giggled. I looked at my certificate. I had carried it over with me in case I wanted to brag to Jake. But next to him it looked childish.

"So embarrassing actually," I said. I folded up the award. I nodded to the bartender.

"A white? Not too oaky, please, no Chardonnay."

"You earned it," he said, taking another drink and looking away from me.

"It's kind of nice, right?" I said. "People want to spend time with me. They aren't trying to ditch me in diners. I'm not so terribly annoying."

When he turned to me his eyes were jagged, slivered, and I was scared. I thought he must be on something. He said, "That's the biggest whore award. You know that right?"

"Whore?"

"Come on, new girl, don't play dumb. Your kitchen boys always send it out to whoever they want to fuck. But, oh yeah, congrats! The big win!"

"Um . . ." I tried to laugh but it died in my throat. Scott saw me from the end of the bar and winked. After so much crying — in bathrooms sitting on toilets, hiding next to the air conditioner in the pastry station, behind the ice machine, into my pillow, into my hands, sometimes simply into my locker — this time I didn't flee. I stayed and the tears came.

"You . . ." It wouldn't come to me. The vicious words I longed for were lost in the flotsam of being humiliated, yet again, like always. "You are mean, Jake. It's too mean

317

for me."

His eyes flashed blue and then collapsed.

"I'm sorry," he said. "Tess."

I nodded. "Please excuse me."

As I walked I forced my heels into the ground. My wineglass burned in my hand. Simone's eyes brushed over me and went to the bar. Yes, I thought, go to him. Comfort him because the new girl with the biggest whore award called him mean.

"Tess?"

I picked my feet up off the bathroom floor to hide from her but I had just taken a line and sniffled. She knocked on the stall.

"You can only come in if you do drugs. Drugs-only zone." I clicked it open. She came in. We were uncomfortably close. We could have stood by the sinks, but she locked the door behind her and sat on the toilet. She gave me her open palm and I put my bag in it. She poured a tiny bump out on the webbing between her pointer finger and her thumb. She inhaled it without taking her eyes off me.

"Please," she said in response to my expression. "I was young once."

She touched the end of her nose thoughtfully and I touched mine.

"I thought it was a good thing," I said.

My hands were shaking. "I really thought, oh, here I am, stuck in an elevator, I better pick someone I really . . . I . . . I picked you."

"I'm flattered."

I pressed toilet paper to my cheeks.

"It's like we're exchanging, going back and forth, just playing. And then he hits me too hard. It goes from play pain to real pain."

"I know."

"Simone, am I not doing this right? Everything feels like a punishment."

"What are you being punished for?"

"I don't fucking know — being stupid?"

"Stop it." She grabbed my hands unsympathetically. "No one is interested in you playing the victim. Get out of your head. If you don't you'll always be disappointed. Pay attention."

I pulled my hands away and she folded hers into her lap.

"Is it too late?" she asked.

"For what?"

"For you to let this flirtation go?"

"I think it's more than a flirtation, Simone."

"It's not, it's a fantasy. Jake knows it and you know it. Can you let it go?" She looked at me impassively.

"Okay . . . I mean . . . we work together . . . so." I paused. "What do you mean Jake knows it?"

"I mean that Jake is aware of this crush."

"You guys talk about me?" I thought I might vomit.

"We don't *talk* about you. It has come up."

"*It?* I thought we were friends. Am I just this big fucking joke to you?"

"You're getting carried away." The way she said it was so matter-of-fact that I nodded. "Now. Can you let it go?"

Fuck them, I thought, I'm going to quit. Then I saw that Simone was right. I wasn't a victim. I hadn't been led anywhere. I had chosen this overgrown, murky path where I couldn't see five feet in front of me — the drugs, the drinking until black, the embarrassment, the confusion. But really I had chosen the two of them — they were the difficult terrain. I understood what she meant by "let it go." I didn't have to quit my job. There had been another route open to me this entire time — a well-lit, well-laid, honest path. I said to myself, Turn around. You do not have to take every experience on the pulse. It's just dinner. I saw the silent elevator, just me. Another voice said, But then you'll just be a back-waiter.

"I can't," I said. "Let it go. I mean, I don't want to."

She exhaled, frustrated with me.

"Don't you remember what it's like?"

She held her face as if it were made of granite. I saw a flicker, aqueous, vulnerable.

"No. I don't," she said. "I don't remember and I don't care to."

"You must have felt like this before. Are you really made of stone like they all say? I don't think you are, Simone. I see your heart." I pointed to her chest, but she looked furious.

"All right, Tess. You want it all? You don't care about consequences? Then it is too late. I could tell you to leave him alone. That he's complicated, not in a sexy way, but in a damaged way. I could tell you damage isn't sexy, it's scary. You're still young enough to think every experience will improve you in some long-term way, but it isn't true. How do you suppose damage gets passed on?"

There was heat coming off her, and I felt the drugs. My blood ran like lighter fluid through my veins. "You sound a little bitter."

"Bitter." She pulled the word through a clenched jaw. She pulled back her shoulders like she was on the floor, readjusting, and said, "We shall see. I'll speak to him."

"Don't!" I said. Will's warning came back to me faintly, about trusting Simone. I had already made myself her pupil, but I had an incision of fear about handing this over to her. Did Jake really need Simone's blessing? Is that what had been missing this entire time? If those were the terms, then I accepted. Didn't I?

"Or, I don't know. Do whatever you want. It's not even a big deal."

"Little one, it is a big deal. You forget how important he is to me. I'm obviously quite invested in you too."

"I know." I looked at our feet and dragged my shoe back and forth across the tile. "I had a dream about you. Part of a dream. It was that we had a secret. You were my mother. And you let me show up late for work, and you came to my apartment and made my bed. But you told me that no one else would understand and if I told I would be punished."

"Odd." That was all she said.

"I don't think you're old enough to be my mother. That's not what I meant. By dreaming that."

"You should pass that along to Howard. He's very good with dreams. Should have been an analyst in another life." She stood and did a small back bend, stretching, cracking. "I wouldn't mind being in an elevator with you. Roomier than a bathroom stall." She handed me a piece of toilet paper. "No more crying at work."

I wanted to ask her if that was love. The blindness, the careening falls, the invisible slow dancing, the longing for real pain, the fixedness. I wouldn't have gotten an answer. She never spoke to me about love from personal experience. Love was a theory. Something that had been embalmed. "Love will do x to you if you let it," or "Love is a necessary condition to y," or "y is a particular brand of love you will encounter in places like z."

Perhaps that's why she was so untouched. She didn't remember. She never got down on her knees on the asphalt like the rest of us, she couldn't tell me about the unspeakably real stuff. What I learned came from the ground up.

He yanked on my wrist and pulled me back from the group I was leaving with. Will made a face that said, Coming? And I held up my hand to say, One minute.

"Text me?" Will yelled as the elevator doors closed in front of his face.

I turned to Jake.

"What? Simone told you to apologize?"

He stared at the carpet. Pensive.

"Pathetic," I said. I pressed the button.

"I was sorry as soon as I said it."

"You're wearing me out. Honestly." I pressed the button again and again. I saw that alternative route, path of peace, of light. I saw the bar, the beer, and the gentleness of being with friends, all of that obliterated when he came near me. I had given him permission to do that. A bell rang and the doors parted. Jake went into the back corner and I stood in front of him, holding the door as everyone crowded in.

"Going out for one, Denise?" I asked Nicky's wife. Nicky told me that she was the first woman who ever talked back to him and he knew immediately he had to marry her. She was a sharp brunette, still pretty but her cheeks were gaunt now.

"No, no. We are heading home. Our best-case scenario is a five a.m. wake-up with the wee one."

"Best-case!" Nicky clapped and turned toward me. "Fluff doesn't get home till five a.m., isn't that right?"

"What's Fluff?" asked Denise.

"It's an old nickname," I said, and my breath shot out of me. Jake dragged his finger down my back. "From high school."

My spine a burning candlestick, everywhere he touched dripping. Behind you.

"I did vote for you," he said softly so only I heard it. And we were back at it: the night buoyant, time elastic, my body forgiving.

"Denise," I said, stepping back closer to him, "remind me, how old is the youngest?"

I straddled him in the backseat of a taxi, leather seats groaning, his fingers inside me, pumping, pressing into a white-hot spot in my stomach. I was struck through layers of intoxication that I might come suddenly. He shifted his thumb and I recoiled, sure I wouldn't come at all. A passage of pushing and pulling, my hair, strands of it coming out in his hand, his shirt collar, him holding me down, forcing me harder onto his lap, the cab hit a pothole and I exhaled.

When I climbed on top of him I momentarily thought of the taxi driver. How far into his shift was he? I wanted to tell him: I work long nights too. Sometimes people treat me terribly. I imagined the taxi driver had a small daughter who called him while he worked. He put her voice on speakerphone and it lit up the car. A glamour shot of his wife hung off the rearview mirror. I assumed it was his wife. She had her hand behind her ear and her head tilted, holding a rose in the other hand. Her lipstick matched the flower. I wondered if the money was good New Year's Day. I wondered if he had seen everything. He slammed the partition shut and turned up the music and Jake pulled up my skirt and I forgot the taxi driver was a person.

I was gnawing on his lips, his ears, his chin, trying to extend the tremor in my stomach, I'm close, I wanted to say, colored lights smudging the windows, it's very close.

Jake grabbed my face and said, "Do you know what you taste like?" and pulled his fingers out of me and jammed them into my mouth.

I didn't gag. I was too stunned to feel anything at first. I'm salty, I thought. I don't taste bad. But I moaned, I ground into him harder. I was completely turned on, switched on, not by my taste, but by Jake's certainty. There were so few moments I had been certain in my life. I was constant revision, constant doubt. What I learned, as he slipped his fingers out of my mouth and back inside me, is that in New York City there are absolutely no rules. I didn't understand that monstrous freedom until Jake said into my mouth, Come for me, and I came in the back of a cab. There were people who did whatever the fuck they

wanted and their city was terrifying, bar-
baric, and breathless.

V

Some men take to vinegar with relish. They delight in the sparkling traces of fermentation. His fingers in the pickles, in the sour cherries we imported from Italy and spooned into Manhattans, his olive-juice-soaked knuckles, one dirty martini after another, his fingers in me, syrupy, astringent, and wait, wait, there it is: briny.

A blue-black wintry dawn crept up the squat roofs of Brooklyn when I left for my apartment. I was in the cab, the car was flying over the East River, the bridge woozy, the car weightless.

I had a small mirror in my bathroom, but it was high and I couldn't see below my chin. I climbed up and curled myself into the sink bowl.

There were marks. A bruise on my chest, above my breast, a nebulous thumbprint. Some chafing on my neck and chin. A red, hivelike oval on the inside of my arm. A cast of blue peeled down my bottom lip. Red dashes on the inside. My underwear felt wet and I looked down — there was my period, days early, like he had pulled a trigger.

My eyes cloudy from wine. The skin under my nose flaking from the radiator. I couldn't stop touching my face, the blank screen that everyone projected onto. Whatever beauty I had, it wasn't self-generated, wasn't rooted. It was permeable. But underneath that, I could just make it out: the face of a woman.

It was my mouth that was changing. This bleak, purplish, inflated mouth. And my left eye perpetually smaller now, swollen, it didn't open as wide as it used to. Tired is what a friend would say. I didn't look new anymore.

I would get tattoos of the bruises. He would be surprised. What did he call his tattoos? A commitment to a moment? Look, Jake, my body is committed. I lay on my mattress, counting heartbeats. I knew it would never be repeated, that night. Never exactly like that again, never as surprising and powerful again. And so I held it, without reviewing it, I held it perfectly still. The walls of my room turned milky with light. I listened to the last of the Puerto Ricans rowdily clamoring home.

Various snowstorms piled up like traffic, snowbanks grinding into sidewalks and rising like new buildings. And indoors the soups kept coming — cure-alls. Santos surreptitiously made menudo on Sunday mornings with the cast-off cow parts. The tripe was sweet and the broth was oily, it tasted like iron, oregano, and limes. Sriracha on everything, even in emergency soups of chicken broth and scallions. Knots in our necks, flus, sinus infections, we passed the ailments between us.

Will, Ariel, and I sat bowed over our bowls in silence while the beginnings of a storm hit Sixteenth Street. Scott made pho for family meal, a recipe he got from an old man in a market stall in Hanoi. It was a gift, steaming, fragrant with star anise, rich.

"You disappeared after the party," Will said to me. Ariel twirled her noodles. I slurped with my eyes down.

"I just went home."

"That's funny. You never usually just go home."

"I was tired," I said.

"How was home?" He sat back in his chair, arms crossed. "Was it nice?"

"Yes, it was glorious." I went back to my bowl. When I looked up he was injured and I was ashamed. "Will, can you act like my friend?"

He looked into his bowl. "I don't know."

He got up and left. I turned to Ariel, hoping for some sympathy. She was also absorbed in her soup.

"It was amazing," I said quietly.

"Gross."

"I've never felt anything like it. I usually have trouble . . ."

"Coming?"

"Well, yes, I mean, it's fine by myself. But hard. At other times. With people. But this time it wasn't . . . difficult."

"Well, great. He's had a lot of practice."

"Don't be mean."

"I'm not, but you want me to act like great sex is the end of the world."

It is the end of the world, I thought. "No. But it feels big. I can't explain it, I feel, womanly or something."

"You think it's womanly to get fucked?" She had her clawed tones out and I retreated.

"I don't want to argue about gender theory. I just feel like something real happened. And I wanted someone to talk to about it. Like a friend."

"Let me guess," she said, tapping the spoon against the tablecloth. "He beat you up a little bit, called you a slut, and you thought that was really edgy, another spoiled white girl who wants to get slapped around because she always got everything she wanted."

"Fuck, Ari." I shook my head. "It must be hard. To have already sized up the world, to already have written it off completely. Is it just so fucking boring all the time?"

"Pretty much, Skip."

"I would rather be called a slut by him than deal with the shit I get from the women here." I picked up my bowl. "Also, you're fucking white. By the way. And you don't get a medal for being gay."

"Listen," she said, her voice calmer. She pouted out her bottom lip. "I am looking out for you. Don't start measuring your life in sex, it's dangerous. Great sex is not a big deal."

I sat back down. "What is a big deal, then?"

"Intimacy. Trust."

"Okay," I said. Those words floated out above me, abstract, romantic, and I wondered what they looked like on the ground. Maybe they were already happening, maybe they were embedded in the sex. Years of wondering if there was something wrong with me. Wondering why sex drove people insane. Years of mimicking porn stars, trying to arch my back in the most flattering way. Years of sex that was empty, never held its shape.

"Isn't sex something?"

She shrugged. I realized she had no idea what I was talking about. When we went to the dish station I put my bowl down and hugged her from behind. I wondered how there was any room for the guests, with all of our hopeful faces and our imposing loneliness.

Let me try this again: it was changeover. He was coming in for the night and I was the beverage runner from the day. It had been snowing off and on, spidery flakes brushing the windows, salt rims on the sidewalks, a tinctured light from a weak sun. I was making macchiatos, but really I was watching Enrique as he stood outside in a huge parka wiping down the windows. His gloved hands held a squeegee and pulled long draws of soapy water up the windows and opalescent patterns slid down.

Jake stopped at the door to take off his cap and shake out his hair. When he touched his own cheeks from the cold it was humbling. All of the most thoughtless gestures were exotic on him. Pulling his keys from his pocket for his front door, hanging those keys — with precision — on a hook inside his house. He looked different today — it wasn't as simple as us having been naked together — after all it had been two a.m. and dark in his room so I didn't know if that counted as actually having *seen* each other naked. No, it was that he was amplified, each vision of him laid on top of another in translucent sheets. Like the collection of Oriental rugs in the lightless cave of his apartment, each rug overlapping another, an uneven terrain of rug on top of rug on top of rug, you only imagined touching the ground. Like his tattoos, none of them quite touching, his skin an image of white space between the images, the private mosaic of him, the sound of his breathing becoming harassed, his uneven teeth, his smells coming loose from skin. I could still smell him in my hair.

I made him an espresso. He stopped to talk to Howard, standing directly in front of me, not looking at me, but when he finished he turned.

"For me?"

"Yes."

He shot it back and walked away. Contentment filled me and I watched Enrique as he scraped the windows into total invisibility.

Six-month review: I bought a dresser from the Salvation Army on North Seventh and Bedford. I had to pay two big kids from the corner to carry it up my stairs. I unpacked my suitcases. I found a Laundromat with two old Korean ladies and an obese orange cat. I tipped them. I got the Saturday night beverage-running shift, with Jake and Nicky on the bar.

We sat down in restaurants after midnight. We went to karaoke in Koreatown when Ariel wanted to sing. Ariel sang them all but her true calling was Alanis Morissette's "Ironic." Will sang "China Girl." One time Jake came and I was sure he was just going to sit in the corner and break my brain, but then he stood and in a low mumble he sang "Born to Run" and I screamed like a teen-ager.

I could place an order at SriPraPhai with my eyes closed. Nicky knew to pour me a big glass of Pouilly-Fuissé as my first shift drink. Simone said I had a palate for "broader" whites, which to me meant they stretched across the width of my tongue. I bought myself a cashmere scarf. I was on track to making $60,000 in a year. I took a lot of cabs.

I walked across the park in numbed, clipped steps. I was going to wait for Jake at the kitschy Irish pub that none of us went to. Jake and I went there now. Paulie, the bartender, was beginning to know us. I was always cut earlier than Jake, and if I didn't want to get dragged to Park Bar I had to leave immediately. Then I sat with Paulie and nursed a beer until Jake came. We were usually still there when the cockroaches crawled out by the beer taps. We batted them away and Paulie swung towels at them like a matador.

That night was the coldest I'd had in New York — Nicky told me he dropped his coffee on the sidewalk and it froze. He said it looked like glass. I wasn't taking my time across the park, but I stopped when I saw Robert Raffles sleeping on a bench. Will used to buy beer and chips at the bodega to hand them off to Robert when we got on the train.

At first I didn't think it was a person on the bench. And though I tried not to look too closely, as I walked I got the vibration of something human, and then I saw Robert's shoes, or the duct-taped and shredded coverings on his feet that passed for shoes. I thought of the coffee on the sidewalk.

So I went and roused him. I gave him fifty dollars. I walked him to a shelter.

No. I didn't.

I sped up to a confused shuffle and stepped past him. I told myself he was sleeping. I told myself if he was still there when I came out, I would call the police. But what would they do? Put him in a hospital? A shelter? If I gave him money, would he use it to get warm? Will said Robert had been living in the park for thirty years. He must be aware of the options, the emergency rooms, the subway stations.

I hit the far end of the park and stopped. My toes were numb, as if I were standing on ice. He was obscured by a trash can, if he was still there, or had ever been there. I ran the rest of the way to Paulie's, my breath in frozen puffs behind me. I ran into the flat yellow light like I had been chased.

"I don't know," I said, "if he's still there when I leave, I'll do something. Maybe . . . actually, do you guys have any blankets? Maybe there are some blankets at the restaurant. But it's like, on a night like tonight . . ." I shrugged. "It's not a blanket kind of night, do you know what I mean?"

Paulie nodded, a small, friendly man well into middle age, light on his feet, a charming Irish accent. Exactly what you wanted in a place where shamrocks hung above the booths.

"It's a jungle out there," he said, filling a small beer for himself. "Kitchen's closing — you want anything?"

"Can I get some fries? Just the basket thing."

I wasn't hungry. But I had cramps in my stomach, like small alarms. The fries came out damp, and took two extra doses of salt, but they were reassuring.

"Fuck," Jake said, slamming the door behind him. "Fucking shit fuck it's cold."

We nodded. He pulled the stool out next to me and I felt guilty about Robert Raffles. But willingly so. It was a jungle. I had to protect my life, my bank account, my commute, my bar stool, some were cold so others could be warm, I didn't create this system, I said, or did I every time I made those little running steps?

"Did you see Robert Raffles in the park?"

"Who?"

"Robert Raffles, the homeless guy that Will is friends with."

"Fucking Will." Jake grabbed two of my fries and ate them automatically. He saw that I was still looking at him, and he pressed his fingers into my temples. "No one was in the park."

Jake slid his cold fingers down the side of my face and started to unwrap my scarf.

"I like to see your throat," he said simply.

No one was in the park. Problem solved. I tilted my chin up when I took a sip of my beer, elongating my neck. What's happening to me? I asked, but not out loud. He got a beer and fed me cold French fries from cold fingers until both of our cheeks turned pink.

Service slowed. At the restaurant, all our affinities waxed and waned, a definite period of waning as the holidays died away and we faced an interminable amount of deaf winter. We were mean, our tones short, we developed strategies against one another, plotted downfalls, worked ourselves up over small triumphs. You could have safely assumed we hated each other.

Veselka, three a.m. I was slowly but surely falling in love with the food of the Eastern Bloc, partly because I finally awoke to the fact that I was living in a city that once housed immigrants from non-Asian countries, countries of endless cold. Mostly though because the food was cheap and Jake hated spending money on food.

Bowls of borscht in front of us, nothing

thin about them, a muscular, magenta soup, sticking to the spoon. Pierogi, boiled, piled with sour cream and horseradish, stuffed cabbage leaking juice into tomato broth. That was how the winter soul was fed.

When I called Jake a Marxist he said I didn't understand the word. When I called him a proletariat, he laughed. When I fingered the holes in his wool coat that hung shapelessly to his ankles, when I pointed to the peeling soles of his boots, he laughed. Hours of my life I never got back, in the most acerbic, unsweetened days of winter, trying to make him laugh.

"I'm buying you a burka," I told him, and he laughed again.

Initially, I didn't bring her up. It was as if I were protecting his feelings, wanting him to think that I thought only of him when we were together. But whenever I saw a new twist in his body, a new tilt to his brows, it felt like I was being shown something that was Simone's. It was a perverse pleasure, but the bonds between them and me were so new I just wanted to reinforce them. And eventually, one of those nights, he sat next to me and said Simone had been driving him fucking crazy, nagging him about his close. He was testing me out, and I said, "Your close is the least of your problems.

Do you think Howard knows you've been late for every shift for six years?" He laughed. Then she was with us, invisible, benign.

"And then she tells me, 'All you need is a knack for understanding light and shade.' Um, what?"

"Keats again!" He shoved a pierogi into his mouth. "She can't help it, you know. She spent so many years with these poets, she doesn't know what's hers anymore."

"Her what?"

"Her words. Her thoughts. She was a poet — is a poet. I don't know. She graduated high school at sixteen. Had a full ride to Columbia."

"She went to Columbia?"

"She didn't."

"Where did she go?"

"Cape Cod Community."

My food stuck in my throat. "No. Fucking. Way."

"Yes, you little elitist bitch. Swallow your food."

I swallowed. "You're being serious." Simone at community college, collecting her straight As, bored, silent, serious. "But why?"

"Not everyone gets the privilege of running away." He glanced at me and relented.

341

"Besides, she had to take care of me."

"Simone turned down Columbia to take care of you?"

"I've given up plenty for her. It goes both ways. I take care of her too."

"What if one of you wants to take care of someone else?" The words came out before I could stop them, and I thought, Please don't answer that. He ignored me. "What are her parents like?"

He leaned back in his chair. "They're nothing like her."

"How did she get like that?"

"She likes to think she sprang from the head of Zeus fully formed."

"But in fact . . ."

"Her dad owned a bar. And her mom was an elementary school teacher with a ditzy, girlish obsession with France, but she never even owned a passport."

I realized that I had my spoon full and lifted halfway to my face. I would have sooner believed that Simone had sprung from a skull in full armor than believed a woman who had never left the country raised her. I put my spoon down, laughing uncomfortably.

"How old is she?" It was something I had been curious about since the first day. I had no idea about the gradation of years, what

342

thirty or thirty-three or forty-two looked like.

"She's thirty-seven. How old are you?"

"Twenty-two. You knew that," I said. I smiled at him but I was doing numbers in my head. "That's kind of old, right? It doesn't make sense. Didn't she start at the restaurant when she was twenty-two? I thought she said she's only been there twelve years, that makes her thirty-four, right? When was she in France? What did you do when she left?"

"I call those my wilderness years."

"How long were you guys apart?"

"A few years, Jesus, I'm bored with this."

"Do you think she's happy? Just working at the restaurant? She seems happy, right? Her life is so full."

"You're really smitten, huh?" Jake tackled crusts of rye toast. "What do you think happiness is? It's a mode of consumption. It's not a fixed state, somewhere you can take a cab to. Simone's dad had a brain aneurysm at one a.m. while he was counting the drop. He wasn't unhappy. Simone has been barbacking since she was nine years old. I don't think she has any illusions about happiness."

I tried to see her as a little girl, busing glasses, watchful. When I was nine the most palpable interactions I had were with my dolls. I played Family with them, but the games always turned out badly, ended violently. Those dolls had to accept the full gamut of my fledgling emotions. They were stuck with me, and they always forgave me when we started over the next day. Which from what I saw of other families wasn't an inaccurate representation. But I was fully isolated from the adult world. I wasn't seen, heard, or acknowledged. It made sense that Simone had been born into it, adapting to the adult rules for conduct, how to be sincere and duplicitous, how to evade, before she realized that technically she wasn't one of them.

I tried to see Jake as a little boy, catching up to her in height, then surpassing her. It was the first time I imagined him as a child. I looked at him across the table and he and Simone — with their history, their rundown parents, their northeastern chilliness, their hardness — felt like the only real people I had ever met.

"What about me?" I said seriously. "Do you think I have illusions?"

"I think you are the illusion." He slid his chair over so he was next to me. Yes, it was a switch in him, radical flips in energy — I could never rest. He pressed his fork into my lips. "Whose lips are these?"

"These lips?" I kissed the fork. "My lips?"

He didn't hesitate, he bit my bottom lip, pulled it, stretched it out. Both our eyes were open, my face padlocked, he bit harder and I breathed harder. He gave my lip a soft kiss after releasing it, and I felt blood, I tasted iodine.

"My lips," he said. "Mine."

He met my gravity with apathy and so began a free fall.

"You love to fuck," he would say, out of breath.

"Doesn't everyone? What does that even mean?" Although I knew exactly what he meant, my thighs were still shaking.

"No, women in New York, they're all up here." He tapped my skull. Then he thrust his hand between my thighs. "They can't be here. They can't be present."

"You've had lots of experience, huh?" I was stuck on the way he said *women* in New York as if I was a woman in New York. "I'm not like a nymphomaniac or something."

"No." He moved his hand higher up and pressed on me. "Don't be embarrassed. Say, I love to fuck."

"No," I said, shrinking away. His eyes shimmered like water about to boil.

"Say it," he said, and grabbed my neck

from the side, thumb on my windpipe. The first rush of vertigo. At the fulcrum point of coming with Jake, I wasn't falling, the world was rising. He hurt me sometimes. He could smell my fear and he would say, Let go. If I pushed myself into the fear, like pushing my face into a pillow, I could come harder, and I did. The steel grates being rolled up by the Chinese guys, their rapid conversations while they dragged the fish trash out, the trucks bleating as they reversed. My body, boneless.

"I love to fuck."

"You're insatiable."

"You're carnivorous."

"You're a tart-lette."

"A wolf."

"A rose."

"A steak, bloody and rare."

"You're inoperable."

"You're terminal."

If he was imperfect it was never in his blue room, never with words, he played them so smoothly, he played me so smoothly. The shit that came out of our mouths was utter nonsense, but. But what? It was a privileged language. If I tried to transcribe it, it would be filthy.

VI

Wait, does cliché mean it's true or not true?
Everyone has a price.
I caught your yawn.
Yeah, mine is anything above twenty
     percent.
Why can't I smell anything anymore?
They've turned into monsters now.
Snow all the time now.
So I said, I'm not paying rent until I have
     some fucking heat.
When does it stop?
It's funny racist, but is it *racist* racist?
He's absolutely jaundiced.
It's the prawns tonight.
'Tis the bourbon season, my friend.
Do you know if Venice is an island?
But it smells like garbage and Fernet in
     there.
They're saying beer is the new wine.
You missed the second glass on 19.
I never see the daylight anymore.

You didn't card them?

That's quite a cough.

Prawns are not shrimp.

And she's not exactly young anymore.

But I never sleep anymore.

Should we call his wife? He's asleep at the
table.

Yes, you suck on the heads.

He never runs out of excuses.

The little vampires?

It's *all* fucking homogenized and
pasteurized.

There aren't any secrets here.

Disgusting.

No, sherry is the new wine.

I need a Kleenex.

I need steak knives.

Like bruises under her eyes.

My rule is that I don't buy it.

And then they asked if we had Yellow Tail.

They froze on my cheeks, just from here to
the train.

Where's the line?

Be nice.

Happy hunting.

Eighty-six the shrimp.

It's an island if it's surrounded by water.

How long until we freeze to death?

How about *wine* is the new wine.

Fucking geniuses.

Another storm coming, even bigger.

Again?

And then I threw up.

It's not hard to like these foods once you open your mouth to them: the anchovies, the trotters, the pig's head terrines, the sardines, the mackerel, the uni, the liver mousses and confits. Once you admit that you want things to taste like *more* or *better* versions of themselves — once you commit to flavor as your god — the rest follows. I started adding salt to everything. My tongue grew calloused, overworked. You want the fish to taste like fish, but fish times a thousand. Times a million. Fish on crack. I was lucky I never tried crack.

"Vee-own-yay."

I didn't mean to correct her. I was only refilling waters on table 30 and I heard Heather stumbling. It was a classic trick, to keep talking while you opened a bottle of wine. No matter the skill level, it was a necessarily slow time in the momentum of service, which usually revolved around a series of quick entrances and quippy exits. But when you tussled with the wine bottle, all eyes were on you, bored, expectant. The only natural thing was to talk through the lapse.

Heather had swayed the guests — rather ingeniously, I thought — from the California Chardonnay they'd requested to a white from the Rhône Valley. It would have similar viscosity and heft, with all the honeyed stone fruit, but without the dominant vanilla and butter of an over-oaked Chardonnay.

The maneuver had the makings of an ideal service experience. They trusted Heather and she rewarded that trust with an education, opening an undiscovered pocket of taste to them. They could spend the rest of the week asking their friends if they knew that the Rhône produced a small amount of white wine. White wine from the Rhône? their buttoned-up friends would say. Yes, had they heard of a Châteauneuf-du-Pape Blanc? No? Then the guests would repeat to their friends verbatim what Heather had said to them: "This wine is fairly obscure, something of a secret . . ."

We gave a similar speech about whites from Bordeaux, Rioja, anywhere that had prestigious red-wine real estate. And we nodded the composed nod of wisdom when they were surprised. A bonus that the wines were pricey and built a nice check, but it was all true — the whites were bold, rich, and a bargain.

As Heather poured for the man in position 1, a woman shaped like a risen soufflé asked Heather just exactly what the grapes were. Heather started strong with Roussanne, Marsanne, but they were the easy ones. She paused. She looked at the ceiling. The guests' trust hovered in the air like a threatening cloud.

"Viognier," I said. Vee-Own-Yay. That's how I remembered it in my head when Simone taught it to me. The room blinked at me, the lights brightened.

"You know," I said, taking a breath, "back in the sixties it wasn't a grape worth mentioning. No one in France wanted to replant it after phylloxera in the nineteenth century. It's such a . . ." I rubbed my fingers together for the right word, ". . . *fickle* grape."

The imagined buzzing of tickets being printed, a clang of glasses at the bar. I didn't want to keep going but I was feeling it now, the ownership that came when the guests entirely submitted to you.

"But they started planting it in California, all along the central coast, and then everyone was like, Wait, what is that incredibly aromatic wine? And then the French said, It's ours, obviously. You know how the

French are."

They chuckled. Position 2 stuck her nose into the glass and jiggled the wine. I leaned to her and said, "I always get jasmine. That's how I remember it."

"I can smell jasmine!" she said to the woman at position 3. I recognized that — the thrill of receiving revelations.

I fielded Heather's look with a shrug. Like it had been a lucky guess. I went to refill the pitcher but I was thinking, What the fuck? I studied. Keep up.

The grayest, blurriest, most miserable weather. Slush congregating in the gutters, lakes welling up in drains, snot and tears mingling on faces, the air like a drill into the head, When will it end? What next?

It happened like this: he asked, rather awkwardly and for the first time, if I wanted breakfast. Neither of us had to go to work that day and I always wanted breakfast. It was too cold to talk as we walked, my lips like slabs of marble.

He led me to Cup & Saucer on Eldridge and Canal, a tiny lunch counter camped out among the mute Chinese signs. It had faded cursive advertising Coca-Cola on the outside, a layer of bacon grease and fryer oil on the windows inside, and he knew everyone.

We had horrid, caustic coffee and I put ketchup on my eggs and I saw the etchings of his wrinkles and they were gray, his golden eyes were flinty, gray, and my hair in the reflection of the window was dishwater colored and gray, the circles under my eyes a lavender gray, and he kissed me, graying daylight fraying and coarse, and he was eggish, lined in tobacco and salt and I thought, Oh lord, oh fuck, is my life becoming one unstoppable banquet? A month of gray and the happiest days of my life.

"You're really developing quite nicely," Howard said to me. His navy suit shone. His tone was light but too direct; I compulsively caved in my chest.

"Developing what?"

"What's your favorite right now?" He eyed the leather-bound wine lists I was wiping down.

"My favorite what?"

"What excites you?" He paused. "On the list."

"Oh."

Simone must have spoken to him. Besides our lessons deepening, I had been studying in my off time. I had a ritual — and having any ritual sounded so mature that I told everyone about it, even the regulars. On my days off I woke up late and went to the coffee shop and had a cappuccino and read. Then around five p.m., when the light was failing, I would take out a bottle of dry sherry and pour myself a glass, take out a jar of green olives, put on Miles Davis, and read the wine atlas. I didn't know why it felt so luxurious, but one day I realized that ritual was why I had moved to New York — to eat olives and get tipsy and read about Nebbiolo while the sun set. I had created a life that was bent in service to all my personal cravings. Looking at Howard now, I wondered if I was becoming the woman with the shopping bags that I had imagined in my interview. If Howard — with his watchful, unapologetic eyes — had seen what I wanted before I did, and had hired me because he knew this job could give it to me.

"The Manzanilla, I think. La Gitana." I said.

"Ha!" He clapped his hands, genuinely surprised. "The Manzanilla, where on earth did you pick that up?"

"Mrs. Neely, actually. She's always asking for sherry for her soup and I thought it was sherry vinegar, but then I saw Simone getting it from the bar and I thought it was a sweet wine — at first."

"And?"

"It's not sweet."

"No, it's not. It's one of the oldest, most complex and undervalued wines in the world."

I nodded, too excited suddenly. "I agree! I've never tasted anything like it. It's like nutty and rich, but so light, bone dry, actually, salty."

"It's the ocean air — that area of Spain is where the Atlantic, the Mediterranean, and the river all converge. You can't make sherry anywhere else, but I'm sure Simone told you that. It's like Champagne in that manner, especially with the chalk content in the soil. They have a name for it . . ."

"Albariza. That's the soil." I liked having answers. And of course he understood about sherry. Maybe that was what unsettled me, the way he spoke in decrees, like Simone, but I was always aware that he was a man. There were no shared sympathies between us. He didn't ever seem to have a question, and I don't mean curiosity, but a throbbing, existential, why-is-it-like-this question. He had already mastered the answer to that Why?

He was the only one who had seen me before the sheer terror of my training, before I had become mute and emerged with a different voice. He was the only one who knew. And always this feeling that he was not just in charge of the mechanics of the restaurant, but that he was puppeting us by cords tied to our unnameable aspirations and fears.

"You were smart to ingratiate yourself with her," he said. He walked around the bar and pulled out the La Gitana from the fridge and poured two small glasses. "She's not like this with new employees. The opposite, actually. I can't tell you how many potential servers she's failed on their trails and we've had to let them go."

I shrugged and smelled the wine. It was as addictive as old books. "I didn't do anything. She picked me."

"Why do you think she did that?"

I thought about those first few times I saw her, how she was so remote and sculptural. I wanted to say that I charmed her except for so long I'd hardly spoken.

"We have a thing," I said finally, inarticulately. It wasn't Jake, but I wasn't about to say that to Howard. "We have something in common, I don't know that I can explain it."

"I think I first met her when she was just a few years older than you."

"Was there even a Park Bar then?"

"There wasn't much. God, Simone and I used to go to this place, Art Bar? Is that still around?"

"It's so far west! What was she like?"

"Yes, we had to travel in those days. Barefoot in the snow, uphill both ways." Howard drank his sherry with his back to the door, and I saw the first guests come in for dinner. I watched as they agitatedly unwrapped themselves from their coats, and I thought I should set up but I wasn't about to stop our little happy hour.

"Would you believe me if I said she was mostly the same?" he continued. "The Owner had her training people twice her age within six months. Everyone was shocked when she didn't take the GM role. Lucky for me, of course."

"Why wouldn't she take it?"

"I know I make it look effortless." He pulled on his cuff links. "But it's a massive job. It's a different kind of commitment. If I remember correctly, she was thinking of going back to school. And then it was adieu, off to France, her first escape."

"You guys all run so deep," I said. "It's amazing, right? I mean, everyone has been here so long."

"Are you happy here?" he asked. Nicky came up behind me, straightening his bow tie, gave a raised eyebrow at my glass of sherry, and headed into the bar. He carefully dimmed the lights.

"Yes," I said. Howard couldn't see what I was seeing. The bar beginning to glow under the low lamps, the music ascending, Nicky opening the house red, jaunty, people shuffling in, the magic of the restaurant emerging as if from a more perfect world of forms.

"Curtain up, kids," Nicky called out and the servers came out of their hiding places, arms clasped behind their backs. Did Howard mean happy *here,* like the restaurant, or *here* in my life?

"I'm deeply happy here," I said.

"Have you given any thought to the future?"

Had I given any thought to the future? Sure. I wanted next year to look like the life I was leading right now. I knew I was drinking too much, and it wasn't without second thoughts that I made the transition from taking bumps of other people's drugs to buying my own, but I figured that couldn't possibly sustain itself, that it was part of an evolution from which I would emerge honed and sharp like an arrow from a bow. And besides, I drank less, snorted less, and fucked less than eighty percent of the people I encountered, though those things tended to affect me a bit more vulgarly.

Did he want to know my goals? Sometimes I made lists that said: explore Manhattan above Twenty-Third Street, buy a membership to MoMA, invest in a bookcase and/or curtains, go to yoga, learn to cook, buy a toothbrush that vibrates. I thought eventually I'd make more friends: urbane, talented, tattooed friends and we would have dinner parties, to which I could contribute because I would have developed a talent for coq au vin, and all the hysterical winds of possibility that buffeted me along the L train would have died down.

I had just started to think about travel. Sometimes I lined my life up against Simone's. I thought that my "escape," my adventure abroad, the one that would make me contemplative and sensual, was still coming for me. I had never been to Europe. Maybe Jake and I . . . maybe Jake and I would become a "we." I had never let myself have that thought in full before — two months ago I couldn't get him to say hello to me — but now, I believed the words as I thought them, that we were moving somewhere together, and it was toward a real "we." A "we" that held hands in the street and became regulars at Les Enfants Terribles around the corner from his apartment. It seemed a little odd that the two of us had never been out to dinner at a normal time, like anytime before midnight, but now that we'd had breakfast, the rest was a matter of time. A "we" that took weekends away, a "we" that went to Europe together, without Simone, continuous days to ourselves, we could fly into Paris, rent a car, travel the Loire River until we hit the Atlantic. I saw the way he looked at me sometimes. Other times it was like I wasn't there, but sometimes . . .

"There are times in life when it's good to live without knowing," Howard said, interrupting what must have been a look of unruffled idiocy. "I mean that we can allow ourselves to live and not really know what it is that we're doing. That's all right. It's an accumulation stage."

My eyes welled up. He took my empty glass from me and slid it into the dish rack.

"I'd like you to be a server here. The Owner would like it as well. You will bypass your coworkers in line for the next position, so you won't be the most popular for a moment. But is that something you would be interested in?"

I nodded.

"Wonderful. I will look for an opening in the coming months and you will begin training. Thank you for your strong work."

I looked at my hands, which weren't terribly clean, thinking they had autonomously produced this strong work. I remembered how scared I had been on that first L train ride to Union Square, and I'd said to my reflection words that had been a mantra all my life: I. Don't. Care. I don't know when exactly it happened, but Howard had changed that when he gave me this life: I cared.

I became obsessed by a pair of tennis shoes, the laces spun in the spindles of a tree outside my building. One day while I was watching the lights come on in the construction sites by the river, I looked down and there they were. I had not noticed them until every last leaf fell away, the tree shedding like a balding head, and there emerged these rotten, brown sneakers. It felt like they had been stuck there a long time. They looked ancient. My thoughts about it didn't go very far, but I was concerned. What happened to the person who lost their shoes? How did they get home? Who on earth was going to get them down? The thought that they would stay there for decades, rotting, gave me an apocalyptic feeling in my stomach.

■ ■ ■ ■

SPRING

■ ■ ■ ■

I

You will see it coming. Not *you* actually because you don't see for yourself yet, everyone is busy seeing for you, days filled with unsolicited advice you don't take and trite warnings you can't hear and the white-washing of all your excitement. Yes, they definitely saw it coming, exactly the way it came.

When you're older you will know that at some unconscious level not only did you see it coming, but you created it, in your own blind, stumbling way. You will console yourself with the fact that it wouldn't have mattered, seeing it or not seeing it. You were a sponge for incident. Maybe everyone is when they're young. They don't remember, nobody remembers what it feels like to be so recklessly absorbent.

When you can't see in front of you life is nothing but surprises. Looking back, there were truly so few of them.

We took walks after work because the winter was relinquishing its fascist hold on the weather. Jake's sense of ownership of his surroundings incrementally increased as we left Union Square. By the time we passed Houston to the south, or A to the east, he was fully in possession.

He took me to his bars. He grew patient, sentimental, nervous. He hated places where the bartenders were young. All the bartenders he knew had names like Buddy, Buster, or Charlie — anything you would want to name a loyal dog. He hated bars where they bought tables or light fixtures to look antique. He liked bars that were actually old, the gloss completely worn off, peeling paint, chipped tile. No DJs. No cocktail lists. He could visit those other bars, but never inhabit them.

At Milady's Jake called the bartender Grace, and stools always appeared for us. At Milano's on Houston, a pit bull asleep under the table, pomaded pro skaters and their model girlfriends lined up by the door. At Mars Bar, the walls were saturated with urine and I was the only girl and no one paid any attention to me. A delicate ecosystem of old men, death metal, drinking, and the most contented kind of anarchy.

At Sophie's on East Fifth his friend Brett ran things on Tuesday, a friend of Jake's from "way back," which I took to mean they were either petty criminals together or in rehab together because neither one of them would talk about it. Brett drank, tamely and grumpily, keeping one eye on *The Simpsons* episode that played on the TV above the bar. Jake kept giving me quarters to go to the jukebox and every time I chose a song he put his hands on his head and moaned.

"Is it genetic? Can women just not understand music? This is shit, absolute shit, you like this?"

"This is a good song. You could walk down the aisle to this song." The aisle and Jake. He covered his ears.

"You're fucking insane, you're making me want to die."

As soon as the song was over, he slid another quarter up next to my beer and I was determined — not for him to like a song I picked, that was impossible, but for him to say nothing.

"You know Ian wrote this for Joy Division before he died?"

"Who's Ian? This is a band called New Order."

"Brett! Brett, are you hearing this? Who's

Ian, she says! This is a band called New Order!"

Brett took his eyes off the screen for a second and sized me up. He was disappointed.

"Who's Joy Division?"

"Fuck!" said Jake. The whole bar up in arms, grown men slamming the wood, someone pointing a pool stick at me. When the song ended another quarter appeared next to my beer.

"You're torturing me?"

He leaned toward me and a lock of hair fell. I pushed it back. That's who I was now: the girl who got to fix Jake's hair. He was getting tipsy, loose, his teeth bared, I could feel him coming for me.

"I like it," he said.

"You like humiliating me?"

"No." He put his hand on my cheek and our foreheads touched. "I like how hard you concentrate when you're over there. You chew on your lips like it's life or death. I like the way you bop on your bar stool even when everyone is screaming at you."

"You like my bopping?" I bounced and his hands found me and pulled me off the stool.

"You ready?" he asked and I nodded, biting his neck. I don't think anything gave me as much satisfaction as when he asked if I was ready to go home. To think that we left places together, that we got to leave all the people to their last calls.

"Brett, we'll settle," he said, one hand pulling cash out of his wallet for a tip, his other hand crawling into my bra, pinching my nipple. Brett shrugged. It was like that all the time — no tab, no consequences.

"ARTISTS USED TO LIVE HERE" it said in graffiti on the plywood covering the chain-link fence around a giant hole in the ground. Demolition crews were inside, breaking up concrete, redistributing piles of dirt and wreckage. Also on the plywood were a series of building permits, and an ad for condos with a computer-illustrated woman in heels and a business suit relaxing, drinking a glass of wine, surveying the Manhattan skyline from her white box in the sky. She was a brunette with vaguely multicultural eyes. Maybe artists used to live here, but this woman was definitely not an artist. Though she was facing west, the ad said, The Dawn of Luxury in Williamsburg.

The wind frothed the river onto the rocks. The grass was brown and bare, the flower beds twiggy. I sat on a bench to look up at the bridge, and felt an acute anxiety. Who was going to buy the condos? Who was going to pay off our student loans? Would our sense of style protect us? And if the poor people used to live here and the rich people were going to live here, where would *we* go?

Two homeless men were asleep on picnic tables. I had become very good at not looking at unpleasant things. I could skip my eyes over any pool of vomit on the train platform, any broken junkie lurching toward the concrete, any woman who screamed at her crying baby, even the couples fighting at their tables at the restaurant, women crying into fettuccine, twirling their wedding bands — what being a fifty-one percenter had taught me was not to let any shock shake my composure. One of the homeless men, in the layers of colorless clothes, was faced away from me on his side. His pants were half down, a piece of shit-covered toilet paper sticking out of his ass crack like a surrender flag. One of his tennis shoes had fallen off and lay to the side of the table.

I looked at him until I couldn't anymore. The sun seemed pensive about setting, and instead of the usual transcendental buzz I got from a change of light, I noticed that the rats were shifting within the rocks. I'm beginning to worry, I said to the river. I checked my phone and walked back home.

When the invitation came it was vague and I was cautious. I waited for her to follow up. But she meant it — she would love to host me for dinner, me and Jake, together. The three of us. I was to arrive at eight. When I looked through my books to see if there was something I could bring to surprise her, I pulled out the copy of Emily Dickinson she had lent me when I first went to her apartment. I had read it many times but holding it in my hand that whole afternoon tumbled back to me with a rush of embarrassment. Not at the memory, but at the ease with which whole afternoons were forgotten. The way thousands of wounds and triumphs were whittled down to only the sharpest moments, and even those failed to remain present. I had already forgotten about the men by the river. Already forgotten what the autumn felt like. My sadness that day when I left her — it only existed in that little book, and even there, it was just a relic.

So, I said to myself in the mirror as I circled my eyes in black liner, not only was I returning to Simone's apartment, but I was going back for dinner, and not only was I going, but I was going with Jake. I wore a cable-knit black sweater, tall black boots, black pants glued to my legs. I smudged up my eyeliner and wrapped my oversized gray scarf around my neck. Surprises in every corner.

"And then she dances herself to death. It's the only way to pacify the gods. It's extraordinary, I make a point to go whenever they put it on," Simone said, pulling a roasted chicken out of the oven. I held a stack of books in my hands that I had cleared off the round table. There was nowhere to put them but the floor.

"Really? That sounds cool."

"This one and her 'cool,' " Jake said, shaking his head. He was flipping through *Meditations in an Emergency,* watching us with a smile on his lips that made me feel gilded.

"I must have heard Stravinsky before," I lied.

"Of course."

"But I can't quite recall it."

"Well," she said, taking off the oven mitts. "I would recommend the ballet — the music is moving, fine, but Nijinsky's choreography, the brutality of it, that was what really antagonized the crowd in 1913. That was the scandal. Will you pull the Chenin out of the fridge?"

She was the artistic director of her apartment. When I came in Jake was already there, there were candles burning, Bessie Smith on the record player, and the fortuitous smell of rendered chicken fat and potatoes. She opened the front windows because the oven made the place steamy, and the mild noises crept in, a swaying spot marking our inclusion and exclusion. She poured me a glass of fino sherry as soon as I walked in the door, and had me sit at the table while she fussed around in the kitchen.

Olives and Marcona almonds sat in patterned dishes ("Tangier," she said when I asked her where they came from) in the center of the table, but she hadn't cleared anything away. Books, halves of grapefruits, swiped-out casings of avocados, pens, receipts, kaleidoscopes of candle wax stuck to the table. And there he was, stalking around like a delinquent in a museum, picking up objects, books, papers, and moving them. When I came in, I got an up-and-down scan that told me he noticed my ten extra minutes of makeup. He was at ease in her home in a way I had never seen him in his own.

"The story has pagan origins . . . but what's always interested me is that the myth of its opening night mirrors the arc of the ballet, which is a descent into the brutal and the primitive. Her fervor creates the same fervor in the viewer. I mean, honestly, can you imagine a riot at the ballet?"

"Who'd you go with?"

"Hmm?" she sang out, distracted. An apron high on her hips, just like she was at work, but her hair was down, elegant, a white T-shirt tucked into washed-out baggy jeans — and I thought, How brave she is, cooking in a white T-shirt. Her face was bare except for her lipstick, which I wanted to think she had applied just for me.

"Who did you go to the ballet with?"

"A friend," she said.

"Howard," Jake said at the same time.

"I'd rather not talk about our coworkers," she said to Jake.

"Not a coworker, *boss,* Simone."

"All right, Jake, will you turn the record over or are you just expecting us to wait on you hand and foot? Your fantasy, right?"

"You and Howard went to the ballet?" I pulled out pewter-handled knives. "These are beautiful."

"Well, I haven't been able to make Jake go to the ballet since the millennium, so Howard is kind enough."

"Was it a date?"

"What a silly question. Of course not."

"They're good friends," said Jake, flipping an hourglass.

"We all have our good friends, don't we, Jake?" she said swiftly. "Now, Tess, I need you to dress the salad, Jake can finish the table."

He instead picked up a sterling silver jewelry box and opened it. He picked up a white pill. "The seven-fifties?"

"Yes, dearest," she said without looking. He popped it in his mouth and took a gulp of his wine. He and Simone had moved onto a Chenin Blanc from the Loire. I couldn't remember if I had ever seen him take a line or a pill, but it seemed so natural, so absolutely charming, that I wanted one too without knowing what it was.

"Are those treats?"

"It's for my back," he said. He picked up a small bust from her bookshelves. He put the face — blandly Grecian and aristocratic — on the counter next to me. "Simone thinks she's going to die reading Aristotle, she had a dream about it once."

"One of Jake's better gifts. You're welcome to a 'treat' as you call it," she said, shifting a tray of root vegetables in the oven.

"It's Simone's perverted candy dish."

"Be sweet," she warned.

"I can't," I said, taking a sip of my sherry

responsibly. "I won't be able to drink if I do." I used two forks to turn the leaves in the salad bowl, but they kept falling out onto the counter.

"Don't be timid," she demanded. "Use your hands." She reached into the bowl and started to move the lettuce leaves into the vinaigrette, soothingly.

"Escarole?" I asked.

"Your favorite," she said and I pulled a leaf out of the bowl and popped it in my mouth.

"True, but I like everything," I said.

"That means you like nothing." Jake dropped the silverware into a pile in the center of the table.

"Anchovies?" I asked, tasting the vinaigrette.

"Perhaps you didn't develop a palate, little one," Simone said. "Perhaps you recovered it."

We moved the plates onto the table and Simone pulled the fourth chair, covered in scarves, books, junk mail, and old *New Yorkers* to the side. Jake put on a new record and propped the cover up — Charlie Parker's sax ran into the room. Someone had told me that when he soloed he referred to the melody only by omission — he implied it. It sounded exactly like New York was supposed to sound.

"Tess." Simone snapped with her fingers toward a bottle of wine on the counter. I had already been eyeing it, the Puffeney Arbois, an eccentric wine on our list, and one of her favorite recommendations for her more intellectually inclined guests. She said it was a wine that stuck in the mind.

"Jura!" I said. "I've been dying to try this!"

"He's the pope of Arbois. That's the Trousseau."

"Moni, where did you find that?" Jake asked, skeptically, grabbing the bottle from me. *Moni?*

"I have a friend at Rosenthal," she said.

"So many fucking friends!" he said and then to me, "This is delicious."

"Have you been there, Simone? The Jura?"

"Of course."

"I want to go," I said, inspecting the bottles clustered on the counter. It was a modest collection but I assumed she had more in the fridge.

"Where the fuck do you think you're going?" Jake said into my neck. He rested his chin on my shoulder and I never wanted to move.

"I don't know. The Jura? I spend all this time studying these maps and I want to see the land."

"You're done with New York already? On to Europe?"

"I'm a quick study," I said. I moved to lean against him but he was gone.

"You absolutely should go," Simone said.

"I couldn't go alone," I said and looked at them. Jake was kneeling, looking into the oven, pressing buttons, and she hovered above him.

"Moni, the light's broken in here again."

"Darling, what do you want me to say? I am not blessed with your amateur electrician skills."

"I'll do it tomorrow," he said.

"Where's your wine key?" I asked, waving the bottle.

"Oh no, you're not performing tonight. Jake will open it for us."

I sat and Jake laid a dish towel over his arm and came up to me.

"Mademoiselle, the Puffeney Arbois, 2003." He opened it roughly, in a manner I could never get away with, a bartender opening cheap bottles on the fly. He and Nicky could get a bottle open in seconds.

He poured a taste and I swirled it. The wine was the color of cloudy rubies, washing up the sides of the glass, audaciously fragrant and crystalline.

"So pretty when it's unfiltered. . . . It's

perfect," I said. Disintegrating outlines all around, the glass, my skin, the walls, a blur of satisfaction that was totally foreign to me. I felt like I had arrived in a room that had been waiting for me my whole life, and a voice in my head whispered, This is what family feels like.

"A toast," said Simone, holding her glass aloft. "The way of life is wonderful; it is by abandonment."

"Emerson," Jake whispered to me, but he was playing too, his glass held up in the air.

"This is to our little Tess. Thank you for joining us."

I laughed at her use of restaurant jargon, the phrase we used as a welcome and a farewell. I always wondered who this ceaselessly festive "us" was, why exactly we were thanking the guests, as if they had provided a service, a contribution. I wondered how it felt for them to be sent back into the embittered, poorly lit outside world.

"Thank you for having me."

We were quiet, passing the plates around. Part of me had expected that they would entertain me. But coming into her home this time, I wasn't spit back out onto the street. I was becoming necessary.

"I had a strange feeling today," I said, tentatively, wondering how people started conversations. Would it always feel like I was intruding with nonsense?

"Did you? Regarding what?"

"I was walking around Williamsburg . . . and it felt . . . ominous."

"Was it the condos?" Simone said, concerned.

"I can't even go over there anymore," he said, mouth full, holding a chicken leg in his hand. He was going to finish his plate before I had my first bite.

"It's happening so much faster than I anticipated," said Simone. "When they changed the zoning laws in 2005, we knew that the end was coming. Friends lost their lofts left and right, but the speed with which it all disappeared . . ."

"2005. So I just missed it," I said. "I thought so."

"We always just miss New York. I watched it with this neighborhood. When I moved here everyone was mourning the SoHo of the seventies, Tribeca of the eighties, and already ringing the death knell for the East Village. Now people romanticize the Alphabet City of Jonathan Larson. We all walk in a cloud of mourning for the New York that just disappeared."

"Okay, okay, but I love *Rent,* is that terrible?"

"I'm going to ignore that comment for-ever," Jake said.

"Treacherous," said Simone. "That kind of singsong nostalgia."

"But I guess I was wondering if it will ever stop."

"Stop?"

"I don't know, the city?" I said. "Chang-ing? Like will it ever rest?"

"No," they said in unison and then laughed.

"So then we just dance ourselves to death?" I asked.

"Ha!" Simone smiled at me and Jake smiled looking at his plate.

"This is so good, Simone."

"It's always the simple things, well exe-cuted, that are memorable. I don't concern myself with complexity when I have guests."

"What was it like when you moved here?" I asked her.

"What was it like? The city?"

"No, I don't know." I turned to Jake. "What was she like at twenty-two?"

She groaned. "He doesn't remember, he was a child."

"She was a heartbreaker," Jake said, "and I was not a child anymore. You had your long hair back then." He was watching her and I wondered if I was going to be the kind of woman about whom they said, She was a heartbreaker.

"Oh god, Jake, don't start. When Jake was a baby he would never let me put my hair up. Hysterical tears, panic. God forbid I cut it."

"Tears?"

"I was very particular about women, even back then," he said, and he nodded toward my hair, which was down. "I still think it's too short."

"Me?" I asked, but he was looking at Simone again.

"Long hair like that is for girls, Jake," Simone said, touching hers, which sat at her shoulders. Mine was much longer.

"I knew you were a girl once! You must remember."

"Yeah, Moni, tell her."

"I remember much forgetfulness."

"Come on," I said.

"The city in the early nineties was rampant with crime. Everyone was still reeling from AIDS, entire communities had been wiped out, and all the neighborhoods were being rezoned for development. Gentrification has always been with us, but these were massive, government-subsidized overhauls, not just a new coffee shop or a block of renovations. Was it so much better then? Do I miss not being able to walk this block in the dark? I can't say. But, as trite as this sounds, it was a very free time. And by free I mean that I felt free to pursue the life I wanted, and I could afford to. There were still dark spots in the city, fringes, margins, and I believed — still believe — that those areas are what make cities thrive. But being twenty-two . . . that was confusing."

"Confusing?" I asked. "Is that the word I would use?"

"Seems to be the age that ladies run away from home," he said. "I never got to see twenty-three."

I hadn't put that together, that Simone and I came to the city at the same time in our lives. Our first escapes.

"You survived," Simone said to him, and to me: "It was confusing because I didn't know what I was yet."

"Does it get better?" I asked. Can it? was what I really wanted to ask.

"Aging is peculiar," she said, moving a piece of parsnip around the plate with her fork. "I don't think you should be lied to about it. You have a moment of relevancy — when the books, clothes, bars, technology — when everything is speaking directly to you, expressing you exactly. You move toward the edge of the circle and then you're abruptly outside the circle. Now what to do with that? Do you stay, peering backward? Or do you walk away?"

"Aren't you in a new circle?"

"Of course. But that circle for a woman is tricky."

"Tricky?"

"It's a circle of marriage, children, acquisitions, retirement funds. That's the culture you're asked to participate in. Now . . . if you decline?"

"You're in your own circle," I said. It sounded lonely, but also fearless.

"It's not so bad." She smiled. "There's a settling of the mind. Think of it as trading bursts of inspiration for a steady, prolonged focus."

"Don't you think you were a bit reckless?" Jake asked sharply. I didn't know which one of us he was talking to.

Simone was quiet for a moment and said to him, "I think I did the best I could."

"Isn't that part of it? Being reckless?" I asked.

They didn't answer. They were staring at each other. The record had gone off and I got up to flip it, and Simone stood and started clearing the plates. When I went to take the bottle of wine, Jake grabbed my hand.

"Come here," he said. He pulled me onto his lap. I looked at Simone in the kitchen, but then put my face into his hair, held his face on my chest. No one had ever reached for me like that, like they just needed me close.

"We never get tired of talking about love, do we?" She was looking at us with a dishcloth over her shoulder. She smiled.

"Sex and food and death," Jake said. "The only subjects." He released me and I stood up, tipsy, confused.

"She said 'love,' not 'sex' — you're such a boy." I turned. "Simone, that was so good, thank you."

She pulled out another bottle of wine, and I realized we were going to get drunk. I wondered if I would ever go back to my apartment.

"Let's try the Poulsard now."

"Liquid dessert, perfect," I said.

"That's not all."

"Oh no, I'm totally stuffed."

"Shut your eyes," Jake said. He pushed me away from the kitchen, toward the windows in the front.

"What?"

"Tess, shut your eyes," Simone said. I looked out onto Ninth Street. People walked obliviously underneath me. Inside lit windows I saw people fulfilling their real lives, I saw minutes that counted. I was expanding, it wasn't just the job anymore, not just the restaurant, but I was finding a place in the world. Someone stopped the record, and it looked like the street was breathing. Then someone turned out the lights and I shut my eyes.

"You can turn around," she said. When I did she stood with a chocolate cake in her hands, with a single candle burning on top. Jake stood next to her, holding a bouquet of white tulips. My hand flew to cover my mouth. I thought, No. I can't take it. I didn't know how they knew, how I didn't think to tell them. I didn't know how badly I had needed them and how I'd been waiting for them, but I endured it, my joy, don't ever forget this moment, and Simone said, "Happy birthday, little one."

II

"Oh, what you think, you can get the pie in the sky and eat it too?" Sasha said serenely.

"Does that translate to you missed me?" I asked. I didn't know how long it had been since I'd gone to Park Bar after work. Nobody asked me where I'd disappeared to, as if they knew that talking about Jake would give me too much pleasure. Instead they kept a chilly distance when I walked in. Nothing had changed in there. Ariel and Vivian were back on and talking about moving in together, Will purposefully flirted with any woman under the age of forty, and Terry was a little fatter but still told bad jokes.

Once I could get each of them in the bathroom we would be in love again, but the only one interested that night was Sasha. I took a line. The coke rutted out my nose and I squinted my eyes. Had it always hurt before? Pain beyond the stinging heat?

"Oh, you got plenty-a time to talk now

the cock outta your mouth? You think I care whatsoever you live or die?" He snorted the peace offering I laid out for him. "You looking very rosy though." He pinched my cheeks and I knew he had forgiven me.

Simone's "cleanses" had a reputation among the staff — apparently she wasn't very nice while doing them. Jake said it was the most miserable time of the year, and Will asked to switch out of dining room backwaiter when she was senior on the floor. I was mostly impressed with how casually and often she said the word *colon*.

"Spring cleaning," she said. She didn't seem mean. She seemed really happy in fact, and her eyes did look brighter.

"Is it all right if I sit with you?" I held a plate of spaghetti and Chef's Sunday sauce and three pieces of garlic bread. Simone had a thermos in front of her.

"Of course. I don't have an appetite after the first day."

"Did your eyes get bigger?"

"That's the wine. The puffiness disappears in the first three days. When was the last time you took time off from drinking?"

"Okay, okay, we aren't talking about me," I said.

"Your metabolism at your age lets you get

away with murder, but every now and then your body needs a break. All the dairy, all the sugars, all the acid — there's mucoid plaque that builds up along the walls of your intestines, it's black, you can actually see it when it comes out, so this is an opportunity to break it down, expel it."

"Simone," I said with my mouth full. "Jesus. Please. Twenty minutes before we do 'mucoid' or 'expel.' "

She took a sip of her tonic.

"How long?" I asked between bites. "Also, aren't you going to make Jake a plate?"

"I'm starting with seven days. I've done thirteen."

"Seven!"

"Tess," she said, putting her hand on my shoulder, "your body doesn't always need to need. There is a still point in the center."

"You. Are. Crazy," I said. The thought of not eating for seven days made me ravenous even though I knew I shouldn't get seconds. Misha the hostess was announcing the soignés that were expected tonight, but I wasn't really listening, I was thinking about how much pasta was left and if I should save some for Jake, but I did hear her say that a Samantha and Eugene were coming in and had requested Simone, and I heard Simone say, "Absolutely not."

We all turned to Simone. Misha glanced at Howard, who nodded at her to continue.

"So I need to move Simone to section 1 because Eugene only sits on 7. . . ." She hesitated to see if that was allowed. "So . . . Simone . . . section 1."

"Absolutely not," Simone said again and picked up her thermos and walked into the kitchen. We all turned to Howard.

"Misha, finish the notes," he said, heading after Simone and passing Jake, who was still unbuttoned, just getting to family meal. He looked at the table expectantly and I shrugged. No Simone, no plate for him. He looked confused as he put his own together.

"Who's Samantha?" I asked him when he sat down and started shoveling the food into his mouth.

"Samantha who?" he said defensively.

"Samantha and Eugene who requested Simone."

"Samantha's coming?"

"That's what Misha just said."

"Damn it." He took my last piece of garlic bread, took a bite, and I grabbed it back. "Samantha and Simone were friends. She was a server here."

"Okay." Simone's "friends" were usually obliquely mentioned and none of them ever visited her at work so I had assumed they didn't exist.

"Okay . . ." I waited for him to go on. "So she quit and they weren't friends anymore? And it was super dramatic and Simone doesn't want to wait on her?"

He wiped his mouth and threw the napkin on my plate. "I'm going to go find her. Are you on the dining room tonight? She could use you on the floor."

Samantha was *meticulous,* that was the first word that came to mind. I didn't believe she had ever worked in a restaurant. Her hair was blown out at perfectly corresponding angles, her cheekbones shone. Her hands, with long, pale-pink ovals for fingernails, conducted their precious stones and platinum with ease. To top it all off, there was stark genetics — she was beautiful. And I was part of a cult that equated beauty with virtue.

"Those are new teeth," Simone said, watching them from across the room. Samantha's teeth winked at us. Simone exhaled and began her approach. I followed with a water pitcher, though there were at least seven tables being sat throughout the restaurant that could have used some water. I took Jake's order seriously.

"I would hardly say we're fresh, maybe fresh off a plane, but I'm sure I look frightful."

"Ah well, you've always been able to hide the damage." Simone pulled her shoulders back. "Are you two still in Connecticut?"

"Back and forth," said Eugene, waving his hands. In the genetics department, Eugene had been shortchanged. He had caterpillar eyebrows, a bulbous nose, and not much hair left. He had to be more than ten years Samantha's senior. I was familiar with older men and their younger wives. But Eugene seemed authentic. He had clever eyes and he narrowed them when he was listening.

"It will change when Tristan starts school, but we have so much freedom right now, I'm trying to enjoy it."

"By enjoy it she means cart a two-year-old around Europe."

"Be nice," Samantha said, hitting his arm. "People make such a fuss about traveling with children. But you can't let them be in charge. Tristan can sit through a four-course meal."

"How elegant, Sam," Simone said. "Of course, Chef would like to cook for you both."

"Oh." Samantha looked at Eugene and pouted. "I'm afraid we can't accept. I couldn't stomach a full tasting, Simone, my jet lag and so on. But perhaps I can pop in and say hello if he's not busy later? And was that little Jake behind the bar? He's all grown up. Remember when you two were sharing that shoe box in the East Village? Eugene, Simone had this place, it didn't even have a proper bathroom, the tub was in the kitchen!"

"I'm still there."

Simone smiled. She smiled so forcefully I could hear her molars grinding together.

"Well, it was adorable. We had a lot of fun there." Samantha looked airily around the room. "Is Howard here as well?"

"We're all here, Sam. I will let Chef know you declined." Simone was stoic.

Samantha pointed to something on the menu and Eugene laughed. "You just can't get rid of the filet mignon of tuna. Like it's not the twenty-first century. Adorable, I love it."

Adorable. I had never seen grown women attack each other so fluently. No one tossed out *adorable* at Simone. No one declined Chef's tasting menu. And yet Simone wasn't stunned — she was braced. I realized that they were women who knew dangerous

393

things about each other.

I shouldn't have been surprised that Jake and Simone had lived together — I knew she brought him out to the city, it made sense within the narrative I had composed — but it was so directed, the way Samantha said Jake's name, probing.

"Eugene," Simone said, turning her back to Samantha, like she had taught me never to do to a guest. "The Dauvissat? We have one bottle of the '93 hiding downstairs. Howard will be livid, but are you interested? If I can find it, of course."

Eugene slapped the table, thrilled. "This woman — when was that dinner? Six years ago? She never forgets! Best server in New York City. Don't get mad, Samantha, you know you weren't cut out for serving. Bring it out, Simone, but make sure to bring yourself a glass."

"With pleasure," she said.

Did I dare to compare them? Of course. My loyalty fierce but not blind. I struggled, wondering what categories they could justly compete in. The physical didn't seem fair. I wasn't mistaken, Simone shrank as soon as she greeted the table. And it wasn't just that Samantha was taller and had posture like a steel rod ran the length of her spine. Simone's shoulders had bowed like a stone had been hung around her neck. She was wearing her glasses, which gave her a slight but mean squint. The total effect was miserly, as if Samantha had sucked up all the grace in the room.

Simone's nails — I just noticed — were clean but dull and the edges were bitten. I could feel the jagged edges when they clamped onto my forearm and she said, "Watch my section, don't move from it, I will find the Dauvissat."

Her bright eyes seemed peeled away from her head.

"Maybe you should eat something real quick. Just a bite." She was on day four.

"I would appreciate it if you focused."

"What if they need something?"

"They're just guests. Get them whatever the fuck they want."

As if I could stay away. Samantha took one sip of her full water glass and I materialized beside her to refill it. Heather was touching the table, she must have known them too, and she excused herself on my approach.

"Hello," she said, putting her hand on my arm to stop me from pouring. Her fingers glittered. "I'm Samantha. You're a refreshing presence here. Heather says you're the new girl."

"That's what they call me."

"That's what we called Samantha once," Eugene said. "Eugene Davies."

"You worked here too?"

"No, no." He smiled politely. "I was a regular. Standing lunch on Fridays, but twice a week toward the end, when I was trying to capture this one."

Samantha smiled, putting all her buffed white teeth into it. Their pinkies were hooked around each other's.

"But," Eugene continued, "when I asked Howard about her — I remember this perfectly — I said, 'Who is that stunning brunette?' and he said, 'The new girl?' And that's always how I thought of her."

"So many years ago, stop!" They laughed, the way guests sometimes laughed or cried because they felt like there was a privacy curtain encircling their table. I was always watching this intimacy, these people revealing their petty, hopeful, or maybe in this case, genuine selves.

"Do you miss it?" I asked.

"The golden handcuffs? Besides the back-breaking labor and turning into a nocturnal zombie and the general cattiness." She paused and appraised me as if I were about to go up for auction. "Of course I miss it.

It's family."

"Yes." I felt a kinship with Samantha. I would with anyone who came in and announced that they had once worked at the restaurant. We shared — even if she had covered it up with jewelry and skin serums — a muscle memory. We had both broken down wine boxes in the cellar, we had both learned how to tell when Chef was heating up, we had the same aches in our necks and lower backs. "I feel really lucky."

"You are. You'll never be luckier." Her and Eugene's touching pinkies blossomed into holding hands, and I wondered what she thought being lucky was. Their eyes moved off me and I knew Simone was coming back. She had the Dauvissat but something was wrong. On her way back up from the cellar she must have reapplied her lipstick. Just slightly, but definitively, she had veered off the mark.

I backed away as she began presenting, something I had watched her do, wistfully, at all hours and from all angles. I looked at the Dauvissat, the yellowing label, its promise of history, of alchemy, of decadence, and the label was shaking in Simone's unmanicured hands.

Within ten minutes of Samantha and Eugene bubbling out into a taxi Simone's section was in disarray and she was nowhere to be seen. I got Heather to help me establish order. As soon as I had a second I found her in the wine room, a bread basket at her feet, thermos in her lap, breathing hard and taking little sips.

"Simone, I need help in your section," I said. "9 is pissed because they wanted the broccoli rabe and polenta sides and Chef doesn't have a ticket, and I didn't see it on hold, so maybe they didn't order it, or maybe you forgot?"

She stared at the wall and broke off a piece of flatbread. She crumbled it up. "It's funny. The people you become."

I exhaled. "You need to get back upstairs."

"You think you're making choices. But you're not. Choices are being made against you."

"Should I get Jake?" It was like car alarms in my head, knowing that her section was falling to pieces, that guests were looking around the room for their server. I saw a red stain down the side of her shirt.

"Did you *spill wine*?" My tone exposed my disgust. She was obviously not well. It had to be the cleanse. "Eat that bread," I said forcefully. "Now."

She ate a square of focaccia, chewing

398

timidly like a child trying a new food, like she might spit it out.

"I'm getting you new stripes. What's your combo?"

She wasn't catatonic — she tracked my words, they just didn't puncture. The adrenalized immediacy of service, the force that kept the restaurant running, had completely drained from her person.

"06-08-76."

I repeated the numbers as I ran up the stairs. Only when I started to input them did I think it might be a birthday. It was the 06 — I remembered that Jake was a Gemini. I did not remember how I'd come to possess that knowledge. It seemed to have passed to me in the leaky drunken hours when information entered but didn't adhere. Maybe this was Jake's birthday — the 76 was a more accurate indicator than my half remembering that he was a Gemini.

I thought of him waking up last June 8, thirty years old, and not knowing that I was weeks away. Neither of them had known I was coming. This June would be a culmination. I'd watch the English peas and sugar snaps come in, maybe I would get a bike and he could teach me how to ride in the city. And his birthday. Simone and I would plan a dinner, and he would be uncomfortable but happy. When I ran back into the cellar Simone was sitting stormily, glaring at the label on a bottle of Saint-Émilion.

"Quick, quick." I barreled past any formality left between us and unbuttoned her shirt. She let me. I forced it off her shoulders. As I did her arms went up and back and I saw a mark under her bra strap. "What's that?"

She lifted the band of her bra, dreamily, still unhurried.

It was a tattoo of a key. Matching. Identical. It was in better condition than Jake's and looked branded into her pale skin. Of course, I thought as I balled up her dirty stripes.

"I didn't take you for the type." It looked ridiculous on her, like an accident. But it wasn't. I wished it had been anything else. A butterfly, a star, a quote from Keats, a flippant tattoo. Now her body was an echo of Jake's. No — his was an echo of hers. It was the first tattoo I had seen on him, back when he pulled me into the walk-in and opened oysters for me, before that body became familiar, before I could find all his tattoos in the dark. Would Jake and I ever have private moments, just the two of us?

If I left her here in the basement the restaurant would be thrown into a tailspin.

One bad night wouldn't ruin her, but the staff would talk. It would be a fissure in her power. I ripped the dry cleaner's plastic off the new shirt, hoping to feel capable again, craving order.

"It's a funny story actually."

"I can't wait to hear it. Another time." I threw the light-blue stripes at her. "You're fucked up there, Simone. One more bite of bread, please."

The fresh shirt hadn't revived her like I thought it would. She smelled stale, or maybe it was the wine room.

"So 11 is mid-entrée, we're running way behind for apps on 14 but drinks are down, I sold a Quintarelli, only the Valpolicella Classico, but not the worst sale, I know it's Italy, but they insisted, maybe if you talk to Chef he can rush the food, I would go straight to 15, Heather was dropping the check for me." I pulled her hand. She was breathing deeply. They were rough, lachrymal breaths that I knew all too well. "Hey. When are the asparagus coming?" Her eyes bounced to me.

"With this weather?" she asked, consulting the ceiling. "Three weeks. Minimum."

"Oh yeah? You think it's going to snow again?"

I kept asking her questions she knew the

answers to. Once she got on the floor she went straight to 15, smiled compulsorily, and snatched up the check.

"We thought you went home," Heather said. "In the future can I get some warning before you cleanse your spirit, darlin'? I'll just plan on taking the whole dining room." Simone didn't acknowledge, apologize to, or thank her. I watched over Simone all night, but she was fine. Her tattoo faded from my mind as service beat on, relegated to the neglected file of weird, annoying shit about Jake and Simone. She got her normal tip average, an unfluctuating twenty-seven percent. The mechanics never failed.

"I thought you guys were such good friends," Ariel said later that night. She was still halfheartedly punishing me for my absence from Park Bar. I told myself to be patient with her and Will, but I was willing to push it with her tonight.

"Wasn't Simone like the maid of honor?" Will asked. Vivian was pouring out tequila shots. "You wanna shot?"

"Ugh," I said. Jake was going to pick me up after he walked Simone home. I had no desire to get drunk, but it was the best shortcut to the reliable Park Bar intimacy. And, looking at them, I felt guilty. I was going to be a server. Howard had no idea how bad it was going to be for me. I couldn't even imagine asking Ariel to get me something "on the fly" in that harried, bossy way the servers did. She was going to beat the shit out of me. "Maybe in a minute?"

"All My Friends" came on, and Ariel made Terry turn it up. I thought she would grab me like she used to and pull me onto the floor to dance. It was our song when we were heading out into the night — the manic, dizzy piano introduction stretching us. The song was all promise — that this night would be different, or different enough.

"You swallow you cunt," said Sasha putting a shot in front of me.

"But, hey guys, it's our song," I said. No one acknowledged me. Simone's meltdown made me miss the simplicity of us getting fucked up together with no ulterior agenda. But I had an agenda now — a walk with Jake, a potential breakfast — things to stay sober for. I considered the shot. If I got too drunk I figured I could throw up before Jake got there. I took it and groaned.

"It's like Samantha represents the life she almost had with Mr. Bensen."

"Now what if *he* came in," Will said, "what if he and his *wife* came in? That would make tonight look like a nonevent."

"Abandoning her section midrush — not exactly a nonevent."

"No, wait, guys," I said. "Slow down."

"Oh, Bensen, the Silver Fox, I woulda done him, double shot."

"And it was like, out in the open, and Simone was putting in her notice without putting it in, like a six-month notice, but still."

"And what?"

Will shrugged. "How does that phrase go? Married men always leave their wives?"

"Oh," I said. "That's not how the phrase goes."

"Poof be gone," Sasha said, and snapped his fingers. "You fuck the servant, you don't take her to Connecticut, 'kay?"

"I think Samantha lives in Connecticut."

"Bravo, doll," Will said. "So a few years later, along comes Samantha — she and Simone fall hard for each other, like school-girl style."

"But Eugene and Samantha fall even harder. She wasn't even here long enough to get a voucher. She and Simone had some bizarre falling-out after the wedding. It just broke Simone for a minute."

"Wait, Ari," I said. "Simone doesn't get broken. Especially by shit like that. She's

404

not like, looking to get married or get validated by a man. She's in her own circle."

Ariel slammed her hand on the bar. "Are you fucking blind?"

"Baby Monster, you need a bathroom break."

"It's like you fucking own me," I said to Sasha, standing up automatically and getting in line with him. I waved to Scott who sat in his corner.

"Back at it?" he said. Mocking and cruel, as if he knew that I didn't want to be here again, in a cycle of nothing nights.

"Like riding a bike," I said and turned to Sasha. "What about Jake?"

"What about my Baby Jakey? He picking up all the Simone pieces like always."

"What about him and Samantha?"

"Why you ask that?" He grabbed my chin and looked in my eyes.

"She mentioned him," I said. But that wasn't it. It was that Simone was so upset by Samantha I felt like there had to be more to the story. A black aura of heartbreak shrouded Simone now. Her poems that no one read, her apartment that she could never leave, her expertise so niche it was skeletal. She hadn't made a choice. Someone else had.

We locked ourselves in the bathroom and

he took out his bag. "Sugar Face, you better off just assuming that Jake fucked everyone. Where's your key?"

"Sasha, when are you going to be happy for me? Also I don't have a key on me."

"Oh look who all grown up!" He pulled out his wine key and took a bump and handed it to me. "You know, you the worst kind, you want to marry the artist and live like squalor, but you wait, in five years you be like, Baby Jake why we eat ramen noodles every night? You a hustler, don't blind me, I see."

The cocaine was an illumination, the bathroom florid, filtered. When I looked at our reflection in the mirror we looked like a photograph. I could see that we were just playing. The degree to which I took myself seriously was laughable. "God, Sasha, it's so dark here. You guys are so fucking dark. Do you not see that?"

"Oh, Baby Monster, please show me the light!"

"I'm just saying it doesn't have to be like this." I checked his nose and teeth for him and lifted my head for him to do the same. He flicked something off my nose and I grabbed his face and kissed him on both cheeks. "This isn't Mother Russia. It's America. We believe in happy endings."

"Get me the phone, lemme call my mama, Jesus fucking Christ, 'cause now I really fucking heard everything."

III

The hungry gap appeared, spreading like a rattled plane in front of us. We extended our use of the word *local*, bringing up soft-shell crab and asparagus from Virginia, blood oranges from Florida. The guests, the cooks, all of us anxious, still shell-shocked from winter and bucking against the restraints. It wasn't spring fever, not yet. We didn't fully have faith that it was coming but we had no choice but to move forward into the protracted promises.

The sun came out for a moment. I stopped and stared at the ends of the branches, willing them to bud. I had just left the Guggenheim and clouds blindfolded the sun again as I walked toward the train. I felt like a stranger again, like I could disappear into any intractable diner or bodega or train station.

I got out at Grand Central, hallowed ground of anonymity and flux, and followed signs for the Oyster Bar. It was a strange impulse — he had been saying that he was going to take me, it was one of his favorites. I don't know whether it was a Kandinsky or a Klee that gave me a curious detachment from my life, but I decided not to wait for him. Simone assured me it was an old wives' tale, but someone said that you were only supposed to eat oysters during months with an *r* in it. So maybe it was the impending warmth, the loss of the chilly *r* months, but I knew I should take myself to lunch.

I got the last seat at the low counter, under a vaulted dome of tiles. I was prepared with my book but I stared at the ceiling instead, inhaled the velvet scent of shellfish and butter, watched the servers and busboys, then looked at the guests, slowly realizing that I was singular in the room. I had nothing in common with the suits and their lunch breaks and BlackBerrys. I belonged, but not because of my age or my clothes. I belonged because I spoke the restaurant language.

"Excuse me," said the man sitting next to me. He was midway through a bowl of clam chowder. He was broad shouldered and fine featured, and I did a double take because he had blue eyes. I raised my eyebrows at him.

"I know you from somewhere."

"Oh yeah?" I put my eyes back on my menu.

"Pardon me, I thought you were someone I know, a French friend."

"You have a friend who looks like me?"

The waitress came up and stood in front of me silently, pen and notepad ready.

"Can I get six Beausoleil, six Fanny Bay to start, and I'll move on from there. Um" — I flipped the menu around, scanning, not wanting to waste her time — "you have a Chablis by the glass, yes? You can pick."

She nodded and walked away, and I fished into my purse for my book.

"You're an actress then. I know I've seen you somewhere."

"I'm a waitress. You've seen me every-where."

"You're going to eat all those oysters alone?" he asked, smiling.

"And then some." I sighed. It was a hazard of my job — or maybe it was my nature, maybe that's what they'd hired me for — that I was too hospitable to strangers. On street corners, in bars, in line, I felt a duty to entertain, as if I were clocked in. I didn't know how to be uninviting. I put my book up.

"What are you reading?"

"Okay." I folded my hands. "I know it's

quiet at your job. You sit in silence at your computer and when you do talk nobody listens to you, so I understand the need to impose yourself on whatever docile-looking female you find yourself in front of, but let me tell you about my job. It's loud. I lose my voice I talk so much. And people look at me, and they stop me, pretending they know me, they say, Let me guess, are you French, and I shake my head and smile and they say, Are you Swedish? And I shake my head and smile and so on. But this is my day off. I just want quiet. If you want someone to put up with you, may I suggest your waitress because that is *li-ter-ally* what you're paying her to do right now."

"So you're sassy, huh?"

"Sassy?" He was still looking at me, jocular, so fucking arrogant. "I have a boyfriend," I said finally.

The waitress came and poured me a heaping glass of Chablis. It was flabby but acceptable and I thanked her. When I looked back at him he was pulling out his wallet and signaling for his check. Did I believe that? That I was available to everyone unless I invoked Jake? By the time I finished my first dozen and ordered another, I was blissed out. I did wonder though, if people would ever start listening to me.

■ ■ ■ ■

"Yeah, it's your karaoke song, but I thought it was ironic."

"Ari, everything can't be ironic all the time or it would lose its luster."

"But you can't be *sincerely* into Britney Spears. Or I guess you can, but you shouldn't admit it."

I was curved on my bar stool, my posture long forgotten, my feet thrumming with the Saturday night-ness of it, the three discordant turns of it, and now a big stunning glass of Pouilly-Fuissé was sliding like glycerin down my throat. Ariel was closing up the coffee station, Will had just joined me, and the rest of the staff was trickling in, beaten up. Ariel was annoyed because she had fucked up too many times and Jake yelled at her.

"Can't my sincerity count for something? Isn't it a by-product of honesty? Of course, I'm not like, holding her up as a paragon of virtue."

"It's criminal that they let her reproduce."

"But, late at night, a little drunk, a little sentimental, I watch her old music videos online. The ones from the millennium. And I cry."

"Did you see the photos of her when she shaved her head?" Will asked. He had his shot of Fernet and a beer, it should have been normal, but he looked so much older than the last time we all sat at the bar for shift drink. I hadn't looked at him, really looked at him, in a long time. "She looked like a fucking demon."

"You cry to 'Hit Me Baby One More Time'?"

"Okay," I said, pulling up the Pouilly-Fuissé bottle from behind the bar and refilling my glass. "I can't explain it when everyone's attacking me. But she's around my age. And when I was growing up I thought, That's what a teenager is. I wanted my body to do whatever her body did. She's so common right? Attainable. She's not that beautiful, not that talented, but you can't stop watching her. That's why it's always the videos, she's not something to listen to, she's something to look at. She's so powerful, knowing you can't look away, and then this glint in her eye that she's just playing. That she's still a child and she's played this fantastic joke on you. And then, it's like, those eyes went vacant. She wasn't in on the joke anymore. Does that make sense? She *was* the joke — she didn't know."

"Oh my god, this is a tragedy for you?

413

That this bajillionaire, white-trash, drug-addict fuckup with zero moral compass has vacant eyes? She had choices, she's a grown woman now."

"But Ari," I said, straightening my spine, feeling angry and energized by the wine. "I don't feel like she let me down, I feel like I let her down. Like I was a part of this mob that cannibalized her. And you're right Will, she looks like a monster in those photos. I'm totally repulsed. And I feel nothing but guilt."

"I can't," Ariel said. She put her hands up. "This is what intelligent women think suffering is? I don't even know you."

"So fucking dramatic, Ari, I'm not crafting a rational argument for 'Why Britney Matters.' I'm telling you how I feel. Are you pissed at me about something?"

" 'Why Britney Matters' would make a great T-shirt."

"I'm just questioning your moral fiber —"

"My moral fiber? Because I grew up practicing Britney choreography in the mirror?"

"You know what she represents —"

"Stop." I finished my glass and when I put it on the bar the stem snapped in my hand. I felt a splinter of glass in my index finger and brushed it away. Everyone down the

414

bar looked at me.

"Come on, Fluff," said Nick, and glanced at Jake, who kept his eyes on the sink he was cleaning.

"Sorry," I said. I held the stemless bowl in my hand and lowered my voice. "She doesn't *represent* anything. That. Is. My. Point. She was a little girl. A human. It could have been any one of us."

"I call bullshit, Skip," Ariel said, "but that's a nice fairy tale." She grabbed an empty crate to stock and walked away. Will looked at me.

"I'm tired of her shit," I said. I collected the pieces of broken glass into the bowl.

"I still like Dave Matthews Band," he said. "That's kind of embarrassing."

"No," I said. "Nothing you do is ever embarrassing. You're not a girl."

I put on my coat, picked up my purse, the broken glass, and pushed off from the bar.

His room in a converted loft was painted a pithy blue and felt like a cave on a cold northern ocean. He had one roommate, a street artist called Swan whom I only ever saw in his robe as we passed each other on the way to the bathroom. He looked through me. In contrast to the rugs that covered the living space, the floors were bare in Jake's room. Tarnished linoleum and a mattress in the center.

He had a wall of windows that got only patches of daylight and looked out onto a fire escape and a boarded-up building.

Touches of an aesthete: the mattress was a Tempur-Pedic and covered in spotless linen sheets. He had collected wooden wine crates and built them into bookshelves. It was an entire wall of books. But unlike Simone, who had everything — sections of poetry, religion, psychology, gastronomy, rare editions of all the capital *L* literature, and a column of art books that cost more than a year of my rent — Jake had mystery novels and philosophy. That's it. Pulpy, sooty paperbacks and leather-bound collections of Nietzsche, Heidegger, Aquinas. Mutilated copies of Kierkegaard in their own stack. Some unreturned NYU library books: William James, Aristotle's *Metaphysics, The Odyssey.* A black book on anatomy that was large enough to be used as a side table. He'd planted an elegant lamp on the floor next to the bed. It was three feet high and had two hinges in the arm, the bulb set in a dome of cracked, wavy glass.

The walls were blank except for a small area above the shelves where he had stuck pins into black-and-white Polaroids. I saw the camera collection when I came in, hung on hooks in the main room with guitars and two bicycles. It took a while before I asked about the photos. There was a mountain range ("The Atlas," he said, "that's in Morocco"). Some grass on a beach ("Wellfleet," he said, "it's called beach heather"). A pile of broken bicycles stacked in a pyramid on a cobblestone street ("Berlin") and her: her hand, actually, blocking the camera, a huge starfish of a hand. The simplistic camera had flattened the image, capturing every line of her hand like it was an engraving. In the underexposed background, I could see — only if I unpinned it and put it under the light while he wasn't in the room — an exposed, stunning smile.

He was asleep and I was crouched on the floor next to the bed, touching the spines of the books. I reached and unpinned the photo. When I asked him about his tattoos, he rolled his eyes. When I asked him about those photos, he barely tolerated me. But the longer I knew him, the more I saw a system of symbols that must have had some sentimental value. If I asked him to tell me about Morocco or Berlin or Wellfleet, he would digress into the Berbers, or this German artist he knew who grew sculptures out of salt, and stories of gruesome deaths in whaling lore. It reminded me, the way he skirted around those photos, of something Simone had told me during one of our lessons: try not to have ideas about things, always aim for the thing itself. I still did not understand these four photographs, the *why* of them.

"How's the investigation going?" he said, startling me. His chest was bare, sheets covering his torso, and he lit a cigarette. I could barely make out his eyes. He didn't sound mad.

"When was this?" I asked. I took the photo of Simone into bed and lay down on my side, leaving inches between us. Still I was too shy to reach out to him first.

"I don't remember," he said. He reached out and pulled a piece of my hair, twisting it around his finger and I thought that we were sinking into the blue, the mercurial hours between night and morning.

"Why do you have it up?"

"It's a good photograph," he said. Ash fell into the bed and he brushed it away.

"Is it because you love her?"

"Of course I love her. But that's not a reason to hang a photograph."

"I think it's the reason to do a lot of things," I said carefully.

"You know," he said, putting his cigarette

out and pulling me onto his chest. "It's not like that with me and her. You know that."

He was distracting me, he knew his neck distracted me, his hands rolling over my hips distracted me.

"Was it ever like that?" I tried to see his eyes. "Simone's not ugly."

"Yeah, she's not bad."

"Jake . . ."

"No."

"How come?"

He grunted. His knees cracked as he got up. He squinted at his bookshelves, and pulled out a copy of *De Anima*. An old color photograph fell out. He picked it up and threw it on my lap and jumped over me back into bed. A woman with feathered, golden hair was smiling, holding a baby that looked sternly at the camera.

"That was my mom."

"Oh," I said. "They look alike."

"Tell me about it. Everyone has their shit. I have Simone. I know it's hard for people outside. But it's the way it is. She pretty much moved in when my mom died. She was only fifteen, but she raised me, in her fucking haphazard way."

I didn't react. I let it sink in and fit into the puzzle I had been putting together of Jake. Motherless. An entire city of orphans.

I looked back at the photo of Simone. What would I have given for someone to come and take care of me? I touched the baby's face in the photo. Those impenetrable, penetrating eyes. "You were unamused even then."

"It takes a lot to amuse me."

"How old were you when she died?"

"Eight."

"How? Did she die, I mean."

I reached out for him. I used my nails to trace his tattoos and his eyelids shut. I felt the bumps on his key tattoo and thought of Simone wrapped up in her sheets, alone in bed. I wondered what the funny story was, wondered why his tattoo looked like his skin had rejected it, and why hers looked like it had sunk in too far. His breathing deepened.

"That feels good," he said. I don't know how much time passed before he said, "Simone told me my mother was a mermaid, and that it had always been her destiny to return to the ocean because it was her real home, and someday she and I would return too. My mother swam away. I think I knew better, even then. I got older, I found the newspapers, I learned what drowning is, I know. But when you asked me that, my first thought was, she swam away and went home. Funny, right? The way we can't unlearn things even when we know they aren't true."

I rolled on top of him, torso on torso, stomachs breathing convex and concave into each other. I thought about saying a lot of grown-up things: I lost my mother too. I think it would have been harder if I'd ever had her, could remember her. I know that trust is impossible with other people, but mostly with yourself because nobody taught you how. I know that when you lose a parent a part of you is stuck there, in that moment of abandonment. I thought about saying, I know you're falling in love with me too. Instead I said, "I told someone you were my boyfriend."

"Who?"

"Some guy who was hitting on me."

"Who? Where?"

"Just some guy." I had never seen him jealous, or even prickly, except for maybe when we talked about Simone and Howard's friendship. But his tone had gone from laconic to lucid. "He was like, a fancy rich guy at Grand Central Oyster Bar. He wanted to have oysters with me."

"You went to Grand Central? Without me?"

"Are you mad or impressed?"

"Annoyed and intrigued. How did it feel?"

"It was totally magic in there, I was thinking we should go back —"

"No, how did it feel telling that guy that you had a boyfriend?"

How did it feel? It felt — possibly, potentially — true. "I don't know. I mean, he left me alone after I said that. So that was . . . good." We looked at each other. I kept resettling my head on the pillow. I was terrified. "How does that make you feel?"

"I'm not big on labels. You like labels?"

"I'm not trying to have a talk about labels."

"But I will say . . ." His hands found me again. He traced underneath my breasts. He traced the round part of my stomach. He traced my ribs. I watched his rings. "I don't want you to eat oysters with anyone else."

"Really?"

"Yes. I like it when you're mine." He pushed me onto my back and my head banged against the wall, hollow. "Now, can I ask you a serious question?"

"Yes," I said, breathless.

"What does a guy have to do to get a blow job in the morning?"

"It's the middle of the night."

"I see three rays of sun over there on the wall."

"That's the neon sign from across the street."

He kept my wrists above my head. He rubbed his chin and lips over my breasts. "Let's see," I said. "I got my eight and a half minutes of cuddling, I got the sensitive-man monologue, I got my bohemian 'nonlabel,' so I guess I just need . . ."

"What else for fuck's sake?"

"A sign," I said, catching his eyes. He made fun of my tendency to invoke fate. Simone made fun of me too, but said it was very old-world, which was a compliment when we talked about wine. Jake and I looked at each other, and I thought, How can you believe everything is accidental when we're together and it feels like this?

Suddenly, dozens of pigeons thrashed against the fire escape, their wings flashing the light, hammering the windows, and I said, I don't think it was out loud, Okay, I accept.

Will came down from the mezz whistling, and stopped to drop off the last round of silver at the bar. Nicky and I were down to one guest, Lisa Phillips, who was on that precipice between tears and laughter. Nicky, in retrospect, probably shouldn't have let her have six glasses of wine, but she was a notoriously exceptional tipper, and her husband, she'd just found out, was leaving her.

"If we can't let her get drunk here tonight, what good are we to anyone? She came here 'cause it's a safe place," Nicky said when I suggested that we should cut her off. So I watched. Her eyes grew unfocused, her mouth gaped, and even her cheekbones seemed to slump.

"Oh, Lisa," Will said to me. "Who's gonna pour her into a cab?"

"I think Nick is on it. It's really sad though. He left her, and the new one is like, my age. She won't even look at me."

"Yeah, it's always about you, huh."

"Hey!"

"Joking," he said, his hands up. Lisa's head dropped onto her arms, and Nicky pulled away the bread basket, then her silverware, then her balled-up napkin. She didn't move.

"Are you going for one?" Will asked.

"Are you cut already? Nick hasn't even gotten me the list yet."

"You want a quick treat for the close?" He touched the tip of his nose with two fingers.

"It's a bit early," I said. I polished the glasses and looked at him. "You're into it during your shift now too?"

"Tonight was an exception. Heather, Simone, Walter — it was diva night on the floor, they ran me fucking ragged."

"Isn't it always diva night?" I asked. "You look tired, babe."

He nodded. I thought of how selfish I had been with him, but couldn't summon the appropriate guilt. It was another instance of something that failed to hold its prescribed meaning. He was just a boy.

"I'll go for one. Save me a stool?"

Mrs. Glass, one of our elderly regulars, approached us. It wasn't my job, but she reached out with a coat check ticket. The hostess stand was empty.

I never had much use for the coat check room. Occasionally I pulled high chairs from there. The door was already ajar.

For a split second I didn't see them. I saw empty hangers, a vacuum cleaner, the mop bucket. But sitting in the corner was Misha, with her fake breasts affixed to her bird-boned Ukrainian thinness, and Howard, as dense and secure as another piece of furniture. Misha was perched on his lap sideways, her skirt fanning out over his knees and to the floor. She had her hand over her mouth, like she was afraid of making a noise, and he had one of his hands on the small of her back like he was a ventriloquist.

425

"Yes?" Howard asked calmly, quizzical eyes. Neither of them moved.

"Sorry," I said and ran out, shutting the door behind me. My head twitched around in a circle, trying to sense signs of movement in the restaurant, but I was unseen. I remembered Mrs. Glass.

I knocked on the coat check door. There was no sound inside.

"Misha," I whispered into the door. "I need Mrs. Glass's coat. I'm sliding the ticket under the door. She's waiting."

I ran back to the barista station.

Mrs. Glass was just perceptibly rocking. She inhabited another parallel time, where all faces, all places had been assimilated. Her days were on repeat. Nothing shocked her.

"People are so stupid," I said under my breath. She turned her ear toward me. "Your coat will be right out."

I mixed Cafiza with scalding water and threw the portafilters in. I grabbed the micro-wrench and very carefully unbolted the hot mesh screens from the group head. I dunked them. I kept my hands moving, but a jittery, unstable giggle hung around me.

"What the fuck, Fluff? You didn't last call. Maybe Lisa wanted one."

"Nicky," I said, my voice loaded, "it's too late for espresso."

Misha came out carrying a short fur coat and Mrs. Glass clapped her hands. They walked in tandem to the door and Mrs. Glass was off into the night. Nick came around the bar and took Lisa by the elbow. She tried to protest.

"Does he *know* what he did?" was all I could hear her say, and I shook my head, trying to get it out of my ears.

"I know," Nicky said, helping her off the stool, standing her up. He put on her coat so gently, and did the button at her neck. There were no tears, but her face was contorted, confused, as if someone were trying to wake her up. I thought about how her life didn't belong to her anymore. I thought of Simone. Nicky kept saying, "*I* know."

Howard came out. I wiped my face clean of expression. He walked behind the bar and pulled down two rocks glasses and grabbed a bottle of Macallan 18. I watched him pour it out, more intrigued than ever. He wore his power so lightly most days, as if he wasn't attached to it, but in fact, it informed every step he took. Highly, highly off-limits, this scotch. He slid it to me and I caught it. It burned my entire mouth.

Howard watched the street where Nicky was hailing a cab in his stripes and apron. He sighed. "It's a dangerous game, isn't it? The stories we tell ourselves."

IV

"Pick up!"

"Picking up," Ariel sang out. I giggled in line behind her. Will elbowed me to shut up and I laughed harder. We were playing Go Fish. Do you have any gin? Go Fish! Do you have any Hitachino White Ale? Go Fish! The person who was without had to find and deliver it — stealthily — to the others. I had just fished Sancerre from the white wine bucket. It was still early in the night, the first tickets rolling lazily through the printer, the servers dawdling in the hutch, all waters topped off. Chef demonstrated the specials on the line, while Scott set up the expediting station. A tipsy, languorous night with my friends stretched out in front of me.

"Order in — soigné, it's Sid's table," Scott yelled out. "So 23, order fire two tartares, order fire sformato, order fire foie." He inspected plates in the window. "Pick up,

13, asparagus, 1, Gruyère 2, I'll take a follow on the oysters."

"Hubba, hubba," I said. "Picking up."

A new ticket printed and Scott glanced at
it while holding out the asparagus special
toward me. The poached egg on top jiggled.
He kept staring at the ticket.

"Piiiiiicking up," I said again, and reached
my arms out farther to grab the plate. He
dropped it to the counter and the egg
slipped off. Chef looked up sharply.

Scott, drained of color, said, "The health
department's here."

Chef set down his knife and in the quiet-
est and most controlled of voices said,
"Nobody. Touch. The. Fridges."

The kitchen detonated. People ran. Chef
flew up the stairs. From all over the kitchen
things went soaring into the garbage: half a
leg of prosciutto and the ropes of sausages
hanging by the butcher station. Bar mops
dropped into the trash like streamers.
Anything that had been out, in the process
of being chopped or even salted, went into
the trash. Potatoes that were being sliced
for fries, breakfast radishes that were being
cleaned, sauces that were being divided into
labeled quarts. Interns ran up from the
basement with brooms and swept madly
from the corners, porters tied off the trash

bags, the line cooks pulled down pint containers from shelves above their stations — inside were kits with bandanas, thermometers, pencil-thin flashlights.

I had never seen such precise chaos in my life, the fear animating everyone. Zoe talked about a two-minute drill, but nobody had trained me on it. I assumed it was above my pay grade. Ariel pulled all the cutting boards off the tables and I grabbed her.

"What the fuck do I do?"

She looked me up and down and pulled the bar mops hanging from my apron string and threw them away. She held my hands and said, "You're going to run the food. Just like you were doing a minute ago. And when you get in the dining room, you smile extra hard, and when you see a man holding a flashlight and a clipboard, you make sure he sees how pretty and happy you are. Don't open the fridges, we need stable temperatures. Don't touch any food, not even a lemon or a straw at the bar. That's it."

I nodded. She threw the cutting boards into the dish station and pulled all of the servers' water glasses. Whatever hair-tingling exhilaration I'd been on my way to churned in my stomach. I thought about hiding in the bathroom. Pretending I had to pee and it couldn't wait, and I would sit in there

431

until the whole inspection was over, and I would at least know I didn't fuck anything up. But I couldn't. My adrenaline kicked into overdrive but then something else did too. My training.

"Picking up," I yelled. Scott was on his knees shining a flashlight under a lowboy and sweeping with a hand broom. When he heard me he stood up and looked at the pass. All the plates were still there. He looked at me, then at the plates again. He moved the poached egg to the top of the asparagus. It had been barely two minutes.

"Pick up?" he asked.

"Picking up," I sang out, my hands unwrapped, open like I was receiving a blessing.

What was the Owner banking on? His reputation? The endurance of tacit understandings from the nineties, a sort of honor among thieves? It was hard to believe that this plebeian man in a dusty jacket had any sort of power over us, that he could cause panic in the kitchen or halt anyone from getting their calamari. He went to the bar first, and I smiled to myself as Jake stubbornly stood his ground, the inspector too large to move effortlessly back there, saying, Excuse me, and turning the coldwater faucet on, saying, Excuse me, turning the hot-water faucet on.

Will said, "That's the essence of his evil. See how quiet he is?"

He was right. The inspector didn't exclaim, didn't interact. He seemed to have the most boring job I could imagine — his weapon was a digital thermometer. He opened a refrigerator door, marked a temperature. He poked into our plastic-wrapped items, and marked another temperature. He fondled the gaskets on the fridges and prodded the cracks in the ones that hadn't been replaced yet. He lumbered down to the floor with a flashlight, nodded as he got back up. He checked the expiration dates on every single gallon of milk, every stick of butter. Looked inside every bulk dry-goods container. He went through his faucet drill at every sink, pumped all the soaps, which were full. He seemed to be moving on an invisible grid, and so I kept forgetting about him. I saw him come out of the walk-in and I thought, That guy's still here?

I had seen my share of disgusting shit, but I was also positive we were the cleanest restaurant near the park. There were stories about the house-pet-sized rats at the places around us, or the restaurants where raw sewage backed up from the street when it rained. Sure, I cut some corners on my side work, but I watched the porters bleach out the darkest corners of the kitchen, and I watched the overnight guys arrive as I was leaving every night. Chef put the fear of God into his crew. I would have eaten off the floor without a moment's hesitation. If the inspector had paused at any table, our virtue would have been self-evident: we put out beautiful food.

We were turning, moving delicately on tiptoe. Will, Ariel, and I weren't getting drunk anymore, and Scott didn't stop sweating, but it was just another service. Howard and Chef took the inspector up to the mezz and sat him at a table, where he wrote a report.

I was dropping off a rack of glasses at the service bar and batting my eyes at Jake when I saw him look past me, which he didn't really do anymore. I turned. Howard was coming down the stairs on his cell phone. It was a fracture — managers never had phones on the floor. No one did. Howard went straight to Simone and pulled her into the back hutch. They spoke with their heads bowed. Her hand went to her chest and she nodded. When I went back into the kitchen it was silent, not like a church, like a graveyard.

Howard came in behind me and announced, "We are ending service for this evening."

"Now?" I asked. No one responded.

"If anyone has questions be vague but firm. We are voluntarily closing for repairs. We will see them all in a few days. I will touch all the tables. Mandatory all-staff meeting in one hour."

We were in a very old building: it was the foundation, the layout, pipes, ceilings, and walls that weren't completely up to the new codes. It felt fundamentally wrong that we could be operative one second and closed the next because of architecture. No one mentioned pests, or rodents, or hygiene — only I seemed to be thinking of the fruit flies, the cockroaches, the foreboding empty mousetraps, infestation humming in the walls, down in the sewers, behind every plaster and asphalt coating of the city. Architecture was definitely an easier — cleaner — problem, but I wondered if the inspector had found the drain under the bar sink, or if he knew that I was too scared to fully clean the espresso machine.

The hostesses were on the phone with our sister restaurants, securing tables for the remaining reservations and the people who had barely started eating. All checks were comp'ed. Pastry made to-go boxes of cookies and I delivered them in little stamped paper bags. Simone and Jake stood at the service bar, whispering, not looking at each other, but holding each other in that magnetic exclusivity. I kept waiting for an outburst from anyone — one of the guests, a server, but everyone moved mutely around the room.

Most of the guests had assumptions about what was happening — they were the regulars, who knew what the Department of Health was, and being New Yorkers, operated on a communal subtext that let them observe life unsurprised. They were put out but flexible. It was the tourists who seemed most perplexed. Howard guided them each step of the way.

The inspector sat at bar 1 as the guests shuffled past. He stared placidly at a midpoint on the wall. Mr. Clausen, old enough to be the inspector's father, rapped on the bar until the inspector met his eyes and said, "This is appalling. You're as punitive and pointless as the damn meter maid."

We held the door open and the air was supple. It may have been the first true day of spring.

■ ■ ■ ■

We sat in the empty dining room, streetlight laminating the windows. An oxidized edge in light that came from routine being disrupted beyond repair. The Owner was all smooth surfaces when he strode in and shook the inspector's hand. I was still waiting for the explosion — a punch, a copper pan flying, a gasp. When the Owner looked out at us, I knew that would never happen.

"First of all," he said, putting his hands together, pulling our focus to him, "I want to thank you all for your dedication and patience tonight. What has happened here is not a reflection of how hard you work, but a reflection of an outdated system, a reflection of an outdated structure. This is an old building, an old restaurant. And we are proud of that. But in keeping up with the DOH, we have a lot working against us. We *still* keep the cleanest restaurant below Twenty-Third Street. And that's a testament to you — to Chef, to Howard. I want to apologize for this upheaval. A lot of you don't know what exactly I do. I sit at a desk in corporate across the street, I give interviews, my photo is in the paper, I open new restaurants. But my only real function here

— and this has been from day one — is to make sure that you guys can do your jobs perfectly. That's all I do. I put structures in place so that you — the blood and guts and heart of this restaurant — can shine. So you can excel. Today I've let you down and I'm sorry."

He put his head down. When he raised his head again, he acknowledged each of us as his equals. "We expect to be closed for three days tops while we do some restructuring in the basement and behind the bar. We will reach out to the regulars and explain. Each of you will be compensated if you were scheduled to work. . . ."

He went on. I felt pinned to my chair. So it was true. I glanced at Simone and her cheeks were wet, Jake standing guard behind her. For the first time in twenty-some years, the restaurant was closing.

I have forgotten exactly what Howard sent me up there to retrieve. I want to say a blue binder containing checklists, phone numbers, policies.

I remember climbing the mezz stairs with a sense of purpose and privilege. I remember that I had on my gold hoop earrings. I remember pushing papers to one side of the desk. And I remember her handwriting. I had seen it nightly — on her dupe pad when she took orders, on the whiteboards marking the counts on specials and wine, in the margins of the wine notes we kept in a folder behind the bar. The extravagant script, cursive that looked engraved, slanting deeply to the left as if it had been lured across the page.

I saw "Simone," I saw "Jake," I saw "sabbatical," "France," and "month of June."

I absorbed the words but not their meaning. I picked up the paper. It slipped out of my hands. My finger pads couldn't grip it, my nails couldn't get the edges up. I heard breathing but I couldn't get any air. Valves shut in me, first behind my eyes, then in my throat, then in my chest, then in my stomach.

This is what happens when the body anticipates a wound. It steels itself. A pliable mind twists vainly to avoid logic, all judgments, all conclusions, if only for a few seconds longer.

It was a Vacation Request Form, the kind of dreary printout that Zoe spent all her hours creating and filing. It was in the handbook: all vacation requests had to be approved by Howard at least a month out. The restaurant was so carefully staffed that it couldn't accommodate spontaneous absences — every service was designed around all the servers' strengths and weaknesses. To take an extended vacation required a radical reworking of the schedule. But Howard liked to retain his staff and hold their jobs for them. He encouraged us to take what he called sabbaticals.

My mind caught up: Simone was requesting a sabbatical to France for the entire month of June and she was requesting it for her and Jake. It had been given to Howard three days before my birthday dinner. I saw the tendrils of smoke off the candles when I blew them out, I saw dozens of burning plates in the pass, rushed drinks on the bar, subway rides, Jake's sleeping face, Simone's satisfied face — the weeks since that night reeled in front of me. I sat down in Howard's chair. The request had been approved two days ago. When I tried to remember what I was doing two days ago it was like running my face into a wall.

I told myself to be calm, gather my information, hold very still. Maybe it was a mistake. Maybe I had misunderstood.

"Hey," I said, touching Simone on the shoulder as I passed to my locker. "Can I talk to you?"

"I'm changing," she said distantly. Her

mascara leached into the lines around her eyes. The changing room was crowded, the whole herd of us in there at once. People were talking about going to Old Town for burgers since it was still early. Then everyone would head to Park Bar. My sense of hearing was off, I heard the overlapping tenors of voices I knew so well, but at a dim, fuzzy volume. Overriding all of it was the ringing of the lightbulbs. I looked at Simone. She was holding her stripes to her chest over her bra and I inadvertently looked for her tattoo, like it was going to explain something, like it was a message written to me that I had missed. And it was. They were marked, weren't they? I reached for my locker to steady myself.

Whenever I'd asked him about that key: "It's nothing, it's not the key to anything, a tattoo is just a tattoo, only as permanent as the body." How I swooned when he spoke to me in that vaguely Buddhist, vaguely nihilist accent. In reality it was a shitty tattoo that was a warning to anyone who looked at them that they were not available.

I kept blinking, my lashes sticking together, my eyes dusty. "Simone, can I borrow your makeup? I forgot my things."

I stood in line behind Heather in the mirror, thinking about setting fire to the restaurant. So what? I asked my reflection. It's just a month in France. It's just matching tattoos. It's just that they grew up together. How many times had I used the word *just* to explain away something that so clearly needed my attention? My eyes said, Stop. This *is* something.

Everything I had ever learned about the two of them bound them more securely, squeezing out all the air, all the light. Why was I the last one to learn anything, and why when I thought I learned something did the bottom drop out of it?

Simone observed me in the mirror. She was attuned to my shifts in mood. No, she was never blind. I put on mascara. I took out her lipstick and it smelled like roses and plastic and was cold when I dragged it into place. My reflection said to her reflection, Yes, I make you look old.

I handed her the cosmetics bag.

"Can I talk to you?" I asked again.

"Can it wait?" She walked away without waiting for my response.

"No," I whispered.

The key, the key, a month, a month. Some white-trash tattoo parlor. He had probably been underage and she had probably been his consenting adult. I wondered how she covered her breasts while the needle hit her, whether she and Jake had locked eyes or if he'd turned politely away. A series of men touching it on her and asking, What's this about? She would say, It's nothing. And a series of women all over his body, ending with my idiotic face, asking, Why a key? Never an answer, never a clue.

When was that? Where were you? The questions they didn't tolerate. The two of them imprecise and evasive. I saw him living in her apartment, hitting his head on the ceiling when he rose from the bed in that lofted space, reworking the electrical wires. I saw her Miami mug and his Miami magnet, this phantom Morocco they both mentioned, the two of them in every corner of this restaurant, watching me with reserve, which isn't something, Tess, some things are nothing, but suddenly not these things.

And now this: the two of them sitting next to each other on a plane, the way she would drowsily drop her head onto his shoulder when the plane took off, thirty cafés au lait and croissants, thirty bistros, thirty languorous afternoons, thirty caves du vin, and Simone's French smothering the rooms they would stay in. My visions of our June vanished. I would long for the two of them to give the days significance, to show me how far I'd come, to reflect my progress, and they would be gone. I would wake on his birthday, and on my anniversary of arriving, alone. These weren't masochistic daydreams, this was the reality I would have to live through.

Simone's voice came back to me, but now it also sounded like my voice, a maxim she had pronounced during my endless, deranged training: "You need to do more than keep an eye out for incongruity. You have a blind spot for the unraveling whole."

The dining room was wrong, misshapen, crude. Howard was texting in the corner where the tables were unmade and pushed together. The restaurant would sit, an empty space anchored in me no matter where I went or what I did.

Jake was at the bar in street clothes. He and Nicky were counting out the drawers for Howard to put in the safe. Nicky said something and Jake laughed. Nonchalantly. And didn't he do everything nonchalantly — he mixed a drink, he kept his sunglasses on indoors, he flipped a knife out of his pocket, he got his stripes wet when he cleaned the sinks, he put on a record, he ordered for you, he ordered you, took down his guitar, held your lips between his teeth like he had been doing it for years, with no

444

effort, with nothing at stake.

"Jake." I leaned on the bar, my voice sedate. "Are you going to Old Town? I heard that's where everyone is going."

"I'll meet up with you later." He didn't turn around. He didn't even stop counting.

"Okay. But I might be busy later. Do you want to make a plan?"

Nicky looked between us. The bills flew through Jake's hands.

"I'll meet you at Park Bar."

"When? Aren't you going to eat? Everyone is going to eat."

"I'm walking Simone home. I'll probably eat with her. I'll meet up with you later?" He didn't even glance backward. I wadded up a bar napkin and threw it at the back of his head.

"You can at least turn around when you speak to me."

"What the fuck is wrong with you?" His eyes had gone lethal.

"Hey, hey," Nicky said. I was ready to climb on the bar and slap him. "Jake, you wanna step outside for a minute? Fluff, be quick, we've still got shit to do."

Outside the air had lost its potential. I crossed my arms over myself defensively.

"I'm sorry," I said. "But you were being rude."

445

His nostrils flared. The wind battered us. I tried again.

"I'm sorry I threw that. But I need to talk to you."

"Tess, I will see you at Park Bar. I've got to walk Simone home. You don't know her like I do."

"No one knows her like you do!"

"What's wrong with you?"

"Me? No, it's what's wrong with you guys. Simone is a grown woman, Jake. Maybe she could occasionally walk herself home, or cope with some difficulty without you."

"Do you not notice that Simone is . . ." He grunted hesitantly. "Overinvested in this restaurant?"

"She's overinvested in a lot of things, Jake."

"I don't have time for this shit, this is a real situation."

"A real situation? It's like free vacation! You love vacation right? We're going to take a vacation? You and me, no parents, no chaperones?"

"You're a fucking child. You know the Owner closed down one of his spaces in Madison Square Park? Do you have any awareness of the industry you work in, of how your paychecks work? You think this is great for business? What do you think

446

Simone will do if this place really shuts down? Where would she go?"

"Where would *I* go, Jake?" Simone could go anywhere, I wanted to say. Then I thought of her being trained in some generic, tableclothed space and I knew what he meant. She had overqualified herself for her own line of work. The thought of her in another uniform was offensive.

"Simone and I can't just put on a skirt and work at Blue Water, Balthazar, Babbo. Make half the money for double the hours, let a bunch of slimy dudes press up against us in the hutch. I know you'll be all right with that. Or maybe you'll finally become a Bedford Avenue barista, your dream —"

"Fuck you!" I screamed. "Your cruelty doesn't turn me on anymore." Suddenly he had me by my shoulders squeezing me, crushing me. I pushed him away and yelled, "I know you're going to France with her."

"So?" he said. He did not miss a fucking beat. He even shrugged his shoulders.

So. It all came down to this insulting, one-word question.

I had been holding on to the hope that Simone was delusional. After all, it wasn't his handwriting. But it was me: I was delusional.

At least he was consistent — his enunciation, his expression said that it was nothing. I was too sensitive, dramatic, hysterical. His certainty always disabled my thoughts, like in this moment when I searched for my words, for my anger, and found a void where my reason had been. Something about how Simone was trying to separate us? Something about how he should be going to Europe with me? The only thing that came to me was, "It's not right."

The wind came up again like a knife in my back and I was disoriented, Sixteenth Street felt foreign.

"We can talk," he said, assessing me. "I will see you later."

I wanted to say, No, I can't wait, but I nodded. He kissed me, unexpectedly, on the lips. We had never touched at work. Never hugged, never held hands under the table at family meal. I was more affectionate with Papi the dishwasher than I was with Jake. He thought it would pacify me, but it was so pedestrian. A trinket offered in place of jewels. God, how many times I had accepted that.

"Jake," I said. "You know that key tattoo you have?"

"Are you serious?"

"Okay, okay. Just please find me tonight?"

"I promise." He held my shoulders and

448

inspected my face. Make it easy, I begged him with my eyes. Fix it. He said, "Take that shit off your lips. You look like a clown."

"Where you from?" Carlos asked me while I smoked outside Park Bar, all my joints soldered together, my body swaying in one monolithic piece. I had a blundering, lost feeling, as if I had been digging tunnels, not knowing if I was going up or down, only that I had no other option but to keep going. My night had gone terribly astray.

I checked my phone again. No texts, just the time. Six hours of drinking, the last four of them at Park Bar. I was accidentally too high, waiting for him, waiting for him. I was sore from the bolts of cocaine flexing my muscles, I was smoking, my nose, throat, and ears burning, he's not coming, he's not coming. Too high for talking, my thoughts elbowing each other out of the way, crowding to the front, to a spot on my forehead I kept touching to try and still them. I understood that the boxers in the painting were a metaphor for consciousness, the way the mind divides, combats, and destroys itself.

Carlos was in front of me, gleaming, his shoes shined, his hair slicked with pomade, his diamond earrings, which he insisted were real. They were his grandmother's in the Dominican Republic, they were on loan because he was her favorite. He and I had grown closer since I'd sold him my car for $675. It was the exact amount I owed the city in overdue parking tickets. I was pretty sure he'd flipped the car for more money, but I got discounts on my bags so it seemed a fair deal.

"Where are you from again?" he asked.

"Have you seen Jake?"

"Which one is Jake?"

"The bartender. Always looks homeless. Crazy eyes."

"Yeah, yeah, your bartender over there. The one that used to hook up with Vanessa."

"Ha," I said. "Yeah, yep, that's Jake. Funny you say that because I was just thinking about the women Jake has fucked and I was thinking we should form a band or something, maybe a book club. Maybe all go on a vacation even."

He held his hands up. "I know nothing. I don't even know when that was."

"Of course, no one *knows* anything, let's not get involved, let's not have a real conversation with dates and facts and names and places because we might be held accountable and that, *that,* would be a catastrophe for some of us, we would have to remove our sunglasses, or lipstick, whatever, the apparatus, and we would have a proper trial, with judges and evidence and verdicts, and some of us would be clean and some of us would be dirty."

"You're pretty up there, huh?" He whistled and it sounded like *cuckoo*.

"I'm done, I'm fine. I can wait it out."

"You want something to help?"

"I don't do hard stuff. Like heroin, I don't do heroin."

"Yeah, I know, none of you rich kids do heroin." He winked at me.

"Why would we when you keep us up to our eyeballs in shitty coke? Don't fucking wink at me."

"Girl, you are mouthy tonight!" He smiled and handed me another cigarette. I hadn't realized I was gripping the leftover filter, pinching it. "I like it, you got your teeth bared and shit. I was talking about Xanax, niña, shit your mama gave you when you got nervous about the SATs. I never seen you so tense."

"My mother never did that," I said. My bones were sharp, my skin wasn't thick enough to hold them, but I enjoyed Carlos and his kitschy moves. Thank god for Carlos. "I will take a Xanax, actually. How much?"

"First time's always free, niña."

"Oh Jesus, you're really going to make me feel filthy about this aren't you? What is that? It doesn't look the same."

"It's a Xanibar. Just take a small piece. Should last you a few days depending on what kind of fiesta you're on."

"I'm not on a fucking fiesta, I'm in fucking hell."

"Still works the same."

"My friends will kill you if I die."

I broke off a piece and chewed it up. I grabbed someone else's fairly full beer from inside the open window and chased it. We looked back through the windows. Will, Ariel, Sasha, Parker, Heather, Terry, Vivian — all listening to Nicky hold court on one of his rare forays to Park Bar. I couldn't face him like this, with my clenched, throbbing molars, my twitching hands. Everyone was there — except Jake and Simone, of course — telling and retelling the story of the inspection, speculating about what had really happened, what would happen. Normally I excelled in that gratifying, circular talk, hours slipping by while we filled space with drinking and reinforcing the same stories, never coming up with different endings.

"I think your friends forgot about you," Carlos said.

"You think that. But I'm their pet. Their puppy. They need me to follow them around." I ran my tongue over my lips and they were serrated. I tasted blood, I thought of him. "Actually we don't even have to call them my friends. Let's call them the people I spend time with. Or actually — this is funny — let's call them my coworkers. It's *just* dinner!"

"I heard about your place. That's really fucking crazy. If we got shut down —"

"We didn't, we voluntarily closed to perform repairs —"

"Steve would have our throats. I mean it, I would be sprinting out the door, never look back."

"The Owner came by."

"Oh shit — who got fired?"

"No one." I thought back to the reverence, the hush, and it was as if I saw him pulling his hands together to calm us and I calmed. "He thinks we're wonderful."

Carlos shook his head. "You drank the Kool-Aid, huh?"

I nodded. Everything. Felt. Better. "I love the Kool-Aid."

I leaned against the windowsill and sipped my beer. The weather was schizophrenic, appealing one minute, aggressive the next, frenetic, like water breaking from a dam.

"Ohio," I said. "Thank you for asking."

"I got cousins there."

"You don't."

"Ay, niña, I got cousins everywhere. Speaking of, one of them is picking me up, we got errands. But he's holding some grade-A shit."

"Enticing. But I think I'm finally becoming happy. I think I mastered life, right here on this windowsill. I don't want to move too much."

"You sure? Where you meeting your man? We could drop you."

"My man?"

Jake was quicksand. Hours ago my plan had been to talk to him rationally, he had promised. Maybe he hadn't bought the tickets yet, maybe he wouldn't go for the whole month, maybe I could meet them. But at that moment I didn't want him. The man I was totally and completely devoted to was going away with another woman, and I was so fucking blind and tolerant that they thought I wouldn't have a shred of feeling about it. Or perhaps they simply didn't care. Finally — facts not colored by the weather or the voices and visions in my head. I didn't want anything: not a drink, not a line, not a snack, I didn't even want to fidget. It was the freest I'd felt in months.

The city does sleep, the windows darken and the streets vacate. New York dreams us. Wild, somnambulistic creatures, we move unhurried toward our own disappearance at dawn.

"Tess, that's not your beer." Will's voice was far away. He was inside the plush noise of the bar and holding a spotless beer in his hand.

"I can't hear you," I said. I reached my hand out to touch the glass between us. I touched his face instead.

"Are you okay?" He grabbed my hand. The day rushed back to me. I fell backward, slapping the ground.

"I'm fine." Will's hands, Carlos's hands, lifting me. "No more man hands."

"Come inside," Will said. I squirmed but his hand was stuck on my back.

"Carlos, are you going east?"

"You're not going with him," Will said, and now his hand was stuck to my shoulder. "Are you crazy? You can't get into a car with a drug dealer."

"Don't be racist Will, now please leave me alone. I'm going east."

"Donde, niña?"

"Ninth between First and A." As I said it a black car with tinted windows pulled up. The front window rolled down when Carlos approached. I pulled my purse out of the bar through the window and put my beer inside it.

"Hi Carlos's cousin," I yelled out. "Simone's house, please." I opened the door and climbed over the seats with astonishing grace.

V

Throwing up mostly water. Throwing up curds in mostly water. Throwing up in your lap. Throwing up in your purse. Men yelling. Red and green blistered lights out the window. Gravitational forces on you instead of a seat belt. Your face smashing into the seat back. You tried to hold on but you were thrown like a doll.

To their credit, I was dropped off exactly where I asked to be and given a bump of grade-A shit. The front of my shirt was slick. The sidewalk felt dented. When I tried to stand up out of the car, my knees caved.

"Don't blame yourself, Carlos," I said. I felt in control as I consoled him. "I made some bad choices, you are not to blame."

Carlos and his cousin sped off sharply, squealing, and I leaned against a wall. I watched a couple walk out of their way to distance themselves from me and I laughed at how bad my shirt smelled. I dug into my purse and it was soaking wet. I shook beer off my phone and it miraculously clicked on.

Hi, Simone, I texted. It's Tess.
Hi!!!
You said we could talk.
I'm outside actually. If that's ok.
I am going to ring the bell probably cause you're not responding.
Oh look whose bike I see!
Hi Jake!!!
Maybe you can just ask him to talk to me, cause I know he's there.
I'm sorry. I know it's late for you. You're old.
I'm not mad about France. No big d.
We got in a stupid fight, but it wasn't that much.
Simone!!!
I'm going to ring the bell again, I'm warning you.
Ok, no one is answering, I'm going home.
Tell Jake I'm sorry and I hate him, whatever order you want.
I'm sorry that was me again, I know you're home.
I see his motherfucking bike.
France hurts my feelings.

I'm leaving.
Also, I'm sorry the restaurant closed. I care
 a lot. Too.
Simone, if you're good at this job, what
 exactly are you good at?

I remember the sickly green Heineken light
in the window of Sophie's. I remember the
bathroom, my hand slipping every time I
tried to cut a line. I remember my eyes in
the mirror. I remember the coke spilling
into the sink. I remember the back of my
thigh being pinched between the trash can
and the wall when I was pushed against it. I
remember someone's tongue, not being able
to breathe. I remember my cheek on exfoli-
ated concrete. The rest is a blessed darkness.

The first time I woke up was a false alarm.
My skin registered clothing, and I reached
into my jeans pocket where I kept pills and
broke off another piece of the Xanibar and
swallowed it. There was a glass of water next
to the bed, but I didn't surface enough to
reach for it.
    When I woke up again it was to a sunset I
didn't deserve. Not just me, no one could
deserve it except newborns, the untar-
nished, the language-less. I stayed perfectly
still and the ceiling was violet. I searched

459

myself for signs of pain, for the inevitable headache. All seemed calm. I took a bigger breath, preparing my body to sit up. My ceiling pinked and blushed. The windows were wide open. The wind had wrecked every book, shirt, or slip of paper. It was freezing.

I moved my neck first, craned it, looking down. My jeans were on. My Converse were off, but my ankle socks were on, evidence of an outside presence. I didn't remember getting to my bed or to my apartment. I sat up a bit more.

From my tailbone the shame started and with it came prongs of pain up my spine until it hit the base of my skull. I looked reluctantly at my shirt and moaned. The vomit had dried but the blood was still damp in spots on my breasts and at the collar. It had already dried and rusted out on the pillowcases. I touched my nose and flakes of blood came back on my fingers. There was a note safety-pinned to my shirt: "Please text me so I know you're alive, Your Roommate, Jesse." I patted the bed for my phone. It was dead and there were beer droplets inside the screen. Movement made me ill. I ran to the bathroom, turned on the shower, and threw up. There wasn't much of anything left. Just extraordinarily gratifying dry heaves. My first real thought was, Shit, what time am I in today?

If I am qualified to give advice on anything, it is probably a hangover. Advil, marijuana, and greasy breakfast sandwiches from the bodegas *do not* work. Don't listen to chefs — they will have you drinking five-day-old beef stock or reheated menudo or pickle brine or wolfing down bags of White Castle burgers at five a.m. Mistakes, all of them.

Xanax, Vicodin, or their opiate/Benzedrine cousins, Gatorade, Tums, and beer *do* work. *Dirty Dancing, The Princess Bride, Clueless.* They work. Bagels sometimes work, but not with anything on them besides cream cheese. You think you want lox, but you don't. You think you want bacon, but you don't. Salt will promote your headache. You think you want Ritalin, Adderall, meth, any kind of speed. You don't. You're fucked for at least six hours, so the goal is to numb out.

Toast works. Before you leave for your night out, leave yourself bread, a big bottle of your preferred color of Gatorade, a handful of prescription drugs, and a note with an emergency contact. I had none of these things.

■ ■ ■ ■

Somewhere in the middle of the night, as I watched old DVDs of *Sex and the City* on my beaten-up laptop, my lids barely qualifying as open, my hangover transitioned into a fever. I was irritated that my computer screen was shaking, until I realized that it was on my stomach — I was so hot that I kept throwing off my sheets, my clothes, but the shaking was me, shivering.

Initially my sheets were stiff, my skin brittle. I touched my forehead and the sweat released. My pillows were wet. Then the heat rose again, chasing me. I couldn't catch my breath. I searched the apartment but there wasn't anything, not even Advil.

I put my winter coat over my pajamas and hid my head under a wool cap. I thought of Mrs. Neely when I was on the stairs, clutching the railing, talking to myself. It wasn't that cold when I got outside. Sweat was running down my sides and from my hairline. The bodega was two doors away, but I couldn't get there standing up straight.

"It's you!" the Pakistani owner said.

"Hello." I held myself in the door frame. He and I had developed a fondness for each other over the months.

"You remember me last night?" He came out from behind the bulletproof glass.

"No, sir, I do not."

"You need to be more careful. It's not safe for young girls like you."

"I'm sick, sir."

"You're all red in the face."

"Yes, I'm sick." I rolled through a wave of nausea. "I need medicine."

"You need rest. You can't live like this."

"I have no intention of living like this much longer." He didn't understand me. "I will rest, I promise, I promise."

My vision faded, browning. I got scared and sat down on a stack of *New York Times.* I heard myself making sounds like crying, but there were no tears on my face, just sweat at my temples, behind my ears. He had his hand on my back.

"Can I call someone?"

"Please, I just need medicine. I have a fever and I'm alone. I need stuff like what a mom would get."

He called out into the back and his wife came out. She looked at me like I was a criminal. He talked to her in another language and I took pauses between each breath, reassuring myself that I was still alive. The wife made her way around the store: Advil, water, a box of saltines, two apples, tea, a can of lentil soup. She pulled down a bottle of liquid NyQuil, assessed me, and put it back. She came over with the individually packaged capsules instead.

"Only two," she said.

"Your girls are good girls. He's so proud of them," I said to her. He had shown me photos of them many times. The eldest was in high school in Queens, applying to Ivy League colleges. I couldn't take her pity when she handed me the bag of items with no charge. I accepted because I hadn't brought my wallet.

"I'm sorry," I said. "There's no excuse."

I don't know how long it took me to get home. I thought about falling down and waiting for the police to come and take me to the hospital. I thought about screaming out, Someone please take care of me. I pressed against a rolled-down steel gate, spitting onto the concrete. The streets were empty. It was just me. So I said, Fuck, it's just you. I climbed the stairs cursing, dry heaving. I made the mint tea they had given me. I wrapped an ice pack in paper towels and put it on my forehead and when it got warm I put it back in the freezer. I shook, I sweat, I cried, I held myself, I mumbled in and out of sleep. It went on like that, more or less, for two days.

■ ■ ■ ■

Do you know what I was, how I lived? That refrain ran through my head as I took the train into work. I was a gaunt reflection in the spotty windows, but possessed of a sparkling sense of clarity. That was a line from a poem I couldn't remember. I don't know when I'd started quoting poems. I don't know when I'd started ignoring the flowers as I walked through the Greenmarket.

I stopped in front of the large window on Sixteenth Street, wanting to see if it looked different. Flower-Girl was conducting her botanic orchestra and behind her they were pulling down the chairs. The servers were congregated at the end of the bar, where Parker was making espressos. How much I had taken for granted: being excited to walk through the door every day, making rounds to say hello to everyone, even in the days when no one responded. Flower-Girl singled out a branch of lilac. I had smelled them since I'd come up from the train: cloying, heavy, human — but unripe, like a cold-climate Sauvignon Blanc. That was the full circle, wasn't it? Learn how to identify the flowers and the fruits so I could talk about

465

the wine. Learn how to smell the wine so I could talk about the flowers. Had I learned anything besides endless reference points? What did I know about the thing itself? Wasn't it spring? Hadn't the trees shaken out their greens to applause? Isn't this what you dreamed of, Tess, when you got in your car and drove? Didn't you run away to find a world worth falling in love with, saying you wouldn't care if it loved you back?

The lilacs smelled like brevity. They knew how to arrive, and how to exit.

"Everyone was worried," Ariel said.

"I came by and rang the buzzer," Will said.

"I told them we speed-dial police if you don't show today," Sasha said.

Whatever changes they had made to the restaurant were barely noticeable. We did have new sinks behind the bar. It was a lunch shift and I didn't talk much. My head was still in the isolation of my rancid bedroom. I was unshakable.

They did not arrive together, though I suppose they never did. Simone came in first. I went to the locker room and sat on a chair in the corner. I had no plan, but when she came in she was not surprised to see me. We were following a script that I hadn't seen yet.

"I'm relieved you're all right," she said.

"I'm alive."

She fiddled with her locker combination. I saw her go through it twice.

"I did not receive your texts until much later," she said, maybe the first time in her life she had been the one to break a silence. "I don't check my phone at that hour."

"Of course."

"I was very worried."

"Of course. I could tell."

"I texted you back."

"My phone is broken."

"Tess." She faced me. She buttoned up her stripes and slipped out of her jeans. She looked clownish in that giant shirt.

"There is so much I don't know. I accepted it. That's life, right? I mean, what do you guys even really know about me? But I am an honest person. What you see is what you get."

"Do you think someone has been dishonest?"

"I think you people are so far gone you don't know what honest means."

"The idealism of my youth —"

"Stop." I stood up. "Stop. I see you."

"Do you?"

"You're a cripple." I was surprised at how accurate it felt. "You don't care about anyone but yourself. You certainly don't care about him."

She paused.

"Perhaps," she said. She went back to dressing.

"Perhaps! You think I'm stupid. I'm not. I was just hopeful."

She moved to the mirror and took out her cosmetics bag. I watched the concealer go onto the dark circles under her eyes. She pressed the matte paste against her crow's-feet. She dropped her chin while she put on mascara. How had I never seen how morose her eyes were? She wore the lipstick to distract from them.

"You are blessed with a rare sensitivity," she said. "It's what makes people artists, winemakers, poets — this porous nature. However." She paused and blinked her mascara into place. "You lack self-control. Discipline. And that is what separates art from emotion. I do not think you have the intelligence yet to interpret your feelings. But I do not think you are stupid."

"Jesus, that's lovely."

"It's the truth. You can take it."

"You both enjoy saying that. You love the truth as it applies to everyone else."

"I never lied to you, Tess. I kept him away from you for as long as I could. I was explicit about what you were dealing with."

"It's not normal, Simone, you both going away like this, not even bothering to tell me. It's not right."

"Jake and I haven't traveled together in ages, it's overdue."

"Was I really so threatening?"

"Don't flatter yourself."

"Why don't you just take him?" I said. "Just take him, have him."

She turned back to me and said, immaculately, "Oh, little one, I don't want him."

I pressed my hands into my eyes. Of course. She wanted a Mr. Bensen, Eugene, someone to deliver her to the rarefied world that she had always been entitled to but never able to access permanently. Not Jake, who wore the same underwear for days on end without noticing. She had been seducing and rejecting him since he was a child, and *of course* she didn't actually want him. And yet, I realized, looking at her — she swiped her lips, she swiped, and swiped, and I still saw her immovable, sad eyes — those men were gone, and he was all she had.

"I pity you," I said. My voice had lost its conviction.

"*You* pity *me?*" When she turned to me she wore the most antagonizing smile.

"You can have your diligence. And your self-control, and your cynicism disguised as professionalism, and your stunted ambition. I mean, honestly Simone, what the fuck are you going to do? Are you going to get it through your head and leave or are they going to have to retire you? I guess we'll never know, all of us will be gone."

Venom rose in her, colliding with mine. I loved it, I could feel her enjoying me, and I was ready for it, for whatever she threw at me because I would have time to revise. She couldn't really hurt me, I was young, buoyant —

Jake opened the door. We both turned to him. He was winded.

"Well, here we are," I said.

He looked back and forth between us. Simone walked out, the door slammed. I could tell he had just woken up. His eyes were unadjusted to light and had a patina on them that could have been feelings, could have been pills, could have been sleep. He reached for me and I went unthinkingly.

"I looked for you," he said.

I laid my head on his chest. He smelled like a deeper layer of earth, a secret blue room I kept in Chinatown. He kissed my forehead.

"No," I said, inhaling him. "No, you

didn't."

I accepted his invitation to Clandestino for a nightcap and an overdue conversation. I left immediately after my lunch shift, skipping my shift drink for perhaps the first time since I'd learned of its existence. When I got home I poured myself a big glass of sherry and waited. The Shabbat sirens shot out over Williamsburg. I watched the sun set and the pigeons loop and swerve and reunite with their coops on the rooftops. I sat and waited while the night attached to the corners of buildings. Drums beat steadily. I ate canned sardines on toast and half a jar of cornichons and waited. He needed me. I hadn't mistaken that. I thought maybe we could survive without her blessing.

I wanted to see Jake repentant. The ugly truth was that I could forgive him anything as long as he still desired me. And, I thought as I walked into Clandestino, that wasn't all of it — the need, the desire. Not anymore. When Jake and I had been fucking these past months, our binges on each other were constructing something behind our backs: the stubborn stains of intimacy marked our hands. I had to see if that could hold us on our own.

"Oh, it's Tessie," said Georgie. "What brings a real lady this far downtown?"

"Meeting my friend," I said. "How's it going tonight?"

"Dead." He shrugged. "First nice night, people are too happy for drinking."

"New Yorkers are never too happy for drinking." I pulled up a stool. "I'll just take a lager, whatever is up there."

"You guys like the Brooklyn, right?"

"Yes, we do." I wanted to cry but batted my lashes instead. "Brooklyn would be lovely."

I realized that "Fake Plastic Trees" was playing over the speakers. I hadn't listened to it in years and when I had, on repeat, in the bathtub, I hadn't really understood what it meant to be worn out. I couldn't shrug the song off. So I sighed and said to Georgie, with my face in my hands, "Misery. Will you just turn it up?"

I didn't even notice when Jake was next to me.

"Hey," he said. There were lilacs in his hand. He apologized for being late. Jake's crooked teeth, the stubble hiding the sharpness of his chin, those otherworldly eyes, the lilacs and their melancholy, narcissism, mystery. He touched my cheek, but I was still in the song. His touch felt like a faded reproduction of something that had once knocked me off my feet. "You're so skinny."

"I was sick."

"That sucks." He nudged the flowers toward me. "Don't you like lilacs?"

"You know they're my favorite," I said. "You want a prize for paying attention?"

I moved them to the side, and Jake put his helmet up on the bar. Georgie set down Jake's beer and retreated from our silence. Jake sipped and I matched him.

"I saw your bike. At her house. One of the few things I remember from that night."

He didn't say anything.

"Because I blacked out." It sounded accusatory because it was.

He turned on me. "You think it impresses me that you know how to hurt yourself?"

I leveled his gaze back at him. "Yes. I do."

He wanted to bite me. He wanted to pull my hair out. I could see it churning in him, his eyes, his chest, his fingers. It was unavoidable: the ignition when he reached for me, how I would strain against my clothes to get closer to him, how his breathing would turn ragged, a sound that made my body liquefy, and we would stop thinking.

"I'm pissed," I said, leaning back from him. That was the first time I didn't throw myself on top of the fire he laid before me.

The restraint made me feel old.

"I'm sorry," he said, as if he'd just remembered the protocol. "Seriously, I wanted to meet you, I was going to. I fully intended to —"

"This is the part where you give me the excuse."

"I fell asleep over there."

I tore off tiny shreds of my napkin.

"You fell asleep in her bed is what you meant to say."

"Come on, you know it's not —"

"Like that. Yes, I know it's not like that. Not everything is something."

He coughed.

"Here's something: She's bad for you. She would abandon you without a moment's notice."

It was like he hadn't heard me. "I know how she gets, but she comes around. You will too. We're all a little off from the restaurant being closed."

"No," I said. "You're not hearing me. I will not be placated, Jake. You two have never let anyone close because you would have to look at how fucked up it is, whatever it is. You would have to explain why a grown man and woman who are *not* together still share a bed, vacation together, or why you've *never* had a real relationship with another woman. You're thirty years old, Jake. Don't you want a real life?"

"There's no such thing as a real life, princess. This is it, take it or leave it."

"Enough with the life-is-short-and-painful-and-you-die-alone bullshit. What a fucking scam that is, you never have to take any risks. You deserve better."

His knee was bouncing; I watched the anxiety tense him, like when he got restless behind the bar. I rested my hand on his thigh and it stilled.

"You shouldn't go to France for a month. You hate the French and their smug, racist version of socialism." I elicited a smile. All my reliable tricks. I had a new one to try on him tonight. It was directness. It was truly my last one.

"I want you to quit with me. Or we can transfer. You need a change and I want to be a server."

He cleared his throat. We kept drinking. I felt alone like I hadn't since before I moved to the city, like I would never connect with another person for as long as I lived.

"Just think about it," I said. My voice was desperate; I heard it but couldn't control it.

"I have." He blinked rapidly. He looked up at the lights. I kissed his hands and filthy fingernails. So many things he never said. I wondered who Jake would be if he said all the things.

"Say it."

"I remember the first time I saw you."

"That's all I get?"

"You surprised me." That was all I was going to get. I said, "I remember the first time I saw you too."

Barbs of nostalgia sank in me, bringing a terrible weight, ringing with distance that I resisted. I had vowed to myself — since that first day of this new life — to stay in the present tense, to keep my eyes forward. I think his hands were on my neck, in my hair.

"I can't leave," he said.

"You can. This is still good between us."

"I can't."

"You mean you won't."

"All right, Tess."

"You're a coward," I said. A cripple and a coward. Wine-Woman and Sweaty-Boy. Simone had been right. Our senses are never inaccurate, just our interpretations. This wasn't on them. It was on me.

"Do you remember that morning you let me pick the record?"

His routine had never strayed: a cigarette, the stove-top espresso, a second cigarette, and the day's record. That morning he had woken himself up hiccupping. He had been

476

so scared, he clutched at me, still asleep, and I kissed his temple. I teased him about his hiccup phobia. He laughed. As a reward I got to pick the record. I put on *Astral Weeks* and when "Sweet Thing" came on he said, This one deserves a dance. We danced, him bare chested in stretched-out underwear, me in his shirt with no pants on, moving in circles on the carpets under the gauze of cigarette smoke. That was the morning I committed the first sin of love, which was to confuse beauty and a good sound track with knowledge.

He should have asked me, What morning? What record? But he said, with clarion eyes, "Van Morrison?"

I nodded, shook my head, nodded. "I know you were happy. I felt it. I *know.*"

God, how I loved him. Not him exactly, let me try again: I loved his ghost. What had he said to me about his mother? How impossible it is to forget the stories we tell ourselves, even when the truth should supersede them. That was why he adored me for a minute. Because I saw a beautiful, tormented hero. Rescue and redemption. I never saw him. All promise — the new girl.

I waited as long as I could for him to say something. He stared at the bar and scratched at his scalp under his hat, a gesture I had consumed and memorized. I grabbed bar napkins and patted them on my cheeks, wiped my nose. I kissed the corner of his lips. He tasted perfect: the salty, the bitter, the sweet. I felt him switch off. I knew I would be fucked for a long, long time. I grabbed the lilacs, said goodbye to Georgie, and slid off my stool.

The lilacs shed as I walked the bridge. My phone buzzed twice and I turned it off. The city was radiant and I felt untouchable. I experienced the boundlessness that ships cut from their moorings must feel. I experienced again that feeling of having money, paying the tolls, of being allowed to enter the race. Yes, I felt the freedom again, even if I couldn't quite recapture the hope. I could have walked all night. All the times I'd been denied entrance, all the times I'd asked permission — but it was my city too.

VI

So what if the gold had rubbed off the feather pin she had in her periwinkle fedora? A lot of important people ate at our restaurant: former presidents and mayors, actors, writers who defined generations, financiers you could recognize by their hair. We had plenty of special-needs diners who weren't famous at all: a blind woman who had the specials read out loud to her, men with boyfriends on Fridays and wives on Sundays, eccentric art-collecting men who sat at the bar, ordered a martini, and then drank an entire bottle of red wine for their lunch. Why did I love Mrs. Neely so much?

She was fragile. A rare, endangered species of bird the way she fluttered in and out with her hats and stockings and kitten heels. Sometimes I would watch her from across the room and she would be staring at nothing. I wondered if I would be a woman content to stare into space remembering her misses and near misses, her history.

"Hey Nick, can I grab the Fleurie?"

"Don't top her off, Fluff."

"Come on . . ."

"She's gonna pass out."

I sighed. "So she passes out. Isn't that the privilege of old age? You can sleep whenever and wherever you want?"

He winked and passed the bottle.

"Thank you," Mrs. Neely said, smoothing a pin curl next to her ear. "That bastard at the bar pours me short. He thinks I don't know, but I know."

"Nicky's all right. He just takes some reminding every now and then. Are you enjoying the Fleurie? It's my favorite of all the crus right now."

"Why?"

The only question Mrs. Neely had ever asked me before was why I didn't have a boyfriend. Her tawny apple cheeks were high in a smile and her eyes were lucid. This was a good day for her and I believed she would keep visiting us forever. I picked up her glass and smelled it.

"So Beaujolais is like this hybrid — a red that drinks like a white, we even put a chill on it. Maybe that's why it has trouble, it doesn't quite fit. No one takes Gamay seriously — too light, too simple, lacks structure. But . . ." I swirled the glass and it was so . . . optimistic. "I like to think it's pure. Fleurie sounds like flowers doesn't it?"

"Girls love flowers," she said judiciously.

"They do." I put her wine down, then moved it two inches closer to her, where I knew the field of her focus began. "None of that means anything. It just speaks to me. I feel invited to enjoy it. I get roses."

"Child, what is wrong with you? There's no roses in the damn wine. Wine is wine and it makes you loose and helps you dance. That's it. The way you kids talk, like everything is life or death."

"It's not?"

"You ain't even learned about living yet!"

I thought about buying wine. About how I would scan the different Beaujolais crus at the liquor store — the Morgon, the Côte de Brouilly, the Fleurie would be telling me a story. I would see different flowers when I looked at the labels. I thought about the wild strawberries dropped off from Mountain Sweet Berry Farm just that afternoon and how the cooks laid out paper towels and sheet trays in the kitchen, none of them touching, as if they would disintegrate, their fragrance euphoric. They were completely different from the strawberries in the grocery store, they were as puckered and pruned as my nipples the one time that Jake had made me come just from touching them. I thought about how I would never again buy tomatoes out of season.

"Can I call you a cab this evening, Mrs. Neely?"

"A cab? Goodness no, I will ride the bus as I have every day since I was old enough to walk."

"But it's dark!"

She waved me off. She was peaceful, but I noticed that her lids were getting heavy, that her head dove slightly each time she blinked. "How will I know you got home okay?"

Something in my voice gave it away, that I was scared I would never see her again. What if she stopped coming? No alarms would go off in the restaurant. How many Sundays would it take before we noticed?

"Tess, don't you worry about old Mrs. Neely. If you ever reach my age you'll find that death becomes a need, just like sleep."

I knocked on his office door at ten p.m. after tracking his movements all night. Howard was such a minor element of service for me but I had unconsciously memorized his habits. I realized that he always came to the coffee station at seven and then spent two hours on the floor and then by nine, barring any emergencies, went back up to his office in order to get out by eleven. Two hours on the floor felt like nothing, a cushy job by our standards, but then I thought about all my lunch shifts, and how he was always here before we got in, and nine a.m. to eleven p.m. on a good night sounded awful. It never showed on him.

"Come in," he said. Howard was settled back in his chair, reading glasses on his head, a stack of papers in front of a desktop computer from the Paleolithic era.

"Tess!" He sat up. "What a surprise."

"I know I should have made an appointment, I'm sorry, I just saw that you were still here —"

"My door is always open."

I took a seat and I looked at him. I didn't know exactly what I wanted, but I knew that I had exhausted my resources downstairs. The phase in which I had existed so happily was over. Howard had put me in stripes, and I needed him to tell me what was next.

"I'm curious. About opportunities. In the company." I was hesitating. With the door closed I felt oddly vulnerable even though the dinner crew was still finishing up. "I'm sorry, I didn't plan a speech." I saw a bottle of Four Roses on his bookshelf. "Can I have some of that?"

He took his glasses off his head and retrieved the bottle without standing up. His eyes never left me. On his desk were random samples of glassware, some of them quite dusty. He picked up a rocks glass and used his blue-checkered tie to wipe it out.

"I don't have ice," he said as he passed it to me. He didn't pour himself one.

"No need," I said, and took a big sip. "You said that I could be a server."

He nodded.

"So. I want to be one. I'm really good at this job. I'm better than all the other back-waiters, and most of the servers."

"You are gifted. That's why I have you first in line." He hedged, not sure where I was going. I wasn't sure where I was going. "Tess, we are totally transparent at this company. You see the server schedule, you know how it works. There's no space available right now."

"Okay," I said. I drained my drink. "Maybe you can make space. Or maybe you can place me."

He raised his eyebrows and reopened the Four Roses. He poured more for me and some for himself.

"I've made a considerable investment in you. I'd like to see you grow with us."

"I would too. Honestly, I don't want to

484

leave, even when I am so fucking sick of this place I could die. It's my home. But I also know that you don't really run this place. Simone does. And she would never allow me to be on her level."

"Don't pass that along to the Owner." He wasn't insulted. He was interested. "You and Simone . . . don't tell me this is a story about a boy."

"It's not. It is, but it's not. It's about me. Come on, Howard," I said, leaning back, trying it out. "I know you don't like Jake or he doesn't like you or whatever. And I know you and Simone are whatever, friends. But I should be a server here. I know plenty of people doing things that they could be fired for immediately. It's not even the drinking and the drugs and the theft. It says in the handbook that if you're more than fifteen minutes late three times then you are to be fired. No one would blame you. Certain people who have been showing up thirty minutes late for years . . ."

"Tess!" He laughed. "You're out for blood."

"I'm not. I know you won't do it. Firing him would be firing two people. But let me tell you, Howard, from the inside, that stagnant water stinks. It's just a fact. And this restaurant isn't getting any younger. We have real problems, the walls are crumbling, the food is stale, and yes, people still come, but because of nostalgia. They aren't excited to eat here. Now some fresh blood — some unjaded servers who actually fucking care — wouldn't hurt the atmosphere, the reputation, or the bottom line." I finished my drink again. "But you know all this."

"I like to hear you say it." He refilled me.

"You might be the only restaurant manager who has leather-bound Freud in his office."

"I consider it an instruction manual."

We were silent while I scanned his books.

"You wanted to be something else? An analyst? Anthropologist? Architect?"

"Why do you ask?"

"The same reason everyone asks. You couldn't possibly choose this job, you must have fallen into it accidentally."

"And yet here you are."

"Here we are."

We fell into silence again and I felt like I was running out of time. All my wants crowded forward. I wanted an ally. I wanted my job. I wanted to hurt them. Someone knocked — Misha poked her head in.

"I'm leaving," she said awkwardly, looking at me.

"Okay," I said.

"Excuse me one moment, Tess," Howard said, straightening his tie.

When he left I stood up over his desk, scanning the papers for any edges of her script. It was just a few days ago that I'd found the vacation request. What if I hadn't found it? No fight with Jake, no night of self-abuse, no fever, no truth. I would be downstairs right now revisiting the Pouilly Fumé. When were they going to tell me?

I heard the door handle and I took my seat again.

"Are you going to place Misha?" It was a card I was unsure about playing, but I couldn't take it back.

"Misha?" he asked without concern. "As far as I know, she's content where she is."

"Oh, I just thought I read in the handbook about like, sexual congress between management and staff not being allowed, blah blah. I don't know."

"I believe that is how the rule goes." He glanced at a clock on his desk. "Do you mind if we pause this meeting? I still have a few hours of work, but I'd like to come to a satisfactory conclusion about your prospects, maybe even a plan for the upcoming months."

"Um, okay." I felt like a failure. "I'm the three p.m. tomorrow."

"You can meet me back here at one."

"One a.m.?" I exhaled. "Okay." My mind spiraled. "I mean they might still be closing —"

"You can ring at the back door and we can meet in the other office. No need to disturb the nightly staff party." He put the cork in the bottle of whiskey. "I'll bring ice."

"All right."

"All right," he said. He smiled and tapped the computer mouse, dismissing me. The screen saver dissolved. It was just business after all.

Even at the time I understood that Park Bar was unremarkable unless you worked in those five square blocks. One of those bars that survives because of its location. Nobody ever went out of their way to go there. It was somewhere you ended up, an oasis for the stranded.

But it was a rarity in the city — not quite a dive, and not quite a nice place. Decent wines by the glass. They were smart painting everything black — you could never tell how dirty it was. The bathrooms let you know that people behaved badly, but when you walked by the open windows and saw people sipping unpretentiously in the twilight, you envied them.

It was nearly empty when I got there, at first I couldn't make out anyone I knew. I had a vision that they'd all stopped going there, that they had a new place and hadn't told me about it. Then my eyes adjusted. Sasha was blinking brilliantly at me. I sat down next to him. Terry gestured toward the bottles.

"I don't know," I said to him. "I'm so tired of drinking. Just pick for me."

Sasha pulled something out of his pocket and slid it over to me. I thought it was going to be a bag of coke, but it was a small jewelry box.

"What you think?"

I opened it to find a pair of earrings, opals set in gold.

"I send them out tomorrow. A surprise for my mama. She's gonna flip the moon when she sees them."

I closed the box. "You miss her?"

"Yeah. She an old cunt, more fucked up than even me, but I love her."

I started crying. Sasha was skeptical.

"You got your health, Baby Monster."

"Do I?"

"Let me tell you about self-respect, okay? When you do the things, you fucking do them, and when the consequences come you take them up the ass too, 'kay?"

"Trust me, I am."

"Now, in the beginning, I think, this girl, not so smart, we throw in the garbage in two weeks, but all right, you a Baby Monster, you a little cunt, you gonna make it, and I say, I'm gonna talk straight to her 'cause everyone else trying to stick the dick in her pants or make her over like little dolls, but okay, I tell her straight. And what you do?"

"I didn't listen." I wiped under my eyes. "You know they're going away for a month? To France?"

Sasha pursed his lips at me. "This my shock face."

"It's fucked up."

"Yeah, they fucked up. You know Simone start fucking and sucking him when Jakey was a Jakey Baby, not like the elevator going up from there."

"Wait, like literally or metaphorically?"

"Whatever the fuck that mean? Oh please, you know all that. I don't kiss and tell. Jakey had looser lips when we used to snort it all and scrape up the table for seconds, you know how I'm saying? Who keeping track of this shit?"

"When Jake was a baby?"

"Whatsoever, who is knowing anything? He was too young when they start fucking each other all up, and Simone not such a sweet-as-pie face like you. But why you liking the past so much, Pop Tart? That shit goes dark then it nobody business, and none matters the least bit."

"None matters the least bit," I repeated.

It was bright in Park Bar. Terry should have dimmed the lights. It was all too exposed, including my beleaguered insights, which began with old-fashioned nausea. Then a suspicion that Sasha was lying. I could never tell with him and cruelty wasn't out of his purview. Then a confirmation I had never known how to articulate: Simone had broken something in Jake — there was anger buried under his attachment. My compassion for that golden-eyed bartender was total in that moment. I thought, If only I had known . . . Then I laughed out loud. I don't know that it would have mattered, even if it was true. None matters the least bit. Sasha kept right on talking.

Apathy blanketed me in the middle of a life I had constructed never for an instant to be dull. It was an unexpected comfort. I didn't even want the cocaine that Will and Ariel offered me when they came out of the bathroom. We talked shit to each other for a while. Good songs came on, then forgettable songs.

Terry was from Jersey, the pretty part. Will came from Kansas. Ariel came from Berkeley, Sasha came from outside of Moscow. What did I know about them? We would occasionally remember each other, laugh thinking about how fucked up we used to get. I saw it all, how we had failed to penetrate each other's hearts. I couldn't blame the drugs. I blamed the job, how it made everything feel temporary and unpredictable. We never had the time to say anything that mattered. The Owner had said, "You can't train a fifty-one percenter, you were born that way. Our job is to recognize it."

The jargon, the tenets, the manifestos — it wasn't just to make the guest feel better about spending their money. It was for us. To make us feel noble, called, necessary. They would miss me for a week. At most. Perhaps the biggest fallacy I subscribed to was that I was — that *we* were — irreplaceable.

It wasn't until I walked into Howard's other office later that night that I recognized — and I mean knew with my whole body — that I had been operating my entire life upon the assumption that most men wanted to fuck me. Not only had I known it and encouraged it, I had depended on it. That did not mean I understood the actual transaction of sex. I only knew how to control it until the point of penetration. After that, I treated my body like a sieve — it all passed through me. With Jake, I wasn't a sieve but a bowl. Whatever he gave me, I could hold. When he filled me, I expanded.

It was said that Howard was a great lover. I didn't know what "great lover" meant. But he was not embarrassed by his age. He did not turn off the lights. We had a drink and he put his hand on my thigh at the end of an innocuous sentence. When he started a new one I slid my thigh toward him. His hand went higher. That was all. A sentence, a hand, a sentence, a thigh. These are the axes upon which we are balanced.

He only unbuttoned his shirt. His chest was covered in dark hair. He stripped me with authority. He seemed less impressed than charmed by my breasts, my thighs, my ass, my shoulders. A plaything. He spent a good amount of time warming up my body before he had me face away from him and toward the bookshelves in the auxiliary office with my jeans around my ankles. Jancis Robinson's *World Atlas of Wine, The Wine Bible, A Cheesemonger's Guide to France*. The novelty was valid, his clean, soft hands, the arrogance with which he positioned me. My only thoughts were: I could come if it was a different position, or a different room, or different lighting, a different night, a different man.

It was quick and he didn't ask me if I'd finished. I didn't think about a condom until he pulled out and I wondered if men were supposed to ask before they came inside you. I remembered when Jake gave me Plan B after that first night, how he passed it to me without comment. I had saved it because I had gotten my period. At the time I had thought Jake was considerate, responsible. Howard handed me a Kleenex that was hidden behind a stack of books and I thought, Why hide the Kleenex?

They would find out. I would never tell anyone, but I was acquainted with the way information trickled down at the restaurant. No one saw me enter and no one would see us exit but someone, somehow, would know. Simone would be furious, irrationally so, unable to explain to herself why. Everyone would sense it and avoid her during service. Jake would be shocked. Not because I was with another man. But because I had hurt myself, humiliated myself beyond the ways in which he had humiliated me. And he would understand how terrible it was that he hurt me. I had wanted to take some power away from him, but — my chest tightened as I threw the Kleenex away — I had made myself so small to do it that I was unrecognizable.

"I was like you," he said, zipping up his pants.

"In what way, Howard?"

"When Simone first started, she used to tell the filthiest jokes. Old fisherman jokes, absolutely unrepeatable, they made me blush. She wouldn't flinch while she told them but then you would see her shoulders start to twitch with laughter." He looked at me while he spoke, but he wasn't seeing me. "I was very serious about her. And I didn't understand the two of them. They repulsed me."

"And?" I clipped my bra.

"Well, it hurt. It hurts, doesn't it? When Fred Bensen came into the picture I suffered terribly. Jake and I had something in common that day when she announced she was leaving us. I often wonder if we didn't drive him away. He really just . . . vanished. She never told me what happened. I thought it might soften her." He shook his head.

"I get it. Now you fuck young girls to punish her?"

"No, Tess. I fuck young women because

they taste better. I don't need to punish her. She built her own elaborate prison here. All I have to do is not fire her."

"Jesus." I had been holding on to the idea that Howard was not one of us. That he was impervious to our schemes and pettiness. I think at that moment I knew I had lost, completely.

"Time passed," he said, finishing the buttons on his shirt, folding up his tie and tucking it into his pocket. "And I realized she did me a great favor. I think you will feel the same way."

"You know what I dislike? When people use the future as a consolation for the present. I don't know if there is anything less helpful."

"You're delightful, Tess," Howard said, sitting on the desk.

"You think so?" I tucked my hair behind my ears. I leaned back on my arms and regarded the empty space between the desk and us. "I think you're strange, Howard. I always have."

"Do you think maybe you're strange also?"

I nodded. My vision blurred around a stain on the carpet under the desk.

I thought that once I got to this city nothing could ever catch up with me because I could remake my life daily. Once that had made me feel infinite. Now I was certain I would never learn. Being remade was the same thing as being constantly undone.

We heard footsteps and Howard shrugged on his jacket. I sat in the chair and folded my hands on my lap as he opened the door to the hallway.

Nicky yelled out in shock, "Jesus fuckin' Christ, Howard, you almost gave me a fucking —"

Then he saw me. We met eyes before I looked away. I saw his mouth harden. I saw his lack of any confusion or faith in extenuating circumstances. Nicky was nothing if not a realist. I saw his disappointment. I covered my face with my hands.

"A bit late isn't it, Nick?"

"Yeah," he said. He held up a stack of bar mops. "Finishing up."

"Tess, we can conclude our discussion tomorrow. You can go out the back."

I nodded. The adults were taking care of it, dispatching me into the night. I wondered what kind of look passed between them, masculine, implicit. I envied them their effortless understanding of the world.

"Sorry, Nick," I said right before I shut the door.

The next morning the blossoms on the trees

blew down like paint chips off desiccated buildings. I stood in the Sixteenth Street window and stared at the park. It was a violently windy day, the trees bent, clouds skipping through a blue sky.

"It's like it's snowing again," I said, but no one heard me. Small flags plastered to the windows, an onslaught of petals.

I was in the wine cellar organizing, a job that had become mine gradually then definitively. No one cleaned up after themselves because they knew I would do it. Simone knocked on the door, holding a boat of potato chips and a dewy bottle of Billecart, and I knew I was being fired.

"Do you have a minute?"

I put down the box cutter and arranged three stacks of boxes in the shape of two stools and a table. The boxes had been so heavy. Now I could lift two at a time. I could toss them.

"It looks great down here."

"I try."

"I thought we could have a treat," she said, shining the label of the bottle at me.

"A treat indeed. It's been a minute for me and the Billecart."

"That's a sin." Simone opened the bottle with the barest whisper. She conditioned two glasses with small pours and then filled them gently, looking at me the entire time.

"I'm into rosé right now," I said. "That Tempier . . . oh man, it's divine."

"The Peyrauds are wonderful people. We're staying with them in Bandol." Her eyes darted to me but she kept going. That woman had no fear. "If people can have terroir, they have it. Salt of the sea, joy of the sun. They come in when they visit the city, next time I —"

"Ah." I stopped her lie. No Bandol for me. And there would be no next time.

"I spoke with Howard."

"I imagined you would."

"You're getting a promotion. Much deserved."

"Am I." I meant to say, Am I? but couldn't.

She sat across from me and I knew her face better than my own. I had studied her so intently. I was sure that nothing — not the passage of time, not distance — would disrupt this intimacy. Thirty years could pass and when I walked into this restaurant I would know its rhythms, its secrets, in my bones. I would know her anywhere.

"You're going to the Smokehouse."

It took me a minute to absorb it. I sipped the Champagne and stopped.

"Sorry, cheers." I touched her glass and then drained my own.

"Of course I'm not going to the Smoke-house."

"Tess, at least consider —"

"Oh Simone!"

I had yelled, it bounced back to me from the bottles. "Barbecue, burgers, and beers? Giant TVs? Why are you going through this charade?"

"The servers make excellent money."

I put my hand up. "Shut up. Let's make this easier. I'm not going to the Smoke-house. I quit. I will stay for two weeks but prefer to go as soon as possible. Now can we have a real conversation?"

"As you wish."

Champagne and silence — the only resting places in the world. I sighed. I wavered audibly in the end but kept it together. I took another full inhale and exhale.

"Those are good breaths," she said.

"Shut up."

She nodded and I spent some more time breathing.

"I got in over my head, I will admit."

"It's perfectly normal."

"It's going to be boring after this." I looked at her, her red lips and unforgiving eyes. I thought, I will miss you.

"Boredom can be incredibly productive. It's the fear of boredom that's so destructive."

"You were bored," I said. "You're bored out of your mind. That's why you fucked with me."

She blinked a few times. "No, Tess. I know why you want to tell yourself that. But it's not so simple. I believed it too — that we were a family."

I didn't know if she meant the whole restaurant or the three of us. It didn't matter. I bit into a potato chip and it crackled. My mouth flooded. The bare bulb palpitated at the same pace as my heart.

"You will be fine," she said. She ate a chip and considered her last statement. "You weren't going to be here forever. You can get a real job now. A real boyfriend. Live in real time. Don't roll your eyes."

"I'm thinking about wine. Like retail, there's a shop off Bedford I like."

"Yes, that's wonderful, you'll be fine there. I know someone at Chambers, I would be happy to make a call. Howard will provide an excellent reference as well."

"I fucking bet he will." I wanted to feel anger at all of them, I wanted to feel used, but it never coalesced. "I have some money. I'm going to take some time."

"That's smart," she said. We both took a chip. "You will be fine."

I don't know if she repeated that for my benefit or hers. I saw this from above, our chips and Champagne. I saw the kitchen, family meal being set up in the dining room, the locker room where I would gather the trash and residue of my locker and put it in a plastic bag in case something became important enough to keep. Eventually nothing would be important and I would throw it all away.

The salt off the chips stuck to my fingers and I tapped them together, the salt breaking off, and I heard someone roll a hand truck through the dining room above our heads. The lingering taste in my mouth was of chalk and content, disarray and lemons. There wasn't a hint of regret. I spoke slowly, not knowing what was coming but knowing it was final. I looked at her. "Of course, I'll be fine. I will never be anything but grateful."

I didn't remember the right things, let me try again: the herds of Hasidic children on the South Side street corners at midnight, the calls of the Empanada Man walking on Roebling while I napped, Empanada, Empanada, hours lost walking in circles on artless blocks with Jake, while he punctuated his thoughts with a cigarette, all of us running outside to the middle of Sixteenth Street to watch that bloodred sun drop into the Hudson, drinking beer out of paper bags with Scott while we hopped the bars on Grand Street, Will teaching me karate moves on the subway platform, the gorgeous, orange, abraded tongues of uni that we spread on toast, Ariel and me on the bridge at sunrise, singing, the commuters pushing against us and we knew a secret that they didn't, which is that life didn't progress unswervingly, it didn't accumulate, it was wiped as clean as the board at the end of the night and if we kept our spirits up, it meant we were inexhaustible.

I think it was Nicky who used to say, "Life is what happens when you're waiting." I don't know, it's a cliché at this point. That doesn't make it untrue. My life had been so full I couldn't glimpse beyond it. I didn't want to. And really, would it ever be as loud? As satisfying? Always this desire for the wildest, the closest to its source, the most pungent, the most accelerated — that's who we were. Even if we forgot the regulars, forgot the specials, forgot to clock in.

It was Simone who used to say, on her better days, "Don't worry, little one, none of this will leave a scratch."

But I see the marks on people. Strangers who sit at the bar alone and order a drink with intimacy, order the chicken liver mousse and chat with the staff. People who pay attention to their plates in a way I want to call worshipful. I see them on myself: the scratches, scars. No, I didn't wait forever, but in that way we were all lifers.

Those flowers are wilting already.
It's just my usual five o'clock abyss.
And *that* guy has a girlfriend.
God, they should make a reality show here.
When will I stop being so moved?
Turns out there are a million theories on
    purgatory.
When will I learn?
Yeah, Scott put in his notice — Chef is
    livid.
And she just went out the back.
But like, there's no arc in a love story.
It's like a pizza place in Bushwick.
Well, style triumphed over content.
30 needs attention.
That's what happens in the city.
Not too sentimental, that one.
The plums are real.
New York has perfected it.
But the cake is imaginary.

You don't have to cultivate cynicism, it
    flowers naturally.
I mean, Stalin was an angel in comparison.
But why would she bring gardenias?
I'm weeded.
35 is helpless.
Move them.
It's too rare, even for me.
You know when you gamble that you're
    going to lose.
I'm dragging, make it a double.
What did she expect?
And win just enough.
I guess you just had to be there.
Three fucking turns.
On a Tuesday.
Jesus, we were slammed all night.

ACKNOWLEDGMENTS

My gratitude is boundless.

To Claudia Herr
To Mel Flashman
To Peter Gethers

I don't know how to deserve the attention, dedication, and hours you've given me, except to work harder. Thank you.

To Robin Desser, Sonny Mehta, and Paul Bogaards. To Carol Carson, Oliver Munday, and Cassandra Pappas. To Christine Gillespie, Sarah Eagle, Erinn McGrath, and Jordan Rodman. To Katherine Hourigan, Rita Madrigal, Lydia Buechler, and the awe-inspiring team at Knopf.

To Sarah Bush, Sylvie Rosokoff, Meredith Miller, Lauren Paverman, and everyone at Trident.

To the MacDowell Colony, Byrdcliffe Colony, and Casey and Steven at the Spruceton Inn for time and space.

To Helen Schulman and Jonathan Dee.

To Mani Dawes for my PhD in restaurants. To Heather Belz and Michael Passalacqua. To Tia.

To Jody Williams, Caryne Hayes, and my loves at Buvette.

To DHM and everyone at USC.

To Pam.

To Christina.

To AGH.

To Car.

To Bradley.

To my tireless readers and supporters: Margaux Weisman, Emily Cementina, Morgan

Pile, Marianne McKey, Waverly Herbert, Mariana Peragallo, Eli Bailey, TJ Steele, Dave Peterson, Alejandro de Castro, Lu and Francesca, Kevin Ruegg, Wendy Goldmark, Denise Campono, and Nancy Ferrero.

To SJD, who read every sentence of every draft, and said the only thing I needed to hear: It's good. Keep going.

ABOUT THE AUTHOR

Stephanie Danler is a writer based in Brooklyn, New York.